NEIGHBORWORLD

DAVE DELUCA

SUBGENIUS FOUNDATION

subgenius.com
P.O. Box 807, Glen Rose, Texas 76043
P.O. Box 181417, Cleveland Heights, Ohio 44118

FIRST EDITION

ISBN-10: 1946529001
ISBN-13: 978-1946529008

DEDICATION

Thanks to Jeff Henning, an artist who died about 15 years ago and who constantly told me *Neighborworld* was cool and I should try to get it published, and to Dave DeLuca (SR) and Maxine DeLuca, my parents.

And praise be to Rev. Dr. Uncle Onan Canobite for kick-starting The SubGenius Foundation back into book publishing.

CONTENTS

FORWARD BY REV. IVAN STANG

Thanks to print-on-demand technology, The SubGenius Foundation can again self-publish. *FREE of CONSPIRACY PUBLISHERS AT LAST!* We have many books planned, utilizing both new material and old, including out-of-print books and zines as well as a trove of unpublished art and writing. Most of these projects are SubGenius-centric, others not especially so.

Even with all that to choose from, there was never any question that we would first publish Lonesome Cowboy Dave DeLuca's incredible novel *Neighborworld*.

I first encountered the Dave Brain on a Cleveland radio show produced by the late Chas Smith: *ESO Swamp Radio* on WCSB. As *Brain Rot Radio Theater*, Dave, Chas and others, including myself whenever possible, performed scripted radio plays and a lot of improvisation. We shared many of the same influences: The Firesign Theatre, Warner Brothers cartoons, The Mothers of Invention, maybe even a little Monty Python!

I incorporated the recordings into my own show, *The Hour of Slack;* in 1999 I moved from Dallas to Cleveland and we all became regulars on each others' shows. Since Chas died in 2007, Dave has joined my wife Princess Wei 'R.' Doe and me every week on *Hour of Slack*.

Anyone who hears this show either turns it off after five minutes as random nonsense, or they recognize that that one guy, the Lonesome Cowboy, talks like no one they have ever heard before. Some might even go so far as to say that Dave can talk like James Joyce wrote, off the top of his head, seemingly without effort. It does take effort to *follow* Dave, and sometimes it sounds like nonsense to me too. But then I listen back to the recordings — and by golly, it wasn't nonsense, it was just too fast and maybe over my head.

I knew Dave worked as a newspaper reporter and magazine writer, so I wasn't surprised when he sent me the text file of a novel he had written over several years.

When I sat down to read it, however, I was flabbergasted. It reads like Dave talks, only richer, thicker, and easier to follow. The first comparison that comes to mind is Anthony Burgess's *A Clockwork Orange*, if only because that novel is also written partly in an invented future slang. (When you read *Neighborworld* you find yourself saying things like, "Wow, I think the President is smearing.")

Neighborworld shares a theme with most dystopian novels: dehumanization by runaway systems and technology. Anthony Burgess and George Orwell didn't know about the Internet, though. To those of us who see dependence on the Net and social media as potentially more destructive than helpful, Dave's vision is perhaps a worst case scenario.

When William Gibson wrote a novel warning about the Internet, he used a manual typewriter, not a computer. He didn't really know much about computers per se. Likewise, Dave is about the least Internet-friendly guy I know. He is not on Facebook. When he has to use email he goes to the library. Like Gibson, he doesn't need to know the details. While the rest of us were admiring individual trees, Dave was acutely aware that we were deep in a forest the whole time.

He's also a very good surf-punk-bulldada electric guitarist, and you can hear some of his songs on the YouTube channel *revstang*, a few music CDs published by The SubGenius Foundation, and, of course, *The Hour of Slack*.

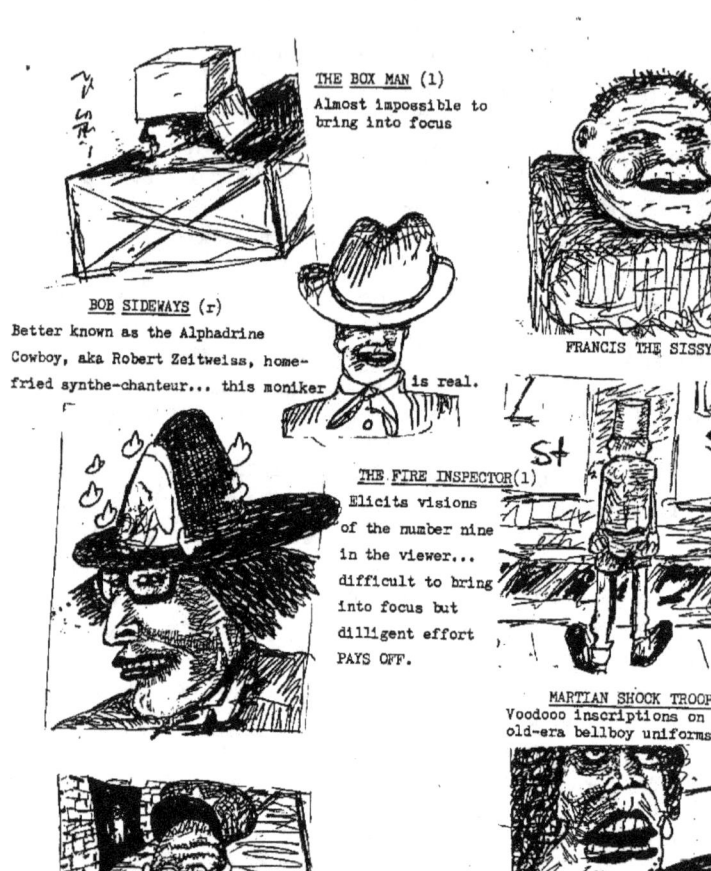

THE BOX MAN (1)
Almost impossible to
bring into focus

BOB SIDEWAYS (r)
Better known as the Alphadrine
Cowboy, aka Robert Zeitweiss, home-
fried synthe-chanteur... this moniker   is real.

FRANCIS THE SISSY (above)

THE FIRE INSPECTOR(1)
Elicits visions
of the number nine
in the viewer...
difficult to bring
into focus but
dilligent effort
PAYS OFF.

MARTIAN SHOCK TROOPERS (above)
Voodooo inscriptions on mutilated
old-era bellboy uniforms. Easier...

THE DREAMER(above)
Also the visited woman, the
sleepwalker, la caltera, la
suenadera, la infinita, etc.,etc.

THE GENERALISSIMO (above)
Comes into focus whenever he pleases.

-1-
"IT'S WEIRDER THAN YOU THINK"

Outside, it was twilight. Evening stars glimmered in the late autumn sky, black clouds poured across the red horizon like puffs of smoke, and wind howled through the empty glide paths. It was a beautiful sunset, but nobody in Local 838 saw it. 838 Neighbors never went outside to zoom the scene, or do anything. That's how it was in most of NeighborWorld.

Inside, it was screen light. Silver glow baked the pale blue walls, leaving the rest of the room in darkness. The song "Ghost Riders in the Sky" blared away from a warped record on an antique turntable. Soon, millions of Neighbors would be crowding into my living room to hear my slant on the story of the Weirds. The rumor mill had it I was in line for an 'Andy' if my take on the Weirds took off. Not bad for fifteen minutes of fame.

I wasn't eager to relive the experience. It almost put me in the unhouse, almost even erased me. But I was a NeighborWorld advo, and the advo's credo is Tell The Truth. I had the uncooked, uncensored shots, the fat and skinny. What else could I do?

"Up the reverb," I told my screen.

The Ghost Riders sound track swelled, all psi-fi spooky.

"Nex-in," I told it.

Almost instantly, Neighbors from around the planet began nexing-in, lighting up the screen panel like a swarm of fireflies. It was going to be a good night, after all. The worst of the Weirds seemed over, so there was no paranoid scram as I stood full up to the source, opened my yakking skull, and cued my credit to the world.

"Welcome, Neighbors," I said in my old-era TV anchor voice. "Mi casa es su casa. I'm Standard Mozuck, with 'Cutting on the Action,' my personal diary and slant on today's hot happenings on the connector."

I goosed the emotion knob. Speak, tweak, squeak.

"So get ready, NorthAm, and the rest of the world, because you can't afford to miss this one. It's time for 'Transdimensional Paradise Or Psychic Hell... Where Do The Weirds Really Want To Take Us?' It's rough, uncut, and gooey in the right places, with all the bleeps left in the mix. So dig it while you can!"

Then the words INTERIOR - LAB - DAY - OVERHEAD SHOT crawled across the top of my screen. They were directions for the opening shot's location, lighting, and angle. Ghost Riders faded quickly, and another music track, some schmaltzy synthetic love song, started weaving into the background. Instantly the first scene appeared, for the whole world to see.

It showed one of the labs that monitored world programming. All the labs looked alike. No furniture, no gadgets, just white walls covered with luminous, full-dimension holo-screens. The interactive screens sampled millions of NeighborWorld shows. They were probably smarter and friendlier than most of the NeighborWorld novice trainees there.

Once in a while, bored, silver-lapelled novices wandered into the overhead shot. They watched the screens blankly, then left to drink coffee, monitor, or get lumed on stimsublim subliminal light patterns, in private lounges. Since nobody left home to work anymore, the lab's only real purpose was instilling team spirit in novices. They didn't show much spirit in this lab security footage, though. It looked like just another droned out workday in the year the old guys would call 2037.

One screen in the lab showed an elderly woman wearing a blue bandana, as she put walnut pastry in a pink brick oven. The show was coming from a small NeighborWorld Local near Athens, Greece. The screen's ethno-box translated, using her voice and manner of speech, while flawlessly animating her mouth to speak English or Spanglo or Spanish words. That way, viewers saw climb potential; not distracting flubdubs. And the pastry smelled good, too.

On another lab screen, a spot coming from a small NeighborWorld Local in WestAf showed a white-bearded, ochre-skinned grandpa selling coconut soda with a drink, a wink, and a hearty laugh.

On yet another, a crewless cargo ship ploughed through the dark green waters of the Pacific. Another screen showed a scene of pine-covered mountains. The mountain scene concealed a barrage of mood-altering stimsublims.

A screen monitoring a spot coming from a small, skin-min NeighborWorld Local in NorthAm's Great Lakes region - our Local 838 - showed two fat, red-haired women, conducting a séance. Suddenly, a man who looked like an animixed cartoon character burst onto the scene. He was sticking out his tongue, and waving his arms in some warning gesture, obscuring the twins.

Then the shot zoomed into an extreme close-up of his gaunt, bright yellow face. He had thick red lips, high cheekbones, bug eyes bulging through dense old-era eyeglasses, and an aquiline nose packed with scraggly hairs. His mug was framed by an enormous, shiny, black poly-wig. On top of it all, like a cherry on a sundae, sat a little red fireman's hat. Then a sunburst blew out in the background, and multi-colored spaghetti erupted from his ears and nose, wriggling like snakes. The screen started shaking violently.

Then, a deep, old-era B-movie trailer voice rumbled, "Their origin...

unknown! Their mission... a mystery! There's no escape from the Transdimensional Weirds! Francis The Sissy! The Dreaming Woman! The Box Man! Martian Bellboys! The Generalissimo! The Fire Inspector!!!"

Immediately, another, more subdued Voice-Over tagged, "Coming soon... To everyone's forebrain! No screens needed."

The shot pulled back to show the lab, from overhead. Below, a chubby, alarmed looking novice was pointing at the berserk holo screen.

"That's not supposed to be there," the novice kept repeating.

Before he could assess his slender female partner's bewildered reaction, all the lab screens showed the Fire Inspector making faces. High-pitched noises poured from the screens, growing into a numbing wail.

"Hey," the novice screamed, almost unheard under all the screens starting to whine, frizz, and blow up. "That's not supposed to be there!"

FADE TO BLACK on my monitor screen.

Then another scene heading crawled by: EXTERIOR - WEIRDSVILLE (INDUSTROS TRAGICOS) - DAY - ANGLE ON WEIRD CALLED FRANCIS THE SISSY

A full shot of the Weird came up, showing the strange little guy sitting in the sun on the front stoop of his weather beaten old 1920s home. Except for his baby smooth cheeks, Francis's face was gnarled and twisted like a tree stump. His buddha-drome noggin sported coarse, irregular stubble and was dinged by bad haircuts. Spotty, black, wild-weed eyebrows were woven above his glistening brown eyes. His nose was the size, shape, and texture of a large moccasin. He wore a bright green sweater made from some old-era material, probably real wool.

"How do you do it?" I asked him.

Francis seemed unfazed by the magnitude of the question I had just asked him. He looked like a kid ready to answer an easy math problem.

"Simple," he said. "The screen goes in my mind. So I make my mind go in the screen. Nem nem nem."

Then, after a short, glassy-eyed stare, with spit bubbles forming at the edges of his mouth, the Weird called Francis The Sissy smiled like the cat that ate the canary. How could I argue with an answer like that, dear Neighbors? And how could I tell my boss that their secret was they made their minds "Go in the screen, nem nem nem?"

SLOW DISSOLVE ON FRANCIS'S FACE, then FADE TO BLACK on my screen.

A long run of my own Hab/Home Diary footage was beginning. The nexing Neighbors were coming into my hab to see my life the way it was, the loose ends and dirty underwear.

"A hab might be a home," I said to everyone in NeighborWorld. "But it ain't always where the heart is. No matter, dear Neighbors. Coming right up, we'll be as one. Let's go beyond feelie-realie, all the way to Point A, to see, experience, and feel it just as I did, and how it truly was. Give me your empty heads, and I'll bring light to the small places."

A new scene heading blipped up: EXTERIOR - SHOT FROM ABOVE OF GEORGIAN STYLE HAB BLOCK - MORNING - ZOOM INTO BEDROOM WINDOW TO FULL SHOT OF ME IN BED, STARING AT CEILING.

For me, it began one chilly late autumn morning, the worst of a streak of bad mornings. A new season in piss-hole Local 838 was under way, and I was working long shifts. It was horrible, real zoom-the-zoombies-from-hell stuff. They had me not only producing and directing Spotlights on 838 Neighbors, but hammering out tech flow problems for nearby Locals, too. That often meant working twenty straight hours without sleep.

I was still idealistic about being an advo. Whether it was a wastewater treatment specialist, or an analysis analyst, or whatever, I made folks look like stars in my Spotlights. I wanted them to know they could climb, that we are all information. They got their fifteen, and I got mine.

To combat fatigue, my fave giga-goo and daily performance booster was stimsublim. I liked Satiscope, alpha-stim, beta-stim, gammadrine, all kinds of patterns. New stimsublim patterns were released every hour, so getting lumed was no problem. Like the commercials said, "No need to think. You need a blink! So zoom the lume."

But I was taking on too much stimsublim, especially Satiscope. Sleep was rare and restless. There were terrible nightmares, where huge, grotesque faces would chase me. Then something would freeze me up, and force me to look at them. They spoke, but I couldn't understand what they were saying.

On this one morning in particular, I woke up, and the faces were still there. I rubbed my eyes, sat straight up in bed, slapped my cheeks, but they didn't go away, for like thirty seconds at least. Frizzing, convinced I was smearing, or something even more nekro, I looked frantically around my bedroom for disappearing faces. I searched up and down walls packed to the ceiling with antique books and old-era media tech, then down the hall, then behind the monitors. Then it hit me. The faces were the same ones we'd been burying in religious stimsublim spots all week, at the special behest of the General Offices.

Right on cue, my old-era alarm started whining in the background. Then 'Mina, The Yoga Lady,' the sweet, sisterly character created to wake me up, and other things, began repeating "Time to face the morning sun, Stan..." over and over.

I was tired. If I wasn't blinking on Satiscope or some other stimsublim, I was always tired. The awful noise, the light squeaking through the tall bedroom window, all made the realization more sickening. The General Offices, the bleeping G-O. Leaking tox-box on Neighbors, another 'experiment.' They were releasing dangerous psychoactive stimsublim patterns in 838, maybe the whole Great Lakes grid. And the experiment probably had something to do with suppressing Weirds.

"I'm awake," I grumbled out loud, shutting Mina up. "Jesus, I'm awake already." My mouth tasted like moldy salami. My nerves were shot, my chems blown.

The G-O was slamming down hard on the Weirds. To the General Offices, it was a bigger problem than programming disruptions or wrecked gear. The G-O knew the Weirds were no ordinary box beaters or malcos. The Weirds scribbled moustaches on the Bigs, made the truth come out of their mouths, and did it all somehow with their minds. At least, that's what I thought. No source could trace them. No recorded images held.

All the genalts thought the Weirds had to be genetically altered, like them, because only splice-babies could head up such juju tech. Most genalts in 838 were frizzed and frothing about the Weird break-ins. Older non-genalts, like my boss, thought break-ins were some kind of mass hallucination, but that didn't explain much. What was really getting the G-O stinky was that the Weirds refused to Spotlight, to become part of NeighborWorld.

I wasn't really a Weird fan. I thought everybody should Spotlight. After all, isn't it 'Everyone information, Everyone In The Spotlight, Everyone A Star?' For the mandatory fifteen minutes, or whatever's right. But I sure admired their guts.

Only the Weirds dared to laugh at satire bans and ridicule NeighborWorld openly, and show the true nekro of the probes and goons. Without getting caught. They sliced through genalt skull patrols like a laser through cheese. Genalts might do some things better, but they're still human. Humans couldn't do stuff like this. Everyone - malcos, frips, and jokers - got caught sooner or later.

So these sweaty dreams, and the nekro fearscape the G-O was running, weren't cutting well into the mix. And although the stimsublim kept me going, it was killing me, too. Add to that my problems with Sylvia, my beloved habmate, monitoring the loud spot in the next room, oblivious to everything but her screen.

OVER-SHOULDER TRACK-ALONG SHOT OF ME WALKING DOWN HALL

"I'm watching it watch me," Sylvia blurted out, to herself, in the background. "Zoom the lume. Lume the zoombie." Some audience laughter swelled.

Sylvia never slept, rarely spoke coherently, and hardly ate. She hadn't cued credit or contributed to hab-maint for over three seasons. I couldn't believe what happened to her in sixteen seasons. She was such a squish, hot focus diva-Jane in the then. In the now, she was a mangled, skull-ripped zoombie. Like most of Local 838's Neighbors, she never went outside to watch Lake Erie's long gray waves smash against the decaying old beach houses, never took a breath of fresh air, never felt the sun or rain. Except in feelie-realie. Oh, yes, dear Neighbors, Sylvia was smearing.

Again, right on cue, the Home monitor buzzed, a stranger wanting in. I was still in my pajamas.

"Come in," I said.

It wasn't a stranger's face that appeared immediately on my screen. It was one I'd seen too many times before, the face of a character with no human relatives, an animixed Surcord goon dressed up like an old-era cop on the beat.

"Knock, knock," he said, looking like he was peering through an old apartment peephole and pounding on the door. "Knock, knock. Who's there?"

"It's Standard Mozuck," I came back quickly. "Associate with Local 838, third step advo. What's up?"

"Hi Stand," the goon said. "Nothing's up. Just a routine check. Have a nice day." Then the cop character blipped off the screen like a code flash, and the screen faded to black.

Another knock-knock spot, the third one this week. This wasn't good, especially with Sylvia in such bad shape. If it wasn't for me, playing amigo with the clean climbers, and the 838 probes and goons I didn't have dirt on, she'd already be in the unhouse for sure. And she'd have plenty of company. Knock-knock spots were putting hordes of 838 Neighbors in the unhouse.

I shielded her from knock-knocks, because when that Sur-goon appears on your screen and says "Knock-knock. Who's there?" you'd better cue credit and say your name in twenty seconds, or you're gone-D. The servo comes and they pack you off to a bio-collective, you're unhouse bound. For Sylvia, twenty seconds wasn't long enough to remember her name. She was whoever or whatever she was watching. She was smearing.

INTERIOR - KITCHEN - DAY - WIDE SET SHOT, ALL SOURCES, FULL ROLL

Finally awake enough to feel hungry, I slumped off to the kitchen. Naturally, with my old-era obsesso, it had the look of a 1950s diner, and the personality of a cranky waitress named Gert. Sometimes, jeri-era obsesso griff made me call Home's prepro a computer. That was the jango in the jeri-then; they called them computers. But could a computer nano-grow our food, clothes and furniture—and do all the flash stuff, too—with remnants of someone like Sylvia's brainwaves still in the mix?

"Hey, Gert!" I barked. "Give me some eggs, home fries, and coffee. Number three, over here. Point 'em up, sunnyside."

Gert's craggy, too-rouged face emerged on the monitor, her heavily lipsticked mouth opening just enough to show a few snaggly teeth, and form a few crabby words.

"Gawd awmighty," Gert croaked back sourly. "Hold on. I only got two hands."

In the mood for Neighborly gossip, I nexed into a diner-style yakker from some Local near Seattle 12. The yakker's diner set wasn't as cool as my kitchen. It made me wish 'Nick And George's,' the diner in CarTown, was still open.

"Hey, Gertrude," I said. "Give us some 'Nick and George' style nose to go with the b.s."

Cafe aromas filled the kitchen de pronto, with a hint of Cubano cigars, my personally designed smells, my own feelie-realie K-flavors. I wanted to jump in and come back on the diner yakker, so I got into character. After putting up my look, a Bogie hat and a gone-gray journo's trenchcoat right over my pajamas, I found an obscure booth in the background and blended into the nex-al-mundo studio ambience. It was time for some yakk about Weirds from out there in the land of cowboy boots and berets.

But the show was limp, and nobody was yakking. It was just an audience of listless peekers and zoombie blinkers and everyone seemed to be smearing. I jumped out just as fast as I nexed in. Something wasn't right with my head, making it hard to stay in focus. I dumped the diner search entirely, unbuttoned my coat, and shadow cooked my eggs, just to do something on my own.

"Who am I?" I asked Home.

The names and faces came up; my ancestry, a perfect weave of every cloth and color. An advo, here on the little north seas, 152 seasons old. A face with dark brown, almost black hair, normal teeth, standard nose, eyes, and ears. Then the screen quick faded to black.

"What, when, where, why?" I shouted at the monitor. "No, never mind!"

It was hard not to worry about what was going on in NeighborWorld. Everyone was unhouse bound; to the bio-collectives, to lose what little individual personality they still had left. I didn't want to fade that way.

"Play something maestro, Gert," I told my kitchen, "And let me serve my own food."

Immediately, Beethoven, the Chorale from the 9th, blasted up and under. Home's weather monitor blended some wind from outside into the background sound mix. I scooped up eggs and homefries and plopped them onto a platter. Gert had already served buttered pumpernickel toast and a glass of cider, which I guzzled in one slurp. I had a fork in hand, ready to eat, when Sylvia started yelling. She was touching down for a while, and for that brief moment, she was super alive.

"Standard! Standaaaard!!" she bleated. "Come here! Quick! He looks like you. He looks like you but he's Japanese!"

I got up, told Gert to keep my breakfast warm, and schlepped into the living room; through the clutter of old era paintings and books, and into the middle of the mess, where Sylvia sat, as usual, facing a screen. She was watching a Shinju, an eroto-slam director, as he babbled about how eroto-slam created a ravenous appetite for consumption, and how boners and buying went hand in hand. The Shinju ranted untranslated, no ethno-box, in Japanese, peppering his speech with little kid words, like ca-ca, and poopy. Who knows what he was saying? He gestured wildly, like I do when I'm really excited, and there was something familiar about his mug, but he was no twin.

"You think he looks like me?" I offered, hoping for some communication.

Ignoring her would have been easier, but I couldn't. I used to love her, and still felt responsible, or something. Soon it was obvious she even forgot I was there.

"Syl," I said, leaning over and speaking into her ear. "Are you still monitoring tech flow for the 'Alice De Malice' show?"

Sylvia stared into the glowing electrofuzz with her mouth open, rocking back and forth, her sandy hair and cherub face giving her the look of an empty-headed child. Glimmerings of recognition bloomed and died in her eyes in microsecs. Then suddenly, her stacks filled and she was with the living again.

"Oh, yeah," she mumbled, like talking in her sleep. "I like it. I like doing that."

I was imagining a huge prop hammer coming down and bonking her out, when her hand jerked away from the connector, and elation lit up her eyes. The Alice DeMalice Show started, inundating us with its loud, goo-goo-malo theme music; a xylophone or marimba horror from some old-era cartoon, with frantic clinks and clanks. On the screen, a grotesque animation showed Alice as a mad-Martian majorette aboard a parade float; sneering, spitting venom and innuendo like a tranced out parrot, smearing Neighbors in the name of info.

Alice DeMalice was aggro-deggro of the rankest kind, nothing but libel, slander, and malicious rumors about Local Neighbors. Every Local had Alice, and Alice always ran the sweeps. The G-O sure understood the numbers. Alice made even near-smear like Sylvia frothy. Sylvia twitched and bit her nails in the screen light, sinking further into the box, merging with the screaming feelie-realie audience, leaving behind only her body in a worn out, overstuffed chair.

Over all that, the mixed-in sound of servo-shrinkers from 838's Biz/Tek Direk droned from outside as they yanked the microdots and replaced them with the new gels. Sixty seasons ago it was pinhead sized discs. Soon we'd all be nexed-in with our brains. The old-era ended so many seasons ago, everything was moving so fast, but still staying the same.

A chilling thought broke in. Maybe being genalt was the only way out of the unhouse. A strange urge to log all my feelings, thoughts, and sensations was peaking right then. Something big was going down, and maybe my perceptions might wind up as wrap-arounds in a spot's narro.

Then the connector buzzed. Was it someone unfamiliar to Home, another knock-knock or someone just being polite, buzzing before jumping into my living room? I rushed over to nex back, deliberately walking behind the monitor source to avoid being seen in the jeri-era duds. Then I turned off its eyes-in, and answered.

"Hello, this is Stan..."

Ngo Blgo, the pasty-faced genalt interested in stealing my job, popped up on the screen. His funny tag was a tribute to genes donated by early NeighborWorld stars. Most non-genalts in 838 called him Nogo Blogo. And I pronounced it No-go Blow-go.

"Why'd you block my eyes, Stan?" Nogo barked, all nasty.

"Because I'm not dressed yet, Nogo. Want to watch?"

"No," Nogo said, and blocked my eyes. "Cerevello's on his way to your hab," he went on. "He's steamed about something. His chems are twisto."

I almost faded to black, right on the spot. I couldn't believe it. Going somewhere to actually see someone was unheard of, except to symbolize the seriousness of a situation. Even with the General Offices monitoring, it was for private, hush mode, in-person conversation. Hearing that my boss was on his way to see me put me in nervous shock.

"H-he's coming here?" I stuttered. "T-to this hab? Where Syl and I live? Why?"

It was barely audible, but it distinctly sounded like Nogo was chuckling.

"Thanks," I grunted, then disnexed.

I walked back into the kitchen, hung up my Bogie and trenchie and sat down to eat. After a few bites, the homefries stuck in my throat; dry and unappealing. The eggs tasted like poly-food models. Again right on cue, Home started playing a slow trumpet paseo.

"Shut up, "I said. Then, thinking about how the sound track might work, I said, "Aw, fuck it. Keep it in."

The morning wasn't shaping up too well. The nekro fearscape was growing in the background. I didn't trust Nogo. It wasn't because he was genalt, or because I was jealous of his talent. It was because he thought average Neighbors were lower than skurd. Sure, most Neighbors were ignorant, and they frustrated advos sometimes. But Nogo hated them. And though we'd only been in-person together once - except Point A feelie-realie - he'd been nexing-in with me every day, for half a season, playing amigo.

Finally, the worst event possible; my boss was on his way here, to talk me into some energy-draining project. Coming right up after this short break. Rubbing my temples, groaning, I looked out through the kitchen window into the dim morning light and saw it was going to rain, maybe snow. The whole day was slanting nekro. I gulped down hot coffee and tried to brace myself, but it was bad focus all the way. With my fists clenched, breathing hard, gritting my teeth, my stress level alarmed Home.

Mina appeared on a console screen nearby, in leotards, her thin, olive face framed by black hair in a bun. A sitar whined in the background.

"Stan, you're upset," Mina chimed reassuringly. "Breathe deeply through the nose. Yes."

Some yoga breathing restored my equilibrium and shut up Mina. But she came back pronto. "Message... a message coming up on the 838 personal monitor. Oh, Stan. How touching... It's in old era text!"

I was thinking of retiring Mina. Then the message came up on the screen. Mierda.

MEMO FROM THE CONSOLE OF
WILLIAM E. "BIFF" CEREVELLO
TO STAN MOZUCK: G-N, STAN. HOPE U NO MIND ME
STOP BY FOR A L C. U-B U-FED!

Stop by for a little chat. What did that mean? What the hell was going on?

I headed upstairs to the bathroom to shave and shower before Cerevello arrived. The bathroom door had hardly closed behind me when I heard Sylvia's grating nasal voice, peaking, filling the whole Hab. She sounded like she was calling me through a twenty-meter schnozzle.

"Standard... Someone's coming. Someone's he-ere."

My head was throbbing. A quick peek at the bathroom screen above the sink wasn't flattering. My unshaven mug looked bloated and emaciated at the same time, my forehead and neck veins were sticking out. The shot of my face was superimposed on a split screen that also showed the hab's touch-lot. Rain was already drizzling down.

Then Cerevello slowly pulled into the touch-lot in his little green e-mag. The electromagnetic vehicle was tweaked to look like a 1965 Carvette, a stunning duplication, right down to four useless wheels. The e-mag mag stopped and Cerevello stepped out, clenching his raincoat lapels together, banging his vid/source - which looked just like old-era eyeglasses - against the bridge of his nose with a free hand. Getting drenched in the thickening rain, he creep-walked to the door.

"Ok, ok. I hear you!" I yelled back at Sylvia. "I'm coming!"

I wanted to watch Cerevello, so I yelled at Home, "Switch, switch! Full up!"

Home switched to another source in the kitchen, and got a shot of him coming in the door. Heading downstairs, I caught his entry on an overhead monitor. Cerevello closed the door, still nervously clenching his coat, and broke wind, loudly. In embarrassment, he looked down at the floor, making rainwater pour off the brim of his beat up hat onto his shoes.

Cerevello was bad focus incarnate, a picture of uncontrolled anxiety. But his motions gave him away as a master manipulator. Hunchbacking, duck walking, and groveling, in a way carefully designed to create viewer discomfort, he understood the arcane secrets of social science. His chemstat was always imbalanced, but he used that defect to make his crew feel guilty, to get sympathy. Always sick, always needing help, always sentimentalizing about the glory days of pills - but still always trying new stimsublims - he only needed a little of your time.

Projecting a unified motion, ready to climb, I strode into the kitchen to greet my wincing, farting, old-era relic bossman, William E. 'Biff' Cerevello. An in-person with Biff required confidence, positive thinking. I began mentally drafting my Upfielding speech. I could see myself at Point A, looking grateful, holding my Upfielding plaque, and thanking everyone for making it possible. I was vividly imagining delivering a wonderful anecdote, about my grandpa telling me how dreams could come true. Then reality broke through.

Cerevello's freaked, jerky movements, and Sylvia's empty-headed stirrings in the other room squashed everything into perspective. Impending doom. No way out.

"Standard," Cerevello whined, still clutching the lapels of his rain mac. "Sorry about overiding and walking right in. You want me to come back later? You know, I can always come back if you're busy right now."

He glanced towards the other room, as if Sylvia and I could possibly be busy in a male-female way, and smiled stupidly.

"Of course not, Biff. I've got time. Stick around," I said, starting to grit my teeth again. "Have a donut. Gert just brewed coffee."

I had time because he was my boss. Cerevello sat down at the table, unbuttoned his mac, and pushed back his old-era journo's hat. Abruptly, the sound from Alice DeMalice in the other room ended. Biff ignored me, while furtively ransacking his pockets for pills. An olfactory spot, a K-Factor, from some famous Chinese garden, started blaring from Sylvia's screen. Most guys Cerevello's age would probably still call olfactories like K-factor 'Smell-O-Vision' or something.

"Nex-in now for K-Factor," the spot's voice-over said. "K-Factor stimsublim patterns elicit olfactory sensations. Nex-in now." Some Chinese violin music swelled for a second.

Trying to feel less panicky about Cerevello's odd visit, I acted like the in-person was routine. I wanted a peek at the new Sino-gush anyway, so I nexed into the K-Factor garden spot, via the kitchen table screen.

"Gonna zoom some of this K for a second, boss," I half yawned.

As soon as the light hit my eyes, the rain sounds in the garden spot swelled in perfect synch with the rain sounds outside my window. Then unexpectedly, sound combined with overpoweringly intense, real aromas; jasmine, lotus, spices, eucalyptus, pine. It was a dramatic demonstration of the power of subliminal light and ultra-sound over human chemistry, and definitely Chinese tech. They used k-factor aromatherapy for everything, for mental health, having fun, even telling time. Like jasmine was 1400 hours, lotus was 1500, or something.

"Ouch," I said, half chuckling. "It works."

The K-Factor was opening me up, making me crack smiles and amigo teeth, but it was still pretty edgy focus. Cerevello had been bragging to the G-O about the two great young guys he had working for him, Stan and Nogo, and how much they liked him. And how they'd do anything for him. This probably meant bringing all the Weirds in 838 into the Spotlight. Going after the Weirds as the nekro skulls of our times was the wrong box, and potentially dangerous. Things always flip. Bad guys one week misunderstood good guys the next. A misdirected m-line on the Weirds would ruin my chances of getting out of 838.

"So how are you?" I asked, still smiling. "In the real live flesh and dirt, once again. How many seasons has it been now?"

I paused, losing the smile.

"What's going on?"

He shrugged, polishing his vid-source glasses with a worn-out snot rag, playing down the visit. The new K-Factor was too subtle for Biff's clogged brain; it was stuck in some time worn convolution. For me it was almost overpowering, and it was twisting my chems, producing strange side effects, like feeling somehow I was with my boss in China. It made me nauseous. I couldn't wait for his answer.

"Uh-oh..."

I bolted upstairs to the bathroom without even excusing myself, all gaggy and listo to toss breakfast pronto. But the queasiness panned, and I held my focus. I walked back down to the kitchen, where Cerevello was still cleaning his antique fashion-prop V/S glasses, squinting at the lenses, still so absorbed in his guilt game he hadn't even noticed I was gone.

"Gert, give us some donuts," I told my kitchen, and instantly they appeared nearby. I plopped the plate of golden indigestion right under C-Man's tortured mug. "Want some coffee, Biff?"

"No thanks, Standard," Cerevello said, frowning. "Sylvia got me some."

Cerevello pushed his unchic vid-source glasses against the bridge of his nose, moved them a little, then rattled an old-era style bottle of pills. I couldn't believe near-smear Sylvia had Gert serve Cerevello coffee, but there it was. Good. At least Cerevello thinks she's still with it. Or bad. Maybe she's not smearing, and she's in on it.

"Stan," Cerevello continued in a sincere, velvet voice. "We want you to know how much we like your work. That is, Alan Dingleman and I. Alan and I have been talking about you all morning. That is, you and Nogo. We really like your work. I just want you to know that."

Dingleman was Biff's way-back buddy at the General Offices. Climb time, baby. Cerevello smiled sheepishly, and banged his goggles against his honker again. For a moment, lame optimism crept into my chemstat, making me glow goofy.

"Thanks, Biff. You know, I've been lucky at 838. Bob Sideways was a challenge, even with the freedom I enjoy here. And …"

Cerevello interrupted, gesturing condescendingly with his left hand, poking specs with his right.

"That's great, Stan," he said. "Great. We like your work. That's why I want your help. Stan, I want you to…"

Biff paused, and sighed loudly. He looked like he was shrinking. His opened mac exposed huge butterfly-shaped perspiration stains billowing from his armpits. After one more poignant poke at his specs, Cerevello looked intently at the donuts, and began stirring his coffee, banging the spoon loudly against the cup. His lips trembled; he was sweating so hard his glasses had steamed over. He stared at me like he was in some great pain only I could stop. Then the K-Factor hit him.

"What's that smell?" Cerevello mumbled doubtfully. "Am I smelling it right, or not? Smells like a damned old-era Chinese restaurant in here. Is that it?" His expression went blank.

"I sure could use a burger," he went on. "Haven't eaten all day. Been sick. Damn stomach's always upset. Worryin' too damn much about the spots is what it is. What do they call it? L-Factor?"

Burgers in the morning, all day? Cerevello working long shifts, too?

"K-Factor," I answered, trying not to sound like he should have known L-Factor was 26 seasons ob. "K-Factor."

Cerevello stared at the donuts, transfixed by some internal argument about how to do whatever he came here to do. The sound of the spot coming from the other room suddenly got louder, like someone had left the connector open, ready to nex and inteleract. It felt like someone was probing. I had to find out without drawing attention. All the shots had to look casual, sponto, un-peeped. Maybe someone got Sylvia to leave the connector open, paid her in new limited access patterns. No, she was too gone-D to handle that. A random nex? No, advos have sacred space, and this was supposed to be a hush-mode in-person. It was frizzing me. I got up and walked around the table towards the other end of the kitchen, changing the mix, trying to throw a little spike in whatever eye might be peeping.

If this were really part of an ongoing spot, the spot in the other room would recognize something that fit its producer's personality - some sound, word, shot, or ambience. And if we were talking about something that might bounce, the sound would get louder, to warn us and give us time to prep for the nex al mundo, or disnex. We would hear them come-back, hear them hearing us.

Already, from thousands of miles from the K-Factor garden, German school kids had become part of the spot's audio fabric. Then, on Sylvia's monitor, a visual of the kids popped into the background. The sound of an African pop song, sung in French, squeezed under - the perfect audio bridge. Some experiments are dangerous, mi padron, we may be next in line.

Cerevello started banging his spoon against the cup again, staring at me without any trace of awareness of the spot getting louder, or any probing or peeping. It seemed incred that Cerevello could stoop to sleazy spy stuff. The older guys all grew up believing NeighborWorld was mankind's salvation. When it came to selling us, sin permiso, Cerevello was incapable of dirty deeds. But monitoring a conversation, to use in "The Making Of Biff Cerevello's Bluebook Retirement Spotlight," would be easy for him. In fact, he probably wouldn't be able to resist that idea, wouldn't even think he was infringing on my sacred.

I couldn't figure how Cerevello's reaction to the K-Factor could slide into that spot's ambience, so I felt even more nervous about looking beat, making bad focus. The paranoid scram had to end. I stared at Cerevello, looked into his eyes, and smiled. Then I yelled, "Sylvia, did you leave the damned connector open?"

After a long pause, she mumbled "Yeah, I mean, no. Uh, what? Oh, yeah. I did."

Cerevello remained impassive, immersed in seven stars and water, plotting some 'pity me' angle, waiting for his moment, totally oblivious to the open nex. He was unhep to NeighborWorld's slimy spy stuff, even after being surrounded by it all these years. He was going to try to nail me with guilt, when all he needed was his beloved tech. That was a relief. Still, someone had to be peeping.

"Want some coffee, Biff?" I asked, still dangerously close to frizzing.

Cerevello raised and lowered his eyebrows, looking bewildered, then pointed to his nearly full coffee cup.

"I already told you, Standard. Sylvia got me some." He paused to give me a withering look, and said, "Are you lumed, Stan? Are your chems twisted again? Are you too lumed to talk shop chops?"

"Oh no," I came back. "No, I forgot. That's all. Want me to freshen it for you? Want a warm up? Oh, no. It's still warm. Still warm. What did you want to talk about, Biff?"

Cerevello was still staring at me, sweating like a sprinkler system. His lips began trembling again. After a short pucker, he mustered a determined expression, and resumed his speech suddenly, gesturing flamboyantly with his handkerchief.

"Stan, you know how good you made Bob Sideways look? How you transformed him? People, I mean, individs, are calling him Starlight material for a big Local now, even calling him the next big head."

Cerevello paused to smile, almost crosseyed, then pushed on.

"Amazing, son. I mean, you've got to know how much I like your work. So I think you must know why I came all the way over here to go in person with you."

If Sideways was on his way to becoming a big skull, so was I. If there was really any way of getting out of here, I had to start making good focus for myself, show some initiative, take command. But mainly, I wanted to know what the hell was going on.

"Does this have to do with Weirds?" I asked.

Obviously, Biff wasn't ready for that, because he stopped staring, looked down with a stupid grin, and started breathing fast, almost panting.

"Because I think they're amazing," I went on, waiting for the next, maybe fatal, reaction. "That Francis The Sissy guy made monitors glow in jumbo-chrome colors all over 838. At least, that's what I see and hear coming back."

My expression was blank as I paused, then pushed on.

"And he made screens dissolve and turn into little holo-zigs that looked like his head. Incredible stuff. I do believe the Weirds are onto something big. Or were. Whatever."

Then, of all things, a giggle escaped. A light-headed giggle, just a goofy glow expulsion, still a slap in the face if Cerevello wasn't comping amigo. It was the K-Factor, making me bravo and eupho, confessing symp for the Weirds to my boss, who hated them, and making me laugh. With the nex maybe open, too. Man, K-Factor really worked. Poor old Biff's face was turning bright red. He looked ready to explode.

"It wasn't just 838, Stan," Cerevello spat back, his whole body trembling now. "It was the whole goddamn regional chunk! The whole Great Lakes! I suppose you don't think that's serious. Do you?" He paused, still shaking, wiped his nose, and narrowed his eyes accusingly.

"I know your views," he said, waving his handkerchief like a piece of damaging evidence. "I hear what you're saying. You're not Hard, but you sure ain't Soft. You just don't fit do you, Stan? How the hell do you know what the Weirds really are? They don't stick around long enough for anyone to know. They never Spotlight, and no one can keep them locked down, or in focus. You ever got one Stan? Hah? Got any Weirds we can look at right now? Real stuff, not animix. Got any?"

So now Cerevello was admitting that the break-ins slammed into the whole Great Lakes area. Officially he'd been flatly stating the Francis incidents were restricted to 838 and 834. He also claimed 838 had recorded Weirds, which everyone knew was crap. The images evaporated in seconds, they didn't hold. We only had memory-generated animix, screw-loaf, cabeezer-hetch ima-gens, not originals. As far as what the Weirds wanted, what they intended to do with their break-ins, or when they were going to happen again; nobody knew. They did whatever they wanted, on their own schedule.

"They got my balls in a wringer, Stan," Cerevello said with an agonized look. "And they're gettin' ready to crush 'em!"

Cerevello's quaint jango was a sure sign of pressure frying his brain. Obviously someone was pressuring him, but he was probably exaggerating. I mean, the G-O monitored Bob Sideways, didn't they? The system actually worked, sometimes. So who were the shadowy pols twisting Biff's balls? Some new genalt cult he'd blipped into, or just a paranoid delusion?

"Who, Biff? Who has your balls in a wringer? Surcord goons? The G-O? Who? There has to be a faction, or a splinter group, or it just won't Go..."

Then the uncontrollable laughter started drizzling out again. There was awareness that all my flap was crap, and that the K was mighty indeed. It made me sincere, like a kid, a novice, and that kind of attitude wouldn't get me out of 838. Another table slapping howl erupted, making me wheeze. Bad focus. I was building my own M-line, but couldn't stop. "Sorry   about giggling, but that k-factor is packing goo-goo grande," I said, trying to make good, serious focus. "It's a real skull-tweaker."

Cerevello's gaze hardened, his jaw jutted forward, making his bottom teeth stick out. He was really pissed-off now, frizzing. I'd stepped on a nerve.

"Never mind that shit, Stan!" he sputtered. "When a guy like Francis or the Fire Inspector stays out of the Spotlight this long, it makes us look bad! It could ruin everything! My Blue Book chances, your click up, Nogo's, everything!"

He paused, and pointed at me dramatically with his hankie hand.

"You have to go after them, Stan. Go after the Weirds. And you have to make 'em look bad. No star crap. An M-line, pure and simple, for all of us, Stan. For all of us."

For a moment, it seemed like the loud spot and the mixed-in rain sounds distracted him. He paused, and crushed his V-glasses against the bridge of his nose.

"You do this one thing for me," he pleaded in a soft, hoarse whisper, "and you're made for life. Alan Dingleman already mentioned your name to some important guys at the G-O."

Cerevello made one of his expressions meant to get pity.

"Myself, well, I don't have long to go. You know, my health. I'll take my thing and split."

Cerevello brightened, smiling again.

"But you… you'll be in all the big Locals, covering all the climber focus, doin' spots about how we're all smearin' out here in the sticks. You'll have it all. Just do this one thing, man. One thing. For me."

Cerevello would never admit little Locals were smearing in a monitored in-person, any more than he would admit the Weirds blew out most of the Great Lakes grid. Something really big was shaping up. Home's wind sounds got louder, then, boom. "Goddamit!" he shouted without warning. "I want it done!"

Begging and pleading shifted quickly into threat and intimidation.

"You're supposed to pick up Nogo so you two can work in-person, like big skulls in big Locals do."

Then he made a worried look, and said, "Can you handle it, Stan? Can you? Because I don't want you involved if you're going to be too lumed to work. You'll lose your edge, or wig out and frizz violent. You're known for that."

Cerevello was talking dangerous talk. I couldn't believe my ears. Frizzing violent wasn't in my nature, it never happened in my entire career. The cold fearscape that was crawling in since the first take of the day was now actually starting to overpower the K. The in-person was going malo, the head was too feelie-realie.

"Since when am I known for frizzing violent? What the hell are you talking about?"

"All I mean," Biff said apologetically, "is if you can't give it your best, step down so Nogo can do something."

Nogo wasn't capable of doing anything, let alone something. He was dry as a bone when it came to real sparks. I came back dark-barking on Biff's scenario all pronto, in my most deadpan mug and metallic drone.

"No, no, no. Not Nogo. He can help or something, but I'm not collaborating with Nogo. Let him be an assistant producer. Then we'll expand the gig so he can grab some good cred. I've got no problem with the guy if we don't have to spend too much time together. I just…"

It was time to plead.

"Listen, if you really want my help with this spot, and it's really that important to you, it has to be my spot. Mine."

I couldn't believe what I was saying. I didn't want to do this stupid spot, but I didn't want Nogo to have it, either. It was a ticket out of here, although doing it this way was dangerous. I made a Biff-like hand gesture, like I was haggling over prices, and schmoozed on.

"Look, Biff... they call them Transdimensional Weirds because they can be in two places at once. Or seem to. They fool every bio-scan or source we throw at them. They're untraceable. That's first off. Then remember, they blow gear with their minds. What's to prevent them from frying the gear? I mean, that's provided I can find them."

I gave him the harried, overworked slave look.

"Then, if I can find them, and somehow keep the gear and focus intact, what next? I can't bury them if they refuse to Spotlight. They've got to come on down, join the Neighborhood, in full focus. If they take a defiant stance, their cult popularity is going to grow. To me, that's worse than wrecked gear. We want M-Line Spotlighters, not cult stars. Right?"

Telling it like it was purged me, made me feel heroic. Then there was that barely audible noise, that pulse, like electro-frogs burping. Were they vipping squares into my skull in my own sacred?

Biff kept blinking and twitching and fussing with his goggle-sources, reacting like I hadn't even spoken. For him, the whole scenario was already worked out and written in stone. Nothing I could say would change his mind, or his slant.

"Alright, alright," Cerevello agreed, too quickly. "The spot's yours." He raised his eyebrows and peered over the tops of his glasses. "And don't worry about Nogo," he went on in a patronizing tone. "He'll do his job. He'll do what we say."

Biff's face erupted into a beaming smile as he began proudly listing Nogo's virtues.

"You couldn't ask for a better sidekick," he said in a coachy tone. "Nogo does all the funny voices for the ethno-boxes, the accents and stuff. And he can repair gear in a right to left brain mode, for Chrissakes! Instinctively! He can feel a shot before it happens. Don't tell me he can't find those sons of bitches.

"And you've got to admit he's not bad at shaping spots and creating slants," he added with a condescending tone.

The only thing I felt like admitting about Nogo was that he was an unscrupulous, meanie-monk, splice-baby worm. Letting him steal the spot was a no-go. I couldn't screw up a chance of getting out of here. I had to do the spot, and do it right.

Cerevello stared open mouthed at the door, smiling oddly. He turned to look at me, as if he was going to say something, then pulled on the brim of his crumpled, still wet hat, stood up, and abruptly walked out the door, leaving it open behind him. Rain poured in, soaking the floor. Then the shot showed me walking over and closing the door, and watching him leave through the window, instead of a screen, like in an old- era thriller, for suspense. The next shot was better.

Rain drove down Cerevello as he walked his beaten walk across the touchlot to his e-mag, his fear and confusion showing through the deluge. The electromagnetic path, made of super-conductive earth, hummed quietly at low freq vibration. Then the e-mag's bottom glowed and he was gone. After all the time I thought I'd never get rid of him, just like that; he was gone.

- 2 -
"GET OUT THE DAMNED SPOT"

HAB INTERIOR - OVERHEAD SHOT – DAY

So the gig was pushed in my face without a choice. I walked back and sat down at the kitchen screen. Another work atmosphere music track began, with ambient nature sound stimsublims buried in the mix; a spacey, bubble-noise and baby-tunes motivator. Wind sighed in the background, highlighting the feeling of doom. Stan Mozuck would play the patsy, the poor sniv selected to save Cerevello's wasted career. I'd have to secure the ladder of ambition for that sneaky genalt, too.

Biff was incompetent, Nogo played con games, and I was willing to work around that for the sake of smooth. But this was different. I had to M-line some Neighbors for common box beating. A very nekro M-line, too; a trip to the unhouse at best, overdub at worst.

Stimsublim was the only thing that could numb the pain. I checked my health monitor, to see what I could still lume on without twisting myself too much. I wished I had a real dog or cat pet. Not animixed feelie-realie, a real one.

"Witch doctor," I said to the screen. "Doctor Tim! How am I doing?"

Dr. Tim popped up on the screen, his long tan 240 seasons face under a green surgeon's O-R cap, clad in green hospital scrubs.

"Oh, ok, I guess," the health voice came back, all folksy country sawbones. "But Sylvia...not so good."

Doctor Tim paused, an uncomfortable pause, looking serious.

"Oh, by the way, Stan," he continued, perking up. "I took the liberty of using her chems to build a good stimsublim P-S-A."

"You did what?" My Health program's independence, and boldness, shocked me. "You put Sylvia in a public service announcement? A P-S-A? What the hell's wrong with you? She's almost smeared. You want them coming after her? Coming here?"

"No, no," Dr. Tim came back sincerely. "I'd never do that. Just the sappy warning voice, that's all I used her for. Oh yeah, also an animix of her staring in the goo-goo with her brain frying. But you can't even recognize her. It's fun stuff. Just fun stuff." He paused. "I hope it's ok..."

The prepro was frizzing down my nubs. Was I talking to myself here, or a little man in a box? What next? Cart me to the unhouse and take over my hab?

"Listen," I said, starting to lose patience. "Don't you dare cue her credit. Go ahead, but do not cue her cred. Cue her as 'Non' or something. I'll take care of it. I mean it's funnier that way, right? And darker, too. Yeah, do that."

"Sure, Stan," my personally created doctor agreed quietly, seeming aware I was still the one who could delete his personality. "Right you are. It's funnier. And darker."

Guilt started swelling, about snapping at Dr. Tim and panning Sylvia nekro out loud. Many Neighbors would find what I said unforgivable. After all, Sylvia and I lived together. We used to eat and sleep together. We had sex, real squish, not feelie-realie, but in the real flesh and dirt. We were more than just hab mates. We used to be in love.

But the truth was that Sylvia spent all her time and cred getting lumed. She blinked on every new stimsublim pattern released. All she ever did was cue cred and tweak her skull. Luckily she wasn't so twisted she couldn't work, or she'd be in the unhouse, in a heartbeat. Maybe she'd even fade to black. Sylvia was probably already glinting on nekrolim, the big nudge, or some other restricted pattern, behind my back. Sometimes she looked faded out enough to scare me. Thank god NeighborWorld kept her on the treadmill, gainfully employed, slaving for relief from slavery. Everyone was information, and NeighborWorld promised everyone growth through information. All I ever saw was a bunch of Neighbors shrinking.

The kitchen still reeked of coffee and painfully authentic cigar stink, pumped in for old- era journo-story atmosphere. Heartburn was killing me. On an in-person with Nogo, without stimsublim, my nerves would blow. My eyes were irritated, and as I began rubbing them, my health profile came up on the monitor screen, ready to roll. The word 'Chems' kept blinking on the sidebar.

"Moderation," the homey doctor voice whispered. "Moderation's the key to success."

Screw moderation. When you needed a cool metabolic, like Satiscope for calmness, or Betastim for creative edge, you sure didn't need Home's nagging. You needed a blink or two, and a lume zoom, zooma-looma.

"Tim, what's going on? Check the chems blink on the health monitor."

"You know what it means," the doc came back. "Stimsublim. You're way above your limit, boy. Way, way over."

Without subliminal fortification, Nogo would boff me. He was a typical NeighborWorld genalt - aloof, suspicious, always trying to make something go. He considered non-genalts inferior, and that justified anything. Genalts just didn't care about average Neighbors. There was no Neighborly love programmed into their DNA. Genalts saw themselves as evolution, destiny. Nogo's opinion probably was "Stan Mozuck is ok, but he's not really built for the future." Maybe the world faced a better future under the Weirds.

The spacey soundtrack was becoming annoying. The babies gurgling and the pinging staccato pulse of tabla drums weren't restoring my inner peace. It was frizzing me. My mouth was dry, my hands itched, my head ached, and an uncomfortable cool sweat was oozing from my body. The task seemed impossible.

I must have been delusional, thinking I could do this. How could anyone background Weirds? They were unknown, maybe not even human, without cred or cue. When you Spotlight someone, or something, you've got the hard and cold, and faces that connect. Here, there was nothing.

The wind outside howled away, still in the mix. Obviously my prophylactic world would be nothing like outside. Outside of NeighborWorld, there were real sounds, real storms, real problems. The natural habitat of the Weirds could be dangerous. But worrying about it was blank screen. It was time to get busy.

"Hey Bill," I told Home's story editor. "Give me a quick composite background on the Weirds. Bring up anything called Weirds or Transdimensional Weirds or Transdimentos or Smooth-brains or break-ins, and put it in historical order, ok?"

Instantly, the spacey soundtrack faded under, and a 1940s-sounding Jump soundtrack started thumping. Then Bill appeared on the screen, all silver-cowled and suspender-snapping, chewing a fat pencil, making his concerned professional face. A real as feelie-realie old-era city news bureau bustled behind him, as he sat in a wooden swivel chair, one foot plopped on his mahogany desk.

"How soon ya want it?" Bill shot back in his grumpy jeri-era "Front Page" voice. "I'm still messing with 'The Making Of Bob Sideways, Alphadrine Cowboy!' I don't want to start bumping stuff around now. You know?"

Home's personalities kept chewing my culo.

"I want it now," I snapped.

"For cryin' out loud," Bill grumbled. "Rule number one. Hurry causes worry. You never gain time, just lose. Corrections, dead end leads, useless research."

"Bill, pan the advice and bring it up. This is full tilt editorial override. Just do it, ok? I'm real and you're not. You're just a fucking tool. Do it."

De pronto the screen showed the old intro art I tacked up when the Weird break-ins first showed signs of hot focus. The fireman's mug, flat white with a bluish cast, shouted out from a close-up, his red coat burning over a canary yellow background, with all the colors goosed. Then shot directions crawled under, and the old title card popped up on top.

WORKING TITLES FOR SPOT ON BREAK-INS: "Through The Looking Glass And Into Your Screen" (OR) "Transdimensional Paradise Or Psychic Hell? Where Do The Weirds Really Want To Take Us?" By Standard Mozuck

INTERIOR - LAB - DAY - FREEZE EXTREME CLOSEUP OF FIREMAN

But nothing else came up. Nothing. The shot's yellow background pattern started to waver a bit, and something looking like snowy static flew from bottom left to top screen right, covering the face. A shot emerged through the blur, an old looking black and white surveillance cam shot of a toilet stall from overhead. A middle-aged individ, female, afri, attractive, was on the toilet.

She looked agitated, gripping a wad of toilet paper with enough force to shred it, then started sobbing and wailing.

"Oh please stop this," she whispered frantically. "Please stop this. Please leave me alone."

Then another voice swelled over hers, a hoarse male voice. "Shut up, bitch," it rasped. "We're not done fucking with your mind. And we won't be done until Jesus H. Christ comes back. Hey, can you imagine men actually find you hot? Those videos of you in the shower are making us tons."

The woman started crying again, harder. "No, no, no," she moaned. "You can't do this to people. It's wrong. It's wrong..."

Then the shot disappeared from the screen entirely, replaced by gray static. I never logged that shot, or even saw it before. "What the hell was that, Bill?" I shouted at the editor. "Where did that come from?"

"Where did what come from?" Bill shot back. "I put up your first titles."

"That shot, the lady on the can. What was that all about?"

"I don't know. I've never seen it before. I thought you were rolling it from another deck."

"No other system's running, Bill. Something's fucked up in there. Find out what it is, ok? See if you can find out where that stuff came from."

"Ok," Bill said. "I'm looking for a lady who is already in the can?"

"No, no, you're looking for a woman on the toilet."

"What does that have to do with the Weirds? Is it supposed to be funny?"

"Bill, you're telling me you didn't even really see it, right?"

"How could I not see it? I get paid to never make such errors. I'm not human, right?"

"Did you see it or not?"

"If it was there, I saw it."

"You're saying you're frizzing or what?"

"I'm saying I saw something, but I don't know what it was or where it came from, that's all."

"That's all? Since you're incapable of errors of omission, how can you see something, and not know what it is?"

"I don't know," Bill said, scratching the back of his neck. "When you get right down to it, I'm just an image generated and animixed by you. Maybe you don't know either."

"That's all, Bill. I'll figure it out. Just look for anything loose floating around, see if you can find it. What if it's a break-in or slant-plant or something? I'm screwed. You've got to at least look."

The leak was blowing my focus. All I could think of was taking it from the top. "Right now, bring up the Fire Inspector footage from the first Weird break-ins."

"Done," Bill said, and immediately another shot of the Inspector froze up on the screen.

The Fire Inspector wasn't fun to look at. Staring at the Inspector induced nervous stomach and metallic-mouth symptoms, and they were swelling up in me. And this was animixed. Imagine what seeing real first generation footage of this character could do. Or worse, a flesh and dirt in-person with him. Ay, yi-yi!

The date of the imprint crawled across the Fire Inspector's forehead: WINTER / WEEK 6 / TUESDAY / 1200 HOURS / (4) SEASONS THEN

The Inspector's face was still frozen there, but I didn't feel sick. In seconds, warmth, bliss, and gooey were overcoming this advo like a double black eye of limited access stimsublim. He looked so tranquil, so comforting. Suddenly, unexpected thoughts drifted into my mind. I was focused. All the gooey tech at my disposal was unnecessary. I didn't need to review the shots to remember how it snowballed. The pictures just appeared in my mind, all under the peaceful, watchful gaze of that idiot in a fire inspector's get-up.

Why did they cancel Sylvia's feelie-realie subscription to "Cro-Magnons On The Beach?" On cue with that thought, an old slow waltz, played on the tuba, began rolling in the background. It seemed an odd choice, but I didn't stop it.

How could things get so out of control in just four seasons? Something happens, just a blip, then suddenly it's the next big. Then, just as suddenly, it's daily crunch, so pervasive it's almost forgotten. Then, like all flesh and dirt, it fades to black.

When the Weird break-ins started, we avoided reporting it to the G-O for almost a whole season. We thought it was just a Local 838 problem, so we let things go until they spiraled, in plain view. We couldn't come up with any slants or shape, and the raw 4-D Weirdness was driving even more Neighbors to the unhouse.

What was your POV, Neighbor? What was psychic terrorism?

Most Local 838 yokels thought the break-ins were just genalt whiz kids screwing around, and that sooner or later, they'd take credit for new tech and pay for damage. But no genalt kid ever cued cred, and the break-ins kept on, like something out of psi-fi hell. The Weirds made faces, and screens blew up. That thought quick faded, tucked under subliminal noise.

What was a crime against awareness, dear Neighbor? There must be justice for victimized Neighbors. If you beat the box, the box will beat you.

So, still without involving the G-O, 838 started looking for culprits. We probed all known Spot abusers and box beaters, slanting on Captain Cortex types with enough gray- grooves to pull it off. And of course, malcos who posed dangerous and demanded more than their fifteen.

All that forgotten hysteria flashed into my mind; the babbling heads being escorted into whacko-wagons, and taken to the unhouse. Besides inadvertently finding a few real malcos with plans, we got nada. The suspects who didn't smear went home. The inquiry collapsed, because nobody matched bio-profiles from the break-ins. Worse, the DNA configs hardly registered, just vague traces. Obviously whoever was breaking-in never applied for a Spotlight. They weren't disnexed or discon, they were totally unknown to the system.

Right in synch with that thought, the tuba waltz faded under swelling military snare drums and tympani. I dived deeper into the flow, sex-death, get funny, the old formula.

After the break-ins, G-O Grandees peddled answers, like the prepros were accruing consciousness. Sure, it seems that way sometimes, but we all know glitches and frizz are within, and only the user's mind is to blame. The G-O was just trying to control tech flow and ideas with cheap, one-week hysteria and demographic splintering. Nobody dared think what was really on the Bigs' minds. There was someone out there with a lot of power, even more power than NeighborWorld.

"No more music for now," I told Home. Instantly the drums were gone.

A stimsublim urge started twisting me. I needed a blink. To keep my mind off my mind, I poured a glass of water and drank it. Wind was whipping through the back yard gardens, spitting thick clusters of raindrops against the windows. The gusts were strong, and rattled my overpriced, Nova-Mas eco-seal bay windows, punctuating each attack with a loud, soaking splat.

I wasn't really prepared to go head to head with nature's raw power. Working outside in this weather could be crazy. But the old-era guys did it. And it would sure make me feel alive. Thinking about it goosed my knobs.

What if the Weirds could kill with their minds?

Feeling alive. It reminded me of a theory about Weirds, called 'Ozzy and Harrier's Last Dream.' It was fantastic speculation, real oddball conspiro-flimmer. The idea was simple. According to Ozz-Dream believers, back at the end of the old era, the nuclear war everyone feared really happened. The world ended. Humanity was wiped out but dreaming - in heaven, or some collectively terra-formed nirvana somewhere. Some ancient calendar prophecy came true.

Dead, but dreaming of NeighborWorld. In the abyss between life and death, we saw ourselves at a global family barbeque by the pool, transformed into good Neighbors on an info-screen. No drunken dads or frigid moms attacking each other with hot dog skewers, no kids trying to drown each other. It was techno heaven.

Actually, limbo or purgatory. The break-ins, Dreamers concluded, were a prelude to the dream ending. Dreams are uncontrollable, especially the dreams of billions of dead souls. As we hurtled further from planetary existence, we'd soon realize it was a dream, and then fade to black. Or the Creator would wake us in paradise, as stars. There'd be no poverty or war, near-immortality, in utopia without toil, where every individ was valued info.

The Last Dream's followers had an artifact to prove their bizarre credo, a supposedly sponto generated image that appeared on 838 monitors two seasons ago. No one cued credit, no bios matched, so to Dreamers, the sponto ima-gen was proof. Techno heaven, dear N's and A's.

"Bill, put up that shot of the Last Dream's holy artifact."

The song "Somewhere Over The Rainbow," played ala 1940's swing section, filled the room. Then an old B-movie, end-of-the-world, hysteria-looking title crawled across screen center - THERE IS NO FUTURE! OR IS THERE? Instantly a mushroom cloud erupted on screen, black and white old stuff, to the sound of a deafening rumble. The image popped up, showing a standard four-person family unit staring at itself on a screen, stark black and white, with bluish screen light.

And that's it. The original run supposedly lasted two hours - with some angle changes - of a modern caveman family staring at itself, in an electronic fire. For a sign of divine intercession from the spirit world, it wasn't too impressive. There was no way to authenticate the break-in. It just seemed phony, like maybe it was some genalt whiz kid, trying to imitate or fabricate a Weird break-in. But nothing on my side, not Home or Bill or any of those guys I created, could make it stick. And I had the good stuff.

It was just instinct. Somehow, the shot was, as the old guys used to say, a Lee-Harvey, a fake, a mind-fuck decoy. Clearly, it wasn't Weird. The Weirds weren't saying we were all dead, or in paradise. But the creepiest thing was that the shot held. Obviously a plant, it didn't evaporate like Weird break-ins. Ozzy and Harrier's Last Dream theory was bogus. So who was planting slant? Could it be the same shadowy pols squeezing Biff's balls?

"Bill, put up the Aliens Among Us theory footage."

"Aliens?" Bill came back quickly, as if he'd been waiting for my next command. "Are you sure you want to sit through a bunch of boring late night Yakk Backs? You think that's going to get you where you want to go?"

"I'm examining all the material, Bill. Is there a better system than that?"

"Yeah, Stand," Bill said, "but it's a dead-end lead. The Alien theory guys have one story. Some Supreme Galactic Council somewhere is fed up with earth culture, or lack of it, and it's blasting us with directives from deep space. We don't understand these directives, so we hallucinate."

"And?" I begged, starting to frizz again.

"Well, jeez. We both know the break-ins aren't hallucinations caused by spacemen."

Editorially, at least, Home was still with me. But it wasn't reassuring, especially if Weirds did what they did with some kind of mind control.

"You also got your judeo-christian-islamic fundamentalist crew who think the break-ins are end-times messages from God," Bill cut in quickly. "Or satanic crypto-babble, depending on their mood. I got 'em all for you, Stan. The thumb-in-butt pure science guys who called it interference from tectonic plate shifts. The guys who said the faces and voices were pure coincidence, exploding monkeys. I got the whole confused pack; the prognosticators, pundits, slanters and shapers. Do you really need to see it?"

"No, Bill. You're right. When you're right, you're right. Did you find the woman on the can yet?"

"Still a ghost, chief," Bill shot back. "I say, if you're in a hurry, let's go with what I've got so far. It's all just stuff you've checked out. Kind of your original intuitive searches, know what I mean?"

On screen, still chomping on his pencil, Bill handed some paper copy to an animixed ima-gen secretary, then gave me his "Let's go get 'em" grimace.

"Bang 'em out for me, Bill," I said. "Time's wasting."

My screen faded to black and the sound of a jazz quartet doing a mod secret agent vamp - with walking bass and smooth sax solo - cut into the room. A title appeared over the black in wispy, ghost-like letters - THERE'S NO CAUSE FOR ALARM. The letters solidified into times roman bold, then evaporated. Then a bust shot of a less harried, almost younger looking Biff Cerevello appeared on the monitor, wearing a dark blue old-era anchorman's suit, without his vidcam specs.

"Neighbors," Biff said with a sincere smile, "There's a sickness going around. But you won't be able to ask your friendly Home/Med system what to do. Some of you are frightened. Believe me, I know how you feel. But you can all go back to living the happy lives you've designed for yourselves, free from worry."

He paused and made a lame attempt at brightening, using the same smile, only with raised eyebrows and a more confused look in his eyes.

"These disruptions are no cause for alarm," Cerevello continued. "Yes, Neighbors, the frizz is within. You are not dead but dreaming, an evil extraterrestrial empire is not controlling your mind, the 'Weirds' - as some of you call this phenomena - do not exist, and there are no powerful cults within, or outside of NeighborWorld."

The shot changed angle, to show Cerevello from a profile, with his unspectacled eyes still facing the source, almost a film noir half-over-the-shoulder shot. It was as disturbing to watch as the Fireman's moosh, but for a different reason. Cerevello was painfully corny.

"You're alive, dear Neighbor, and safe," he said, turning to front. He narrowed his gaze, as awkwardly as an old-era car dealer reading a prompter's card. "You're just hallucinating." He smiled stupidly. The director (not me, dear N's and A's) must have told him to smile knowingly.

"Recent studies have shown," he went on, "That there is a threshold written into our DNA. And when it's crossed, we hallucinate. Global self-awareness might be more than we all can chew. Some of us just can't function in a society where we're so nexed together."

He paused. Then, like a punch-drunk boxer, he reflexively banged the vid glasses he forgot he wasn't wearing against the bridge of his nose. He smiled with the wounded look of someone who just had dental surgery.

"It seems that after NeighborWorld's novelty wore off, when confronted with the horror of planetary self-awareness, the collective mind balked," he went on. "We're not dead; we're just having a global nervous breakdown."

He raised an eyebrow, and the shot zoomed into a close-up extreme enough to bring up dark circles under his eyes. "Neighbors," he said. "We must control our minds. Or they will control us."

FADE TO BLACK. Immediately another sound track began, ear-bludgeoning jeri-era satan-metal. The spot's title popped up on screen; a rip-off of a homemade old-era conspiracy 'zine cover. A target, like a hypnotic whirlpool, swirl-faded over a stark title, proclaiming: AN EVIL CULT IS IN YOUR LIVING ROOM. It faded, and the first shot began.

It was institutional surveillance-cam stuff, showing a lounge in a bio-collective. Two smeared skulls at a snack bar table were yakking about the Weird break-ins on a makeshift 'in-house unhouse' show. The interviewer, a thin faced middle aged euro man with salt and pepper hair and big hairy ears, had an old microphone and recorder set-up, and kept pushing the audio mike - which probably didn't even work - in the other guy's face. The other smear was a little younger; smaller, darker complexion with double black hair; asian-subcon descent.

"Are evil culties using advanced technology to destroy NeighborWorld?" the interviewer asked him, and an imaginary audience. "Neighbors are panicking. Who are the Weirds, and what are they trying to do?"

"They are crushing my brain," the man being interviewed said, off cue. Then he rolled his eyes back, as if trying to look into his own head. The smeared interviewer stopped a moment, like he forgot something, then ranted on about mind control and Weirds destroying life as we knew it.

The Hard School depicted the Weirds as a menace with muscle, and definitely generated fear. The unhouse yakker was an example; no small feat for smear who couldn't remember their own names. A war to win the minds of the mindless was on.

"They will crush every brain, up and under," the smear being interviewed screamed.

FADE TO BLACK. The image of a candle appeared on the screen, Home's way of saying it was break time. The rain had let up but the room was filling with chiaroscuro, shadows, and gloom. The feeling that psi-factor and spy stuff were playing under the theme was hard to shake.

The sound of cowbells and moos started blaring away, the beginning of a Nanny Cow commercial. Then the animixed cow popped up on my screen. Even advos in sacred space had to endure at least one personalized, monogram commercial every shift.

"Mooooo! Moooooo!" the brown dappled Nanny Cow bellowed. "Who wants a cheeseburger and a shake? Who wants chocolate pudding and a t-bone steak? Tacos carnitas and a nice cheesy pizza. Mooooo!"

A beautiful pasture filled with farm animals appeared on screen.

"Nanny Cow is like having a farm in your own hab," a young mother character quipped. "Nanny Cow nano-grows any specialty meat or dairy product you can dream up, without killing one precious animal."

"You're a vegetarian who loves meat," youngish dad said, joining her. "So you love Nanny Cow. Order or renew now and get Prepro Porky included for just the price of your Nanny Cow subscription."

"Moooo!" Nanny Cow tagged. "You'll be glad to meet me, and you won't have to eat me!"

FADE TO BLACK

Then another shot of Cerevello popped up on the screen. It was a short break.

The Softies cranked out countless spots during the break-ins, aimed at teaching Neighbors to cope with constantly being in focus. Control. Nirvana was in the screen. As if that could stop break-ins.

"These Weirds are intangible, nothing more than eruptions from an unruly collective subconscious," Cerevello squeaked in a tense, high-pitched voice. "They're just hallucinations. They can be subdued, or at least tethered, by deep breathing and meditation. Neighbors shouldn't hallucinate," he said sternly, then paused. "Unless they want to." Then he released a higher pitched cackle.

It suddenly popped into my mind that this Soft School spot was probably loaded with quirked-up stimsublims. Both Hard School genalts and ultra-Softies like Cerevello were heavily into restricted subliminal research then. They got me involved in it, too. Who knows how many lists I was on. Hopefully I hadn't seen enough of the spot to twist my chems the wrong way.

Quickly the screen went black. Then Nogo's moosh appeared. He looked frightened, like someone was ready to jump him. Then the image froze, with Nogo in mid-sentence. A spot I-D crawled under him - TO: INFOTECH RESOURCE UPGRADES - NEIGHBORWORLD GENERAL OFFICES - -EMERGENCY ASSISTANCE REQUEST.

Nogo unfroze and resumed, clamoring for help.

"As far as I'm concerned," Nogo said tersely, "the Weirds are psychic terrorists. Local 838 can't stop the break-ins without help. We're underequipped. I believe the Weirds are trying to destroy NeighborWorld, testing it out in the little Locals. There's definitely a conspiracy. We can't find anything out. If this isn't contained somehow, it will become a global threat."

Nogo was the first guy at 838 to inform the G-O, as if they didn't already know. Nogo's plea quickly faded to black, and another pinch began - this time an animix of one of the Weird break-ins. The screen went gray, and a title crawled, in blue letters in the old computer generated style; FRANCIS/APOLOGY.

Since there were no traces of original take, we had to turn to brain scans to produce it, as well as animated donations and warped meanderings from every frip, malco, joker, and snaker in 838. The renderings of 838's whiz kids were priceless. Children had great digital memory; they were clean-brained, innocent. There were five kids in 838, a lot for such a small local, and we used every one. So with all the tech, art talent, and imagination we could muster, we snagged a pretty true likeness.

There was Saint Francis The Sissy, in all his ancient baby-faced glory, spewting and slobbering wit and wisdom. An electronic pulse, coupled with some white and pink noise, quavered faintly behind Francis as he spoke.

"I'm just human, sillies," he lisped. "I don't care about no stupid global eye. Nem nem nem. We didn't wanna hurt no one. No. Or break no silly stuff. No. Because my sister says 'no.' So, I says no. Nem nem nem. Sorry."

Francis's face slow-dissolved.

Nogo and the Hard School's portrayal of the Weirds didn't play. Francis was saying he was real, not a hallucination, and there was no conspiracy, because frizzing gear and scaring Neighbors was an accident. Francis was apologizing for the break-ins. But it didn't explain the Weirds' behavior, or why they didn't want their story told. And it didn't look like the Weirds had leaped off the evolutionary map, unless it was a leap backwards.

Another pinch of an animated Weird break-in began, showing a wide overhead of the CarTown area near Industros Tragicos. The music bed was a circus calliope. The title, FIRE INSPECTOR/ORIGINS, crawled under the wide shot, as it zoomed into a shot of a house on fire. Smoke plumed straight into the lens as the shot tightened on the rooftop, then panned over to show some people watching the house burning from across the street. CarTown near Industros Tragicos was still old-era. Bad homemade wiring and old wood stoves caused fires.

Suddenly the shot was on the street, with fire victims telling their stories to servo Surgeons and 838's servo street-beat reporters, while servo fire fighters battled the blaze. None of the individs were injured, but they looked emotionally distraught enough about losing their homes to make good focus. Then, all together, they looked beyond source, with an expression of happy recognition. This is where animix begins. The original shows them reacting to just a blur.

The Fire Inspector, pedaling furiously on a huge red tricycle, appeared center screen. The tricycle had a pickup bed, laden with disposable cups, water bottles, clothes, coat hangers and racks, and boxes filled with salves and bandages. Clad in his usual fireman's attire, beaming a ridiculous smile; he stopped, dismounted, walked to the back of his tricycle, and began dispensing cool water to the victims. He also offered to take their charred clothing. They declined.

Then the pinch cut to the victims being interviewed about whom or what they were talking to. The servo sources didn't know, since only a blurry image was registering. They told the sources that it was a man they'd seen before, often at fires, but they didn't know his name. They said sometimes he slept in the rain, and never got wet; that a sparkly little cloud hovered around him, and seemed to protect him, like a force field. Then they said some things that were more disturbing.

They said sometimes he was hard to see, even off screen, like a bunch of red, blue, and green phosphorescent lights, electron dots, were amassed without substance; a very crappy looking holozig. Naturally, this made all the Hard School guys say someone had rigged a photon gun, like the kind used in old-era TV sets, to some kind of weak field generator. To me it seemed like he was tenuously holding himself together with an act of sheer will.

Then they talked about seeing nine little red fireman's hats orbiting his head like a nimbus or halo, then sailing in formation directly into their foreheads. Most of them became obsessed with the number nine after the experience. They found patterns in arithmetic systems based on nine instead of ten, discovered arcane symbologies in the number, had only nine pairs of socks.

Overexposed Neighbors remained apprehensive for weeks, expressing doubts about staying in focus, in the Spotlight, even in NeighborWorld. Half of the individs ended up in bio-collectives, with no return ratio. It was a hush-mode rumor for a while that somehow the smeared ones were erasing themselves, leaving no imprint, stealing credit and gear.

Long exposure to break-ins must trigger some unknown biochemical reaction, maybe caused by strong electro-magnetic waves.

All this begged the question; were the Weirds dangerous? The Fire Inspector had his schtick, and Francis - who made screens drip with vibrant colors before they exploded - had his. But were these pear shaped, middle aged nomads capable of real damage? They never hurt anyone. The exploding screens evaporated into thin air, zero space.

But they were definitely dangerous to the system. And unless someone was planting rumors and spinning stats, break-ins could make folks smear, become obsessed; even uproot their desire for NeighborWorld.

A new pinch began, with a title crawl labeled THE SPINNING WOMAN. The sound of Afro-Cuban polyrythms did the rhumba full tilt into the room. La Caltera, The Snake Lady, La Culebreta, The Spinning Woman, La Suenadora; she had lots of names. And there she sat, center screen, in her somnab state, twitching slightly, on a bench in an old-era subway station. The garbled sound of a stationmaster announced times and destinations, then "Please stand clear of the doors..." crackled through a loudspeaker, and over the rhumba. A subway train roared off, and La Suenadora stirred from her slumber, her dark blue mascara-shadowed eyelids drooping. One wide eye pointed left, and the other, squinting, pointed right.

"Diablos!" she screamed in hoarse, fitful whispers, getting louder, peaking. "Diablos!" Then, with her voice modulating into strange, contrasting high-low tones, she began hollering "Angelos! Angelos!" Then she laughed, and cursed the unseen devils. "Chengan les!" she yelled, "Puteros y putas! Putas!"

She looked around at the station platform malevolently, then spat. She rustled a bit, then began snoring, completely asleep in two seconds. Then the image dissolved into a slow circle wipe, and she was gone. La Suenadora had more fine tuned control of her break-ins than the Fire Inspector. She was easy to animix. Everyone who witnessed it saw a perfect old-era slice, with no rough edges, no blurry Weirds, no colors. As an accurate scene from a bygone time - of a crazy woman in a subway station - it was scarier than all the rest.

The screen faded quickly to black, and another pinch started, showing a freeze up of the Weird we called the Generalissimo. On a split screen, it showed him in his two disguises; one more afri-am, the other more euro-am, as identical black and white chessmen. Either way, the guy looked like a hamster in military dictator gear. The Generalissimo wore an ascot scarf and beige riding pants, and his huge epaulette-shouldered jacket bore an explosion of incongruous, seemingly meaningless military emblems, medals, and insignias. He would have looked menacing if it wasn't for that smiling, furry critter face. With those almost crossed eyes gazing behind old-era era tinted prescription glasses, whether afri or euro, with watery blue eyes or double brown, he reminded all witnesses of a chubby rodent man.

My screen faded to black again, and a sinister sounding surf guitar solo started weaving ju-ju in a sound bed. Paul Grayleaf appeared on screen, wearing his monogram western shirt and jeans, sunglasses, headband, and long black hair. He was in the middle of a monologue, moving around the stage like a cat, pushing his hair back, working the mike like a pop star. Paul Grayleaf was my favorite underground comic before he disappeared.

A Huron with a little French-Canadian blood, born on an old era reservation, Greyleaf had a gift for social satire, enough to snag a 'Lenny' before he was 35, and still alive. But Paul wanted to do more than succeed, and like the real Lenny the award was named after, he began getting more involved. A performance he did made some Bigs look real bad, and they did more than threaten lawsuits. His wife committed suicide under mysterious circumstances, someone tried to kill him twice and botched it twice, and finally, they never let him work again. So he went boinky, or so they say, and wound up in the unhouse. He smeared.

Then he disappeared. No one in the bio-collective knew where he went, or how. He's there on the surveillance monitor one minute, then, after seeming to blend into a group of smear, gone the next.

The screen faded to black. Before Bill had a chance to put up the next bit, it struck me that Weirds might be political dissidents, like they had back in the old era. The thought made me feel uneasy, trapped.

"Break time, Bill," I said without hesitating. "Break time."

The candle appeared on my screen again, so I decided to go for a cross-country run while waiting. A few wayward splotches of rain were still tapping on the window, and Home mixed in some more nature sounds; seagulls cawing outside nearby, the raw wind rushing overhead. In the other room, Sylvia was somnab, between spots, and her screen was in hush mode. It was almost comforting to not hear Sylvia's moronic noises, almost stimulating to hear the wild weather. It was a nice two-minute stimsublim run, but it didn't help much.

Maybe some of the bad stims in Cerevello's Soft School spots, or maybe some of Nogo's stuff, had seeped in. Thinking was getting difficult, labored. My focus was fragmented, like some invisible hand was pushing down on my head, forcing my mind away from the truth about the Weirds.

Lost in nekro thoughts, I reached for my coffee mug. I grabbed it, and was slowly raising it to my lips, when something came up on the screen. It was another old surveillance-cam shot, like the woman being harassed in the bathroom. I'd seen this start up shot before, long ago, while a novice. There was Bing Whizzer, the old-era computer voting-machine baron, sitting on a metal folding chair, bound and gagged with duct tape, surrounded by gun-toting people wearing ski masks. But not for long.

Within seconds, the money shot goes down. One of the ski masks walks up behind Whizzer, says, "For crimes against humanity!" and blasts him behind the ear. Whizzer kicks twice and dies.

The footage, showing the 'people's court' execution of one of the bigs who supposedly helped rig old-era elections, was a Lee-Harvey. And definitely not part of my research flow.

"Bill," I shouted at my editor, "What the hell's going on? What are you running? I said I needed a break. Is this like the woman being peeped, or what? Where's this stuff coming from? I didn't ask for this, did I?"

I took a deep, distracted drink of coffee, only to discover too late that Gert had warmed it for me, while I was in the research flow. The scalding hot coffee seared my mouth and throat.

"Ptwaaahh!!" I screamed, spitting it out onto the floor. "Too hot! Gert! Cold water! Please! Help!"

Gert cued up ice water pronto, which I downed while pounding on my chest, making most of it slop all over. Home cleaned the mess quickly, but it was a pitiful joke on me, no matter how the edit went. Who knows who was probing, slanting nekro on the flow?

"No, sir," Bill said quietly, after unobtrusively reappearing on my screen. "You did not. I saw that one. But I'm sorry to say I have no idea what it was. I think we're being peeped, or seeping somewhere. We must not be locked down."

"Haven't you checked it all out?" I asked, already afraid of the answer. "I need my sacred space."

"Down to the last," Bill said bluntly. "All I can offer is that you said it best."

"How's that?"

"The title, Stan. 'Transdimensional Paradise Or Psi-Fi Hell.' "

"Yeah, right. With that profound, incisive, Stan Mozuck touch. Bill, this isn't working for me right now. I need to take on a betastim pattern to regain a creative buzz."

"Don't worry, kiddo," Bill said reassuringly. "I'll find the leak somehow."

"Somehow," I added.

Bill blipped off, and I got busy with what I was really good at; getting lumed. The betastims were goo-goo this week, freshly tweaked. Just a blink, zoom the lume.

"Satiscope stimsublim patterns, please, Home," I said, like an old-era alkie with shakes ordering a shot of medicine at the bar. "And Series 12 betastim."

A green dot appeared on my screen. A deep female voice intoned directions for use and the usual warning which no one heeded.

"Focus your attention on the spot upon your screen," she said. "In a moment, scenes and sounds will appear, and the spot will vanish, but keep your gaze where it was. Maximum suggested use is one minute. Overuse may cause psychological dependency, difficulty making decisions, lack of interest in minutiae and details, and anxiety."

The light was my friend; warm, inviting, always there. And I took advantage of the friendship. In the glow there was oblivion, safe haven from the peeping eye that saw everywhere. The brain got the message first; release, relief. Then the body followed, as the lume seeped further into the entire nervous system. This batch of stims was goo-goo grande, and all the gates opened quickly. It was powerful enough to put me into a Stage 2 introspec in seconds, and new angles and slants were rushing into my expanded head like a river.

On another monitor, I saw an overhead shot of myself looking like a corpse, my right foot tapping slowly, with that ridiculous, open mouthed, blinko-blanko-Joe mug. I was lumed out, immobile, taking it all on, when Sylvia started snoring loudly, shattering everything.

Right on top of that, in perfect synch, Home's delivery system broke in with an announcement.

"Something's coming, honey," the sultry female voice sizzled. "Oooh... Stan. It's coming!"

The corny Voice-Over was something I put in two seasons ago, when I was still trying to talk Sylvia into feelie-realie sex. We hadn't squished in the F and D for a while.

My screen showed an 838 Biz Tek Direk delivery mag as it approached my dock. Home's eyes followed the e-mag van on the path past the touchlot, through the garden, and up to my eco-seal dock. The vans had been frizzing lately. Almost every day, fancy chocolates, intended for some love-starved near-smear, had been coming to my house. Returning the stuff was becoming annoying. So the lume was blown.

"Check address!" I yelled at the van. "Check for correct address!"

Too late. The van had spurted the delivery into my dock. Then, like a post-coital whale, it lumbered off to its next destination. Two huge silver eco-seal eggs were laid on my dock. They were too big for chocolates. It had to be the costume gear I'd ordered. I should have had it all nanoed directly into my hab.

There was lots of gooey stuff, like old era style journo's trench coats and hats - weatherproofed and insulated to 20 degrees below zero, with microdot vid-sources that had 20 kilometer ranges. It was all for a potential spot like Transdimensional Hell, something with atmosphere, a look.

Home cued the containers up on the table right next to me. A check of my costume look seemed like the perfect thing to get my mind off the peeping and seeping, but it was still scaring me down. Frizzing, I ripped open the eggs, then quickly started trying stuff on, starting with a hat, then a coat, to match. I put the look right on top of my work tunic and pants.

The outfits and look looked silly, the poses looked canned. I started laughing a stressed out whimper, then a mad loon laugh escaped. I ripped the clothes off, threw them all over the place, and collapsed on the sofa, with the internal red light blipping.

What was a crime against consciousness?

Obviously, someone was monitoring, even though an advo's locked-down workspace was supposedly sacred. It was bad focus. They were probably already slating me for personality erasal and overdub in a bio-collective named Larry or Linda. Or worse, Trotsky, for troublemakers, dangerous malcos. There, they'd blend, or grind, Stan Mozuck into the 'Wider Angle.' I'd be another blinko-blanko unhouse Joe. There'd be nothing left of me but a living product I-D, a human commercial.

Then a scene of myself - as a Linda - came up on the internal monitor; with me as one of the male characters in the 'Country Good Cookies' campaign. There I was, mindlessly singing the Linda's Cookies jingle like an invocation to God, my personality merged with the winking, straw-bonneted Linda character on the label. Mmm, mmm. Home style.

That creepy, liquid fear sweat started pouring out again. Monitoring the pertinent bits, digging deep into the story before confabbing with Nogo was critical. Whoever was peeping already had enough strange focus to build a whacko-wagon m-line. There was no way I was going to Nogo's without being in control. His powers of recollection were incredible; he could destroy me during event reconstruction.

His great memory wasn't the product of personal achievement, though. It was stamped, templated into his DNA. Geezers like Cerevello fawned and gushed over biotech miracle genalts like Nogo, but I wasn't so impressed. I was careful, though. Nogo already had all the available research, and a working slant. And he wanted my job.

A smell crawled into my nose, the crisp, palm-oily odor of ... what? Spicy Bahamas fried chicken? Then all these tropical fruit, flower, and spice tangs wafted in, strong enough to put me there like feelie-realie Point A. Sylvia was taking on a Caribbean cooking show, with the new K-factor.

A steel band played in the background as she shuffled half somnab, with her mouth open and eyes smoking in their sockets, towards me from the other room. She was trying to speak, and as usual, speech was prefaced by a long, pained stare.

"I know, I know," I said without blinking. "Time for me to go, right? That's what you came in here to tell me, isn't it?"

She agreed vacantly, nodding like a frizz-glitching doll. Sylvia was a one-spot gig gone malo, a face popping out of a P-S-A on everything you want to escape. Lack of self-control was destroying the human race. Genalts, splice-babies, were replacing us everywhere. But the fact that Sylvia was losing it made me cultivate will power. As she started back towards her screen, I looked back at my screen, almost as much to avoid looking at her as to dip back into the flow.

It didn't turn off the feelings of isolation and fear. The panic grew, into another sickening jolt of realization. I was different. I wasn't smearing like Sylvia, or some non-genalt advos. Sure, genalts didn't smear. But I didn't suck up to genalts, like most non-genalts. My v-u on the Weirds and break-ins was different from other 838 advos'. Maybe I was on to something. That would explain Nogo's amigo teeth and Cerevello's frizz. And maybe, who was peeping, and why.

Nogo and Biff had been muttering nekro ever since the day real Surcord agents came to 838, after the break-ins subsided. Except for transporting dangerous hot focus malcos to the unhouse, Sur-goons never go on location. Never. They're stay-at-home spies, drinking gourmet coffee and chomping beignets in front of screens, like the rest of us. We all thought they came because Nogo squeaked so hard, they had to oil the wheel. But the G-O already knew all about the break-ins.

"Bill, put up my animation of the Surgoon interrogation. I'm ready to work again."

A wide shot of the windowless room in Tech Center's basement where the Surgoons questioned Biff, Nogo, and me, appeared on my screen. It showed as much as I could ima-gen from memory; the smooth brown floor, the single door, the pale blue walls, the harsh light. No bubble hats, vid specs, scan monitors or sources of any kind, allowed. They even searched us, like common smear or malcos.

They questioned us for almost five hours. There were no stimsublim breaks, only two comfort breaks, and one poorly prepped bio-collective subsistence meal; overcooked pot roast with carrots and spuds. Even without sources to record what happened, my memories were crystal clear.

Most of all, I remembered the face of the goon who kept hammering away at us. He appeared on the screen, a big, goofy shock of reddish brown hair crawling over his face like a tarantula, a huge jaw, leathery tanned skin. Just as I recalled, and animixed.

"How come nothing works out here?" spider top kept asking with a crooked smile. "Everywhere else we've had these problems, genalt whiz kids come up with something that works. Sooner or later, the banditos wind up smeared in the unhouse. Maybe you're just not applying yourselves."

Then the goon looked at his compadres knowingly. One smiled, like 'gotcha,' and the other nodded. What a bunch of morons. Obviously they were looking to us for leads, like we had previewed global focus, and must have known something. But we didn't have their tie-up. They could have done anything to us down there. They could have shoved us in a whacko-wagon and hustled us off in the dark to a bio-collective and dubbed over our personalities. And there'd have been no trace.

Instead, they changed gears to good cop, got all soft and fuzzy, and treated us to an expensive dinner in Tech Center's VIP Lounge. It was a lonely, paranoid meal, in a painfully empty place. Besides the goons, Biff, Nogo, and me, and one non-servo, near-smear, live-in waitress who looked like a mummy, the joint was vacant.

The animix showed her sitting at the other end of the cavernous, rarely used 300 seat lounge, squinting at a monitor with a no-smoke dangling from her wrinkled lips. Then she got up shakily and picked up our order, carrying the tray as if it weighed 100 kilos, and placed it on the servo serviette. Then, in her decaying fuzzy pink slippers, she slowly inch-walked along behind the serviette to bring us our orders. No cheapo-servo in a classy bistro like the Lounge, right? At least the old bird had a gig and a hab.

Nondescript, nauseating music - as well as I could remember it - played in the background. Nogo zoomed the goons suspiciously with his brow furrowed and eyes narrowed, occasionally tossing in a pro profile or some teeth. The goons acted smug, and except for the needling, almost ignored us, like we were supposed to grovel because they cued credit for the meal.

"I'm not just spouting dok," Nogo said over and over to them, squinting from trying to avoid eye contact. "It's psi-terror. We need more resources. We can't fight something this big alone."

The goons smiled, like they knew where he was coming from, and more about it than he did.

"It's just part of the human condition," Biff added with conviction. "I still believe most of it is hallucination."

"Then where'd all the blown gear go? The screens, the boxes?" the redhead with the spider-top asked accusingly. "You know this argument is bunk, and yet you keep repeating it. What are you, a poetry lover? Or are you just hiding something?"

Cerevello, paralyzed with fear, managed to mumble indignantly, incoherently, about poetry and repeating the hallucination slant.

"Maybe they don't really understand how much trouble they cause," I joined in.

"Oh yeah?" the red goon shot back quickly, eyes opened wide.

Oh yeah. I ranted on. I laughed and did the goofy advo. Forks fell out of my hands and banged onto the floor, wine made it half way into my mouth, and the area around my plate was littered like a baby's high chair platter. The goons stayed snotty and aloof, but little smiles were creeping into those cold mouths.

The scene's tag line was simple. Only Stan Mozuck had the offbeat credo, the original ideas about Weirds. He wasn't just tired; he was nervous, he knew something. If I didn't help 838 squish some Weirds, I'd be m-line meat. Crunch, crunch, crunch. The screen went blank, like my mind, the scene unresolved but the memory intact.

Right after the goons split, for no apparent reason, they bestowed mucho production gear and credit on 838, with specialists zooming-in assistance. This is where the production credit for "An Evening With Bob Sideways, The Alphadrine Cowboy" came from. After thousands of deadend Spotlights, it was my first solo as Producer/Director.

So maybe I owed Biff and the General Offices. Regardless of my feelings, Nogo was good. If I could get him to do the parts without imagination, the drone work, and keep him from stealing all the credit, the quality would be there; without his splicer, meanie-monk slant.

My nerves were still shot. Doing a full cycle of a cool metabolic stimsublim was definitely la cosa mas importante. Not just a blink of Satiscope. Then, flashing on Weird rumors and spec with Nogo wouldn't be so stressful. He'd sense the relaxation, come back with stuff that screened his deepest, and preview his slant with his schtick. And he would find out about trashing the Hard School later. Too late to do anything, or he'd sabo the spot.

The stimsublim pattern in the middle eight of Bob Sideways' "Ghost Riders In The Sky" was pure relaxation. The viewer got a nice alpha wave stim, and a good beta-endorphin dose. The pattern was hidden in background b-roll animix behind Bob, as he performed on different sets; in clouds, cactus flowers, and tumbleweeds.

Bob was a rare find, rare enough to get someone Upfielded. I was resolved to monitor the pattern, even if I had to do it in Nogo's touchlot. But it was only for the sake of smooth, so Nogo couldn't pull anything without me comping immediately. To serious blinkers, any anxious situation justified zooming the lume.

The rain was letting up. Another scary scene of myself in the unhouse appeared on the internal monitor, and I forced it out of my mind. I thought about the full day ahead and rubbed my eyes again. They would probably be bright red by afternoon, making more bad focus.

Dish-eyed Sylvia stumbled into the kitchen again, and stared at a spot somewhere beyond my head. She struggled to speak, her mouth formed words, but no go. Her brain was still in the other room, filling stacks, and it would take a while before anything intelligible could froth out. By this time in the combo, I didn't need to read her mind.

"Standard... you should... it's almost time. You..."

By the time she said my name, my coat was on. Before she was done fumbling for words, the door had closed behind me.

-3-
"MEET NOGO BLOGO"

Droplets of chilly rain hammered down relentlessly. Icy mud splattered on my shoes and pants as I dashed across the hab's touchlot. I almost dived into my mag, then paused to shake off the first bitter wake-up call from the cold, wet, real, outside world.

"Hello," I said to the mag. "It's Stan. Let's go to Nogo Blogo's hab."

My shocked looking face was in the dash panel monitor, but it didn't seem like a close-up could make it any worse, even with nervous zits popping up in all the right places. There was no way my ride wouldn't be totally monitored, so zaniness seemed like the right button to push for more upbeat, offbeat climb recognition. I puffed out my cheeks, crossed my eyes, and started mugging. Then the hover brake popped off, and slowly, the nano-replicate of a red, yellow, and silver 1969 Thunderbird - my mag - drifted forward.

To most of 838's screen-sucking Neighbors, watching the weather change, enjoying the outdoors, was a lost art. Electromag paths were almost noiseless, and except for nature sounds, the outside world was silent. No tourists or shoppers roamed through, no one went to see a friend. Only servos, and maybe one Associate in an e-mag, glided on the paths. Rain beat softly against the mag windshield as it swooshed through the thick, soggy air.

The mag's voice intoned "Thirteen minutes to destination." Then the sound of music swelled through the mag; a song called "El Chimpy," with surfy, psychedelic guitars, a Latin edge, and screeching chimpanzees.

The mag accelerated, and leveled at fifty kilometers an hour. When I was a kid, cars could go a hundred miles an hour. You could go anywhere. I'd rented cars in Car Town, but the speed limit was 35 miles per hour down there. An e-mag was a servo, a computer car riding the neural circuitry of an immense transport grid. It could be driven manually, steered to the left or right of the path, slowed down, and stopped. But it was still part of a closed system, totally nexed-in, like everything else NeighborWorld.

Rows of habs fast-forwarded by, filled with Neighbors who had never seen their homes from the outside. Wet leaves were smeared all over the hab windows, but that was ok; no bored kids or horny teenagers ever peered out of them. The Neighbors' world was in the screen. Images and sensations passed through Neighbors at light speed, and they traveled anywhere on light. They didn't need to go outside. The global Neighborhood was in their living room. They were all dreaming in unison.

To me, though, gliding in a red, gold, and silver e-mag was nice. It was like being in a big Local, where Neighbors went outside sometimes, to live spots, to plays, to full saturation enviro-parks. In big Locals they knew how to live. Not like 838's zoombies.

The rain stopped suddenly, completely, like it used to when weather control was big, when folks still went outside. The sun started peeping through the thick gray clouds, invigorating me, dropping-in instant eupho teeth. Daydreams about living in Toronto Metro or Manhattan One or LA Pinpoint filled my skull.

Then green markers flashed on the path as the mag approached 838's Business and Tech Directory. BizTek Direk warehoused and dispatched everything entering or leaving Local 838. Inside BizTek Direk was a five square meter cubicle housing the prepro that conducted shop-at-home sales. The prepro, a tiny silver ball filled with glop, contained everyone in 838's credit information. Everyone but the Weirds.

As the mag buzzed by the BizTek Direk, I fantasized about working in LA Pinpoint, the last step on the Ladder Of Lights. It was almost unimaginable, even scary. It was easier to think about why I wasn't there already. Twenty-six seasons ago a friend of mine, the famous Hairy Larry, went international just by being in the right place at the right time. Still known by his real tag then, Larry Ramirez, he was monitoring CentAsian Locals for tech leaks. The Japanese are notorious leakers. Leaking new tech before international standardization format clearance, and social impact testing, is prohibited, no-go.

NeighborWorld's dik-dok is that Locals should neither run ahead nor lag behind. Advos called leaking 'premature jerk-u-lation.' All leak monitoring was boring, ungratifying work, but his full-time was better than mine - monitoring Northam tech laggers like 838. So Ramirez wound up as the famous Hairy Larry, and I wound up in 838.

One day Larry watched a Japanese advo, as he told his audience how to access stimsublims that would let them actually smell the programs. Larry tried one that not only let him smell beer being brewed, but imparted some of its flavor, and high. Larry had inadvertently monitored Tokyo Ichi introducing K-Factor on a private broadcast thread - before its creators, the Chinese. The Japanese were clearly infringing on K-Factor, which the Chinese had packaged and were ready to market, as 'Blissful Aromatic Infusion' or something; a whole line of psychically stim-sim sense environments. It had to be reported.

Larry, with hardly enough climb in his profile for one good spot, was sitting on hot focus. Luckily for him, the new 'Democracy Rules' rules obliged him to inform everyone on the shift what he'd discovered, even low-on-the-pole guys like me. Before the new rules, if you told just your supervisor, he could write you out and steal cred for the spot. I helped put together research and interviews for Larry's K-Factor leak spot, but my name never even made the credit roll.

The urge to monitor stimsublim was becoming unbearable again. Thinking about Larry's success was all it took to make the wrong juices flow. It made me no better than Sylvia, who constantly balmed herself in electro-salve and faded the real world. Thinking about the spot, putting up possible opening shots was the only way to fight it. The establishing shots needed warmth, maybe a nice autumn color scene, something that created empathy for the Weirds.

"How's the weather shaping up today?" I asked my mag. "Bring up Fat Frank."

Immediately the glowing face of Fat Frank, Local 838's weather guy, popped up on the dash panel monitor. Bloated, blue-haired Frank was one of Cerevello's old-era cronies. He was real, not feelie-realie.

"Good morning, Neighbors and Associates," Frank bubbled enthusiastically. "It's 8:38 a.m. in eastern NorthAm, and this is Fat Frank with the all day all night weather and traffic report!"

Fat Frank's facial color changed from pale cream to pale blue, and a little cloud materialized above his head. As the cloud drifted away from his head, it spat out one last rain drop.

"The rain has subsided in Locals 838 and 834, and the afternoon's forecast calls for clear, sunny skies with increasing cold and a chance of scattered snow flurries by sundown."

With some animix that seemed far too goosed to be Local 838's, Fat Frank's head became the front of an e-mag.

"Traffic on Local glide paths is light," Fat Frank continued, "With some activity near the Business and Technology Directory."

Of course it was light, fat-ass. No one went out in 838. Just servos. And me.

"And the gas guzzlers are running again in CarTown! So come on down!"

Earlier this week, during some paranoid scram, Cerevello said the guzzlers' days were numbered. It probably had something to do with the CarTown credit scandal. CarTown or Industros Tragicos had something to do with this spot, too. It seemed illogical, but the feeling was hard to ignore. Thinking about it was frizzing me, so Frank got ye old hook and gong, in mid-sentence.

There used to be spots on how to work outside, but nobody had easy access anymore. They just seemed unimportant. It would be nice to know how to do this. The best track seemed to be get the location stuff quick and early, then go to the conference lab to size up slants with Cerevello in person. He always had to have creative control, his overview. Going on location to do an interview was important. Advos hadn't played with this for many seasons. Making this spot was making history. Hopefully the

Weirds could fool gear, but not the naked human eye.

"Give me green markers to Nogo's hab, and arrival time," I told the mag.

9:02 popped up on the monitor screen. There wasn't enough time to monitor both "Today On The Connector" and the stimsublim I needed. TOTC was an ongoing global programming index, a scramble-down of every spot shown in the world over the last 24 hours. It was ultra-limited access, for advos above Step One only. Taking on TOTC saved time, but it took time, too.

"And bring up Today On The Connector and enter Weirds," I added.

What year was it, anyway? 2037? But years weren't numbered in 2037. It was just last season or this season or next season or three seasons from now. No numbers. Seasons - and years - were merely green access markers that turned amber after you passed them. Time was relative, wasn't it? The past and future were one. There was no common era. Only then, now, and shaping up.

TOTC reads started flipping by on the monitor. Pages of useless stuff; then one, then two spots positively I-D. Then a long pause. Only two spots about Weirds on the entire planet? Jesus, that didn't seem right. It searched again, but still could I-D only the same two spots. One was from Africa Central called "Weirds Are Evil Sorcerers." Good old witch-scourging mundo magneto from Ma Africa, but too predictable for my purposes.

The other thing was from Local 884, right next door, directed by my old boy Cax Grimoire. Cax had a Weirds obsesso, but his profile was flat, no climb. All he did was push telekinesis, which was only part of the story. If some cryo-man slant popped through during a global interest dip, I'd scoop the loop. If Cerevello could be schmoozed into slowing down the production schedule, in a couple days my spot would be a climber. But for now, let light bring focus to the smalls.

I wanted to grab the sunlight, so I stuck my hand out of the window. I got a jolt of arctic air instead. Could Great Lakes weather, those quick, drastic changes from sun to snow, connect somehow? Either the Weirds liked shitty weather, or they didn't squirm it for some reason. Maybe they had cushier weather-mod systems than ours. Or psychic environmental control, selective to about a meter's width around the controller's body space; the Fire Inspector's trick.

El Chimpy started blaring again. The mag, in its best 1960's B-movie trailer Voice-Over, said "Destination in focus." Green markers flashed in the distance in Nogo's touchlot, contrasting with red markers in the background. The green lights turned amber as my mag drifted into the touchlot, then turned red again. The mag slowed, then stopped at a spot in the empty lot near the tall, dirty gray, metalloid hab.

Monitoring the Bob Sideways spot suddenly became urgent. So I tried to access it, while glancing back at the building, moving around, pretending to be looking for some misplaced item.

"Bring up the middle eight of Bob Sideways," I mumbled to the mag, trying to look like I was swearing about losing something, as if everything wasn't perfectly seen and heard. Just a blink would straighten me out. But either the mag was glitching, or Home, or someone, was denying access. Maybe nothing was secure now. It didn't matter, because Nogo had to be faced sin-stimsublima, without fortification.

I pulled myself out of the mag and trudged towards the hab, coughing frozen breaths and shivering. Dying, brown evergreen trees encircled the deserted lot. Snow clouds, big moisture laden noobers, were rolling in off Lake Erie. It was a hell shot, a scene that could fit easily in a demonic possession spot. The security eye perused me.

Goofy old songs were pushing through the anxiety. "Increase your size, poke out your eyes, let's do the sex-death polka!" Sex-death, the basic subliminal formula.

Voosh! The door flew open all abrupto.

"Yow!" I croaked an absurd yelp, and jumped into the air with my heart pounding.

The eye had let me in before voice recognition. Nogo was waiting for me, blowing nerves because I was late, taking the edge with punctuality, even though he screwed off the whole time he was on the job. Anxiety returned, full field. Holding my hand over my heart, I shlommed in.

Inside, on the way to Nogo's place, it felt like a grimy, opaque filter was panning everything. Nogo's vidpaper glowed on the walls, his jerk-off systemic music blared away, but nothing registered. If Nogo asked me what I thought of today's decor and sound ambience, there wouldn't be a good focus response coming back. The hall was long, and between vidpaper sequences, the light was dim. Clashing with all this were the sounds of numerous spots blasting away in different parts of the building. Nothing was in hush mode. The noise grated on me, zooming the apprehension.

As I stepped into the mag lift, a new vidpaper progression began and the interior appeared to burst into flames. Thousands of red, blue, and green dots licked at the walls in different patterns, in time with Dvorak's "New World Symphony." Nogo was all go today, eager and ready to work.

I needed a blink. Stimsublim was the only way to survive this.

"Stan?" a voice behind the surveillance eye whined, as I walked into view before his door.

Then, voosh! The door flew open again. As I walked into his living room, I noticed time readout on the white wall right in front of me. 9:05. Good. Not too late. On a huge white couch below the time display, Nogo was curled up, almost in a fetal position, shaking his head, scowling.

"Hey-hey Nogo," I babbled, with all the amigo teeth I could muster.

"Here we are, in the real live flesh and dirt. Real work for real advos. My knobs are goosed to go."

"Goddamn it," he groaned. "Why do you always have to be late? You know it drives me nuts. Please. I like to start early, so there's enough time to do it right. Can you at least try?"

He knew my profile, knew I was late for those depressing Point A feelie-realie conferences, sometimes unfocused. The only time we'd really been together was when the Sur-goons were zooming us. He was already reading my mind, zooming my skull.

"We're still on top of it. I was... uh..." I couldn't come up with a good excuse.

Nogo scowled a little longer, then he sat up abruptly, quickly rearranging his mug into a radiant grin. He had shifted into partner's mode without pausing for a breath.

"Hey, kiddo," he oozed, all synchro-sweet. "How's 'bout some breakfast? I've got the new Agricord double yokers, bagels, fruit - you name it. A feast. Climbers need fuel."

"Oh yeah," he went on, pointing upwards with his index finger. "Remember Manfroed Oonga? Old Oonga-foot just nexed-in with me. Said he had a real steak and beans follow-up for our spot. Said he'd come back on it later."

Just as abruptly he stopped grinning and gazed at me with a concerned, sympathetic expression.

"How's Sylvia?" Nogo glommed in a care-care-servo's drone. "Still having trouble? Too bad."

His eyes looked like they actually got misty. Then he lowered his head. Once again, unexpectedly, he sprang to his feet with a smile on his mug, and trotted off into the kitchen.

"No, hombre, I already ate," I said, but he wasn't listening. "Nogo? I'm not hungry. I ate breakfast at home."

He emerged from the kitchen wearing an apron. With a weakened expression, holding a spatula in one hand and an orange in the other, he started turning it on.

"What will I do with all this food, Stan?" Nogo asked with a disheartened whine. "I made enough for a whole crew."

He was going to force me to eat, after all the coffee, eggs, toast, and doughnuts I choked down while chewing Cerevello's ultimatum. On poquito stimsublim, without even a good lume. The discomfort level was going to be high, all day.

"Sure, what the hell," I came back, like a mind-controlled near-smear. "You are the best chef in 838. I might not get another chance like this. Sure. What the hell. Climbers need fuel."

Nogo's dining room ceiling was covered with lights. It was the brightest joint I'd ever seen. He kept it meticulously clean, and his taste was unsettlingly quirky. Everything was in black and white. There was no color anywhere, except on the numerous Info screens. It created a cartoon atmosphere, only bleak. All the screens were barking. Nogo was taking on five spots at once. A real climber. But it was distracting, and scary.

My focus was coming undone. As Nogo turned and went back into the kitchen, I stared down at his pristinely white carpet. The place was making me nauseous. The odor of food became so strong it overpowered everything. All I could think while I tried to keep from getting sick was that Nogo was nuts. He had a bad splice or something.

Nogo blew back into the room like a lunch hour waiter in an old-era restaurant in a big Local. He flipped plates onto the table like a poker dealer, and started serving food lightning fast, precise. There were omelets, peaches in brandy sauce, espresso, toasted bagels, parsley hash brown potatoes, orange and grapefruit juice, and blueberries with honey and cream.

Nogo was showing off. His Home system was quicker; he was the best, even as a freaking food service worker. He and Cerevello were conspiring to knock me off with fatso slow-mo and indigestion.

"Best meal of the day," he grunted to himself.

Nogo was a good chef, sure, and a good artist, composer, director, whatever. Everything he laid his splice-baby, new-lizard hands on cued cred. Naturally. Or unaturally. He was genetically altered for art, for right brain dominance, but a goofy glitch whispered-in the opposite. Imbalance. An unexplainable left brain dominance flawed his work.

"The past and future are one, advo," Nogo said with a smile. "There's only then, now, and shaping up. Seize the moment and ride the zoom."

It was like God superimposed a slapstick reminder on the artificial prodigy, a memo from the Executive Producer to disregard all this genalt crap. Meaningless patterns blasted through his all-systemic visual art, searching for significance. He couldn't cook without prepros and measurements, compose without tone and pulse standards, or make art without matrices and interfaces.

"Ride the zoom," I agreed.

He was gifted ironically, with a brilliant bio-program but no intuition. Nothing about his work was unique. Nogo was the brotherhood and BizTekDirek in the F and D. How could he be touted as the best there was?

"Bon apetit," a young, female Voice Over with a slight East Asian accent intoned through the monitor system. "Let's have a pleasant meal, shall we?"

"Climbers need fuel," Nogo said, rubbing his palms together. Then he winked and said, "Dig in."

I was impervious to most of Nogo's oblique strategies, but mommy guilt was a new one. I sat down and surveyed the enormous glut of food. I began poking at my omelet, and tried to sound enthusiastic about stuffing myself.

"Mmmm," I said. "This looks great. Hey Nogo, if we get Upfielded for this spot, let's wear our 838 bowling shirts, right in focus al mundo. Hilarious, right?"

BREAKAWAY INSERT: OVERHEAD LONG SHOT OF BOWLING ALLEY - FEELIE-REALIE ZIG OF 838 TEAM ROLLING GUTTER BALLS

838 had the worst sport game teams in NorthAm. Even with full muscle simulation in the animix, the best shoes, and the best feelie-realie, we couldn't roll strikes. Our bowling team was a global sport game joke, dating back to old-era 'Me and Mind-Game' days. We were derided everywhere. Just to utter the number 838 was an international sport gamer's insult, and our only claim to fame.

"Great," Nogo snarled sarcastically. "That would give them something to remember. But they can't remember anything. Remember?"

Nogo liked to make folks ooze sedition, malco, and info-crit, and then entrap them. He was a provocateur who catalyzed trouble, like someone who started a fire and then anonymously reported it. You had to be careful what you said.

"What?" I blurted with my mouth full. "Nogo, it's just a joke. We'll wear the bowling shirts in focus. What are you talking about? Who can't remember? The G-O? The Weirds? The Neighbors? Who can't remember?"

The only way to handle Nogo was to confront him directly, like when dealing with Cerevello. I looked right into his eyes and he looked back for a second, then away. He flinched. Nogo was hiding something, and I saw it. This made me the alpha now.

Pale skinned, watery blue eyed Nogo; the sympathetic ear, the phony jerkoff on the make. A music track started up on the monitor, some bongos playing in slow rhythm, and then the lights dimmed. Nogo's eyes narrowed as he closed his focus in on me again.

"You know what I mean, Stan," he said. "Everyone. It's everyone, man. What difference does it make what we do? Cerevello determines the content, the G-O and Concord determine how it goes down the path politically and economically, and then the Neighbors forget it all ten minutes after they see it. You know it's true, Stan. You know it."

He was the new lizard of the old newsroom. It was too early to trash the Neighbors. The game hadn't even started yet.

"So what the hell does that have to do with wearing our bowling shirts?" I barked back. "Who cares if they forget? Most Neighbors don't climb, they just forget."

"That's the point," he hissed acidly. "They never climb."

He looked genuinely sad. Genuine feelings from Genalts were rare, so when one came up, I paid attention. Seemingly right on cue, a walking bass joined the bongos in the sound track.

"Forget the bowling shirts, Stan," Nogo said, like the world was about to end. "The point is that all those folks are just amoebae. They're like some single cell creature feeding off some more complex creature, never knowing what they're doing, or why. Most of them can't even remember their own names, for chrissakes! How can they retain all the info-drizzle they connect into daily? It's meaningless to them. It's like psychic fiber. It passes right through them, man. Right through 'em!"

He looked away, then crossed his legs and folded his arms across his chest. He rubbed his shoulders, and twisted his skinny frame into a question mark. Then he rolled his head around slowly and looked at me.

"I've been thinking about the job lately," he said bluntly. "That's all."

When he said 'all' a large piece of egg slid out of his mouth and landed on the table. Good shot. He lowered his eyes and stared at it for second, then casually brushed it into a disposal shaft. Strange behavior. Was he frying his skull on some new restricted patterns, the hush mode lumers only inner circle splicers are hip to, or concealing something?

"Look," I said, trying to fathom the deep water Nogo had us swimming in. "We're like old-era journos. We Spotlight events, or individs, or info. So what if the world is asleep? We can't change that. All we can do is supply the package and hope the cream rises. God, Nogo. You should know that axiom. You're Genalt. I mean, didn't they cue you for social science?"

Sex-death, the oldest control formula.

I took a spoonful of cereal, and held it my mouth without swallowing. The light above Nogo's head was burning right into my eyes. I swallowed, put the spoon down, and then started stirring my cereal into little mountains and whirlpools. Nogo wanted to say something then, perhaps, but held back.

Then, right out of the blue, the bongo and bass thing stopped, and an old-era doo-wop song started blaring through the monitor system. And right on cue, he started talking again, like he'd picked the music for his Voice-Over.

"Standard." he droned emotionlessly, "How many years are we into the Nova Century? And yet..."

He put his hands together as if praying, and looked thoughtfully into a nearby monitor source.

"And yet everything's the same," he said with a condescending smile. "The looks, the slants, the hep and unhep - they're all from before. Everything's arranged, so average Neighbors won't flip, to keep them from smearing into the unhouse. But why the arrangement, Stan? Why?"

Here it came. The argument was recurrent, incorruptibly pure, born into different shapes, over and over. Nogo believed that non-Genalts were useless in the Nova Century. Except, of course, guys like Cerevello and me. We were different. But for everyone else, it was simple. Assist evolution by selectively eliminating gear and tech in troublesome parts of the Neighborhood. Get rid of folks who won't Spotlight, abolish the bio-collectives; let the smear fend for themselves. In short, let it all dry up.

And as for people, or things, like the Weirds, it was simpler still. Erase them all.

"They're incapable of assimilating new info, Stan," he said, as if announcing some important secret truth. "NeighborWorl has fabricated a comfortable transition century for a bunch of amoebae. Our celebrated Nova Century is nothing more than a regurgitation of the past, attractively packaged to keep a dead race thinking it's alive. They're not asleep, Stan. They're dead."

His eyes got really wide when he said "dead." Then he started clicking his tongue in time with the music. I knew the slant Nogo wanted for the spot. The Neighbors' garden needed weeding. But cutting off the system would devastate average Neighbors. Everyone relied on it, depended on it. Agricord grew food, Transcord delivered things and repaired habs and paths, and Surcord peeked. But it was all NeighborWorld. NeighborWorld marketed everything.

Sure there were enviro-saturation commercial parks, places like Old Bedford Mall, but shopping was extinct. Local folks went to those places every once a year or so for the illusion of human contact, to walk the concourse and smell the sweat, but it was historical vacation time in a museum, like at Car Town. If Neighbors didn't have anything to offer for the set-up, they should fend for themselves. And without the set-up, most Neighbors would fade to black.

"What do you think's going to happen next, Stan?" Nogo asked with a look of wide- eyed wonder. "I'll tell you what's next. Nothing. Literally. End of story."

Nogo was still Hard School. But why try to convince me? There was no tweak in my DNA. The old-era music was driving nails into my head. Nogo was right about one thing. There was no Nova Century. We were just passing time in purgatory, waiting. Nogo wanted me to defend my beliefs, but that would only expose them. Arguing had to be resisted. He was trying to frame me with Cerevello.

"Ah, that's crazy," I said quietly. "You can't really want to dry up and fade so many Neighbors just because they've got no climb in the old profile. That would be like genocide or something."

It would have been better to call them people instead of Neighbors. Or even individs. But the point had to come across somehow. They needed subsidy. They had no talents beyond one Spotlight. After that they monitored tech flow, getting ready for a StarStep that usually never came. Tech flow could be monitored by prepro systems dumber than mine.

"Besides," I added before he could speak, "all that genocide bleep is such a long shot, such an L-S, it's not worth putting up."

The room seemed to get brighter for a second, and Nogo appeared further away, like in a bad stimsublim reaction. His body jerked when I said "genocide." He glared angrily at me, and went through the motions of suppressing rage, real or scripted. Nogo jumped to his feet shouting.

"Oh, so now I'm the villain of the age," Nogo yelled in a high voice. "At least you didn't call the Neighbors people. I know about your snide remarks; like how I'm not really 'people.' I'm more people than they are, Stan. I'm what people should be."

"You're more people than they are?" I snarled back. "What does that mean? How many people are you? Are you schizoid, or what? And whatever happened to infodemocracy?"

The big bark must have shocked him, because he came back much smoother.

"You know what I mean," he almost pleaded. "Selectively withdraw support from segments of the Neighborhood that don't enrich the fabric. Whether it's smear - who are too stupid or too low on the ladder to hep - or political groups, like the Weirds, I say dry them up. They contribute nothing."

Then he sat back down, sneered at a sausage, picked up his fork, whacked the sausage in half, then stuffed half in his mouth and made a nasty smile, like he was on to something. When he called the Weirds a political group, I almost choked on my cereal.

"Weirds aren't political," I screeched, sounding hysterical. "They're different! Totally different!"

My nerves blew. I started choking. The lights began spinning, I almost passed out. Coughing, wheezing, I pounded on my chest until my breath came back. The room stopped moving, but my eyes were watery and my vision blurred. I looked down on my breakfast, embarrassed, redfaced. Nogo chuckled.

"Easy, boy," he said. "You're taking this conversation far too seriously. You must need a blink."

"I need to stop arguing," I said. "The Weirds don't connect with the slant you want. The Weirds aren't political. And even if they were, you couldn't dry them up. They're not NeighborWorld. They're not in the system!"

The way Nogo made individs say things, and moved them around like pawns, was sick. It was frizzing me.

"I hate this kind of crap, Nogo. I'm too upset to talk now. If I don't calm down I won't be able to work."

It felt creepy having an argument with a near stranger, someone I'd only been in-person with once. Sure I worked and interacted with him, saw his face and heard his voice plenty. I knew his views and background, but not him, really. This much hostility was very unprofessional. The only way out was stimsublim.

"Nogo, where's the bathroom? I'm going to monitor a pattern."

"I knew it," he giggled. "Sure, third door down the hall, on the right. You mind if I monitor you, while you monitor it?"

A strong wind picked me up and blew me down the hall. There was revulsion, for this so-called human being and my own weakness for the light. I was a bird dog, whatever the hell that meant to old-era junkies. Just a blink or two will do. Inside the bathroom, with its walls covered in greyish purple vidpaper and kitschy looking gold ornaments, it dawned on me the act wasn't solid.

"Nogo, let me access 'Ghost Riders In The Sky' from your stump," I called out. "I'm bubbled up somewhere at Home."

"Como no, senor," he snickered. "Just talk to the mirror over the sink. Access is cued everywhere, ready to go."

"Go ahead and monitor," I said, zooming in on the sink and mirror. "I don't care."

"Keep your eyes on the screen, Stan," Nogo said, laughing. "I'll time you."

Nogo's laughter suddenly got more staccato, punctuated by sharp hiccup sounds. He was a twisted man in the 838 spiritual desert, too. My chemstat was bent, the whole deal was frizzing. I needed a blink so bad the gag machine was churning, and in a rush to get relief, I smacked my knuckle against the sink and cried out in pain. Nogo erupted in hysterics.

"This is Standard Mozuck, NeighborWorld advo step three, looking for access to my Home chew of Ghost Riders In The Sky."

"I know who you are," a nasal, sarcastic female voice griped, and the screen went blue with stars and sagebrush on the horizon. Nogo's home prepro was much faster than mine. The first warped chords wove their way into my ears. I smelled a little sagebrush, my own primitive K-factor. Luckily, the volume was loud enough to drown out Nogo's obnoxious laughter. The brown-beaked genalt probe was peeking.

Then, like water for the thirsty, the beatific countenance of Bob Sideways, The Alphadrine Cowboy, popped up on the screen, looking like an icon of Christ. With his oversized chaps and fifty-gallon hat, his snow-white hair and moustache, Sideways would be my savior. I'd be a sorcerer, clothed in light, armed to the teeth, ready to boff Nogo or Biff or whoever else got in the way.

Another wash of color filled my eyes as Bob started singing. The close-up of Bob tracked back to show him looking like a cowboy snowman, standing center screen in a full shot, aping away and flailing his hands across his guitar. Then the pattern started, a starburst, and I was gone, lumed like a zoombie on weatherproof vacation, carried away by the light.

When I returned to our planet, the last few bars of Ghost Riders started fading into oblivion. There was one last apparition of the ghostly white cowboy, and then he exploded into ultra-blue. The Alpha 6 wave was freaking fantastic. Who knows how long it took for me to crawl out of the bathroom; ten minutes, maybe fifteen? Time was unimportant during a giga lume like this. The bliss was both mental and physical.

Then Nogo banged on the bliss, but it was like the world wasn't so dehumanized and bleak and fucked-up after all.

"This alphadrine pattern is complete," Nogo said through the monitor, sounding like an old-era synthesized Voice-Over. "If additional subliminal stimulation is needed, please say 'Review.'"

I was relaxed enough to appreciate Nogo's nostalgia humor, something we shared a little. I cracked the bathroom door to look out. Nogo was still cramming food into his skinny head, watching a cooking show from Spain.

"Hey, where am I?" I chuckled. "Who, what, when, why?"

I fell out of the doorway and onto the floor, a great slapschtick flop. Nogo chuckled through a mooshful of food. Synchro-time, the guy on the cooking show laughed too, and yelled something. I rolled around to squeeze the gag a little, then jumped up prontito.

"Was I in there long?" I asked. "How long was I in there?"

My jaw was aching, my face tingled, but I giggled on.

"You were in there two minutes after the pattern ended," Nogo said. "Hey, Stan. Come in here and take on some of this internap. The K-factor is great."

He was still interested in food. Genalt to climb, and climbers need fuel. He'd stopped giggling, but his expression looked harmless enough, so I kept laughing. Actually, it was hard for me to stop. The lume felt great.

Forgiveness was in order; for my noble Associate Nogo, for myself. What great genius every individ possessed, even Nogo. If I could only master my chemstat, I'd share that with the world. Yeah, I was lumed, and gooey in the right places, and everything and everyone was inspiring. But the Weirds were real inspiration. The world was their playground; anything was possible. That was going up slant, no way around it. It would stay in hush mode for a while, though.

Stimsublim was a miracle, but there were some sorry side effects. Feel sexy, afraid, goofy, smell things, be reprogrammed and refreshed - all with a little dose of light. Just a blink. Get lumed, and anything could be enhanced to a theoretically unlimited level. It enriched appreciation, induced thought flavors. Could the Weirds do the same thing, without NeighborWorld? Was it all redundant?

Along with that thought came a flash of panic. Some paranoid scram was making it feel like Nogo was reading my mind. That was impossible, though. Nogo could never stop the chatter in his own mind long enough to sit in on someone else's, even with a neural link.

"Nogo, are we ready yet?"

That brought another chuckle. He'd been ready for hours. He put down the last croissant, and turned from the holo-screen. The connector had been open the whole time I was in there. But there was no time to worry about that. I acted like a jerk, but basically had done ok. No great consolation, but reassuring.

Nogo got up and grabbed his bag without turning towards me and walked right for the door. I followed, like a mind controlled smear. We walked out and towards the lift, and the vidpaper changed abruptly. As we got down the hall he finally acknowledged me, smiling in the strangest way. We stepped into the lift and the walls began vibrating in that unmistakable ultra-blue. The door closed, and in seconds Bob Sideways appeared on all four walls, floor and ceiling. Ghost Riders kicked in.

The mag lift dropped like a feather towards the first floor and touchlot. Nogo smiled on, totally out of character. Then he turned, put his left hand on my shoulder, and extended his right hand in to shake mine. Suspicious and confused, but still all gooey and willing to play right along, I shook hands with Nogo.

"To success, Standard," he said. "To our success."

-4-

"SHAPING THE PATSY"

Sunlight was blaring through the big window of the hab complex's never used lobby, but it wouldn't be sunny for long. The lobby looked good, the servo crew had taken care of the potted plants and rugs and windows and kept the time and weather monitors working, but anyone who'd ever seen a big Local could tell nobody ever used the place. Something about it was hollow, forgotten, antiseptic but on the verge of decay.

As soon as we stepped out of the lobby, Nogo popped on a bubble hat source and started posing. He looked off towards Industros Tragicos with a brave smile, like old-era propaganda of soldiers ready for the front. Nogo's music over track for the shot was probably full of tympani drums and a male chorus. In my head, all I could hear was that creepy Alice DeMalice xylophone music.

For Nogo, no shot was good enough nude. Everything had to be animixed, fucked with. No scene was specified by nature, nothing was by grace of average Neighbor or God. Who knew what he was up to or might run by this chilly morning?

EXTERIOR - NOGO'S HAB - DAY - FULL TWO SHOT OF NOGO, ME

Our feet made sloppy crunching sounds on the frosty wet green poly-turf as we plodded across the touch lot. That triggered a servo, which appeared from screen right and began cleaning after us. The servo did its best to serve but too late for the gig. Then it frizzed and froze, probably from nonuse.

Nogo and I moved into view of the mag's monitor source, and did a leaving-for-the-war two shot, for all the young diva-Janes we'd never meet in the flesh and dirt. We got into the mag, and it was already cold. What was up with the mag's insulation, the eco-seal? My teeth started chattering, and I rocked back and forth, rubbing my arms to warm them before popping the mag into forward. Then the mag path hummed, and we drifted away from Nogo's hab.

Nogo wasted no time. As if the whole situation wasn't totally extraordinary, he barked out his cue.

"Should we nex in with Cerevello?" he asked, like it was routine. "Or should we just go to Industros Tragicos and see what we can come up with on our own?"

Why would I believe Nogo really wanted my opinion?

"Cerevello's peeking right now," I said. My mouth was getting dry again. "Isn't that right, Biff? What should we do first, jefe, where should we go?"

I smiled, that was good focus. Intuition es muy importante. Nogo didn't get a chance to come back. He'd just taken off his bubble top, when Cerevello's face blipped up on the mag's monitor screen. It was a medium shot, showing him with one hand waving a bottle of pills, and the other holding a coffee cup. He had the 'not funny' look emblazoned on his skull.

"Yuk, yuk, yuk," Cerevello said. "I appreciate your support. And, your trust. But this is the best my wunderkindergartners can squeeze out when I'm not directly nexed-in? I'm trying to help you two Associates, and you give me full shots and close-ups. Thanks."

Cerevello banged his goggle sources and winced.

"I'm sending you two wise-mouthed jerk offs to the bio-collective named Dave," he said in a convinced sounding tone. "You know, where they make the underwear. Maybe for some good slant stuff, funny bits we can dump or m-line the Weirds with."

"What?"

"Now, I know how you feel, Standard," Biff added with an apologetic smile. "So I won't explain. It's just in case we need it. We're going after it old-era style, just the way you want - with live shots, not too much edit or animix. I agree one hundred percent. But we don't really know what Weirds are. So it might be advantageous, even necessary, to do what we're trained to do. Superimpose and animix."

He beamed happily, as if he'd just given long-winded jefe-slam, confidently, for the first time. He was executive producer, and sometimes they needed to be assertive. He held the smile too long, then abruptly yakked on.

"Let's not forget, we're advos, not holy men," he said. "Being all high and mighty is one thing, but sometimes you got to get right down there with the element you're dealing with, and ride the nekro zoom."

He squeezed out another slap happy mugger.

"Go see what the smear are grumbling," he ordered. "Chances are you won't get nothing. But just maybe you'll get that one shot that's the vast enchilada, our campaign emblem."

The smirky sneer, snurky-smear dump, the m-line for sure. Going to the biocollective named Dave was originally my idea. It's where Bob Sideways used to hang, as a near-smear aide, before I Spotlighted him. Now Biff was cueing cred for it. It didn't make sense.

Nogo, who probably wanted to animix the entire goober anyway, sat motionless, expressionless.

"Biff, I want to find Bob Sideways," I jumped in. "A former smearoid, and now a face. The hush connector has it that Bob was an aide at Dave. I want to go face-to-face with him, Live focus."

"Face to face," Cerevello came back, barking from a medium shot. "I know that's your angle. But I don't think Bob ever met any Weirds, though."

Nogo looked uneasy. Maybe, like me, he wished Cerevello would shut up.

"It's not in vogue, I know," Biff driveled on, "but I still don't think they're real. Maybe they're real, but they ain't for real. Weirds are a hoax, a con. Or a secretly induced and controlled mass hallucination. Maybe it's a conspiracy, maybe not."

Biff was all over the place. He took a breath, with a hard swallow.

"But one thing I do know, is that no matter how the cards are stacked, I've got a team I can depend on," he slobbered. "A team that will bring back a credit roll that will put us in good financial shape. In fact, one that will put us in the land of milk and gravy, til it all fades out. So I'm literally banking on your instincts as advos, boys. If you think Bob can help find Weirds, goose those knobs, break your legs, and do it."

Cerevello looked like he had something stuck in his throat. He was gulping, soundlessly, and blinking.

"Alright," he shouted like a sergeant, "That's it! On it..."

The e-mag dash screen went black.

Suddenly we were on our way to an underwear warehouse unhouse, looking for someone who knew Bob Sideways, who might have known Weirds, on a rush cue. My instincts said dead end lead.

The smear can't remember their names, and somehow we're going to get good focus from the first one we zoom? This project needed a solid week of pre-production. Not an hour of randomly asking Neighbors without memories their recollections. Maybe there were smear there who could still recon and yakk about it a bit, maybe not. It wasn't something to count on.

The dash panel flashed 'New Destination Entered' and then the mag's V-O said "Thirteen minutes to the biocollective named Dave. Dave is located in the southwest of the Local 838 region. Dave monitors the manufacture of Dave's Underwear, and is made possible by a generous charitable grant from Dave's Underwear. Please select a preferred route."

"Select any route," I said. "They all take thirteen minutes."

The mag's prepro picked a route with a lot of woods with big, old trees along the way. Home understood my slant and zoom, knew I went for nature shots. Some Bob Sideways music swelled in the background, and we were loping along to "You Don't Know What Lonesome Is 'Til You Get To Herding Cows," an old country swing hit with yodeling, ki-yi-yippie-i-os, and mooing cattle. Soon we were dogie-ing under huge oak trees somehow spared the tox of the industrial old era.

A long rear shot showed the mag from behind, with a profile of Nogo through the back window, reacting in bewilderment.

"What is that crap?" Nogo said sourly. "I think I'm going to be sick."

"It's Bob Sideways, giving us a background swell, for the scene change,"

I said. "You know, get the bad guys. We're the posse, out to catch them damn renegades who robbed the Red Rock Bank. Funny stuff for fill."

Sex-death, the basic formula. Polka music, old country music, get laughs.

"Come on, Nogo," I went on. "Get funny. That's got to go up slant. Think of it. I mean, we're heading for an underwear factory that's really a mental institution for scanned out smear who can't cue their own I-Ds. We should be wearing fifty gallon hats over our eyes and gigantic fur chaps and freaking luminous cowboy boots."

He looked puzzled by the idea.

"The quest," I gabbed on, "the holy parade into oblivion, to nobly save someone's ass while sacrificing one's own. Only we're framing up some poor skurds for box beating, and saving the wrong butts."

"No problema," Nogo said contemptuously. "The Weirds never did anything for me, and Cerevello's harmless, and your flimmer is crap. With our conflicting viewpoints, it beats the hell out of me why Cerevello teamed us up."

He paused to zoom me.

"Go ahead," he said. "Zoom your skull's tunes. Get funny."

"Why all the bad focus, pardner?" I came back. "My flimmer's crap? Touchy, touchy. Maybe you need stimsublim, a nice Beta-stim or Satiscope. Maybe I can peek."

"Get funny," Nogo repeated, with a nekro look.

"M-lining Weirds is ridiculous," I barked back pronto. "We don't know if they're bad guys, or something totally different. Always avoid hysteria. The truth will write our ticket. Cerevello's wrong, and I'm right. We can come up with a better slant, with more climb."

Nogo looked at me in disbelief. I'd promised a better shot than el jefe, right in focus. He probably thought I was lumed, blinking restricted patterns. Cueing deep-field in front of the world felt scary. Cerevello saw me say it, but advos had more privacy than Neighbors. Unless some double Big was peeking. Either way, flapping malco was looking for trouble.

"I mean," I said all apologetic, "when you use your own initiative, you always come out with climb. What if Biff - bless his heart - does something we don't want our credits on? It's possible. We are at his mercy in many ways, right?"

Then there was a painful silence, and both Nogo and I made real bad focus. He looked like he was trying to come back, but no-go. Then he skwacked.

"Cerevello's given us the gold op, man. He thinks we've got climb. What do you want us to do? Take off on foot? Scan this. This spot will help my career. If you don't want to give it your best shot, jump out, disnex. That way a bad slant or spin won't ruin your credit roll."

"I completely appreciate what Biff's doing, and thank him for the gold op," I said, trying to save my culo. "But we should make up our own minds. What if Weirds are hot focus, and we m-line them? We've got a moral imperative, or something."

He started jabbing at me with his finger.

"I don't make the friggin' rules," he snorted. "I do the job, cue my cred, and point towards the goal, Point A, Pinpoint. I don't want to be in this skin-min skurd hole any more than you do. But we play by the prevailing rules."

He vipped up sincere teeth, a medium close-up shot. He trashed the Neighbors in focus. He panned 838 in focus. Something was Go.

"Work with me," he said softly. "I promise not to bring down a nekro m-line on your beloved Weird skulls, if they're good guys. But forget the simpering flimmer, doff the role, and play it. You're an advo. And you can bring the smooth to this spot."

"Ok, ok, ok," I agreed. "Concentrate on the job. Advo, doff the role, and play it. We're not holy men. We are advos, tribunes of the somnappers."

Shaking his head, Nogo put up an icy close-up. I turned up the Bob Sideways volume by hand, instead of commanding. Nogo seemed startled by it.

The mag plodded by an automind, an automated greenhouse and container factory. Suddenly I had an urge to jump out of the mag, grab a rock, and then throw it at one of the automind's surveillance eyes, just to sooze the stay-at-home workers' reactions. Wake those agricultural and industrial heroes up a little.

The Weirds were away from all this, living in the ruins of the old era, with battery powered radios and pig dung or french fry cars. Real old-era, more authentic than our spin. Probably with books and movies and recorded music, too.

Who wouldn't want to toss a rock at the peeper, keep it as a bleeper, and not get caught? Disappear like the green screen, and not get lost.

"Well, do you think Weirds eat?" I asked, right out of a chroma blue. "Do you think they have sex, either flesh and dirt, or feelie-realie?"

I leered, kind of bad focus, but there it is dear N's and A's, for all to see.

"Imagine it. Weirds freaking on sloppy wet and cryo-cry. With visualine stimsublims squirting directly into the brains. All the while, the ground rumbles and the lights go off and on, and it's the best private access ever. Weirds having supernatural sex."

Some advo, some Associate, should have comped to that lucrative focus many seasons back. It could have been me, but I wasn't into sexplo.

Man, it must have been frightening meeting women in the F and D, back in the jeri-era, and actually being with them before, during, and after sex. Sylvia and I were together five seasons feelie-realie before meeting in the flesh and dirt, and then becoming hab mates.

Nogo was nexed with some diva-Jane named Andrea who dressed, and undressed, like an old-era spy chick. He wasn't squeamish about sexplo. She looked genalt for eroto-slam. Like everyone didn't know.

"Nogo, do you and Andrea ever do it in the flesh and dirt, or just with all that expensive feelie-realie gear? Blink blank and wank, skank. Better living through genetic engineering."

He looked like he wanted to punch me.

"You're the blink-blank wanker," he snarled. "You're so lumed most of the time you can't find your dick, and Sylvia has the erotic focus of a nano-grown beef product. Who would want to see that? You're the blink wanker."

It wasn't an attack on his sexuality or Andrea, or genalts. It just felt good to tweak his skull. He took everything too seriously.

"Ok, ok, sorry I got personal. Just going for the twist. Actually, I don't know what I was doing. I'm sorry."

Nogo's body relaxed, but his face showed reluctance to accept the apology. There would be no violence for the General Offices, or whoever was peeking. I relaxed too. Nogo put on a pair of wrap-around sources and started taking on something, ignoring me.

I felt isolated. I had no idea how to get anything out of the smear. Some weren't so bad. They were like Sylvia, you could roust them, bring them back for a while. Maybe, if I talked to them like I talked to her, asked the right questions, it could work.

"Man," I said. "I never should have told Cerevello I wanted to talk in person to the smear. I just wanted to find Bob Sideways and congratulate him in person. Like big heads do."

Bob got his Spotlight, and his set-up, but he never nexed back in with me.

"Now," I said, "it seems he's been erased somehow. His address, gone. His imprint, gone. Even the gear and the van and set-up, gone. Of course, you already know. Strange, huh?"

I didn't like the idea of Bob Sideways, my own gold op, being out of focus, disnexed, like a Weird, with a credit scandal happening. But how did Bob stay out of the Spotlight so long in the first place?

"Not strange," Nogo said, with his eyes narrowing. "Weird."

"Nogo, if Bob's Weird, I'm Weird," I came back. "He's just a character. He's a crackpot romantic in love with the old era, when guitar was king. Sure, he's stuck in the lifestyle statement. So I saved him from himself, and oblivion. I showed him his music was viable, that he was info. And that's what advos do."

"Wait," Nogo cut in, taking his wraps off. "First he's a possible lead, then a character, then a romantic, or doomed whatever. I don't care. Advos are supposed to do their jobs, not play head shrinker. Does Bob know Weirds?"

"How the hell should I know?" I snapped. "I hardly know the guy. He just walked into my hab, and made me listen. I didn't know who he was or where he came from, or how he knew I was an advo. He'd never registered for a Spotlight before that. He played all his songs for me, in-person, like at a jeri-era living room gig."

Nogo looked attentive, but obviously he knew the details better than I remembered them.

"When I asked him if I could put it up on the monitor, and he told me that's why he stopped by. He wanted to come into focus and register for a Spotlight. I told him to look into the source and cue his credit. He said his name was Robert Zeitweiss, but he wanted to cue his credit as Bob Sideways, the Alphadrine Cowboy."

Nogo started fidgeting, glancing out the mag window.

"After I registered him, I went to the other room to see what Sylvia was up to, and when I came back, he was gone."

"That guy is Weird," Nogo popped out. "You'll never see him again. All your fantasizing about breaking him in a big Local is quick wipe. He's gone."

"Put it this way," he went on, pointing with his index finger. "If we can find Sideways, and he's not a Weird, I'll sign a binding contract to do any spot you want. Free. Think of it. He walked to your hab. How did he know who you were? You know so little about him. Why do you think he's into lifestyle statements?"

Being in the mag with Nogo was like being in a cage with a poisonous snake.

"I don't know, I don't know, "I stammered out. "I filled in the blanks, since he was so out of focus."

Nogo looked like he doubted my honesty, and was wrestling with it. He panned my gaze and looked out the window again. Like someone planted a lie, that Bob was Weird and I was too.

The mag took a turn onto a bridge, over a brook enclosed by yellow leaved willows. Lots of great nature shots there. Inside the mag, it was stifling.

"Let me watch Sideways coming into your hab," Nogo said. "I can tell you whether he's Weird or not. I can run scans that will tell what kind of baby food he ate. I can tell if he's trying to fool the source."

He paused and looked directly at me.

"Obviously, you haven't done this yet," he said dryly. "You weren't too lumed too take it all down, were you?"

"Of course not," I said. "Got it all. I just didn't mess with the pre-performance stuff. He's genuine. I guarantee it."

Nogo laughed.

"What the hell does that mean?" he asked incredulously. "You're so naive. He's Weird. He used you. Weirds fool sources. He dazzled you to make you think he's some wandering minstrel who just dropped in from green screen, or some old-era chroma-boing backdrop. Then he goes internap, climbs the ladder, and fades us to black with his Weird powers."

He smiled like it was just that simple.

"Nogo, what the hell would a Weird do with credit? Why would they climb the ladder if they could make their own? Weirds don't need credit, fame, or the system. Besides, I don't want to look at that stuff until after I check it out myself."

"So what?" Nogo snickered. "Put it up. It's information and I've got a right to see it. Tell your Home you want to see it right now."

"I don't see how it's going to help anything," I said.

Then there was a painful silence. Somebody; maybe the General Offices, maybe genalt Hard Schoolers, wanted to hang poor old Bob with the Weirds. The idea was probably to get some color at the biocollective, the smear in their sorry state, and then superimpose Bob as some nekro climber, conspiring with Weirds.

If I didn't put him up, they'd say I was concealing information, get an access order, do whatever they wanted, and leave me on the m-line list. But Bob Sideways was my bundle, and I had to protect him. Somehow.

"Just ask Home," Nogo said threateningly. "We're almost there."

"Alright, alright, alright," I said. "Watch it. Watch it real good."

Then I commanded the e-mag to nex-in with Home.

"Home," I said directly to the monitor screen. "This is Stan."

Immediately, Stansville, my private corner where my shots were logged, vipped up on the e-mag's monitor. Near my main work console, Sylvia was half sprawled on the couch. Home drifted into a close-up of Sylvia's stubby, bare left foot.

"Yes, Stan," Home responded in a secretarial female voice.

"Play the entry shots of Bob Sideways, when he came to register," I told Home.

I smiled at Nogo, and rubbed an itchy eyelid. Then the mag's monitor screen faded to gray, and suddenly Bob Sideways's face exploded onto it, supered over a scarlet background. Lariat-rope letters spelled out Bob Sideways, the Alphadrine Cowboy.

Then the playback of my first encounter with the Alphadrine Cowboy began, just as Home and I saw it.

The first scene, a shot of the area near the hab touchlot, vipped up. It was separated from other random security shots, because Home sensed something unusual about it. Then it blew up a solitary figure walking across the touchlot, towards my hab. He was carrying luggage, some kind of long case.

It was Bob Sideways, wearing a bright red and black checked hunting jacket, and matching moscow fur hat with the flaps down. As he got closer and blew up more, you could see him rolling his tongue in his cheek, pushing out the peculiar scar that ran across the right side of his face. In matching red and black checked pants and green hunting boots, he looked like an outdoorsman from hell. Staring vacantly, with a mierda-munching grin, he trudged full blast across the touchlot.

With his almost translucent skin and blue silver hair, Zeitweiss looked albino. It was a youngish face, mustached with a white rooker, under a stately, well-proportioned nose.

The cowboy arrived at my door, and knocked on it. Really knocked on it, with his hand. Home didn't understand, and could only respond by saying, "Stand! Someone's hitting the hab. What should we do?"

Then I actually got involved and walked to the door to see who or what was hitting it. The source switched to a shot of Bob in front of the door, looking like an old-era horror movie character about to pick up his brain-eating prom date. Then there was an over-the- shoulder shot of me approaching the door, and opening it by hand.

The shot on the mag's monitor screen showed Bob's face getting redder by the second. His lips parted and formed an embarrassed, toothy horse grin.

Nogo and I watched him as we passed into a tunnel cutting through a ridge near the Lake Erie shoreline. Entering the tunnel, the mag faded to black for an unsettling moment, with Sideways's face on the luminous screen becoming the entire focal point.

Bob said, "I'm a p-poet, backwoods philosopher, and c-country song stylist."

The shot tracked back to a full shot of Bob entering my hab, and a long shot of me closing the door behind him. Ironically, in Dave's Underwear, with mussed up hair.

"You're what?" I asked, bewildered. "Who are you? What are you doing walking around here? Where's your mag?"

Watching was no fun. I was forced to relive the whole traumatic experience. Imagine it. Someone unknown coming to your hab, unannounced, in the flesh and dirt, transported by his feet. Nogo was right. It was more than strange.

The screen scene showed me in a three quarters shot, a standing profile, as he stepped forward. Sideways rubbed a little snot from his nose and made a slurping sound.

"I said I'm a p-poet, a singer," he said. "You know, advo. You know. Yup."

Screen scene showed me turning to the source, frizzy and querulous, kind of a double take.

"Come on in," I said, looking peeved and confused.

Then I turned and walked into an extreme close-up, then off source. Bob Sideways followed, the same way. The empty room stayed on screen scene a while, like Home had somehow become confused and forgot to follow the action.

Maybe it was waiting for someone else. Maybe Roberto was skritchy-glitching it with his mind. Maybe Home was smearing. It had a loose, sponto, rough edit look.

Then Home jump cut to show me from a full shot, putting on clothes in my bedroom.

A close-up of Zeitweiss came up right after.

"I want to play some songs for ya," he said. "I'm your main source for the nekro-baddest, cryo-chilliest focus ever beheld. These songs is s-s-special."

He leaned over and unsnapped the latches on his case. It was a guitar case.

"S-s-spent lots of time on 'em," he said, taking his guitar out and strapping it on. "F-first one's called 'G-ghost Riders In The S-s-sky.' Sure you heard it before. But not like this. This here's unique."

Then he nodded solemnly, like the word 'unique' had some secret, sacred significance.

The guitar was an old acoustic beauty bearing a scar near the sound hole from years of hard playing. The ebony pick guard glistened with flashes of tortoise shell scarlet and green. Zeitweiss strummed it, a big G major chord.

I remember that my hab suddenly smelled like burning leaves or a wood fire then, some kind of natural K. The odor got stronger, as Sideways played a haunting E minor chord, and gave me a serious, sincere close-up.

"Or I could sing a silly little d-ditty called 'You Don't Know What Lonesome Is 'Til You Get To Herdin' Cows.' Reminds you of them guys on the range so long they'd rather have an animal than a Dodge City filly. Too much saltpeter in the pork and beans."

Then the cowboy whimper-laughed, like his brain hurt, and slapped his knee. Then he played an arpeggio C major chord. Another source picked up a full shot of me scratching my head in confusion.

Then Nogo cut on the screen scene action.

"Wow, man, freeze that up," Nogo said, totally absorbed in the shot. "That says it all. Stan is frizzing."

Nogo smiled, looking at me with droopy lids, like he was getting ready to lecture.

"I don't understand why he chose you, a yakking artichoke, the vaguest advo in 838. When he went looking for you, he went looking for obscurity."

Nogo frowned.

"Even your own cult can't understand you, Mozuck," he said finally. "Your friend here must have something to hide."

"He was looking for an advo," I spat out. "Someone to Spotlight him. I don't know how he found me."

"Right," Nogo chuckled. "Right. We'll see."

On screen, I was telling Bob where to stand while I took him down.

Sideways said, "I want to play muh songs for ya. I got a CD of music for under muh singin' and playin', but I want to perform live."

CD?

No problema," I responded, worrying about my antique CD collection. "But first tell me who you really are. And how you found me. I'm in Local 838's private directory. You've got to be recommended by a NeighborWorld Associate. See, I'm Step Three. I get to do my own stuff. I don't really take unsolicited Spotlight registrations anymore."

"Oh, sure, yup," he agreed. "But you can sign me up for a Spotlight, can't ya? I c-c-come to the right guy, didn't I?"

"Yeah," I answered, still hoping to find out what was go, and get him out of my hab. "But I only handle folks who've shown some climb. Uh.... like pros, real accomplished at what they do."

Zeitweiss boomed out a beautiful chord change, and then riffed some incredible blues licks. Man, nobody played like that anymore. Nobody even had guitars like that.

"Where's the box?" I asked. "How do you get that sound?"

"Ain't got no box besides my git-box, right here," he responded, tapping his guitar.

He zoomed me disappointedly.

"Do you want to hear s-s-something nova-cent, cryo-man, and different, or d-d-do ya want to spend the rest of your life in 838? You're lookin' at your ticket to climb the ladder, young advo. Just give me a listen."

"Ok," I said. "I'll do it. Give me your music."

It was an old-era CD. Mint. No dingies. It bore a logo; the same art I would later use.

"Wait," I said. "This is a CD, right?" I laughed nervously.

"Yup," Sideways answered with a stupid smile. "I got a portable if yours ain't workin'."

"No problema," I barked back.

Poor Bob Zeitweiss. Nogo saw all Bob's smiles and goofy barking as a glimmering of something devious, and he reacted predictably.

"Blow him up," Nogo said. "I want to check his blink cycle. Liars stick out right away, no tweaking. If he's lying he'll blink, stress drinks up eye fluids. Let's peep a close-up."

I needed a blink.

The image was as closeup as it would go. The Alphadrine Cowboy's pores were craters, his nostrils caverns, and chin pimples volcanoes. I tilted his face up manually, to show his huge, shiny eyes. Bob barked on, without any awareness that compact discs were obsolete. Except to old-era collectors like me..

"Careful with that," Zeitweiss said. "I ain't got but a couple hundred more." He punctuated the comment with another pained-sounding, sideways giggle.

Off source and screen, my voice broke in.

"Hey, man, how'd you know I have CDs? That's hush - just between a few advos and Associates and me. What's going on, Neighbor?"

I had just remembered. Thieves can't break into your hab anymore, but they can get in if you let them in.

Then Nogo yelled "ECU, freeze!"

I froze the image. If Bob was lying, that would be it for me. I'd be ready to move into the unhouse myself. We microzoomed the extreme close-up of the cowboy's eyes.

"Roll back slow," Nogo said. "I'm going to count the blinks."

"Home," I said to the monitor, "Time this sequence. I'll cue to start. Ready?"

"Ready," Home answered.

"Go," I said, and numbered seconds flashed across the bottom of the screen. Bang! The cowboy's eyes slammed shut like a fortress gate. Long seconds before another, then a long time before another. Maybe he'd been trained to lie.

"He isn't blinking much," Nogo said. "Either he's for real, or he's Weird."

"That's what I told you, man," I said quickly. "He's for real."

"We'll play it your way til we know better," he said without any opposition. "We'll see."

"Home, forget the rest," I told the monitor, and we were spared more of the bizarre comedy; with me running to find my 40 year old CD player, teaching Sideways to follow hand cues and monitor digital scans while I registered him, and him playing the songs that were my gold op. And me reacting to him disappearing. Nogo didn't care to see any more, and I was glad. The mag monitor screen faded to black.

The mag emerged from the tunnel, into late morning clouds and light. Below us, off to the right, we could see the pastel pink and blue, silver-domed building; the biocollective called Dave. The unhouse was perched above a stream gully, surrounded by knee high wild grasses. We rode parallel with the gully for about half a kilometer, then the mag wound around and onto a converted old automobile bridge, over the stream, towards Dave.

Dave was built at the end of the old era, and had that corny, futuristic, outer space hotel look. It was a breast and phallus rocket ship, rudely giving God the finger, ready to spurt pioneering humans into the universe. Only now it accommodated smeared guests, who thought they were somehow part of Concord, shareholders of a global corporate trust, somehow working, somehow alive.

We floated into the unhouse touchlot, located on a fifty square meter plain adjoining the grounds. An old brick wall, overgrown with dark green moss on the bottom and half frozen yellow flowers on top, surrounded the lot. It looked like Dave was built near an old settler's mill from centuries ago, over some Native American town before that. There were overgrown shapes all over the grounds.

Dave was a dull-shine monument in the woods, a corroded metalloid and polypast medicine lodge. It was stained with algae. The algae were all rendered harmless by mutantia-flap tox-scrappers, but it still looked unhealthy. Even the tiny air conditioning box was stained green by pacified polyplast algae and molds. The waste disposal area was leaking something bright orange. Flies buzzed in the cold morning, circling a heat leak somewhere, loud enough to hear over the whirring mag. What a great place to care for 838's psychic casualties.

-5-
"A BIOCOLLECTIVE NAMED DAVE"

The whirring stopped and the mag plopped gently on the soft wet dirt. But a great humming persisted, dear mind's-eye Neighbors, coming from inside the joint, the sound of the whacko smear in grand choral unison. Not one human in this entire automind dreamsville thought he-she was anything but Dave, or Davina. And not Dave or Davina Someone, either. Just "I'm Dave (or Davina). Hello there. Stylish scanties with a trad flair. Come on, Neighbor, try on a pair!"

The Dave biocollective made garish, racy, and wholesome originals, like Dave Birthday Suits; full body ultra-light, transparent thermalwear. And the usual crotchless panties, working-diva panties, boxer shorts with big red hearts, briefs, old-era looking longies, and naughty lingerie for vorbed out near-smear combos.

The place was a vast nano-prepro tech lab, with Daves dreaming up proto-panties, using the prepro system, and then the automind spitting out the undies. Then, smeared Daves approached the garments reverently, and gingerly searched each one for imperfections, the tiniest flaws. Not that the automind couldn't do all this by itself, better, and more cost effectively. But the smear added something human, a personalized touch, to product manufacture. The smear thought they were doing something necessary, and felt useful. There was an illusion of a job, of individual worth.

That was the plan, based on sound social science. But the Daves hobbling around under the big silver dome had their lives transformed by ego death, by merging their personalities with a corporate I-D. The individual I-D requires maintenance and nurturing. To meld, to merge, is easier.

I thought it was still a good social program. I wasn't sure it worked; there were more smear every day. And having thousands of people in psychic limbo, on the public barbeque, was an obvious drawback. You got fed, and a bed, but you were discon. Still, it was better than letting them fade to black.

We walked into Dave without nexing with anyone. The prepros must have known we were coming, because we weren't stopped or made to cue I-D. We had on bubble hats, taking on the place in 360, trying to get a total feel. The concourse area right under the dome looked like a giant bird cage. Smear were milling around in slo-mo.

Nogo looked reluctant to walk towards the concourse, like the smear were tweaking his skull and he wanted to leave. After a while, he mustered enough courage to tag along, but he had to keep whispering cruel jibes about the smeared zoombies all around us in my ear.

Inside, the place was glare white, with potted plants everywhere. There were bits of blue, green, and red trim, like in a nursery backdrop key. The smear mostly wore opaque white versions of Dave Birthday Suits. That part of their attire was monochrome and monotonous. But many were wearing underpants as hats, an odd, unexpected display of individuality.

One guy wore stiff red striped boxer shorts on his head, another bright blue briefs. An enormously fat elderly woman wore tent sized grandmotherly skivvies on top of an old-era beehive hair-do. A pink faced old hombre with a long nose drooled by, wearing hot-thong scanties draped over one eye.

As Dave would say, "Always on my body, always on my mind."

The shots had a goofy dream quality. With our bubble hats on, we fit right in. Scanning through the hats, we were picking up smear behind us, overhead, every perspective on every level in the place, full 360.

The slow place of the smear, the droning sound, the overwhelming shot processing of the bubble hat, made me feel drained. I had to sit down.

"Nogo, I've got to catch my breath. I'm going over there and sit without the hat for a bit."

"I'm with you on that one," he came back. "This place is frizzing me."

We headed towards an oasis, with a little jungle of tropical under-plants and a stone bench, near a fountain. The drone sound was quieter there.

I sat down on the bench, pulled off my hat, and disnexed my fingertip source. I could hear the music better with the hat off, and I finally realized what it was. "Twilight Time." Perfect. The smear were working to "Twilight Time."

"Purple evening shadows are falling, it's twilight time," I sang out of key.

I almost showed some happy teeth, but Nogo appeared paranoid. I looked the other way to ignore him, and zoom the smear with naked eyes. Then, I noticed the perfect yakking skull for the scenes, sitting right on the other side of the fountain. The guy noticed me noticing him, and tilted his head back with a look of curiosity.

Alert smear?

The jeri smear hopped to his feet from the bench like a nimble teenager, and walked over, with his white-gloved hand extended. Somehow his underwear hat looked like a hat, not a crazy person's head decoration. He was a wiry old gelf, probably almost 360 seasons, but well preserved. With his stiff brushed white crew cut and leathery mug, he had the kind of skull that climbers love, to create color.

"Name's Gerald Purselips," the smear said. "Funny I-D, I know. Around here I'm just called Old Jer. Been in this dingbat cave almost twenty seasons now, longer than most."

Old Jer continued animatedly, waving his hands to highlight points of interest; a conversational frog jumping all over the place. There was none of the lethargy of his smeared brethren. Only one in a hundred in this mind control garage could converse functionally, let alone whip out a narro like jeri-era Old Jer.

"I'm a volunteer," he said, meaning he locked himself in. "I like helpin' out the new fellas. Gettin' real bad lately. Nobody remembers their names or how they got here or nothin'. They think Dave's family somehow. At least, I know who I was and how I wound up here. So I'm Dave because I want to be."

"And I'm only Dave when I'm workin'," he added with a smile. "I can see plain as day you're Associates, real advos, too. So how can I help?"

Nogo and I didn't have time to respond. Old Jer babbled on.

"There's somethin' funny goin' on in here," Jer said. "More Daves in here now than I can ever remember. Don't know where to put 'em all. Come from everywhere. And a lot of 'em are fadin' to black. Maybe from the emptiness of bein' here. Maybe they're gettin' a hold of nekrolim. Nekrolim makes your eyes all screwy and you go in a coma for a week. That's what some of 'em done in here. And they faded to black. Yessir, that's your story. How are the smear getting nekrolim?"

My mouth dropped open. If he was right and smear had access to nekrolim, it would be as big a story as the Weirds. Even better, maybe they connected somehow.

"Well, how?" I blurted. "Do you really know what that stuff is? It's restricted. No access. Illegal. Because it can kill you."

Nogo made an unfriendly face at the geezer.

"I ain't sayin' for sure it's nekrolim," Jer said. "But something's screwed up in here."

Nogo poured on the evil eye. Old Jer made an expression of recognition, then acted like he remembered something horrible.

"Findin' out things is your job, not mine," he said flatly. "I ain't sayin' no more about it."

"Well, it's my job to ask you. What makes you think smear are croaking from getting their hands on nekrolim?" I paused, long enough to savor the thrill of sounding pissed off.

"Ever see any restricted patterns in here?" I added. "You got me burned-in and image- locked on this thing, and now you're not saying anything more about it."

Old Jer remained expressionless. Then he blinked rapidly about ten times and nodded.

"A fad, folks turn blue," he said. Then he blinked again. "All flesh and dirt, you know?"

"You're a joker," I said, waving my hand and starting to walk away.

"You're not serious."

Nogo laughed, and it sounded a little forced. The geezer followed right behind me.

"Hey, advo," he shouted. "I just don't want to talk about that right now. But you want to know what it's like in here, don't you? I'll tell you what it's like. Dave is cracking up! Too many left over personality traits overcrowding the automind's prepro. Dave's confused."

"Hey, hey, hey," he said falling behind. "Don't you want to see what living here does to folks? What happens when the lines blur? Look! Here comes a real Dave. Talk to him. Let me help you."

Old Jer grabbed the smear by the arm and presented him to me.

"Hey, Dave," Jer said. "Come and talk with these two nice advos. Tell them what Dave's working on today."

The blotchy-skinned Dave was self-absorbed and squinting, preoccupied with Dave obsesso-griff, some delicate issue in delicates. Like other Daves, it was always on his body, always on his mind.

"Is this a spot?" the Dave asked us, his eyes darting towards Old Jer for reinforcement. "Is Dave In The Spotlight?"

Then the Dave looked at his feet with an absorbed expression. He'd already lost his thought, forgotten the context, even the conversation. This Dave was definitely biosmear of the forever kind. Nogo, disgusted, almost horrified, was barely handling being near him.

"Dave," Old Jer said in a teacher to child tone. "These advos want to know what Dave's up to today, and what it's like bein' Dave, and how we like it, things like that."

The Dave looked up from his feet and back towards Jer. He acted like someone waking from angry sleep, like me.

"Before I was Dave, I was nothing," he said, like someone converted after a miracle. "I was just a Neighbor who dreamed of being somebody. But the more I dreamed of being someone, the more I became a nobody."

The Dave squinted hard, like his eyes were imploding. His mouth was moving, but no sounds were coming out.

"Then I became Dave," he blurted out finally. "Now I really am somebody."

Nogo slapped himself on the forehead, like the Dave's reasoning was ridiculous. Which it was. But the poor Dave was freaking sick, you know? In frustration, or something more nekro, Nogo stormed out of the oasis, towards the main access area.

"The dome does that to them, sometimes," the Dave said, transfixed by his shoes again but pointing upwards. "Genalts, I mean."

"How did you know he was genalt?" I asked in astonishment. "How'd you know that?"

The Dave started squinting and pushing sloppy air out of his mouth again, then barked.

"If it wasn't for Daves, the underwear wouldn't be human," he said, now wide-eyed and enthusiastic. "But nothing would be, without the ones like us. Inhuman furniture, inhuman food, inhuman habs, inhuman clothes and gear. Inhuman humans! There are problems. I know. I can feel the market share..."

Then he stopped, and looked at his feet again. He thought he was a collectivist capitalist, little Mr. Grandee Big, when in fact he was smeared, in the unhouse. He was fed and bed, in a panty hat, on the public barbeque, imagining he was a visionary entrepreneur.

"Oh yeah? Tell the advo how much you knock down a season, there, General CEO,"

Old Jer ham-jammed, laughing. "You and the other Bigs doin' pretty well, are ya?"

"How'd you know my partner's genalt?" I pressed on.

The Dave kept staring at his pooty-boots. Old Jer laughed harder.

"It's a strange and wonderful sight to behold, dear Neighbor," Jer howled, wagging his head like a lab monkey on nekrolim. He slapped his thigh, and hopped up and down. Jer was a different kind of smear, voyeuristic and shallow. He stopped laughing long enough to sop it up.

"You won't get nothin' more from him," Jer said with a satisfied tone. "He's done. See, even though Dave's made up of a couple thousand folks, he's still a real person. Alone, we can't dream up great undergarments for millions of folks, or understand their underwear needs. We can't even be who we really are anymore. But Dave's slant is our slant. And Dave is."

"Dave is," the catatonic Dave chimed in, looking like his brain was shorting.

"Always on my body, always on my mind," another nearby smear answered in a church mass sounding response. Others in earshot mumbled along.

In a long shot, close to the main access area, Nogo stood with his arms folded, laughing. The close-up: a disdainful sneer.

Jer stopped the wheezing snorts, and smiled like a buddha. The forever smear went deeper into Daveness, and it was a vast ocean. Just like Jer said, he was done with the world that wasn't Dave. I started walking away, and old Jer followed, holding his chest.

Then his bony hand grabbed my arm from behind.

"Listen," he whispered hoarsely. "I know what you're here for."

I turned slowly, ready to play with the old head one last time for color's sake. But there would be no more beglitched stumpers straggling behind, raining on the shots all morning.

"And why might that be?" I asked sarcastically. "Got any more hot tips for us advos?"

"You got me all wrong, sonny," he barked back pronto. "I ain't about to spill my guts in front of that splicer. Think I want to commit sewercide? You saw him lookin' at me. I can smell them splicers. That poor smeared feller back there probably didn't even know what he was saying, but I did. Splicers give me the willies. But I'm telling you. I know why you're here."

"Then spill it, man, or stop wasting my vee-tee."

He got real close, stuck his face almost right against mine.

"It's Bob Sideways, ain't it? You're here to find him."

My knees got weak. How did a spent piece of material like Jer figure that out? Someone somewhere was running us while we worked. But how did smear know as much as we did? Maybe he saw the Alphadrine Cowboy spot, and somehow remembered it. How?

"Pardon me?" I answered, trying to not look frizzed.

"Why the Alphadrine Cowboy, the master of song himself," Jer said, without batting an eye. "A new fad, someday. He knows Weirds, too. Calls 'em Smoothbrains. He knows 'em all. That's what you want, ain't it?"

"Hey, Jer," I came back, frizzing. "Keep a lid on it. I doubt if you even know what a Weird is. So fade the volume. I don't need someone screaming about Bob knowing Weirds. If you want to say something, say it quietly. Jeez, man."

Jer drew even closer. The bony finger emerged and touched my nose. "Twilight Time" whispered-in under the big Dave dome. Blurry Daves plodded by, marking time in a trance.

A giant overhead monitor screen under the dome showed smear lovingly carrying quality checked, market approved underpants to mag van loading zones, or nano replicator tubes.

"Listen to me," he rasped. "A whole mess of Weirds live around here. A whole mess."

Old Jer panned around over his shoulder, in a wary spy-guy move. "Never can tell, when you're dealin' with them splice-babies." Then he turned back, blinked three times, and sputtered out more of his tune.

"They love it down there," he said. "Don't have to worry about Spotlighting. And since everyone else is all nexed-in now, they get to stay invisible."

Jer stopped abruptly. Then, with a surprised expression, flapped out more.

"Weirds think fryin' gear is fun," he said. "It's like a game to 'em. Makes 'em laugh. And the harder they laugh, the more the screens blow up. I know. I seen it. That was long before all the trouble, before Dave. I even seen Bob Sideways down there, eggin' 'em on, singin' and playin' his twanger. And I still sneak down there for them spacey smoothbrain jam sessions. That's why I'm still with it. I know how to sneak out and have some fun."

It was too much to take on all at once.

"Where do they live?" I asked. "What's a smoothbrain?"

"By the way, Mr. M," he said with an old-era tone of familiarity. "I like your spots. You're the only advo in 838 with any spunk."

"Why do they think it's funny to fry gear? Wait. First. How do you know Bob Sideways? And where is he right now?"

The excited smile drained, leaving Jer without expression, blank. His lips looked ready to shoot out the next palabra, but no-go. I was losing him. The lines were blurring. Dave was stronger than Old Jer.

"Hallooo, Neighbor!" he said in Dave mode, as if meeting me for the first time. "It's about foundations. The first thing you put on and the last thing you take off. Alpha, omega, the world in briefs. Let's talk this season's new luxury pantyhose."

And he did, for almost five minutes, with no cut in the action. I tried vainly to get him to refocus, but he was as bad as the other smear. He babbled on about pantyhose, his throat pulsing like one of the nano-tubes that grew the poly-plast grundies. He almost shouted, refusing to let in the tiniest bark from my side.

Jer had blended into Dave, his nice pensioner's community service gig forgotten. He had blended into the enviro he'd chosen, a victim of happy-sappy bones and automind living. A Neighborly moron, a Dave.

"Jer, this is your last chance," I said, like talking to Sylvia. "Cut on the action, and dim the diva light. Do you remember anything about Bob Sideways, or Weirds, or nekrolim?"

"There's nothing like donning the moudons that lift the spirits, the boulder-holders that give special confidence," Jer said, turning from me, drifting away. "That's why Dave's fall line has so much sponto, so much freedom of expression. It's for living in. Think about it, Neighbor. Think about it."

Twilight Time suddenly became revolting. I wanted to kill Old Jer. His mind had frizzed, and there he was, spewing bizarre-badge, reduced to imbecility without pausing to twitch. Another forever smear, wearing a long-johns turban, walked up and stared at Jer like he was a guru, and sat to listen to his spiel. I could feel Nogo's cold hate stare burning through the back of my head. I pivoted on my left heel, and face to close-up before the nearest outside source.

Then I careened out of that joint, fast forward, right past Nogo, out the door, and into the touchlot.

The touchlot seemed warmer. Probably the genalt polyplast algaes making their own climates; a blue sludge was now noticeable, seeping through green. A vapor lingered, a stink, making me walk quicker to avoid it. The mag door opened, I climbed in.

Nogo walked to the mag, and got in. He looked at the time, above the monitor. Time was running out.

How could I find Bob Zeitweiss? If I didn't shake out something prontito, they'd animix the whole show to m-line the Weirds. They'd say Bob was one, too, and m-line him, and then me. I'd get bumped from the spot, then dropped a rung on the ladder. Then I'd spiral down, like Sylvia, and probably wind up at Dave, or Linda's Cookies, or fade to black. Unhouse blanko-Joe.

The mag hummed, and we were off again, this time with even less direction.

-6-
"POINT A."

The gray fall rain was squeaking back into the scene. Nogo and I sat silently. No friendly facade, but no dark barking. We were strangers, in MrMz Av Neighbor 838. Alone. Nogo, Son of Science and Stan, the apeman, both out of place, out of synch, and off cue in 838.

El Chimpy started banging through the monitor, and Nogo smiled. So did I.

"Well, we can always just head for Industros Tragicos, and look for Bob," he said.

"That's as vague as it gets," I said. "Sounds good to me."

"Sorry I called you vague earlier," Nogo said all buttery. "Just trying to twist."

"Yeah, since when are smear reliable?" I said, accepting the apology humbly. "But maybe Bob can still help us."

Nogo must have been peeping on Old Jer and me, so he knew what I did. But not everything.

"I found some old maps from the 838 History Club," I said. "Home should be able to get us close to something that makes sense."

You didn't have to be genalt to be a climber. My research would put a fire under his ass. The hottest focus was still Bob Zeitweiss and Standard Mozuck.

"Home, take us to the end of the line," I commanded. "Closest to Industros Tragicos near CarTown."

On the mag screen, Home displayed graphics of the route. Home created the display to impress Nogo, or someone like him. I barely understood the graphics, but acted like I was studying them carefully.

The narrow mag path followed a shale rock wall along the crooked river that ultimately wound through Industros Tragicos, to the Lake. Silent delivery mags glided by, carrying things to Neighbors, willed into existence on threads of light. Neighbors dreamed of products, and autominds created them.

The products existed only to answer the BizTek Direk Associates' only question. Is it Go? Will the credit roll be huge, with Neighbors rubbing their nubs down to stubs to order first? Act now while offer lasts. Discharge the noble fruit of commerce hermetically, automind to mag or tube to hab. The new pony express was no glitch, no worry. Neighbors and Associates complain? That's info-democracy. Where's my fall line gear? Look directly into the data base warehouse, at the thousands of products stored on screen, and check for yourself, Neighbor.

If you want to stay in L-838, or L-7, you butt-shield and apologize. If you want out, you deliver, you produce. What's the buzz in the Neighborhood? What's the Neighbors' POV? What if Nogo had the link hidden, and was reading my thoughts?

El Chimpy had faded. The mag was silent. Nogo turned to me and smiled again, then looked out the window without speaking. We were pretty high above the river. In the old era, people probably had better coordination, to drive cars. Without e-mag holding things down, I would have driven off the cliff. Nogo daydreamed, distant, in his own spot.

A simple life, complicated beyond comprehension. Constant communication, light stimulation, merciless self examination. Above all, relentless, total consumption. Without Agricord automind farms, without Concord deliveries, without NeighborWorld connectors to nex with, most Neighbors would indeed fade to black.

The mag began slowly ascending the river gorge, to the top of the banks, past tall pines and weeds. Off to my right, a wide shot of Local 838's perfunctory buildings came into view. A large raindrop struck the mag windshield, then another, through the mist. Nogo sat undistracted, deepening in his own gray.

Gleaming edifices of poly and metal poked through the drizzle, but they were only monuments to the new creator, MrMz Av Neighbor. The left-brain babbling of notes and promises to the body echoed throughout its creation. Welcome to 2000 something, a Nova Century of science and idiot mind chatter. Humanity's bright future had faded. Everything was a re-animix of the then, blown up for the now.

Nogo kept staring, like he understood the hopelessness. Those buildings were basically just backdrops. Real and feelie-realie were not the same. The only well used real buildings were unhouses. And only NeighborWorld Associates were free to come and go. The Neighbors lived on threads of light, projected off the map, into unknown worlds where future and past were one. They crudely examined each other and created maxims.

I was an advo in a brotherhood of light, bringing tiny-shiny focus to the smalls, illumination to those kept in dark. Wish, command, deliver. But this was a job for an illusionist, a parlor hack, a man with wires. We lived in a world built on illusion, an imitation of an imitation of an imitation. It's a world without war, without peace, without end, and the basic formula is sex-death. In the old era it would've been called a rung on a ladder in hell. We're lumps of flesh shackled to threads of light, living in forgotten places in the mind of God, where our lives appear to improve with each new unaffordable toy but actually get worse. Most Neighbors and Associates were just glowing turds in a global toilet.

My introspec deepened, tuning out the mag and Nogo, sinking the stage set city of prepro buildings into the background. The light coming from under the mag dash panel contrasted with the gloomy spit outside. The glow cast shiny patches on our chins and throats, making Nogo and I look like two toy devils in a gift box.

We both sat there so long, lost in our own spots, it seemed like they must have been beaming mind control squares into our heads, through the light. The only sounds were the low mag hum, a slight rain slosh, and an occasional breeze.

"Mind of God damaged during Big Bang?" I rumbled like an old-era newscaster. "Some scientists think so. Details at 11. "

"Some day, you're going to look back on this and wish you would've taken it more seriously," Nogo said sourly.

The view of L-838's neo-fake buildings came up again and faded. Nogo looked at me and took a long hard breath. The mag buzzed past more pines and weeds, then into a small forest of oak, maple, elm, and other trees with yellow and brown autumn leaves, or no leaves. Nogo didn't know how hard it was to have your own thoughts, to keep your individuality in 838. Young genalts had it easy, and always got upfielded. I'd probably end up stuck here, like Cerevello, m-lining Neighbors for a bluebook gold spot.

Show me another Associate as dissatisfied as me. That Neighbor with long lids and droopy shoulders never had it so good. He-she has climbed as far as possible in the world of then, now, and shaping up. For those in little Locals who smooched buns, the rewards were hefty. Unlimited time with limited commercial interruption. But all the signs pointed inward. No way out.

Another mag passed us, going the other way. A busy day, it was strange. I could see the Associate, a pretty, dark brown-haired, light brown-skinned diva-Jane. Through the drizzle, and the mag's static glow, those on the glide outside acknowledged each other with just a look; without losing track of the spots they were taking on. Skin-min Local 838, a cluster of poly-block and poly-wood habs on an inland sea, preferred inside. Art is social science. Who the hell was she?

Then, clicks and snaps were heard. The mag was sealing. We would be locked inside it until the script shaped up, until the construction had a good foundation. We were going up to Point A. Nobody really believed I, or we, could do this alone. We needed guidance, a feelie-realie conference, with all the lume that made it complete. We would be as immobile as corpses when we went up, but safe, warm, protected, and sealed in.

"Oh, not now," I complained, feeling unprepared.

"Here we go," Nogo said, looking excited about it.

The rain stopped again suddenly, and the outside seemed very still. The dichotomy of time - of then, now, and shaping up - jumped out stark naked and made obscene gestures.

Then, raining. Now, still. Rain letting up, day shaping up. Point A was rushing in on Nogo and Stan like a maglev bullet train, pounding light squares into our eyes via the mag console's holo-screen. Woosh. Count the seconds til we're there; a long, short time. The feeling of being in the mag started melting away. Soon we would believe, no, be, in one of those prop buildings for a pep talk. Together in feelie-realie, as real as flesh and dirt, but we'd be deaf-egg, in the mag.

Suddenly, the feeling and knowledge of being in the mag was gone, and there was an Associate next to me. Not Nogo, someone I didn't know. Then I saw scores of Associates around me in the 838 Convocation Hall. Nogo and I were seated at a panel table. I could feel Cerevello around, but couldn't see him yet. The Associate smiled, and we both thought 'Today is really shaping up, isn't it?'

That's how it hit you. First time and POV flattened. Then tunnel vision blocked the physical environment. Suddenly you were interacting with someone totally out of context with your real surroundings. An overwhelming feeling of pleased-as-pie acceptance got you there. Subliminal chemistry provided the smooth segue into gooey gravy and motherly warmth.

The 838 tribe had been called together with subliminal drums pounding on the hypothalamus, called to an artificial council lodge, with electronic fires burning. How long had it been since someone got flattened by Point A, right in the middle of a shift? Long. But before there was a chance to zoom that thought, more space filled in.

We were all on the same monitor, wearing dress white, with multi-colored, differently shaped step lights glowing, in a high vaulted cathedral of internal truth. In the balcony, in pew-like rows of seats, at the panel desk, how did we know where to sit? Not for us to know. Point A was high above average Neighbors, but far below the Bigs, the Grandees, where the air was rare.

"The spot on Transdimensional Weirds jives well the real foundation," some guy sitting in the balcony said. "It has that certain something we can all build on. Give it plenty of wet and cry. Make it a horror psycho-thriller preview of things to come with an old-era slant."

The Weirds spot had been given prio-uno. We were on to something Go. In the then, bad focus worrying about how this all might turn out. Now, things are shaping up.

Someone was watching, taking it all on. Was it Cerevello, perhaps Nogo, guarding the investment? No, it was feelie-realie warm. Maybe diva-Jane X?

The feelie-realie building and Convocation Hall were so beautiful, it got me all wet and cry-mooshy. The brass, the vaulted ceiling, the gold leaf and almost-burnt wood brought up the mood, colored the mystery.

The Neighbors loved it, too, but were forbidden from taking on Live Point A. They were humbled away from the solemn missal service, allowed only edited peeps at home. Only Associates, advos above step one, shared the experience. I was getting frizzy about the warm peeper. As the creator-producer-director-writer-star of the hot focus Weird spot, I had sacred space.

What a great place. In the old era, advos would've tried to steal silverware from a joint like this. But ha-ha, no silverware, not even the joint itself, was real. In the Nova, we Associates made the loaves and fishes in our minds. Milagros pasan. I rose to my feet.

"I'm greatly touched by this eliquid gathering in my v-u," I said to one and all. "And feel one with my brothers and sisters, and the mystery of light."

There were a few peppy-peeper cheers and whistles, and scattered applause. It felt hot at Point A. Under the table, my finger was outstretched, my fingertip source bringing light to the smalls. Who was monitoring me so feelie-realie close?

Suddenly I saw her, but couldn't really make out her face in the animixed dress white, or something. She looked kind of like the Associate we passed on the path. Maybe she was with us on this, somehow, an ally in the cathedral of light.

"I am also honored and touched, and feel one with the light," Nogo answered, "And the finest, smartest, best looking folks in the world."

There was laughter, applause, and lots more cheering. The nex with the spy chick went cold, the moment faded to black, just like that. Who was she?

Above my head in the cathedral of light, in a huge mural, were enscribed the three Tractors of Social Reason, the tenents we buttered our bread on both sides with.

Every Individual Is Information. The Privacy Of Every Individual Is Sacred. Every Individual Who Participates In The System Is Entitled To Its Fruits.

These lofty ideals frowned down wet and cry on some, and garnered good gov and good focus for others. That was life. Some used the tenents as a mask, hiding their true face and motives. They eschewed the real and Live, but their art was illusion. Supposedly, the true light dispelled even that.

The warm diva-Jane had deleted herself, but she kept popping up on the internal monitor. She must have been there for a reason, but it was ruining my chemstat. The eliquid gathering was starting to bore me. Then she was back, on the real monitor, just as fast. My heart was thumping in time to old-era rockin' rollin' pubo-mash. But was she a flirting Associate whose face I couldn't match, or someone without private access, probing around loose? Like a Weird or something?

I mean, I was in the mag with Nogo, right next to him. But I was at Point A, at least twenty meters from Nogo, with my Associates. Had

Weirds figured out how to get into Point A? Had they broken-in to the most sacred space?

Then she quit again. Oh well, the spot must go on.

Suddenly the veil lifted on Mr. C. The big monitor showed Cerevello as the voice of Point A. If he never got any further, he wanted us to remember him. The Bluebook, and hasta luego, compadres. He wanted the Spot that prompted this convocation to honor him, too, and give him the respect that entailed. Cerevello was the opener, but he sounded like the closer.

"Some day, when I'm gone, like from the then, you will remember me," he said. "And the stacks will fill and I'll come up on the internal monitor, just like I am right now here at Point A."

Cerevello paused.

"Or maybe not."

The stately council chuckled graciously at the self-aimed pot shot. The rush was on. My brothers and sisters were clambering for a taste of the new Weird self-cooking pasta. The genalts stirred, as Biff cleared his throat and banged his vid sources. The evil children of science were plotting some contrivance, some familiar crap, to shake up my spot. I had to show off the flesh and dirt genius somehow.

Biff smiled weakly.

"We all must face rejection," he said in a comforting tone. "Some of us here today have worked long and hard on Spots we thought would Go. But we all must look into the monitor to find the smalls sometimes. And work on those smalls even harder. Because that spot will air someday. To those of you who've given your creative blood, sweat, tears, the whole of your creative being, to projects that will not go on the connector today, I offer sincere feelings of respect. There is a time for all things in the future."

Biff cleared his throat again. The gathering grew completely silent. Suddenly at the end of my nose on my tiny hand monitor, was Nogo's face. Not in the mag, but part of the freeze up at Point A. Smiling, with those horrific, energy-sapping teeth. Nogo may have known the light and the dark were there for each other, but he didn't v-u like me.

Suddenly everyone was bringing me up on the big monitor at Point A. As I sat in the mag and stood in the hall, I almost felt frizzy. Then Cerevello's voice boomed out.

"The spot for This Day On The Connector, Local 838's special contribution, is none other than Transdimensional Hell, by Standard Mozuck."

I popped up on the monitor, all shy and bravo. Hands were flapping, clapping, ringing peals of Live sound. The minute long convocation, compressed as it was into our brains in this second hand way, was still a powerful experience. I felt humbled before this pow- wow of charlatans and lume zoombies. Point A was so beautiful, so clean.

An Associate across from me in the audience fiddled with something on his hand monitor, then everyone brought up Nogo again. Nogo wore a scarlet gem ring that squeezed out splashes of bright light. The ring rested easily on his finger, like on a crooked holy man or pol. A glance around the hall revealed more scarlet gem rings, all on genalt nubs. A bad Go in progress. What did they mean?

"I personally feel very confident," my patron saint Cerevello said. "I've invested in the brightest stars in 838. This old-era-style treatment, Stan's brainchild, has real possibilities. So let's all get behind him with our best spins and marketing."

Cerevello peered left and right in a salamander like move and banged his goggles. Then he looked directly at me and said, "As long as I'm the guy who supplies the steps up, and approves the spots for our international offerings, this is the way it will be, amen."

There was no other reason for this final absurd utterance other than Cerevello letting me know he was peeping when I had my outburst in the mag and offered Nogo a more climber spot.

Strong emotion rippled through Point A, threatening the simulated environment, even over the waves of stimsublim accompanying the experience. A collective sigh roared through the concordium like a strong wind. A sigh of relief or disappointment among the captain-cortex steppers like myself, a grunt of disapproval among genalt stars. The regulars, C-man's peers, seemed surprised. But nothing was broken; a storm had cleared dead wood from the trees.

I was back in the saddle, but Nogo was shaping up as a lot more than an assistant. I didn't need a co-director, especially a genalt. I only needed an assistant. So much for my old-era atmosphere; the splice-dork would be goosing knobs at every turn.

The last image of Point A came up on the monitor. Associates began disappearing from sight like lights going out, being psychically jerked back into their previous routine hunga-dunga. One, two, four, ten, fifty, one hundred, then all the rest except Cerevello, Nogo, and me. Nogo and Biff vipped off, then I could no longer see myself on my hand monitor. The giant gates of the cathedral of light were closed. After seconds, or minutes, or whatever, I was back in the mag with Nogo.

-7-
"AT THE SHRINE OF ROBERT ZEITWEISS"

"Damn it," I groaned. "My leg's asleep. I wish they could come up with a better way of reminding you of your body. I always come back from Point A with aches and pains."

Consciousness designer tech didn't have all the wrinkles smoothed.

"What are you complaining about?" Nogo came back prontito. "Your spot's going up on the connector, everybody's looking to you for slants and spins, and you're frizzing because your ass hurts."

Jealous noise from him felt good. It reminded me he was still human. Before going up to Point A, he'd been ignoring me, like I wasn't important. A huge blotch of rain splattered across the window near his head right after he spoke. Light reflected back against his head, giving him a creepy aura. Being genalt didn't buffer him from disappointment. Gift of God or science, talent still didn't like being frustrated. I almost felt sorry for him. The light and dark of the shot, the sincerity of Nogo's emotion, was flukey.

The mag's dash monitor rang a message preparation bell; a nice touch. I lowered my eyes to see what was coming up, instead of confronting Nogo while he was upset.

"Heeeeere's Bob!" Home said like a silly old-era announcer, setting up a game show. Home's animixed face was chubby, goateed.

The mag slowed down, then lurched to a sudden stop. Nogo and I looked around, behind us, off to the sides of the path, trying to make it out.

"What's up?" I asked the mag prepro. "This is it? Where's Bob Sideways' house?"

"This is the best I can do!" the announcer snapped angrily. "I'm not supposed to do your job, too." Then the monitor faded to black abruptly. Home was losing it, or the Weirds were screwing things up.

"That's what happens when a wise ass gives his Home prepro his personality," Nogo said, shaking his head, chuckling, doing his monogram moves. "They start resembling their creator. They grow egos and become overbearing."

Ignoring him now, I looked out the window. The mag chose a place about fifty meters beyond a dirt road. This area wasn't part of the CarTown parcel, so I lit up pronto, taking on the smalls on either side of the mag path where the dirt road intersected. It looked long enough to be an actual road; used, not overgrown. Who the hell was walking around or driving a guzzler out here?

"Look, Nogo. Some kind of road, or path. Over there."

Nogo looked too self-absorbed to turn his head, but slowly made an effort to look around.

"I don't see anything, Stan," he said, as if he could make it go away.

I didn't wait for him to acknowledge the road, I just opened the mag door by hand and got out and started walking. It was chilly, but not enough to keep me from checking it out. Maybe Home really had done its homework. I felt more confident with each step. It was something.

Sure enough it was an old narrow road, muddy but still accessible, stretching deep into the damp yellow woods. I wondered which way to explore, then heard Nogo pop open his door and approach the road.

"Stan," Nogo said in the closing distance. "Why waste time doing this? We can't find Zeitweiss this way."

"Why not? This is a freaking road out here in the nowhere, a used road. It has to lead to the Alphadrine Cowboy , or something important."

Nogo's whining pushed my body into a reflexive search, for something to prove I was right. I pointed my finger source down both sides of the road, as far as it could scan. Then, I saw it. On the right side of the mag path, about another fifty meters down the road into the woods, was an old stump with a homemade sign on it. The sign read 'Steak-And-Beansville, One Half Mile.' What the hell?

"Full up, compadre," I said, pointing at it. "Look at that!"

The hand painted sign was actually perched, balanced, on one tiny piece of weather-beaten board sticking out of the stump. It must have been put there recently; even a few minutes of this weather would have knocked it off. Someone knew we were coming. Steak-And-Beansville?

Nogo stood right behind me, hands on his hips, staring down at the sign.

"I suppose this is another example of Stan Mozuck humor at its best," he said. "I'd never crawl around in a place like this to squeeze one lousy gag."

Nobody would be slopping around out here out of focus, not even an advo or Sur-goon, unless it was a set up. Or Weirds were involved. No way Nogo could really believe I did this.

"What… You're actually saying I did this? Come on man, you know I've never been here, any more than you have. Somebody lives around here. Or more Neighbors wander off into the woods than we think."

Nogo pursed his lips and looked down the path. There was no paranoid scram, he knew I hadn't put the sign there. And he knew it was recent.

"I wonder what the hell it means," he offered, nervously zooming the nearby woods.

"I don't know what it means," I said. "Except someone lives around here."

"Someone must be fucking with us," Nogo barked back. "How else…?"

"If something is Go that advos can't know," I said, "we've got problems. We're patsies for an m-line. But Bob must live around here, or

Home wouldn't have come up with this as the best lead."

Nogo needed mucho reassurance. The outside didn't agree with him somehow, like it was twisto to him.

"Come on Blogo, let's go for it," I said. "Bob lives somewhere near here. Maybe we can't get any closer with the mag. You said you'd help me find him. Don't frizz on me because your nombre won't go on top of the credit roll. We're in deep with something. We owe it to ourselves to find out what the hell Steak-And-Beansville is."

"Yeah," he said, almost whispering. "Before the wolves find us."

Nogo was hard to figure. The splicer genius came up short in an old-era quiz. The woods had returned somewhat from old-era tox, and wolves and bears and coyotes managed to be less endangered or whatever, but what chance would we have of encountering them? We weren't in a forest preserve; we were in some woods near 838, a little out of focus. Nogo's fear of hairy predators was in his spliced genes; a fear of natural, non-man made things.

"Birds, man," I said. "That's all we have to worry about. Birds shitting on us."

I drew myself up and stretched my arms over my head to unkink my back, and took a few big breaths. Then I started walking towards Steak-And-Beansville.

The rest of the scene was just shots of us walking up the muddy path, with Nogo lagging, looking over his shoulder. We passed through raw nature, walking over crunchy nut husks. In places the road was literally covered with acorn shells. We walked past rose bushes that were too beautiful to be wild, like someone tweaked them. Then we pushed up a long slow ascent, to where the woods had a strong, funky scent of autumn leaves going back to nature. I was digging the natural odor but Nogo was repelled by it.

The woods seemed more golden, and redder, in globs of color. It was nothing like what the sources sent back from CarTown, and more beautiful than anything we'd seen in the mag on the way here.

Nogo was puffing like a man Cerevello's age, whatever that was, goffing powdered steam into the cool air. My breath was barely visible. The woods felt warm, it was relaxing and invigorating at the same time, like a good blink of Satiscope. A full shot from behind showed us trudging past some raspberry bushes with berries still on them. Berries. Unburnt by snow or cold rain, just lightly glazed by cool moisture.

"Jeez, man, looks at this," I said. "Wild berries. Can you believe it? Let's try one."

Apologies, again, dear Neighbors, for such unpro focus. The correct format was, of course, to take one berry myself, for examination, and inform Nogo more matter-of-factly.

Pronto, pronto, Nogo barked back nekro. "No berries, Stan. This place used to be polluted as hell, hence the apt nomer, Industros Tragicos. Because it's growing doesn't mean it's not tox."

He waved his hand menacingly and walked on. I stuffed a handful in my mouth. It's funny how so many realities can slide in micro. At first the berries exploded in my mouth with a delicious sweet tart bang. But after a hint of ripe alkaline taste came up I started sweating it, thinking Nogo had the interior on the berries in his warn. Then the goodness of the berries invaded my brain. I could really taste them.

"Nogo, these are great! Try one!"

But no go. Spliceman continued towards the hinterlands. He faded from the wide shot in moments, leaving me standing by the berry bush, looking unfocused on spot, goofy.

I ran to catch up with him. He was marching down the path without looking to either side, acting like something might creep up on him. I grabbed him by the shoulder and swung him around. He looked into my eyes in terrified shock. It was like some old-era dance, or a cop escorting a student from an unruly demonstration on jeri-era TV. Nogo quickly snapped out of it, and walked on beside me. We got to the top of the path's slow incline. Then it happened.

Center screen, medium close, out in the woods: the remnants of an old neighborhood.

There was an old gas station for guzzlers with old grocery store attached, and right beyond that, niched between giant fir trees, an old car motel. The motel had to go back four hundred seasons, a hundred years. In front of those wooden buildings the path-like road broadened into a well-manicured boulevard. All its cracks and grooves sported low cut grass. In other ways the road had been smoothed down, cleaned and repaired by hand, or non-servo tools. That little chunk of street probably gave guzzlers a smoother ride than the poshest high tech highways of the jeri-era.

There, in clear sight, a very camera-looking old NeighborWorld source sat perched on a rock, like the sign on the stump, held in place by sticks and rope. Who the hell could have done something like this out in the woods?

I source-tied into the ancient vid-cam. The scan showed it was dead, or without batteries. Was this place in focus, maybe eighty seasons ago, then olviday por la carta, striken from the grid, by a prepro frizz or something? Two thoughts jumped into my mind at once; an archaeologist discovering something that couldn't be explained, and a jeri-era commercial showing repairmen with cool uniforms and pointy, leather-brimmed hats.

"Holy shit... holy shit," Nogo kept repeating. "Holy shit."

He stood there staring like we'd discovered some ancient lost city, then started pointing and wagging his finger source at the place, as if he could make it go away by scanning it. My more measured, restrained reaction was better focus. My knees got weak, then my butt hit the ground, hard. I just sat there with my mouth open, staring in disbelief.

After that, we moved slowly at first, walking faster as the road got wider, with awe turning to excited curiosity. As we arrived at the entrance to the gas station and grocery it became obvious that the weather worn look of the place - as seen from a distance - was an illusion. It had recently been painted a tawdry gray.

There were old signs; one in the shape of a wolf's head, another a lion head, a bear, and one that looked like a jumping deer. They proclaimed automotive products sold at the station. The signs, too, were restored, painted many times. Only a light layer of grit and dust made them look as old as they were. The gas pumps were ancient, but rustless and recently painted. Except for the grocery store's boarded-up window, the place looked open for business. I knew the camera was dead, but it felt like someone was scanning us.

Nogo stood at the front of the station, and didn't budge. I inched my way around to the back of the building, thinking someone was going to jump me the whole way. There was an air hose for inflating guzzler tires on the right side of the place. It looked usable. There was a shovel, a heavyduty push broom and dustpan, barely concealed under a rust-colored dumpster in back. There were some tires stacked against the back wall. They were all filled with water and leaves and spiders, but they looked ok, not decayed.

I looked back, and Nogo was running sources everywhere. Hopefully he wasn't running some hush-mode spyguy mind link. He looked scared, and was doing what he was trained to, stressed, and in a hurry.

There was cardboard over one window near the back. I hadn't seen cardboard or spiders since I was little. It felt strange seeing all this stuff at once. I reached around behind the dumpster and found a stick. Then I started poking the cardboard, trying to dislodge it to get a peek inside. A spider dropped right near my hand, and scared me nekro. I jerked my hand up, and smashed a glass window behind the cardboard, and sliced my hand.

I howled. A little blood splattered on the wall, on my coat and tuni. An angry bite but not too deep, just messy enough to remind me the outside world was a pellegro, dangerous place.

Nogo came back pronto on the yelp. "Standard! You ok? What's going on?"

"Yeah, yeah. Nothing. I banged my hand on something. I'm fine," I came back just as fast. I didn't want him coming over to see what happened, or overturning something I might find in the smalls by myself. "Just keep an eye out for me in front of the place."

"What's it like back there?" he asked, sounding scared.

"There's a little garage," I shouted. "I'm going to check it out."

I knew Nogo wouldn't be eager to crawl in the smalls with me.

"Ok, Stan... I've got your back."

I turned quickly and pushed the cardboard away from the broken window with the stick. Then I tugged on it and it popped right out, leaving a wide, unobstructed shot of the garage interior. It was like the CarTown museum. There were one hundred year old soda machines, all gloss painted and functional looking, and wall posters from the 1930's of girls in ski outfits drinking cocoa and coffee, of girls in bathing suits sipping lemon-lime soda. And around a hundred one hundred year old guzzler license plates.

"Nogo," I yelled trying to keep him at bay. "There's nothing in the garage."

I took the corner fast as I double-timed it to the front of the building. He was nervously pacing without really looking at anything.

"Hey," I said. "Let's not hang around here forever. This place is starting to give me the creeps. We should check out the other buildings, too. Did you get everything? Good shots?"

"Yeah, let me see what you shot back there," he commanded.

I instinctively stuck my hand up - the one I'd cut - to wave off the idea.

"Nothing that great," I said.

"Stand, your hand is bleeding," Nogo said like a mommy. "What happened?"

"There was a broken glass window," I answered. "I hit my hand on it."

"Did you get shots of it?" he asked. "What's in the garage?"

"It's empty and creepy," I lied. "Let's check the next building. Maybe Bob lives there."

"Yeah," he said. "Let's keep moving. This place creeps me, too."

Whether Nogo bought my lie about the garage or not was nada. If he linked while I was screwing around, he saw the same things I did, and knew I was lying. He must have actually been doing his job for once. So the spin on the 1930's garage would be mine, with more good focus for me. If I trusted the guy more, maybe I would've let him in. But this was the first indication Nogo wasn't spyguy sliming, so I considered myself lucky for now, and kept my mouth shut.

We walked on the asphalt garden road for about a hundred more meters to get to the motel building. By the time we got to the front of the building, the whole perspective had changed. It was bigger than it seemed from the other end of the road.

Right in front, a painted old wooden sign, probably standing a hundred years, showed a chartreuse 1930's automobile parked in a pine knoll, with a sailboat on a lake in the background. Above this scene, written in a pine tree branch logo, were the words 'Evergreen Tourist Apartments' and below it, 'Ph. No. 226-4089.' At first both Nogo and I couldn't figure that part out, thinking it was some chemical number or acid-alkali gradation.

Then it hit us simultaneously. A telephone number. The glimmer of kinship made me think of cueing him up about the garage, but I resisted.

Large, stately pines still loomed over the place. It looked like an arboretum. I was alone in the wilderness, but I felt bolstered, secure. The old L-shaped, two story, clapboard apartment building/motel was so weatherbeaten it looked like the wooden longhouses of the original natives living here thousands of years ago, in the history spots.

The rain had stopped, and just for that moment, there was a bright, cloudless, blue midday sky. A full, orange sun hung over the motel. Nogo and I walked through a pine corridor to get to the alcove in the elbow of the L-shaped building. Like with the gas station, I got the impression the place wasn't as beat up as it looked from a distance. As we passed by, each one of the rooms looked used. Each one, like someone was looking back through the dusty windows. Nogo was taking shots of the glass windows, but didn't look too eager to peek through one.

Suddenly I got the strangest blip - not on a monitor, but right in my ear - sounding like Bob Zeitweiss saying "Come on in, partner. Welcome to my home." Then I saw Bob's mad grinning face shining from the darkness. Nogo saw it, too, and did a double take. Shaken, confused, we entered the alcove. We walked past an old soda pop machine, on a cement floor cracked into thousands of mosaic pieces, peppered with low mossy grass. Then we came to a large gray metal door that bore a red sign that said 'Private.'

The Bob Sideways appeared from the shadows, dressed in cowboy work duds, smiling. He opened the gray metal door, and with a hand gesture, invited us in.

"Nice hat," he said, perusing my journo-look hat source.

Not knowing what else to do, half doubting we were actually at his home, we walked in. The only sound was the sighing of the wind and occasional cooing of doves. After the heavy metal door slammed behind us, there was no sound at all.

What we saw next was a cross between a mystery grotto and some horny thirteen-year-old boy's old era clubhouse. The only light in the dark cavern emanated from shrine-like displays, lit in numerous ways - with Christmas tree lights, votive candles, even garden lanterns - all illuminating hundreds of old photos.

There were sepias in gold leaf frames, sharp black and whites in art deco yellow and white, blurry color photos in 1950's aqua, some 1960's looking psychedelic instant snapshots, photos made into jeri-era photocopies, newspaper and magazine cutouts, and chalk and oil crayon sketches of someone playing guitar in different period costumes. Someone who looked like Bob, but it couldn't have been him. These stills were 200 to 400 hundred seasons old.

Scattered all over the floor were 1960's, 70's, or 80's girlie magazines, the ones that showed everything, and hundreds of detective-style mags from the 1940's. A fortune in antique sheef, all arrayed for Bob's auto-eroto amusement - any time he needed.

As we converged on the brightly lit kitchen we saw the most miraculous shrine of all, one photo of the musician, looking much older, holding a baby. It looked like a holy card or renaissance painting. Then there was another late 1980's video snap-out of the same musician, almost 90, beaming proudly over a young lad in a cowboy hat, playing a guitar.

The boy was clearly Bob, sin mustachio, and the guy in the period costume was clearly his stringman father, who must've had a long career before settling down to sire bambinos. There was no continuity break, all the stills chronicled a march from 1930's jazz bands right up to the early 2000 period.

Then there was Bob, appearing from nowhere, a git fiddle on his hip. That made Bob at least 200 plus seasons old. He seemed much younger, like his ageless, holy jamming dad, who probably died having flesh and dirt sex, at four hundred seasons. Everywhere in the dark room, all the shrines to his poppy's career pointed to the culminating shrine, which illuminated the passing down of the holy relic, the guitar.

We passed into the kitchen and saw a different kind of votive shrine, marked by the guitar itself, a stack of antique vinyl records, and a giant cardboard cutout of Bob banging on his git-fiddle. Arrayed underneath was a stack of print sheef from all the Locals who picked up "An Evening With Bob Sideways, The Alphadrine Cowboy." Frozen on a tiny, one hundred seasons old monitor was the spot's electro-blue opening. Poor Bob. Poor, brilliant Bob. In-fucking-credible stuff.

Scanning it, being in person with it all, had an exhilarating effect on me, but Nogo seemed perplexed, nauseated by it. He looked ashamed to be part of the same human race, as if we'd discovered the den of some rat boy or dog man. I could tell Nogo was considering the possibility Bob was Weird. So far, Bob hadn't said a word. Then two old era style real pets, a fat brown dog and a fat yellowish cat, approached us, looking inquisitive. I was a little startled by the real animals, but Nogo froze in fear.

"Mangey, Fleabag, go lay down!" Bob commanded. "Leave us alone for a while."

The F and D pets trotted off. Bob continued through his shrine. He stopped to look reverently at certain photos, gestured with his hand and eyes, and walked on. He finally stopped by the kitchen table, a goosed-up picnic table, and extended his arms in an invitation to sit. It was time to go to work.

"What's up, advo?" Bob asked, looking sheepish.

"Well, Bob, you don't call, you don't write," I said, smiling enthusiastically, hoping to grease him up with jeri-era jango. "What the hell's up? We had an awful hard time finding you."

Zeitweiss shrugged and smiled.

"Come on, man. Where you been? You pull a vanishing act, right when we're starting to make waves."

"Who's your friend," Bob shot back, eyeing Nogo suspiciously. "I thought you'd c-c-come a-callin' by your lonesome."

"Well, Bob," I said, totally unaware of what he was talking about, "I don't ever recall saying anything about coming to visit you. In fact, you left my hab without leaving any way of getting in touch with you. You disappeared, man, you jumped 838. So here we are."

Bob stared with his lips slightly parted, ready to ask the question again, but I spared him the sweat.

"This is Nogo Blogo," I said, gesturing over my shoulder with my thumb. "He's an advo, too. We've been looking for you all day."

"N-n-nogo Blogo," Bob said, mouthing the name as if it were the answer to a trick question. "Nogo Blogo. If that don't beat all."

Nogo walked past me and shoved his hand right out for Bob to shake. Bob blinked, grabbed the hand, and shook it vigorously.

"That's my name, pardner," Nogo said in a surprisingly authentic folksy jingo vip.

"Don't wear it out," I added.

"Howdy, howdy, howdy," Nogo continued, while Bob squeezed his mitt.

It caught me completely off guard. This was the same guy who was grimacing at Bob like he was poison, turning up his nose at everything in the apartment like it was disease ridden.

Nogo was a first class genalt schmoozer, made for con job and jive jango if it suited him. He was going to gain Bob's confidence, maybe to use his words against him. It didn't matter, though, because Bob wasn't having any.

"Well, now we're all n-n-nice and acquainted," Bob said, lowering his eyes, starting to frown. "And now I'm supposed to t-t-ell you why I ain't been around. All right. I been busy. Makin' me a b-brand new alblum."

His pronunciation of the jeri-era term 'album' made me laugh out loud, but Nogo stayed in character, pretending to be interested in Bob's album.

"That's remarkable," Nogo barked all friendly, feigning disbelief. "Such an old format. Guaranteed retro impact. You're such a ... a... a..."

Nogo searched for the word.

"Such an archivist," Nogo said with satisfied finality.

"A what?" Bob asked with a hostile tone. "You talkin' 'bout my puddin' pulp?"

Nogo was dumfounded by the response, but being more of an archivist than Nogo, I knew what puddin pulp was - those old girlie mags.

"No, you horny galoot," I came back pronto with amigo teeth. "He means you like old music, and you've got a nice old fashioned style."

"I know what he means," Bob said, seeming unaffected by my explanation. He paused a second, then added "I know exactly what it m-m-means."

Zeitweiss looked at me, hoping for reassurance. Nogo wasted no time trying to get back in good with Bob, quickly mumbling, "Yes, yes, you have an interesting v-u, such a solid deep field, such an exciting approach."

Bob seemed too anxious about Nogo being around, so I changed the subject, in a quiet, friendly voice.

"Bob," I said. "Let's hear some of your new material."

"I ain't old f-fashioned," Bob said, staring at Nogo.

Then he abruptly reached over towards the shrine and grabbed his guitar, and without so much as an intro, went into the first verse of one of his new songs.

Nogo looked on thoughtfully, now knowing a warmer reaction might produce trouble. The next twenty minutes went on like that. Bob sang, and we watched with phony interest. It was his best stuff, pure genius. Unfortunately we were there for other reasons.

For the first time, I was exposed to Bob's complexity, his real personality, and suddenly I was overwhelmed by the clinical coolness that the whole experience had taken on. We waited for the genius to stop, so we could politely applaud, then interrogate him.

I was going all gooey, thinking this individ was alive in the flesh and dirt, in front of me. I was ashamed. His voice had the gravely roar and ancient gullah twang of an early 20th century blues singer from four hundred or more seasons back. Where the hell had he been all this time? Who was he really? I only hoped this fine human being wouldn't be hurt by Nogo's dark science. We were bad. We had no right. What we did was wrong.

A trickle of sunlight crept in from a far window, onto an old white coffee cup and a few glass jars on the table. The cup bore an amber blotch, a drawing of a cactus, and the words Souvenir Of Grand Canyon. The sun moved through the clouds outside the window, and Bob sang on. His blues licks erupted into our ears. He tilted his head back and howled like a wolf, he jumped up and down. There was Mississippi mud on his cowboy boots.

Where had he learned all this? From the holy stringman father? Did he have stacks of old 78 records no one had ever heard of? Nogo must have known we were sitting on the gold op.

Nogo was too smooth to listen politely all afternoon. He finally broke Bob off gently, like a dad waking a kid, saying his name over and over, getting louder.

"Bob...Bob...Bob... we'd like to talk to you a little now. Bob... Bob..."

"Yeah, Bob," I agreed, almost sounding sad.

Zeitweiss kept plunking his twanger, shouting the words, firing off dissonant chords to highlight them, clinging to his show even with the audience in revolt. He didn't want to talk. He wanted to communicate. I reached out and grabbed his hand, stopping him from strumming. He held his guitar above his head and began stomping his foot. We had no right. What we did was wrong.

"Look at 'em!" Bob yelled. "Two of the biggest queers in the world. Actin' like two prissy little girls!"

Bob was impugning our sexuality. As an expert on old private dick and psychedelic sci-fi genres, I knew that. But ranting about our sexuality didn't make sense. He meant we weren't men in another way. It wasn't sexist or ho-pho. He was calling us cowards, and somehow not real human beings.

"Designer genes used to mean sissy-pants bluejeans," Zeitweiss added, staring at Nogo, looking almost like a lumed zoombie.

The jango was lost on Nogo, who had grown impatient with Bob's ramblings.

"This is going nowhere," Nogo said, slipping totally out of character. "You can't even understand what the hell he's babbling about. Let's get out of here. If he doesn't want to cooperate, we don't have to make him an offer. Let him bubble under for a few thousand more seasons. He'll come crawling."

Here's the bonus round, dear N's and A's; Nogo playing nice cop/mean cop, the worn out routine of old-era on-camera cops and burnt toast journos. Even Bob wouldn't fall for that. But I'd had houses-are-bricks instilled in my smallbox since childhood, so I was a team player. I didn't have to act. Simplicity was the key, staying close to home, grounding the new reality in your own emotions, not becoming someone else. Besides, there was no time for character development in the frizzy instant interview we were about to do. Just play the part, advo, and ride the zoom.

"Bob," I said. "You're going to have to listen to us now. So just sit down and relax. We need to know something, and we think you can help. It's about these people called transdimensional Weirds. You know, Weirds, transdiments, smoothbrains? You do know what we're talking about."

"No, I d-don't know what we are talking about," he said, looking betrayed and nervous. He sat down in a reluctant stop and go motion, eyeing me cynically all the way down. "What are we talking about?"

Bob didn't seem to understand I was just a team player, it was nothing personal. Naturally I'd cut him some slack. I still wanted to work with him, still thought he was a climber. And I wasn't going to let anyone m-line him. I was only doing my job.

The fact that Bob couldn't understand this irritated me a bit. It made me wonder if he had ever had a job. Then I broke character.

"We're talking about the crew who cooked the monitors all over the place, compadre. The ones who make things blow up and disappear. Know anything about who they are, where they come from?"

Bob led such a pure existence out here, strumming his guitar, and his groin. He had no idea the compromises folks in focus made to survive. We lived in a fishbowl, whatever that was, and anything we did was held up to scrutiny. Staying sane and alive in it called for a subtlety he couldn't understand.

"Bob, we want to help you," I said, grounded in my own emotions. "With your career, to get your songs shown and played. But you split so fast, man. How'd you jump out of focus like that? What kind of place is this? There's nothing out here. At least in Car Town you can jump in and out. Why do you want to live in the woods?"

"Hey, Stan," Nogo said, punching up the contrast with a mean cop threatening tone. "If this guy's hiding something, I know some guys who will come down here and take him out of focus for real. He's got to be hiding something. He's got climb, but he's ducking the Spotlight. Maybe he's hiding Weirds in crawl spaces. Or maybe he's one."

"What if I was one?" Bob spat, without remorse or fear. "I don't know what they are, but if'n you don't like 'em, maybe they're not so bad."

Nice cop, mean cop. Good guys open up; bad guys break down, make deals.

"I told you, Bob," I said. "They're the ones who've been wrecking our gear. Don't tell me you don't know what they are. Everybody's heard of them."

Bob looked confused, almost devastated. Nogo smiled like he knew Bob knew something, but I just felt bad for the poor guy. I had to learn where to find Weirds without incriminating Bob.

"Listen," Bob said sincerely. "I don't know about no Weirds. That name don't mean nothing to me. And I don't know about wrecking no gear. As far as livin' here's concerned, it's better than b-bein' in that damn Spotlight. I don't like it. So I leave, plain and simple. But that don't mean I'm wrecking equipment, or know anyone who is."

But then there was the look that sunk, dear N's and A's. Bob's face couldn't hide a thing. He knew somebody different. It was sweating from his pores in extreme close-up. I wanted him to stop cooking so hard, but Nogo kept jamming him up tighter on a little hand held monitor, pushing the source right under Bob's nose, digging watching him squirm. Too much, enough.

"Ok, Nogo, get that source out of his face or I'm going to shove it right up your ass."

"What? What the hell are you talking about? Just mind your own business. I'm trying to get something out of this creep."

I was out of character, grounded in my own real time delusions. I grabbed the source and vipped it off.

"Hey, you idiot, give me my source."

I tossed it dramatically on the table, hard enough to tweak in some frizz.

"If it's broke, you're going to pay for it, you moron," he said.

Boom! I slapped it with my hand, hard enough to tweak in more frizz. What was I supposed to do? Ask him how much it cost?

Bob sat back in surprise, almost slipping off his seat. Nogo wasn't sure what to do; he just stared with his mouth open.

"Just leave the poor guy alone," I said. "He hasn't done anything. Why are you threatening him, sticking sources in his face? We're just supposed to ask him a few questions."

Incriminating questions and incomprehensible answers, maybe. Not questions for a misunderstood genius.

"Bob," I said directly to him, "Give us anything you think might help. I think we can still do biz with the songs, so don't worry about that for now. Just please, if you know anything. It's not illegal to know someone or something."

Nogo was still seething about his source, but he was letting me work.

"No, no, no," Bob kept repeating, shaking his head slowly.

I hoped Bob was smart enough to keep his friends out of trouble without sounding too smooth. The close-up was on him now.

Bob got up, put his guitar away, and walked slowly towards the kitchen sink. He grabbed the two glass jars and the coffee cup, and walked back with them, looking dejected. He plopped the cup and jars down on the table, sat, and stared at Nogo.

"You guys are goin' at this all the wrong way," Bob said after a pause. "Callin' f-folks f-funny names and blamin' 'em for everything goin' wrong. You ain't goin' to learn nothin' that way."

Again, he rose slowly and walked to the antique wood stove and grabbed a coffee pot. He started back to the table before remembering something else, and turned back and this time walked over to a cupboard. He opened the cupboard and pulled out a glass bottle, and stuck it under his armpit. He walked back with a lazy lope and sat down.

"You're off base, cumpaneros," he said, pouring us coffee. "Reality can't be moved around. Unless somehow everyone agrees on the outcome. Or if something higher's workin'. See that's what's wrong with your NeighborWorld. You can only change reality for a moment, because there's nothing higher working. Everyone might agree on the outcome, but sooner or later, it'll all collapse."

Then Zeitweiss wrinkled his eyebrow like that's that, blew into his coffee, then took a long slurp. Then he pulled the bottle out, unscrewed the top, and poured some into the coffee.

Pew, what a smell. It was alcohol. Maybe Scotch whiskey. My nose recognized that smoky odor from old-era detective stimsublims. Yeah, when I was younger, I got lumed on subliminal whiskey, had feelie-realie with the red-haired sexretary, and solved the crime that never occurred, in my own mind. Except now I was in an ancient motel in the woods, out of focus, smelling the real stuff.

"See, I got to have that first drink of real joe," Bob said. "Sober up a little b-before lighting another fire."

Then Bob smiled broadly, and I noticed he was shy a few snappers. He smelled like real sweat. He stirred the whiskey into his cup with his finger, licked his finger, and took another huge drink from the cup. He smiled again, glowing, and burped softly.

"What the hell's going on, Stan?" Nogo barked all nasty. Nogo's pallid cheeks were growing a little glow from anger.

I didn't know what to say. I didn't know if alcohol was still legal. Nobody needed to actually drink the stuff anymore. Whiskey stimsublims didn't cause headaches, or damage your liver, or make you act crazy. They were a mild subliminal experience, nothing like real whiskey. But so what if the guy wants to drink the stuff? He might hurt himself, but it's none of our business.

"He's drinking booze," I said flatly.

"He's what?" Nogo asked with an almost hysterical lilt. "What the hell does that mean?"

"He's getting lumed on alcohol. Drunk. Remember they used to get lumed on alcohol? Drunk?"

"I ain't drunk," Zeitweiss said contemptuously. "Takes more 'n a groggy joe to splatter the Alphadrine Cowboy."

"I know what it means," Nogo shot back. "I can't believe this! So what happens now? Is he going to fade to black on us, or attack us, or do we have to clean his puke, or what?"

Bob shook his head with an amused look. Nogo made a look of discovery.

"That proves it," he said. "He's Weird."

Nogo kept flopping on the cowboy.

"Shit! Now we're not going to understand a damn word he says."

Nogo's ignorance was going to frizz-glitch the whole send down. Anybody who did old-era research would understand one simple thing; Bob was going to drink, and that would loosen his tongue. He'd tell us anything we wanted to know.

"Nogo, just pay attention and I'll teach you something. Bob doesn't have anything to hide and he doesn't mind talking with us. Do you, Bob?"

"Hell if I don't," Bob growled, frowning. "Nothing I'd rather do than throw you two crumbs out on your behinds. But then I'd really be in for it, w-wouldn't I? So I'll just sit here in my own d-domercile, rousted by teevee-net thugs, and try to keep some dignity."

He took another slurp of groggy coffee and smiled. He licked his moustache and poured more booze into the cup. Then he winked.

"If you guys n-never seen anyone get drunk before, you're in for a treat," he said. "Maybe I'll even roll my eyes around and pass out for ya. Choke on my t-tongue. Hah!"

Bob laughed uproariously and smacked the table. Then he rolled his eyes around and grabbed his throat, pretending to be choking. Nogo had never seen anyone act like this before; his mouth was open in disbelief. Something about Bob reminded me of my grandpa, when I was little. What else could you do out here, out of focus, besides get drunk?

"You're both pansies!" Bob shouted. "You don't know the first thing about real life. L-look at yuz! Never been drunk. Bet ya never smoked the ganj or had real sex with a real woman, either. Bet ya never had food growed from your own g-garden, or had to fix a meal on your own. You're pop-up people, there's nothing real about yuz! Rot in hell, f-for all I care!"

Bob folded his arms across his chest and looked at us like we were spoiled kids. I didn't know what to say. It occurred to me that if we had a drink with him, he might relax and talk. Maybe he was challenging us, anyway, to see if we were worthy of trust. Like in old era dicks, when the hero would be asked to drink with the hood or cop. Never trust a man who can't hold his liquor, right?

Or maybe Bob wanted to put some concoction in our drinks to knock us out.

"Where the hell did you get that stuff?" I asked, smiling. "You make it yourself?"

"Where else would I g-get it?" he asked back with a perturbed look. "Down at the liquor store? It's smoky peach brandy, my own special recipe. Don't ask for none 'cause I ain't got much left."

Bob held out the green, half full bottle, and shook it lightly. Wind rattled the kitchen window, a log popped in the wood stove. The ancient sounds made Nogo jerk a little, but to me they seemed to enhance a growing quiet.

"Well?" Bob asked.

"Oh great," Nogo fumed. "I suppose now we have to get lumed on booze. Stan, we've been out of focus almost half an hour. I can't nex with anyone in focus, and nobody's nexing back. Let's get something out of this detour or move on."

I smacked his source too hard. We were on the frizzy glitch, out of focus.

"What do you mean you can't connect?" I asked. "Use another one. I'm sorry I wrecked it. Try another one. Can't you at least link with the mag?"

"No," Nogo said, all fearscaped. "No, I can't. Something's frizzing all our stuff, not just the source you smacked. Check your own sources. Your guy here must be doing it somehow. He's got to be Weird."

Static, on all my stuff, only my own personal audio-in was working. But nothing was going out. Now I fit into the fearscape.

"What's going on, Bob?" I asked. "What the hell's up with our gear?"

Bob erupted into an insane snaggle-toothed cackle.

"Hah! Hah! It ain't me you boxhead! It's these here w-woods! None of your crap works around here. Why else would I move back down to my old man's place? I wanted to get away from all that. I don't want no computer teller-vision delivering my f-food, or turning off my lights, or s-spying on me. I got me f-few old p-programs on my telly and a mess of fine old radio shows, and there's all these records and books. And my m-music! That's wonderful for me. Because none of that NeighborWorld crap works down here!"

Bob looked smug. Nogo muttered to himself, trying to unglitch the gear.

"Why? Why doesn't it work down here?"

Bob smiled cockily, and suddenly the room felt like we were going up to Point A. Then it was like he was talking right into my brain, but his lips didn't move and there was no sound. Like Bob was somehow trying to become Weird, and his power was growing.

"You're almost done with 'em, ain't you?" Bob said inside my head. "Just like me, you're going to walk right on out."

Then, still in my head, he said, "Do what you want to me. This party's almost over. Purdy soon, there ain't going to be no more of your wonderful NeighborWorld."

Then, out loud, he said, "I guess you do need some of my smoky peach. It ain't right to be inhospitable."

The gear didn't work, Nogo wanted to cut and paste, Bob could talk into my head, nothing made sense, but I wanted to drink with the cowboy, and listen to him, silent. To sample another world, the past, and learn. To hear, without tooth noise, to have real freedom whisper-in over the lies.

"You're going to get too lumed to produce," Nogo said, pacing around the table. "It's not going to work."

"Why doesn't gear work down here?" I asked again. "Why?"

"Here," Bob said, pouring a drizzle into my glass jar of coffee. "You can have some, but don't get stupid on me."

Then he raised his eyebrows, hinting the mind link was real, and took a long steamy swig.

"Ahh, that's damn good stuff," Bob sighed.

"Go ahead, drink the damn sloo if you want," Nogo bellowed dramatically. "It's what you've been waiting for. Drink it."

Nogo scowled, showing the tops of his bottom teeth. Then he raised his hands in a supplication-to-the-lord gesture.

"I'm not used to this kind of disorganization," he said. "You do everything on hunches, wild leads. You spend too much time aimlessly poking around, not sure what you're looking for."

"It's a success-proof formula," he went on. "Everything backwards. Right now, when we're out of focus, frizzing - right on cue."

He shook his head disdainfully, a medium shot deaf and dumb show for the nonfunctional monitor source. He was working out of habit. Nobody was peeking, because the gear took a dump.

"Maybe he only wants me to have a drink, so just drink your java and wait for me to do what we're here to do," I said.

I smiled at Bob amiably. He was going to make us rich and famous now, going to hint and whisper in where the splicer techno-dork could not hear. And we were going to have some smoky peach brandy.

Bob unscrewed the top again, and let a shot drizzle down the side of my coffee jar. The alcohol exploded in my narz in a rich, warm, hard to describe explosion, a both alluring and gaggy smell.

"Thanks." I said, cutting the flow of booze with a hand gesture. "I've never done this before. Don't want to get too lumed."

"I only put a taste in there," Zeitweiss shot back. "Think I ain't looking out f-for ya?"

He winked again. I was going more intu, and Nogo was getting more lost without his stuff. I took a nice long sip, smiling back at Roberto.

It was warm, too warm. My tongue burned, my sinuses burned. It was nothing like the stimsublims. They tasted sweet, real palatable, an illusion brought out by subliminal light and sound and K-factor. Water, whatever, tasted like the experience. This stuff tasted horrible. But the smoky peach aftertaste was soothing, luscious.

I felt flushed and friendly, and a little jerked around. "Bob," I said. "I congratulate you on your smoky peach concoction. It's quite... different."

"Alright," Nogo barked testily. "Give me some, too."

Nogo shoved his coffee jar in front of Bob, standing in one place, but still nervously rocking on his feet. His bravery shocked me.

"And I congratulate you, Nogo, on your courage," I said. "I didn't know you had it in you."

I was punching up Nogo's ego, but his eagerness to jump in suddenly had me worried. Bob seemed a little startled, but didn't hesitate to slop some amber brandy into Nogo's coffee.

Nogo tasted the groggy coffee carefully, flaring his nostrils to cool the smoky fumes rushing into his forehead.

"Hooh!" he snorted. "Woah... This is vile. Ouch."

Nogo patted his chest, then rubbed his eyes. He looked at me, smiling.

"It does make your chest feel nice and warm, though. How long does it take to work?"

Bob laughed out loud.

"Like watchin' boys become men," he said, scratching his neck.

Bob was a character alright. He'd never punched a cow, or maybe even rode a horse, but the character was real. So who was Robert Zeitweiss? The Q shot was good; the bottom of Nogo's cup, and Nogo's genalt Adam's apple, while he sucked the liquid down.

I wasn't going to let some splicer out-drink me. Man, it felt so flesh and dirt real.

"Hit me again, cowboy," I said with a serious close-up. "Let's have a real drink."

"Hey, hold on," Bob said. "I ain't cleanin' up after some damn nazi boy scouts tryin' to outdo each other." He frowned.

Nogo laughed, and held out his jar. This was the unknown factor, the X cue, coming up on all monitors, a bunch of mierda, the wild howl of randomness. Nogo stared intently. Bob poured coffee, then brandy into Nogo's jar. Bob poured more coffee and a little brandy on top of mine.

I drank it quickly, the booze scorching the intake line all the way down. This time the repulso-griff was banging away on every part of my mouth, a strong gag reaction. Then the warmth and flavor again. Then, a pleasant, silly feeling vipped up. It was much rougher than the ones in the stimsublims, and I definitely felt lumed. In the dicks, Mr. Protago-nex drank it all day long. How could anyone do that?

Nogo brought the jar to his lips, staring almost cross-eyed into the liquid, then downed it. He emerged from it with a friendly flush this time.

"Well, let's talk, then," Bob said. "I hope you don't mind if I ain't eager to chew the fat and drink the last of my best with you two brown shirts."

Bob reached into his vest pocket and pulled out what appeared to be a cigarette like in the jeri-dicks, but it was thinner. He put it in his mouth and lit it with a kitchen match. He drew heavily on the smoke, and held it in, rather than expelling it.

"Don't suppose either of you ever got zooted," he said in a high silly voice, releasing the smoke. "That would be a treat to see."

He held out the cigarette to me.

"Go ahead," Nogo said with an encouraging tone. "Smoke some. I will if you do."

Not to be outdone by my fellow nazi boyscout, I puffed on the finger bone like cigarette, just as I'd seen in the jeri-spots on screen. It had a distinctly flowery taste, almost wholesome, and then it expanded in my lungs. I coughed so hard I thought I was going to fade out.

"If you're going to slobber on my shoes, you're cut off," Bob said with a stern smile.

I started to feel another lume on top of the brandy, a glow around the top of the head, a feeling everything was going to be all right. It felt a little spooky, like a kid going to visit grandpa, with the world at his feet. Out of focus, we could drink his strange concoctions and smoke his magic herbs without the big bark and bite of spying nekro heads. We were future, and future, ok. So let's drink and talk, you goofy old retz.

Nogo banged on the flowery, piney herb cigarette with fervor, like a headband and long rock-locks had sprouted from his head. Genalt for art, he was running on chameleon nature now, in the deep water of his own DNA. His genes were tweaked so he could write like Faulkner or sing West Side Story in the little Local stump show. Like he could smoke this stuff and handle it, without experience, because of an occupational safeguard written in over a hundred seasons ago. Ancient biomagnetics were being tested on a nova-cent splicer.

"Pahooo!" Nogo coughed violently. His lips and eyes protruded, as he lurched around like he was choking. The cough faded in and out, and the smile got sillier. Luckily for the little shirker, his helixes took the biggest hit.

"Man, that's some killer shit," he said, like he knew what he was talking about. "Definitely one puff is all you need."

Nogo made a lame sweet close-up, and passed the stick to Bob.

"Damn," Bob said with a friendly grin. "You can't always tell from lookin', c-can ya?

Then Bob leaned over and patted me on the shoulder. The mystery man was too complex. Must get the jump on Spliceman, pronto. Bob took an enormous puff on the cigarette, squinted and grimaced, then handed it to me. Still holding in the smoke, he took a long slug of brandy coffee.

"Groggy coffee and zooter pie," Bob sang like a lullaby, slowly releasing smoke. "Make a man happy til the day he dies."

Then he chuckled and hummed the rest of the unintelligible words, up and under the background sound of the room in the wild woods. Trees sighed in the wind outside, and the wooden floor creaked under Bob's holey socks as he tapped his feet in time to the tune. More groggy coffee for the boys. Pull out another one of them fingerbones.

"Bob, does anyone else live around here?" I asked. "I mean, how do you get along out here? We're all info, Bob, all part of the fabric. Human beings need each other to survive. How do you do it?"

I took a puff and held it in, and it was easier. It even tasted lovely, but still blew up in my lungs. Man, this wild-and-free out of focus reality was so crude. Everything cartoon animix. Bob laughed while I hacked and coughed.

"I sure do seem like a loner with a boner, though, don't I?" Bob asked gleefully. "Makes you w-wonder what g-good all your tech is. I'm happy as a mollusk without it."

He took a busy drink of the groggy and yakked on.

"Why don't you find out why so many folks are losing their m-minds with all yer teevee-net this and that." He burped again.

"God," he continued, shaking his head in disbelief. "I thought it was bad in 2013 with them thousands of channels and virtual reality computer this and that always shoutin' at you, tryin to get you to buy any damn unnecessary thing. But this!"

"And you two are too damn young to know any better," he said quickly, before we could argue the point. "You don't even know right from wrong."

Bob released a grunt, and looked off wistfully. Nogo slid into character number 648 - Helpful Articulator; Type: Dude; subtype 'Hey, dude.'

"But this is now, Bob," Nogo said. "And this is the future, shaping up. The future is now. Things aren't perfect, but at least we're not squatting in caves. Your homegrown and home brew kills your lungs and guts. I can do the same thing with light, and not hurt myself. You're in a cave, depriving yourself, and others who want to hear you."

Nogo paused to point at Bob.

"I do everything you do at home, better," Nogo said. "I don't have to worry about chopping wood or growing or cooking food, or playing an actual guitar. I'm free. And you're a slave. A slave to survival."

I wished I'd said that. Bob was incensed by Nogo's argument of us having greater freedom. Zeitweiss writhed with each word Nogo said, struggling to keep from yelling out.

"You don't know what the hell freedom is!" Bob shouted. "We have no survival problems out here. We got all we need, all we want."

We. Who was 'we?'

Here was the touching part, dear N's and A's - Nogo did not vip into this slip of the jib-jabber's jango, this word, we. It lightly touched the soles of his feet, then vanished out through his toenails. He was totally lumed on the coot's zooter-pooter, whatever the hell it was, and alcohol. Zeitweiss was saved by Nogo's genalt-for-art genes, with all that F. Scott Drunk and F. Stoned Rocker schlock so neatly tweaked in. Nogo was so totally absorbed in the lume, he wasn't really listening, nothing but his ego mattered. And his coordination was frizzing right along with the gear, too, making that task harder for him.

"That's garbage," Nogo said in a loud, arrogant tone, sounding a little slurry. "Your house smells like smoked meat and bad coffee. Booze tastes like shit, you smell like shit, and you don't have any credit cued anywhere."

Nogo laughed loudly, gave Zeitweiss a shaky salute with his coffee jar, and looked towards me and winked. The winking contest. I felt like a freaking princess.

"Face it, Bob," Nogo slurred on arrogantly. "You've got sugar deal talent. Maybe you're the gold op. But you'll just never go anywhere with it. And to me, that's a terrible waste."

That freaking idealistic ad man whiner scruff was shaking out of Nogo's spliced up genes like dust from an old rug.

"I get satisfaction from what I do," Bob said nervously, pushing aside the slip of the lip, the word, we. "I make enough CDs and tapes and alblumens to pass on to generations to c-come. Someday somebody will h-hear 'em."

This innocuous croaking didn't frizz me, but it totally frizzed Spliceman.

"How can anyone listen to you?" Nogo howled. "How could anyone know about this? People haven't played tapes or alblumens or CDs or DVDs or whatever the hell you call them for so many seasons it doesn't matter. You're extinct, and nobody even knows you existed."

I now think this, dear Neighbors and Associates, that those drugs were tweaking Nogo to max. The marijuana made him think he was just, right, and good. And the booze made him just want to win the argument, even if he didn't know what it was about.

The two lumes together created a brusque contentiousness, an inability to shut up and observe. I was above that, even though I was just an old fashioned human, without tweaked genes. Evolution meant survival. I could still gather food and hunt, do my job, while I lumed like the caveman. Nogo couldn't.

"You know anyone down at the Dave's underwear biocollective, Bob?" I asked coyly, twirling my finger in my warm drink like he did. I thought of him inciting Weirds with his guitar, like black turtle neck sweatered bohemians in caves - only no protest march, no revolution, just mass hallucination. Psychic terror attack, brains turn to pudding across the Great Lakes.

"Is that what that old smear said?" Nogo asked, just as coyly. But the smoky peach pride overtook his train of thought. "That's impossible. Zeitweiss wasn't in focus long enough to connect-in with that guy. That smear was forever kind; he had no idea what he was talking about. Random parrot parasite stuff."

Nogo was so strong in his beliefs, and so lumed, he failed to understand Bob was part of a community of some kind. To Nogo, humans couldn't exist outside the system, and Bob was just some malco on the lam in the smalls, soon to see light-bringer.

To me, it was earth-shaking. There were new wrinkles in the fabric, new quirks, a mass nervous breakdown on the way everywhere, and we were future, ok? Not malcos and near smear communing on some prehistoric connexo.

But were the Weirds maybe los admirabiles, the gifted ones, the smooth line in the helix everyone except the genalts have been waiting for? Let's censor that from the format, bury the story, and m-line the individs. No, let's not.

"Bob, at least let us know if there's anyone else we can talk to," I commanded. "Someone who might have had a Weird experience."

Zeitweiss looked relieved, but a little pissed off.

"What you fail to realize," he said, making an expansive gesture with his hand, "is that everything comes and goes. Even pricks like you g-guys. And the low lifes you work for. These people - if they are people at all - are lower than reptile dung. And you're doin' their b-biddin'!"

That was it for Nogo. He straightened up and started walking towards the in-focus world, where gear worked and Bob was ready for the m-line.

"I'm leaving, Stan. If we can't get any cooperation from this guy, I'm going to make sure the friendly Neighbors in our own backyard, 838, hear about this lonely place. It won't be lonely for long. And neither will you, Bob Sideways. You'll be in the unhouse. I don't care."

Bob looked scared a bit; Nogo threatened the homestead. Zeitweiss didn't really look made to play spyguy. He was a twanger who puffed and drank and barked bizarre-badge that was Go. A genius. Not tweaked spunk, like Nogo. But what a noble ape is el hombre. Out of the stink and pinch, Bob's survival instincts clicked in, and a fierce innocence erupted.

"Ok, you don't like my hospitality; then leave," Bob commanded. "I'll talk to your partner here. You can't hold your liquor, kid. I'm just talking painful but true trash. No reason to get all alarmed."

Bob rose and walked with the coffee pot and flask to the stove, and put them back. Nogo looked at Bob in confusion, halted by Zeitweiss's inability to take the threat seriously enough. With a grudging scowl, Nogo sat back down, appearing to want to give him another chance.

"I want to tell you two birds a little story," Bob said, walking back to the table, rubbing his belly. "It's about a king who steals his countrymen's homes so his crooked duke cronies can have more popirty and gold. The countrymens don't have nowhere to go, so they erect their own kingdom, without a king. So he tries to kill 'em but there's too many. So the king just says they don't exist. So that's just wonderful for them."

"Come on," Nogo moaned. "Where is this going? Is there a punch line, or is it like everything else around here?"

Zeitweiss came back prontito, gesturing wildly, rubbing his moustache, licking his lower lip, his pale blues as big as dishes.

"I'll tell you where it's going, stupid," the cowboy said. "Back in 2013 there was twenty million homeless people hiding out in your beloved goddamn Northam, and in 2020 there was over a hundred million. Can't you see it plain as day? Where did all them people go? Where?"

Bob banged a spoon down on the table.

"If that don't mean something to you, get the hell on out!" he shouted.

Zeitweiss was so pure; he had cunning and courage, and actually believed in something. He didn't just entertain an idea, he lived it. But what the bleep was he talking about?

"See, he's smearing," Nogo said. "You can't understand a fucking word he's saying."

Nogo had gulped the last drop of his groggy coffee, and Bob's babble.

"Wait, wait, wait..." I said. "You mean there's millions of individs walking around out of focus, or that something happened to them we're supposed to know, or what? And what does this have to do with us?"

Nogo scratched his head.

"Yeah, what do you mean?"

Bob cupped his left hand over his face, resting the index finger on his brow. The glimmer of a smile poked through the shield of hammy hand meat. He was having fun at our expense, knowing guys our age were ignorant as hell about old-era history. He could have said everyone back then had green hair and pink teeth, for all we knew. He made the figures up.

"Ain't it obvious?" Bob implored. "Can't you just use your heads?"

"Bob," I said firmly. "Give us a hint where we can find folks like you, folks living old-era style, like before CarTown got support. We need to talk to more individs like yourself."

CarTown, especially the out of focus chunk called Industros Tragicos, was the right place to start; it had all the nooks and crannies for hiding in, it added up. But Bob was a blob, staring blankly, unresponsive. He mumbled something unintelligible through his fingers as he petted his moustache, then resumed the stare.

"Go on, get out of my house, right now," Bob said abruptly, all sullen and disappointed looking. "This conversation's r-run its course."

"CarTown slopes down to the Lake, doesn't it?" I asked, not giving in. "Down there means a geo description, doesn't it?"

"Out, out, out," Zeitweiss repeated, pointing to the door.

Bob wasn't going to be a good scout and lead us to his tribe's village, unless this was it. We were going to have to do more hunting and pecking. And we couldn't use anything from our talk with Bob except the audio, and animix, because it all happened out of focus.

Nogo and I looked at each other, confused about being ejected. We got up and shuffled towards the door silently. Bob was behind us as we walked through the kitchen, past all the shrines. Bob said nothing as we emerged into the portico and cold air.

We hit the outside with goose flesh, flash dipped in ice and embarrassment. A slow dull headache was conjuring itself up. We were humbled, and there was little difference between us now. Sources don't always create reality. The events at Zeitweiss's cave shrine were subjective now, open to interpretation.

I was glad the sources frizzed in there. But now, in the cold, walking back to the mag, still lumed from the brandy and marijuana, I felt nude, impotent without them. How could I prove things really went down the way they did? Nogo's animix would be more convincing, even with my audio.

We both smiled, chilly vapor seeping thorough our chattering teeth.

"Bob's a strange guy," Nogo said, rubbing his arms to keep warm. "Notice I didn't say Weird."

"No, you didn't," I said, rocking from foot to foot to keep from freezing. "No, you didn't." He blew into his cupped hands, and the freezing breath curled around his head.

Bob was no spoon bender or box beater, just someone who wanted out of the system. Strange but not Weird. Strange. What an understatement.

Overhead a chain of dark clouds had become lodged from horizon to horizon. Nogo walked ahead of me, eager to get back to the world of frizz and spin. Bob's world, the one we left behind, seemed more attractive to me with each step I took. It took every bit of internal drive to keep walking away from it. The wood smoke, the groggy coffee and zooter pie, the motel cathedral in the forest, the hours alone playing guitar and creating, instead of being bitten by thousands of small voices. Why would anyone run, like Nogo, back to the world in focus?

"Stan, everything's working again," Nogo exulted like a kid. "Woo-hooo!"

I looked at my finger point monitor, and it was perfect, all things shaping up.

"Yeah, we're back in focus," I said, almost disappointed. "We're out of the woods, out of the dark."

The air was colder. The ground crunched under our feet, our breath threw long vapor trails across the path. We were stiff legging - a rare, exhilarating, and irritating experience. The distance from the motel to the break in the trail looked shorter than on the way there, but it seemed to take hours getting back to the mag. The trees were glazed with light frost, and the crystal covered leaves and big pines and chilled mossy rocks were communicating with me. Stay, they said. Time slowed. The uneasy certainty we'd find what we were looking for near CarTown, in Industros Tragicos, gnawed through everything. There were probably hundreds, maybe thousands of people like Bob in Industros Tragicos.

We got back in the mag, and the dash monitor was beeping. Home had been trying to regain contact. Cerevello, Nogo's hab, everybody was in the stack.

"Your destination is CarTown," the mag's deep male 'alert' voice kept saying. "Please return to the path and resume travel to your destination."

Luckily the mag was still on the path, and soon we were slow zooming towards the target zone.

-8-
"INDUSTROS TRAGICOS"

EXTERIOR - DAY - TRACK BACK TO WIDE OVERHEAD OF MAG ON PATH

It took eleven minutes to get to CarTown theme park, on the edge of Industros Tragicos. Nogo fussed with his stuff even though it was perfect, and said nothing. He just made satisfied sounds whenever something worked.

CarTown was the last place Francis the Sissy and the Fire Inspector and the other Weirds were seen. During the last break in, some individs working for CarTown were taking on an internap spot, when Francis's face burst through the screen and moved right on through a wall. They said it scared them to death, but the whole event could have been staged.

CarTown wanted to be a Local, like 838, but was still too skin-min, there weren't enough skulls down there. But Soft School wanted to give them autonomy, after a trial period with 838. Hard School thought the whole chunk of flesh and dirt was Weird. No genalt wanted them in NeighborWorld, let alone having their own Local.

"Do you want to say something to me, Nogo?" I couldn't stand the silence. "You just keep making those sounds."

"I want to take a guzzler, Stan," he said with an embarrassed look. He froze up the shamed face a while, then lowered his eyes. "I don't know if I can lug gear around all day. That visit with your buddy Bob tired me out. I guess I'm not in very good shape."

CarTown's touchlot was the last on 838's electromag system. There weren't any paths in Industros Tragicos, just old guzzler roads. Nogo wanted to interview the guys who had the Weird experience, then rent a guzzler to get down there. I wanted to walk, with no facilities, old-era scenario, right out of the twentieth century. Nogo would have to lug gear. And he couldn't.

"Look, you go rent the guzzler and I'll get the stuff out of the mag," I said. "Try to get a van, ok? If we can't hike, at least we'll get some old-era atmo with the guerilla news van look."

The sun was in my eyes as we got out of the mag. We only had two tiny bags of gear and he was worried about lugging them. Everything fit on our bodies. He was just a lazy splicer, with no feel for atmo. How could he help me shape and slant my way?

I reached into the back of the mag to get the tiny bags, and as I turned my head, looked towards the park. Out of the corner of my eye I saw the strangest thing. The whole of Industros Tragicos appeared to be elevated above the land around it.

Impossible. Industros Tragicos was a geo depression, river flats, surrounded by low hills sloping down to the Lake. It was mostly underneath old bridges. But as real as feelie-realie, the whole chunk of F and D seemed to rise like an island, to the sky, suspended by long tendrils of light. The light strands were different colors and magnitudes. The island stretched up for quite a distance.

Blinking, trying to fit the shot into my brain, I moved to get a better look, then just stared. The vision or whatever it was lasted about ten seconds. Then everything shrunk down, with all the old factories and warehouses undulating, waving, pulsing back down to their foundations. I thought it was Bob's concoctions or blinky chems from the Nogo stress at first, but knew it wasn't. Maybe Weird mind control, or a naked eye break-in.

After coming around from the vision, the first thing I saw was Nogo staring at me. There I was, standing with hands outstretched - I'd dropped the bags - and my mouth wide open. With his pale face and dark clothes, silhouetted against the CarTown ticket shack, he looked nekro indeed, like murder. From his expression, he'd been watching.

I had no desire to communicate with him about it. I decided to wait for his reaction.

The air was still, and each step on the way to the ticket shack made crackling sounds in the frozen grass. The shack was only about fifty meters away, but it was slo-mo getting there. Nogo kept slowing down, looking apprehensive, like the whole scene was frizzing him. Finally, he stopped and pointed at the freeway bridges.

"Standard, did you have a source pointed at those bridges?" he asked. "I swear, some kind of energy was blipping up there. Is that what you were looking at?"

"When?" I asked. "Oh, yeah. I felt something coming from over there, but I didn't put it up. Hey, can't we get the CarTown shots later, from close up? Let's just get the guzzler and get started."

I walked into the ticket shack to rent the guzzler. Nogo stayed outside. He forgot about interviewing the guys who witnessed the break-in, so I forgot about it too. For Nogo to forget, or not want to do an interview, was inconceivable. I thought whatever was blipping energy at us must have affected him somehow.

The guy in the shack was a short, mostly euro, blonde haired young man, who seemed inconvenienced by having to be there in-person. The interior was old-era rustic, even built from boards and things. But the antique cash register was really a biz pad that recognized my face and voice and sweat.

"Hey, how's it going?" I asked the kid. "Renting any guzzlers this week?"

"Yeah," he said, looking like he hated me.

"Really," I said. "Who?"

"You," he said.

"Where's the boss?" I asked, sensing the kid was no lead.

"Sick," he said. "I'm just filling in."

"Were you here when they had the break-in?" I asked.

"Nope. I'm just filling in."

"Ok, I want the van for a few hours. That ok?"

"Yup," he said.

"Am I recognized? Is my credit cued?"

"You're all set to go," he said, handing me the keys.

No lead, worthless. Good. Nogo would have tried to persecute the poor near-smear. I walked back out of the shack with ignition keys and a map, to find Nogo strewing the gear all over, looking for something.

"Hey, they don't know anything in there; it's just some kid filling in."

Nogo barely acknowledged me. He put all his stuff back together, and we walked towards the van. We got to the thirty-year old white, rusty guzzler and climbed in. For a second, he looked evil-eye. I turned the key and started up the van. Since I actually had some experience with guzzlers, and knew how, I was the driver. Nogo pretended he didn't know how, and chose to be chauffeured. The guzzler fired up with a sputter and loud pop, and a big cloud of black smoke shot out of its tailpipe. The tank showed a quarter full, lots of gas.

The van guzzler shook and banged all the way from CarTown to Industors Tragicos, but at least the heater worked. After the CarTown credit problems, the original car maintenance people disappeared, and the new guys still didn't know much about engine repair. Taking the guzzler was fun, though, and I got into the feel with an old-era anchor voice.

"This is Standard Mozuck in the heart of Industros Tragicos, in pursuit of the elusive Weird known as Francis the Sissy," I said. "How long can he stay out of focus? No one knows. It's called Day One, so stay with us."

"Did you see light down there, Stan?" he asked. "A lot of light?"

Nogo couldn't quit.

"No, just an ambience in the light. Why? What did you see, Nogo?"

"I didn't see anything. I just felt energy coming from there. I know he's there, Stan. I can feel it."

"It's strange hearing you say you can feel it," I said. "You don't like to play hunches."

"I don't think it's a hunch, Stan."

Industros Tragicos was a squalid, beaten down world. Decaying smoke stacks and rusty communications towers poked up everywhere in the background. Narrow old streets, filled with holes, spiraled down to the waterfront in a series of tiers, giving the place the look of a brick and dirt whirlpool. We were on the second tier of the descending spiral.

We pulled up in front of a tall, dirty, six hundred seasons old brick warehouse, pocked with holes and moss. Graffitti was scrawled on its longest wall, leading down a narrow alleyway. We walked over to read it, and get shots of it. There were letters - STV on top, YCTO below, and a whirlpool design in between. Right through the design ran a slash. It looked like a street gang tag or revo-group agit-prop from the jeri-era. We read the translation of the obvious threat to outsiders.

"Scary TV You Can't Turn Off," it proclaimed.

Below that was another tag; the letters AFAD-FTB. The translation next to it read "All Flesh And Dirt Fades To Black."

We looked at each other and smiled, as Biff might say, scared shitless. Without saying anything, we turned and walked through the long alley towards the bluff behind the warehouse. The bluff had a great panorama of the old harbor area. We decided to warm up and get our bearings there.

"Spray the scene," I told Nogo. "Every angle. We'll drop in standups later."

Nogo put up some sources and scoped a few shots. He superimposed a close-up of Francis over a long pan of the old waterfront houses, dubbed in some audio, stuck in a few titles and incidental graphics, and logged it. The stuff looked good, so we tried working with it.

I wanted to move to the houses below us, and felt vaguely panicky about staying in one place to long. The vip was like I could be trapped in an alien perceptual landscape at any time without warning. Maybe the Weirds knew we were here, and were secretly manipulating the enviro. Francis, the Fire Inspector, they were powerful. They could smear us, right?

Nogo kept nervously fussing with the audio dubbing, futilely trying to shake loose a buzzing in an audio stack. He got more frustrated, and started bleeping, his eyes big, looking ready to pop.

"Hey, hey, you ok?" I asked all mommy. "Take it easy, the day's almost young."

I was showing concern, for the splicer who laughed in my face when my chems were blown. The buzz stopped and he quickly resumed a superior tone.

"Please don't shout when I'm having problems," he said. "It slows me down."

"Well, are we frizzing again?" I shot back, taking control.

He gave me a withering look and started fooling with his animix. Whether he corrected a real frizz, or something Weird happened again, he wasn't offering clues.

"Point some sources at the row of houses directly across the waterfront," I told him. "I've got a feeling something's going on there. Maybe we should just go over there."

The houses were actually close. An elevated mag line would've put us there in four minutes, but there weren't any mag lines down in the 20th century. We'd have to drive all the way around the harbor. We could shave a few minutes by taking a freeway bridge, but it would be dangerous. I didn't want to drive, but now, with Francis on the loose, I was glad we weren't walking.

Nogo had about ten antique shab-hab row houses in focus. Next to them was a large rusted out old metal machine, probably used for shuttling coal or iron ore, from Great Lakes freighters at the waterfront docks to railroad trains. If you angled on the third house from the foreground, a green house, the rusty brown machine looked like a huge demon's head. A fantastic shot.

"Full up on that machine thing, full up!" I shouted. "Do you see it?"

"Yeah!" he shouted back. "I see it, I see it!"

Nogo and I marveled at our good luck. This shot alone could probably destroy the Weirds. Now all we needed was Francis the Sissy in the diva light.

"I think we should pack up and head over there, Nogo," I said. "Let's head right for those houses."

"I don't know if I feel like looking for him," he shot back. "It might be easier to pick up some more atmo-color shots, and construct the spot with what we've got. I think we should head back to 838."

"No, no, I've got to see what's going on over there," I said. "I've got to."

Nogo didn't disagree. He just started tearing down his gear.

It could be nekro, no matter how we got down there. But danger was part of the spot's old-era flavor. We packed our tiny gear, logged some shots, and took some on. Nogo froze up the shot of the green house with the demon machine beside it.

We started walking back to the van. We were taking on the demon shot as we walked through the alley, when I noticed something funny about it. It was slowly deteriorating into disconnected dots. Before I could adjust the playback, a new shot was emerging through the dot fuzz. It was a close-up on the green house's window, the window closest to us.

Although his back was turned, I could tell the central figure was Francis. Seated across from him was a young woman with dark hair. Then, at the far end of the table, a very old woman with gray, almost white, hair.

"Nem, nem, nem," Francis mumbled. "Nem, nem, nem."

From the center of the table, a rose colored glow emanated, contrasting with the little room's light green walls. Francis and the other two appeared to be staring at the light, or at least, their attention was connected to it somehow. They smiled at the light, and it grew brighter. Then they looked at each other and it dimmed down.

Totally dumfounded, I turned to catch Nogo's reaction. As I turned, it seemed that my body shifted into slo-mo. Stopped in the middle of some meaningless action, Nogo was no-mo, motionless. I turned back to face the monitor, even slower than before, to see everyone in the little room enveloped in rose colored light, staring directly at me. They were pulling me, drawing me towards them with their eyes somehow.

It felt like my consciousness was being sucked into the monitor. Then I found myself drifting into that room. It felt like I was physically merging with one of the chairs at the table. Almost instantly, I was there.

The room's perspective was totally distorted, but I could make out objects, like an old timepiece - a cuckoo clock - and a dark wood cabinet filled with blue and white china cups. In the next room I could make out a red love seat, a wooden dressing table, and a fat old-era leather suitcase bearing a tag marked 'CLE/BUF.' There was a standing mirror on the dressing table, with six lit candles below it. I tried to recognize some other features in the room, but then they turned and began calling me with their minds again. They were focusing on a spot between my eyes, creating a warm, pleasant sensation there. My consciousness was drifting again. Soon the rosy light was surrounding us all, growing brighter, until it filled the whole house. What was left of my rational mind began having questions about my survival.

Then instantly everything got clear and sharp again. I could clearly make out each person's facial expression. The white haired old woman looked grimly determined, the dark haired young woman seemed to be experiencing erot-slam rapture, and Francis looked like a drooling, ancient baby.

"Six beautiful angels climbing a vine to the sun, nem nem nem," Francis said with his eyes half open. "Six messengers, a cross and a circle, a cross and a circle, nem nem nem."

Then the hands on the clock started turning, very fast. The light grew and grew, while time seemed to race. Everything looked hazy, the table and people began vibrating. There were waves of different colored light framing them up. And here's the twisto. Strong ripples of static electricity crinkled my hair. I had no idea how much time passed. Everything looked like a Weird break-in, as seen from the inside.

The Weirds could not only alter perception, they could also change time. The experience didn't stop there, though. After the clock raced and the light grew more brilliant, time appeared to stop entirely. The clock froze.

Naturally, this worried me. It seemed like the bizarre-badge would never end, that I'd never get back to the dream of 838, and advo Standard Mozuck. There were many other lives in the Weird dream, many worlds coexisting. It was like one life was just a spot on the connector, and the spot could be forgotten or misplaced. The brilliant light began dimming, and the Weirds were visible, in their normal shapes and sizes. They were looking at me. Not calling me with their eyes, just staring.

I felt relaxed, unafraid, and happy to be with these people, but I didn't know who they were, or why I was there. I knew I was a NeighborWorld advo, and maybe they had something to do with that, but I couldn't put it together. The young woman was familiar somehow, like I had recently met her on the connector but couldn't place her. I glanced to the right, and there she was, electric hot flesh, pink lips and double black hair, the v-u of breakthrough eroto-slam. Then she spoke into my brain, like Bob did.

"My name is Laya," she said. "I hope you come and see us again, Standard."

The rose colored light streamed in through the windows, instead of emanating from the table. Strands of light purple burped through the schlom like toothpaste. Twilight. What was the name of that stupid song? I tried to turn to Laya for an answer to all this, but couldn't move. I was enthralled by the sunset, the same hue as the tabletop light. The Weirds were synthesizing twilight somehow, to change sense and temporal perception.

I must have been staring out the window for quite a while. When Nogo burst into the room, I recognized his face but had no idea who he was.

"This is the fourth and final time I'm coming in here," Nogo rasped frantically. "Let's get the hell going. This place is twisting my chems. I've got to get out of here."

It was a shock seeing Nogo. But it was more of a shock to see no one else in the room but the old lady. Francis and Laya were gone. Nogo turned and stormed out of the room, past the old woman. She waved, as he left and headed towards the van. As soon as he got into the van he started honking the horn. The old woman stuck her fingers in her ears and puffed out her cheeks in a grotty grimace.

I got up, and as I walked out past her, she came close to calling me with her eyes, but only that, close. I walked out of the little green house and got into the van. I still didn't know what was going on, but knew enough to start the van, and start driving back.

"Where's your look, Stand?" Nogo asked. "Where's the hat and trenchie?"

I had no idea where I'd left them, or why Nogo hadn't reminded me before I was in just my tuni.

"Back there?" I asked. "I must have left it back there."

"You want to leave expensive gear with some Weirds during scandal times?" he shot back, sounding incred. "It's your ass if you do."

"I can't now," I said. "All I can do is drive."

So I drove, looking straight ahead, not once at him. It wasn't until we got back over the bridge again that I realized I not only had no idea where my look was, but where I'd been or what happened.

"Man, you did an incredible job of driving over that bridge," Nogo said sounding duly impressed. "I thought we were going to drop right into the river, but - I can't believe it - you pulled it off."

"I did?"

A shot of everything he said vipped into my head, center screen, but it didn't connect.

"And the way you pulled right up to his house, without even having to sniff, I have to hand it to you, Mozuck."

"I did?"

Once again, a shot of what he described popped into my head.

"How did you know that was the house?" he asked, seeming in awe. "You just stared at the window, and he came right out. How did you know?"

"But I don't remember anything about all that," I said. "All I can remember is being in that room, and then you coming in."

"You can't remember interviewing him on his front stoop, and talking him into a demonstration?"

"No."

"You don't remember the girl and the old woman coming out and telling him not to do it, and you schmoozing it smooth? Man, that was deep stuff. You've got to remember that, no? He created hallucinations, or little break-ins, right in the house.'

"Nothing," I said. "You got it, though? You got it all?"

"Don't worry, I got it all," he said. "All the gear was working, no frizzes. Great shots, great shots. You sure you don't remember anything about it?"

"Nothing."

The van clanked and banged and popped. I struggled to remember what happened but all I could think of was the clock going fast and backwards. I must have succeeded in being in two places at once. Confessing I had no idea where I'd been or what I'd done made Nogo even more suspicious I knew more about Weirds than I let on.

The rest of the ride back to the ticket shack was a blur. Revamping into mag mode and taking the mag back to 838 was blurry, but something was coming back. Something.

EXTERIOR - LATE AFTERNOON - WIDE OVERHEAD SHOT OF TECH CENTER

It was almost dark when we glided into Tech Center. Going back to work seemed almost physically impossible, but I had to. We both insisted on visiting the lab before taking a break. It wasn't necessary, but for the best limited-access gear, and a real old-era look, we included Tech Center's lab.

"This old era schtick is starting to be fun," Nogo said, sounding excited.

"I'll just run in and run back out."

Nogo hopped out of the mag, and jogged into the lab's huge door, dwarfed by its high arch. He was just going to be in the lab long enough to drop off some shots and take a few more, so I just hovered and didn't bother looking for a place to touch. Big snowflakes were piling in from the northwest, whirling around the mag. Ominous feelings about the Weird experience were crowding the upbeat projections.

The big digital monitor above the Biz Tek Direk building was flashing 1700. Time for the end of a work shift, but no throngs crowded through the tall stained glass doors. It was an empty, monochrome shot. All the ways Nogo could set me up and trash the spot raced through my mind. I wondered if Cax Grimoire, another guy with ideas about the Weirds, was in the lab. But I didn't know why.

A Surcord mag kept circling the buildings, which made me almost blow nerves. The lab and Biz Tek Direk building were depressing to v-u in any light, but the snowlight made it painful. I didn't want the surveillance mag picking up anything that might look unusual. They were monitoring me. The Surcord mag slow zoomed into close-up, and I could see two surgoons inside it staring at me.

"My partner had to drop something off at the lab," I said, knowing full well they could hear me in their mag.

The two goons smiled, satisfied with my words, and the mag fast faded off source.

The goons didn't have to zoom me. Everyone knew what everyone was up to, and the abrupt encounter was just to make their presence known, for their own, or someone else's spot. The goons had sources all over the place, but hot scandal focus and elevated paranoia needed more than flat angles from stationary sources. It needed that slow zoom, gliding mag, covert look.

The all-seeing eye loved goon nostalgia as much as my jeri-era schtick. So now the goons were connected to the past, too. The surveillance footage matched my spot. And I basically knew all this, especially after Point A. I knew Nogo would go in to drop off dupes - just for show - and then surgoons would start showing up in the F and D, wearing trenchcoats and sunglasses sources.

But it was still creepy, especially since we'd just returned from an out of focus place near CarTown. The CarTown credit scandal was a possible vamp. Why wouldn't Nogo, and even Cerevello, use the credit scandal against me? They could use Bob Sideways Zeitweiss to deflect their stupidity - how they lost so many Neighbors in CarTown, and how they let the Weird break-ins pre-empt the credit scandal.

Cerevello and Nogo had come up with the hottest focus ever when they discovered CarTown, and brought that chunk of flesh and dirt into focus.

Cerevello was so wrapped up in his Bluebook spot, trying to put notches on his retirement gun, that he didn't pay attention to realities. CarTown was the in-focus chunk of Industros Tragicos, the civilized side of the Neighborhood. How did it stay out of focus so long before that? Why did every living soul in CarTown, just like Bob Sideways, have such an eye-peeling package?

"Home, bring up everything I've got about the CarTown credit scandal, and new Neighbors," I said to my mag, starting to worry.

Naturally everyone heard the request, but what else could I do? All of a sudden, my editor, Bill, appeared on the monitor.

"Not a second too soon, my boy," Bill said with a paternal tone. Then he vipped off before he could reprimand or give me the 5-W.

The crawl appeared on the mag's dash screen: CARTOWN NEW NEIGHBORS - SERIES OF SHOTS - ALL ANGLES, FS LIGHT.

The first shot showed a scene of the CarTown family that was so deformed by jeri-era tox mutations that you had to angle the source left to v-u them face-to-face. This amazing genetic offering knew about guzzlers, how to maintain them and keep them running, even restored them to their original condition.

The next shot showed fifty restored guzzlers parked in a hidden lot near the marshes, all looking jeri-era beautiful. A new shot snapped a medium overhead of the family renting the guzzlers and selling snacks to the few 838 Neighbors who visited CarTown. Cerevello loved that slap-faced family. No wonder he hated Weirds now. Then another shot showed footage of 838 Neighbors driving the cars around, listening to teenage rock and roll, taking on jeri-retro stims in their surfer-spy sunglasses and interesting haircuts and the look. Stop in for a doo-wop hot dog or guitar burger. And we few replayed the experience at home, even came back for more. The slap-faces gave Neighbors hand drawn maps, let them listen to old radio and watch TV - with old-era, small town programming and commercials - in a sandwich shop.

That was the beauty part. CarTown was prepackaged; Cerevello and Nogo didn't need to build an infrastructure. Soon anyone in the world could experience the place in feeli-realie, and Nogo and Cerevello would be rich. It was so beautiful, they never once considered how strange, maybe how Weird, it was that no one except Bob had ever applied for a Spotlight.

The next shot showed the colony of ancient drug suckers in the veterans' social hall. It was great stuff. These sideways gents could beat any feelie-realie game we put them up against. Cerevello did spots on them, Nogo helped create feelie-realie games to beat them. The promo alone, showing genalt whiz kids losing to them, put them both on top for a while. The guys from the social hall never lost.

Before coming into focus, the CarTown Neighbors never used screens to get lumed. They'd never seen connectors, or ate hab-squeezed food, or knew much about NeighborWorld. They grew the herbs that lumed them and the food they ate, by themselves. And they certainly did not comp to Concord or the credit system. They bartered or used old era currency. After C-man and Splice-man turned the place into a theme park, they came into the system. The old currency became prop money.

The screen crawl read SERIES OF SHOTS - FAST FORWARD/SWIRL ZOOM.

The first shot showed a scene from CarTown cooking shows - with old ladies from various Slovenian, Polish, Italian, Guatemalan, Jamaican, and other ethnic social halls roasting the fattened up pigeons that roosted under the bridges, and serving them as a delicacy. Urban squab, as big as an Agricord chicken. The show was a success for a week. Then, one by one, the formerly robust, healthy old ladies faded to black. The show went classic.

The next shot showed the sleight-of-handers and jeri-era magicians and their tricks. Then it quick cut to mutantia throwbacks turned eroto-slam for private access. Suddenly, there was a Q-cut to the strange crew that divined the future. These guys predicted what would happen to them, and Cerevello and the genalt, too, in their last spot before disappearing.

"The world you know will come and go, it came and went, just like this show," they said in unison.

Then they stopped and made gurgling baby sounds in the backs of their throats, then smiled and said nothing more. They disappeared in a flick right in focus.

It was the biggest haul of climbers with bizarre talents in years, but nobody cared that the place might be crawling with Weirds. Success was all that mattered. Usually, when someone comes into the Spotlight, they stay. They're contract obligated, they have to be paid. If you hook them on gear, stack their humble habs with the newest tech, let NeighborWorld do everything, cook their house, clean their food - then you've got them.

But cred alone will not put a climber in your pocket. The trick is hooking them into scrawling a credit line with your gear, endorsements, and name in the producer's slot on the credit roll. Newly brought into focus ones cannot stash, in a few months they're broke again. But if they're connected in, they're part of your reservoir. And if you keep the information hot, the credit stays hot.

Being clever political jerks, Biff and Nogo poured on sophisticated access gear that made it possible to wish products into existence. All those CarTown climbers were suddenly in debt for huge sums of credit. Then it all went up in smoke.

The last shot in the swirl zoom popped up on the monitor. It panned around an empty old-era house, in CarTown. The connectors were all wide open, beeping, with no one around. The quickening series of shots showed open connectors in other empty CarTown houses, more, more, more of them.

Nogo assumed it was just blinky tech at first, because how could fifteen hundred individs disappear with the gear running? He kept working on it, and it kept coming up working. He walked feelie realie through the rooms, even the yards outside, to see if they were hiding. A not so Neighborly welcome. The CarTown climbers had gone on a wild shopping spree, and vanished into thin air. Someone had beaten NeighborWorld out of a lot of credit. El info-scam. But who? The Weirds? Who rightfully owned the credit? Us or them? The Biz/Tek Direk had screwed itself. The credit and gear disappeared with the climbers.

Cerevello was in a panic about losing his bluebook retirement, so he made up his mind to erase that bad take any way he could. Like putting up Shaping Vistas spots that went after the Weirds as nekro, and Soft School spots proclaiming they were hallucinations.

Thinking about it was making me frizzy. Nogo was taking a long time. All these goons and probes nosing around had something to do with it. At the height of the squirm, Nogo burst out of the lab, laughing, waving his fist.

"That's the guy, Stan," he crowed as he climbed into the mag. "We got him dead to rights. We are in."

-9-
"FRIZZ OUT IN THE LAB"

I released the mag's hold control, and we started gliding slowly forward. Wet snowflakes plopped against the window in dense waves, but it was mid August in the lab. Soon we'd be buzzing along with no stop til prepro destino. The world began tilting towards Industros Tragicos.

"Stop!" Nogo yelled.

His eyes were fixed on a spot in the distance, like we were headed towards doom. My hand jerked back on the hover control, stopping the mag abruptly, making Nogo's head lurch forward.

"Where are we going, Stan?" he asked. "Don't you want to see this stuff?"

Nogo turned towards me in liquid slo-mo. His face was wet; maybe from the snow, maybe he was sweating too. He smiled empty-headedly. My hand tightened on the control lever. I felt sick.

"Back down to Industros, I thought," I said. "For the look. Then connect with Cerevello and do what we must, right?"

"No I've got a little surprise for you, in the lab," he said sweetly. "Besides, it's getting too dark to do that again."

"What surprise, Nogo? What's Go? Who's in the lab? What's in the lab?"

A claustrophobic zamp was thundering in. The mag's culfa-foam interior made it feel like a coffin again, smaller, darker, with tiny windows.

"Go ahead and put up what you've got," I said. "Put what you've got on the monitor. We don't need to go back to the lab."

The snowflakes drummed on the mag, impending catastrophe in Industros Tragicos evaporated, and words of an uncomp nature seeped from Nogo's smile, or maybe I was just confused again. It felt like half of me was back in Industros Tragicos.

"No, we don't need to go back down to Industros Tragicos," Nogo said, all smirky-mug. "Everything's much better here. Better for you, too."

"Why better for me? What's going on?"

"I think you're changing," he said, looking superior. "Something's happening inside your body you need to be aware of. I think you're changing and you don't even know it."

Still looking down his nose, he shook his head, leaned over me, and popped the mag into reverse. The mag drifted backwards, to the front of the lab. Then Nogo jerked it into hold.

"Get out," he whispered. "Don't just sit there like smear, get out."

A thing's nature can be determined by its motion. It was all uphill motion now. The fade was a darker gray.

"I want to go back down there," I groaned. "Let's pick it up again in Industros Tragicos."

"Never mind that mierda, Standard." Nogo snapped. "Did that woman touch you? Did she touch you?"

It was an odd time to notice again how angular his body was. He looked like a freaking triangle. I started chuckling, but it sounded like weeping. It was a bad dream. Was Laya the diva-Jane at Point A?

"Who?" I asked. "The diva-Jane? Laya? I didn't touch her. Why?"

"No, you moron. La vieja, the old woman. Did she touch you?"

"No, no, no," I mumbled. "I didn't touch her and she didn't touch me. We had our hands on the table at the same time, though."

Obviously our experiences in Industros Tragicos were different. For me, it was uplifting. For Nogo it was a dangerous trap we were lucky to escape. He must have had the hush mode on something.

"Hey, man," I said. "A Surcord mag and two goons zoomed the mag while you were in the lab. Is that just coincidence? What are they doing here? You pulling some slime, or what? This is my spot, you know. Mine. Or weren't you there at Point A?"

Nogo stroked his chin. He looked like he was waiting for me to do or say something. My throat felt like a rock was blocking my speech.

"Why do you want to know if she touched me?" I asked hoarsely. "Who is she? Did she poison me?"

Nogo smiled.

"Who is she?" Nogo drawled a la spanglo. "She my mother, meng. If you touch her, I keel you. Orale, te matare!"

I started laughing, but I was frustrated and confused, and wanted control back.

"Yeah, mine too," I said, with extra snot. "And everyone else's, you jerk."

What was I talking about? Nogo frizzed.

"What the fuck? Get out of the mag, you asshole. Get the hell out."

Nogo started pushing me out of the mag with his hand. He didn't seem to care noses were probing, zooming the action.

"Hey, jerk, stop pushing me," I growled, raising my fist. "Stop pushing."

He stopped and withdrew his hand.

"I'll go, I'll go," I said. "Who's in there? What the hell's going on? Is Cerevello in there? I want to talk to him. This is my spot, man."

"You still don't know what's going on, do you, Stan?" Nogo sighed. "Your body's changing, trouper. From the Weirds. I didn't run any patterns into your head, so stop threatening me with Cerevello. Right now, you should be worrying about what the Weirds did to you."

So I do the perfect comeback.

"Is she really your mother?"

Nogo looked at me contemptuously. I had made eight hours of the spot's construction. Now it was Nogo's, and I was the assistant, the tag-along, the dummy box.

"You just don't get it, do you?" he sneered. "You don't see what's going on."

The Weird ju-ju was too strong. What was happening to my body, anyway? The Weirds singled me out. They knew I'd get all lumed and flakey and jeopardize my job. The Weirds conned me into giving them the velvet glove, then made a fool of me. Laya was the girl at Point A, the disappearing Diva Jane.

"The old bitch poisoned me, right? The table was a bio-source of some kind, and she was blipping squares into my skull without me noticing somehow. Is that it?"

"Yeah, yeah, yeah," Nogo came back, mugging smarmy. "Something like that." His eyes narrowed. "Hey, Stan," he warbled on, all cocky and tooth feisty. "How many fireman's hats are there? You did a spot on the Fire Inspector, didn't you?"

No one ever brought a Weird into the Spotlight. I used Cax Grimoire's scrimps, his favorite silly break-ins, in my research flow this morning. Is that what he was talking about? Either Nogo had been peeping me before I picked him up, or we were taking on completely different realities; edited by Nogo and the Hard, or Cerevello and the Soft, or Francis and the Weird, or Bobby Z and the whatever he was.

"What's this Fire Inspector shit?" I asked in deep frizz. "Nobody ever brought them into focus, let alone into the Spotlight. Fuck the worms and meanie-monks. I'm going to tell the truth. The credo thing, you know? If Francis and his crew pull up a bad crawl, so be it. M-line him. But this spot is mine."

Blurt on, dummy box. Nogo looked at me in disbelief, like I knew more than I should, or less. With a determined expression, he started up again.

"Stan, how many firemen's hats are there?"

"Nine," I said, this time without hesitation, from another square blipped into my skull, from somewhere.

Nogo looked startled, then relieved.

In my mind I could see nine little firemen's hats swirling around the Fire Inspector's head, shining through a gray nimbus. Shiny red hats. They looked like the childhood ones. No, the stimsublims. Yeah, level nine Satiscope. But there was no level nine. What the hell did 'nine' mean? Why did I say nine?

"I want in on whatever's going on," I said quickly, again without knowing why.

"Hah!" Nogo exclaimed all self satisfied. "You don't know what's happening in your own body!"

"What are you talking about?" I came back up and under. "I need answers. What's wrong with me? Answer me!"

Nogo laughed and opened the door. He got out, chuckle-chuckle spliceman all the way, and headed for the lab.

The day wasn't even over and it seemed like weeks had passed since the morning shift. Now that it was almost over, it seemed like the weeks had shrunk to minutes.

"If you aren't smeared now, you will be," he called back. "Go ahead, stay there by yourself. Or go back down there yourself. But don't expect answers from Cerevello. He's as dumb as you are."

He disappeared into the lab. I realized time was changing again somehow, reality had shifted. There were feelings of frustration and anger over Nogo treating me like smear. Still vainly trying to portray myself as the hero of the show, I opened the door and headed for the lab, to save my spot.

The whole scene was atmosphere, none of it connected with me. I was an actor; the lab was a set, a background. Some goons moved around, for the shot. I walked in little steps against the waves of snowflakes, totally numb, blank to the world. Until I hit the lab.

The lab's production room opened up in an intense eruption of yellow glint, dear N's and A's, and the aging young director stood before whatever awful truth was waiting. My clothing was drenched in a malodorous chicken-food sweat. Fear-frizz oozed from my pores. A charcoal stink from the zooter-pie, and a rancid sweet stench from the brandy had seeped into everything, making an unbearable blend. The focus was horrible, but advo played the part, and rode the zoom, full up.

The faces of the Associates greeting me were distorted, turned down at the sides, peering and bulbous, elongated, sad and happy, blown out of focus. All probing snatches of an insane, crooked, unreal world at odds with a sane, smooth, real world.

But the room itself was in sharp contrast, and the bright yellow light made it look too real, square-cornered and desolate. With all the chromium and phony blue-veined marble, the lab looked like a huge, high class old-era lavatory.

Cerevello's hat was on half sideways, smearing his face into an unhouse close-up. Two nekro looking unknown goons, with dark emblems on old-era dress gray, were present.

Cax Grimoire, looking fearful, was waving frantically to get my attention. The short, ruddy euro, with curly light brown hair and a spade-like widow's peak, was the only friendly mug on set.

Then Nogo jumped towards me, flashing teeth, babbling success. I should have known.

"Standard, I told you we're in, didn't I?" Nogo asked, his voice disconnected from his body.

Then jump cut to exaggerated embraces from Cerevello, and the sound of his hand raining down on my back; his source glasses shining into my eyes, stained teeth sloping upwards, shadows in the creases on his beaming skull.

"You did it, my boy!" Cerevello whooped like a kid. "You packaged the whole spot! What a team! Get ready for big things."

"I took the mag over here to congratulate you in person and help wrap things up," he babbled on under his beat up hat. "We're mighty proud of you, sincerely said, and I mean that."

"Packaged who, Biff?" I asked, still confused, trying to keep track. Everything still looked like shots. "I got Francis, I guess, but I still don't know how I got him. Biff, what's happ..."

Nogo broke me off mid-word, materializing from the shadows behind Biff's smodging mug. He interrupted with authoritative restraint, and no tension in his voice, smiling. His personal manipulation skills were an obstacle to telling the truth. His power over Cerevello was growing and mine was waning.

"How are you now, Stan?" he asked. "Feeling better?"

When I was nine years old, I used to watch Toy Town. All the toys I could ever want right before my eyes, on screen. Toy ice cream wagons, dump trucks, fire trucks, parading by. Only now, in my mind, I was seeing the Fire Inspector, as clearly as any memory, like he had somehow co-opted my childhood.

"So what did I do?" I repeated. "What happened? Can I see a playback? I'm still confused."

My spirits were low, even with all the backslapping and fake gooey concern. Nogo kept repeating, "Are you feeling better?"

The words 'never' and 'nunca' and 'mai' kept repeating in my mind. Snow from my feet was melting, making shiny puddles on the floor, but I kept walking further into the lab, towards Cax Grimoire. A cacophony of signals, squares from everywhere were slamming into my skull.

"I'm ok now," I lied, nervous and trying to control my mouth muscles. "I'm ok. I'm just confused about what happened."

Sound track X played through the lab's monitor. I had reasons for being wary of Grimoire, doubting his true motivation, but he seemed genuinely glad to see me. Maybe he could help. He extended his hand and chuckled.

"How's it going, kiddo?" he asked, all warm and gooey in the right. "You look like you could blink on few hours of choice stims."

"Oh, no tan bueno, Cax," I said. "Not so good. A little under the wa-wa, close to a big frizz, maybe. But I'm here. How goes it with you?"

The room seemed hot. The slick of sweat on my back was growing. A big brown sofa near the console panel looked soft and inviting. I walked to the sofa and plotzed.

"What's wrong?" Cax asked. "This stuff is great. Without animix. How the hell d'ya do it?"

"I give," I said. "How? It doesn't make sense yet. Show me the playback. Can I see it?"

Cax looked bewildered.

"Sure," Grimoire said. "But didn't you watch the sources and monitors while you were on the job? You got to do a little grunt work yourself, Mister Director. Don't expect Nogo to do everything."

Grimoire raised his eyebrow, to highlight what he said to me, private access.

"Cax," I said. "Is it possible someone could beam stimsublim, or slam squares into your skull, without a source? Is it conceivable?"

Grimoire looked even more bewildered.

"Without a source of any kind? I don't know. Isn't that what we're here for? Don't you know?"

Nogo interrupted again.

"Hey, what does this have to do with the spot?" Nogo asked. "Let's deal with the playback, and forget politics and tech talk and supernatural crap. Let's deal with what we've got."

My survival instincts were still intact. I was mustering anger, almost losing my temper.

"Look, blow-go," I dicted all snotto. "These questions are pertinent to my experience, the director's experience."

I looked right at Cerevello.

"By the way, Biff, I am still the director, right? Is it still my spot?"

Cerevello smiled almost crosseyed, and yanked off his source glasses.

"Why it's yours, my boy, yours."

With one eye pointing north and the other south, Biff put his glasses back on, facing me, but fading me with the wayward eye. He pulled out a hankie and gave a long slow blow, grimacing. He tugged at his nose, then mumbled, "Uh... and Nogo's."

"What?" I exploded. "You said it was mine! What in hell's going on?"

"Never mind whose spot it is," Nogo barked all nekro for the m-line. "If you think Weirds vipped squares in your head, and that's why you're acting so fucked up, say so."

Nogo looked at Cerevello with a satisfied smile.

"That should prove the Weirds are dangerous, right there," Nogo said.

"You're the one whispering into my head," I said, argumentative and frizzed. "It's got to be you. You and your anal retentive, splicer dark-bark."

Cerevello withdrew his hankie slowly, eyes focused on Nogo.

"I told you," Nogo said, waving his hand in disgust. "He's paranoid.

Gone-D. Smearing out or just nuts. Babbling the usual screwball crap. Crazy fuck."

Then Nogo raised his hand again, this time a phony threat to slap me, and I raised my fist, threatening right back. This was potentially great focus. We got drunk and took drugs and were totally out of focus, and now we were going to actually fight, in the F and D.

"Stan, Stan!" Biff said quickly. "Hold it, stop!"

He made an expression of suitable alarm, then concern.

"Stan, you are behaving a bit weird," he said, with a forced chuckle. "No joke intended there. But are you seriously accusing Nogo of spot sabo? By beaming mind-control stims into your head? I mean, we're all advos and our skulls are private. Have some faith in sacred space. And trust, for God's sake."

Satisfied we weren't going to really fight, Cerevello sighed.

"Besides, how could you prove such a thing?" Cerevello went on. "You've got to know how this makes you look in focus, if you can't prove it."

Nogo looked angry, betrayed.

"If you think Nogo's taking over the spot, I say good!" Cerevello said quickly. "Healthy competition distinguishes us from animals, doesn't it? Am I right? Fight for the control. Why not? This spot's bigger than all of us now."

Cax laughed, a loud eruption. Nogo pinched the bridge of his nose, disgusted with everything.

"You're both important!" Cerevello boomed, trying a mommy tactic. "Both of you! That's what I've been telling Dingleman all morning."

"Both? Competition? You admitted it!" I yakked, frizzing my nubs down. "This morning you told me it was mine! I didn't even want to do this freaking m-line. Why did you do this to me?"

I lost control and kicked a disposal box near the control panel, and almost fell down. I was acting like violent forever smear. The control panel recognized the unusual action, and instantly replayed it on the overhead monitor. Kicking props, inspiring confidence.

"What difference does it make?" Nogo bellowed. "You're losing it, man. Why should it be yours, anyway? You're smearing or turning Weird or having a nervous breakdown or something. Step down."

"Let's worry about that later," Cax interjected prontito. "No time for egos right now. We're in deep with this credit scandal. The G-O thinks we're in with the Weirds somehow, or that we're the Weirds. We're shaping up as the guilty party."

"We're in up to here," Cerevello said, holding his hand under his chin. "Cax hears the G-O is going to start leaning on us to churn out spots on the Weirds and the scandal. If we don't come up with something, maybe today, they could plop something on us."

"We got to put our differences aside," Cax said, looking at both Nogo and I.

"We can't be caught in the cold when the storm rolls in," Cerevello glommed on. "They'll m-line us. If the Dingle Man can't dingle-dangle and slow things down at the G-O, it's back to monitoring tech flow for all of us."

"Alan Dingleman knows about all this?" I said, puffing up. "How could you be so stupid? Who told him?"

"Alan doesn't know about all this," Nogo said, all misterioso. "He knows about the CarTown credit scandal, and he knows we're having problems with Weirds. He doesn't know about this yet. And we're not going to tell him until we have to."

"I never told him," Cerevello jumped in. "I only told him we'd have a spot that would help us all out. I asked for enough time to do it right, and he agreed. He's keeping anything about Weirds off the connector for 48 hours."

He rubbed his chin.

"Internap, Local, everywhere," he driveled on. "That's why the only things on TOTC were by Cax, and that one that slipped by from Central Africa, somewhere. It wasn't a real Local, but we're checking it out. It's ok. Really."

"But even zombies and somnappers will find it somehow," I said desperately.

Cerevello held his hands upwards, with a look of resignation. Cax stared impassively. Nogo looked amused. Salty sweat poured from my upper lip. I was frizzed.

"Man, you guys covered your asses and brown-nosed so much," I said, "you screwed us. You're acting like common yammer heads, not real advos."

There was that sound again, in my head, like thousands of electronic frogs cheeping, with that vibra-blue insect drone. Squares in the forebrain, whispering-in everywhere.

"Well," I said flatly, "how much of this stuff are we going to use?"

Sex-death, the old formula, based on the principle of Thanatos and Eros. The visual threshold, the gateway to the subconscious, is blasted away by scenes of sex or death. Violence or procreation opens the door, letting subliminal information invade. That's how we did it.

"Enough," Nogo said with a threatening smile. He squeezed a dirty look my way, and gazed into the overhead monitor.

"Nothing," Cerevello blurted abruptly, then, apologetically added, "Only the stuff you just got. We'll have to animix the rest. No time for old-era Live nostalgia. We got enough on this guy and the others to run one hell of an m-line. But we got to do it here, and now."

He rolled his eyes and said "Pressure, pressure." It sounded like he said 'frissure.' Yes, dear N's and A's, pressure everywhere. Nekro clamps running down my spine, Weirdness invading my poor beaten on skull. Through the big window behind the control panel, I could see the muted halo of a demagnetized sun, going down; a wide angle shot without clouds, or blue, or places between. Just a blanket of equally dispersed gray light from horizon to horizon.

Cerevello rambled on incoherently. I couldn't understand him. In my mind I saw stills of everyone, the Weirds, all the idiots I'd come to hate here in 838, Sylvia, everyone. Standing by the control console was smiling Biff Cerevello, the former idealist corrupted by time and circ. The poor buffoon sweated every word from the G-O, ran back and forth like a confused rodent. And now they were going to frame me up like one of those stills.

"There are two kinds of individs in the world, dear Associates," I said with a grandiose ancient radio tone. "Those who breathe through their noses, like this..."

I started doing my yoga breathing, taking long draughts of air through my nostrils.

"Ahhh. And then there are folks who breathe through the mouth like this..."

That's when I dropped down on all fours and began panting like a dog. I tilted my head upwards to face the overhead monitor. "Who cares about doing what's right, anyway? Who cares? Woof, woof, woof!"

"What the hell is he doing?" Nogo yelled, banging his hand down on the long console. "Get rid of this guy! He's nuts!"

Blogo stormed out of the room.

"Get up!" Cerevello dark-barked. "You're going to ruin it for all of us. Get up!"

"Conspiracy," I said, getting to my feet. "Conspiracy."

"Fucking idiot!" Nogo shot back from the next room..

"What conspiracy?" Cerevello asked, seeming incredulous. "We're in the dark as much as much as you are, Stan. The G-O won't let us know anything. That's why we need to help each other."

"We need to embrace the positive, Nogo," I yelled back at him.

Cax laughed. Cerevello banged the glasses against his nose.

"Nogo doesn't know any more than you or I do," Cerevello whispered loudly. "He's grasping at straws."

Biff drew closer, almost making contact.

"As far as what happened down there," he spurted, "maybe they're for real. They were all good focus, and I have no nekro feelings towards them. The old lady was charming. It's too bad we have to do what we have to do."

"So Nogo doesn't know anything?" I posed. "That's bullshit." I wiped the sweat from my lip.

"What happened to me down there? I don't feel like I was even there. But it seems like I'm still there, not here. Understand?"

I grabbed my drenched shirt and pulled it out.

"Check the wet tuni," I said. "Look at me. I'm dripping with perspiration, and it was like zero out there, freezing. And Nogo thinks I'm smearing, all because he thinks he knows what happened and I don't."

"Where's the old-era trenchie and bogie?" Nogo shouted from the other room. "Where's your look?"

"Well, you're making a good case for that smearing thing," Biff said. "Seriously, take my hab-mate Jeanette and I. Take her, please. See what I mean, Stan? People don't always see eye to eye. It's give and take."

"Will you shut up and listen? Nogo and I experienced different things down there. We were in entirely different spaces, doing different things."

"And in this other dimension, he was Mipgip Bloogy, and you were at LA Pinpoint, havin' a beer and a stimsublim," Cerevello said.

The lab's fake marble and chromium steel were making me nauseous. The light had far too much silver in it, too much phony futurism, like in the biocollective. Biff straightened his sources on his nose.

"Is this usable slant or just more jabber?" he ranted on. "Because I don't need a dark-bark narro on bad chems. Or screwball dissertations. Either you get back to work, or I open the Surcord connector. Who is taking all this down anyway. Then it's detention monitoring, and a big Step down and backwards."

Biff glanced towards the goons, who had blended well into the background before, but were now loud as red monitor lights. And smiling. One said "Woof, woof," and the other laughed.

"I want you to stick with this and help us all out," Biff said. "But if you can't, or won't, you're on you own."

Nogo rematerialized like a vapor, to watch closer.

"I want to do this my way for a good reason," I said, staring down Nogo. "If we don't use the discovery aspect, we're not getting all we can out of it. And we'll all be m-lined within a season if we don't."

"So the old-era slant makes sense," Nogo said, nodding benignly. "The feel works, but the brain jerks. Which is why we must apply smooth to it. Right here. Animix now."

Nogo looked intently at the overhead monitor, then back at us.

"We should veer away from the depressing parts," he said.

"No," I said. "There's no compromising about the old-era stuff. That's when the Weirds probably got started. Something must have happened to them then."

"Oh, not all that bleak stuff, no," Cax chimed in, siding with Nogo. "All that junk about media and government and banks and energy companies all secretly conspiring to start NeighborWorld. Never proven. And hush-mode conspiracy theories about them whacking and rigging to pull off the scam. Never proven. Bad focus."

"It's sick, paranoid crap," Nogo said. "Go hot, forget artistic merit, and jam a bunch of conspiracy flimmer down everyone's throats. Shock for shock's sake. It's blaming the system instead of the guilty, the malcos."

He cleared his throat.

"Why come up with a wet and cry that makes the Weirds look gooey in the right places?" Nogo pleaded. "Can't you tell they're no good? It's obvious they made you hallucinate and feel sick. Forget them, Stan, and climb with us."

Cax and Biff nodded in agreement. Soft brain and Hard body were reconciled. The Weirds were dangerous.

"Anything more?" I snapped. "Anything else to help bridge the gulf? Why're you trying to convince me? Do what you want. You're going to anyway."

"I will," Nogo answered. "I don't suppose it ever occurred to you that you can't do the spot you want by yourself. You need us more than we need you. Either you're with the flow that's shaping up, or you're out."

"Yeah," Cerevello chimed in. "Go with the prevailing flow, Standard."

"Can't you idiots see the big monitor, the future?" I posed. "The big monitor says the Weirds are some kind of breakthrough. It's not an m-line on the old-era guys who created the brotherhood. That's just a backdrop, the b-roll, how they got this power. I mean, Christ, it's telekinesis or psi-factor or something."

"All tech, Stan," Nogo said softly. "They've got ahead tech and they're breaking it prematurely. And they take our credit, and leave us. They're thieves, and malcos running ahead. That's beyond limited access. It's illegal."

"How they do it isn't important right now," Cerevello yakked along. "The most important point is, it's illegal. They're disruptive. And they messed with one of our own, boy. You! What are we supposed to do? We're supposed to protect our brotherhood."

"All we have to do is find a tie-in for the credit scandal," Cax said. "It's obvious they used some kind of ahead tech to hurt one of our own on the job. That's you, Standard."

"Suddenly, a promising young advo, bringing light to the smalls, protecting and promoting Neighbors, is hurt by the Weirds," Cerevello said too soon. "Isn't it obvious they'd kidnap Neighbors, and steal credit from us? Maybe they were going to ransom you, maybe they poisoned you!"

"But there was just one interview," I said firmly. "With the goofy little guy and his mom and sister. They put on a show. They're not thieves or malcos."

"Don't be naive, Standard," Nogo added. "They're already stealing from you. Where's your boy Bob right now? Right where we left him. Didn't he take off and leave you holding the bag?"

"Bob owes me nothing!" I shouted, frizzy edges growing sharper. "And he's not Weird. You even said it. He's just strange. Although that's frowned on, it's not illegal yet. And it still butters our bread on both sides."

The claustro-zamp was growing in the lab. Hot sun in fading snowlight, the augur of truth.

"I want out of here, too," I said. "I want to climb. I just don't want to wind up m-lined and smeared into the unhouse. We can't lie. There has to be death. I mean depth. There has to be depth."

Sex-death, the old formula, vipped in daily. Subliminal squares are the building blocks of the Nova Neighbor. Then the 1940's song "All Of Me" and a garbled old-era radio Voice-Over were crosstalking in my skull, along with those freaking electro-frogs. This gig, the advo gig, maybe it wasn't really my thing.

FLASH CRAWL OF MISSING ASSOCIATE ALERT.

My yakky skull opened to source one on the big monitor with no fear of the outcome. Visions of violent old-era cartoon characters, like Dapper Ducky and Swollen Sam and Wanky Peckerwood were flipping by, like the stills before. I was harried and eager to fly away. My POV shifted to the hottest focus; nekrolim.

"Sooner or later the big monitor will not only bring up the origins of the Weirds, but also the nekrolim scandal," I said. "What if smear are glinting on nudge? It'll look like we ignored it on purpose."

Nekrolim reset the retina, put viewers on day long, death-like lumes, the ultimate inward. As the retina reset, they gradually came back to life. Some faded to black. No one, especially smear, could handle the big nudge, nekrolim.

"What about nekrolim?" Nogo asked. "What do you know about it?"

"What?" I asked, rethinking talking about it.

Bootleg nekrolim everywhere now. Neighbors are smearing in epidemic numbers. Hang the nekrolim traffic and credit scandal on the Weirds - two, three birds with one stone - with me, the stone going against the flow. I was a stimsublim abuser, known. As an advo I had access to restricted patterns. Frizz frizz frizz.

"Well?" Cerevello pestered.

Patsy for the m-line. The sweat got colder, the fever hotter. Boing-boing-boing went the bells in my head.

"I don't know any fucking more than you do," I shot back. "You know, this is going nowhere. Just forget it. I want no part of this. I'm leaving."

"You're what?" Cerevello asked, incredulous. "To where?"

The goons laughed again, then one covered his mouth with his hand, and the other coughed. Their faces were cut starkly into the background haze, one skinny and long, one lunar and round.

"How you going to do that?" the skeletal goon asked.

The fat goon laughed again.

"Alright, Stan, that's it, on it," Cerevello commanded in a trembling voice. "You're off the spot until further notice. That's it. You're off."

"Biff, don't do this now," Cax implored.

"Hah!" Nogo exclaimed.

"No, I'm not!" I yelled. "I'm going back down there."

"That's it," Nogo said solemnly.

"You're going home, damn it," Cerevello yelped, face red and ready to pop. "And you're staying there under limited access until you see things clear."

Cerevello took off his glasses and waved them in my face, shaking violently. "These guys are going to take you there, so there's no foolin' around. We got your Home and your prepro all jimmied up so you don't try nothing. We'll have your mag follow you, unless we need it. Now that's truly it, on it. Amen."

A time to meet new friends. The goons waltzed up next to me and asked me to dance, proclaiming their peaceful intentions. My thoughts weren't too clear, but I recollect the motion itself did the work. I declined their offer with a graceful stoop to the floor, then crawled on all fours in a geeky fast forward towards the door.

The goons swooped down and tackled me, crunching the breath out of my lungs, and scaring the remaining crap out of me. I instinctively started kicking, landing a nice thwap on the chubby one's cheek. Fear-frizzing they were taking me to a biocollective, I did scram. But the hands got me, and we kicked and clawed, they tugged on my clothes and skin and smacked my head with forearms. Cerevello and Cax looked on, ashamed.

All the clawing and choking in the world couldn't hold me back. Something was clicking deep inside. There was nothing for Standard Mozuck in 838 anymore. I squirmed from their grip as easily as if I'd planned it. I didn't know where I was going, but I ran towards the door and shouted out my cred.

"Standard Mozuck, NeighborWorld advo, step three!"

The door opened and I burst out of the lab into the darkening cold afternoon in a goose step gallop. It felt like the bad dreams; frantically running and getting nowhere. Panic, flight, but no distance between myself and the horrible faces, the goons.

Then the distance did increase, somehow I moved further from the lab and somnab habs of 838. The goons pursued, but adrenalin must have been on my side. Stim abuser or not, I was gaining speed, moving instinctively towards Industros Tragicos. Then I heard the pop of the bubble drones going off, and knew it could end badly. But I didn't stop.

I felt nothing as my feet pounded cold puddles, patches of snow, mud, wet dead weeds. I was possessed by one overpowering need - to get as far as possible from the goons, bubble drones, e-mag servo-whacko-wagons, whatever might chase me. Their cries to stop blended with the sounds of mucky running to form a dim background noise that seemed meaningless. I had no idea what I was doing. The sky got darker and many minutes passed before I actually realized what was happening.

-10-
"CONCENTRATION CAMPER'S DIARY
- DAY ONE"

It slowly dawned on me I'd been running hard and fast for a long time, with all my awareness focused only on my physical senses - not the goons. Primal animal exhilaration, with no pain. Beep-beep, out of my way! It was like running in a feelie-realie game. An old overgrown sidewalk, an e-mag path, a few somnab habs, and a weed field appeared and faded - all just props, parts of Escape From 838, Game Level One.

MUSIC SWELL - VERDI'S "AIDA" MARCH - UP AND UNDER

Stars swirled by in the dark, late afternoon sky, as the beat thundered on. The bubble drone, with its Surcord red eye, and the triggered servo wagon couldn't catch up with the action. The goons were out of reach but still in v-u. The pounding of my feet, the roar of air rushing in and out of my lungs, penetrated everything.

It seemed I could run in the dark without tripping or twisting my ankle, which brought on a strange instant physical recognition, like I could even close my eyes and pour it on.

"Fuck you, you sick fucks," I screamed at the goons in a hoarse screech.

I looked back, but one by one, the goons had dropped off or plopped to the ground holding their sides. The last one running got smaller and smaller then dropped to one knee. The red- eyed bubble floated closer, but slowly, just enough to make me keep running. A laugh jumped out, and I closed my eyes and ran harder.

I sprinted fast forward on mute, leaping over rocks, jumping over holes, like a wild animal in a nature spot. The goons and bubble drone faded into b-roll then were gone. And so were the bleeping, frizzing, burps and echoing shouts of the skull squares.

I could feel Industros Tragicos getting closer. A dirt path covered with crunchy leaves appeared, twisting into pinewoods. I followed it, and jogged in. There was no slush, no mud, inside the sheltering tree line.

Then just a few steps into the forest, fatigue slammed into me. My sides ached, my skin burned, there wasn't enough air. Unable to control myself, I slowed down, walked, then stopped and collapsed onto a bed of pine needles. My body heaved, squeezing out whimpers, invol emissions, exorcised demons. I quivered and shook as the reality of my run overtook everything, with cramps, spasms, chest pain, shortness of breath. Shit. I was going to fade to black.

FADE MUSIC UNDER

Pine needles poked through my tuni, stinging me everywhere. I was drenched with sweat. The goons had hurt me; there were big brown and blue bruises on my arms and ribs. My legs seemed crippled. My breath was coming back. Mucus drizzled from my nose. The odor of real pine trees was overwhelming, and different from K-factor pine scent. I was actually smelling, breathing, tiny particles of fragrance. I wasn't going to fade to black.

Some raggedy clouds tracked under the early moon and stars. My body was cooling down, but the breeze and ground felt strangely warm. The few wayward snowflakes that penetrated the grove evaporated midair. I knew I had to keep moving, but my muscles just weren't ready. All I could do was sit up.

A strong breeze shook the pines and late autumn oaks, startling me nekro. Bright, full moonlight filled the grove, though it was hard to see things in the shadows. Birds, maybe crows, cawed constantly. The forest was full of wind sighs and other nekro sounding noises, and everything quickly shaped up fearscape again. But I kept staring at the changing sky, waiting for enough strength to stand. The triangular blue light on my chest, my step light, had gone out.

Then the distinct odor of wood smoke, and food being cooked, filled the air. Then the sound of voices, singing. I struggled to make it out, and scanned around, but no go. My finger source was frizzing, too. Suddenly, some crushing inertia, a paralysis, began taking over my body. I couldn't keep my eyes open. Almost instantly, I fell into a big, deep, empty sleep.

Chilly wind rustled the leaves and woke me up. Morning light was creeping in. I remembered where I was and what had happened, and felt lost, scared, sick. I changed position to cover myself from the cold, and found myself at angle from under left - staring directly into the face of the most dangerous Weird, the Fire Inspector. He was leaning over me in extreme close-up. ECU, ECU.

"No!" I sputtered.

Two black, burned-in, hot-haloed lenses shined in his skull, under dark framed glasses. Those eyes could smear you into the unhouse, with one glance. They were weapons.

I was frozen in fear, transfixed.

"Oh, yes," he said in a deep voice, wearing a tombstone smile. "Si, si, si."

His nose was big, bony, slightly humped. Coarse dark hair bushed from his schnozzle and floppy-lobed ears. Shocks of black polyplast wig hair popped out from under his fireman's hat. His lean, middle-aged face was light olive, and needed a shave. His breath reeked of garlic.

The Inspector tracked back to a medium shot. His black, red, and yellow fireman's coat bore lettering - New Bedford VFD. The old-era coat looked authentic, but his fireman's hat looked like a child's toy. His body odor was a complex weave of gaggy aromas, a wild smell.

The Fire Inspector raised his thick, dark eyebrows and parted his full lips. He looked like Pete Numeros, the math teacher on the old era TV show, Toytown. Only possessed by demons. As he tracked back further, I could see sparkly little streamers of blue and pink light dancing around him. He touched his thumbs together, and framed my mug into a shot with his hands, like a director or advo. His movements were quick, frantic.

"What's it like living in a controlled environment?" the Inspector asked, interviewing me, pointing like an advo with a finger source. "How do you feel knowing your mind is controlled? What's it like being watched all the time?"

He spoke in a clipped singsong. His mature, mid-tenor voice had odd baritone dips and soprano peaks.

Everything was happening too fast. Where were the goons? Suddenly, I was in the nekro woods, in the F and D, with the Fire Inspector. I was frizzing and queasy, but felt I had to answer, to come back, somehow.

"Nine," I blurted out, without knowing why. "Nine is the answer. The number nine."

On cue, before I could ask myself what I meant, the Inspector's red fireman's hat rose and floated a few centimeters above his wig. Nine little fire hats burst from the back of his head, and vipped into orbit around it.

"Nine what?" he barked. "Nine what?"

"Who are you?" I asked, trying to comp like an advo. "Are you the math guy on Toy Town?"

The little hats disappeared. The wind went still, no sound from the trees, as the sun rose over the pines. A solitary beam shone on his spit-smeared face.

"Nine whaaaaaat?!" he bellowed.

"Purple moons," I said; not hats, not knowing why. "Lunatics."

He stared blankly. I pointed my finger source at him, but nothing came up. It was dead. Monkey-mocking, the Fire Inspector, pointed back at me. Then he pointed down. A jeri-era, small-screen TV appeared by his feet. The screen was gray, flickering a slow pulse hypno-pattern, maybe 7.83 Hz.

"Now watch!" he commanded. "Now watch!"

"How'd you do that?" I asked.

"Now watch!" he screamed.

I obeyed and looked at the screen. The voices I heard earlier were laughing. The screen's flicker rate increased, and my vision got blurry. The laughter cross-faded into soft murmurs. From the screen, male and female voices, in unison, recited the Neighbor's Prelude to the Advo's Credo.

"We are a tapestry of many cloths and colors, woven from bright light, illumined from within. We are information; protected by light bringers, who preside over heaven and earth, with gifts differing, in the grace that has been given them."

Immediately, nightmare visions with howling sound effects exploded across the screen, dear Neighbors and Associates, in a series of shots. All the horrors of the old era were replayed, in lucid, vivid, chroma-boing, like I was there, feelie-realie, Point A.

There was a scene of hundreds of corpses, and I could see myself as one of them, being bulldozed into a ditch. It was followed by a quick shot of rich diva-Janes and Joes on a yacht, watching air strikes on a coastal village, from a safe distance. I was one of them, too. Another shot showed my face among scores of starving, dying people.

The last scenes showed Bigs getting richer. It looked like footage from the days when NeighborWorld first got going, over a hundred seasons ago. My face vipped-up on a Grandee, stepping from a closed conference into a flurry of camera lights and questions from old-era journos. Then I saw my face on a protestor, being shot by policemen.

The murmurs outside my head grew louder, echoing into a babbling reverb. Suddenly, the screen disappeared completely, leaving me staring at the ground. Then, silence, except a little breeze. Leaves and pine needles were in my hair, nose, ears, everywhere.

I rubbed my eyes, looked up, and there was Francis The Sissy, gawking at me, his ECU mug at an angle from under, with a questioning look.

In a tattered pale blue watch cap, matching scarf, and green turtleneck sweater, Francis's face resembled a giant potato, with stubble. His chubby nose was crumpled in the middle, coated with bright red rosacea. A lack of teeth gave him a huge underbite, and twisted his chin to the right.

"Nem nem nem," he mumbled. "What're you doing way out here then?"

Francis covered his mouth with his hand and released a high pitched cackle. He smelled of rancid body odors and sweet perfume.

"I think I needed to talk to you some more," I said.

"Oh," Francis said sweetly, pleasantly surprised. Then he scratched his temple and struck a pensive mug. "I don't think you need to talk, nem nem nem. You need to listen and watch."

"Yessir, yessir, yessir," the Inspector repeated, moving into a close two shot. His eye whites popped around his glasses, tusky hair waved from his flared nostrils.

The murmuring voices faded into indistinct resonances in the air. Then the wind rose, covering everything in a rich hum. Thick, needly pine branches rubbed together in a dull crunch. Oak, hickory, maple, and elm limbs screeched, with the clattering of dead leaves. The sound swelled, then zoom faded, leaving faint, tinkling overtones. Francis disappeared, quick cut from the two shot, poof, into thin air.

The Fire Inspector's face zoomed into just a few centimeters above mine. His left eye darted as he surveyed me from extreme close-up.

"There's no use pretending," he bubbled. "We know who you think you are. But who are you, really?"

"My name's Standard Mozuck," I said. "I'm a NeighborWorld advo, step... uh... step..."

I pulled my step light from my tuni and looked at it. "Step three. Who are you?"

"That's just what we expected you'd say," the Fire Inspector chirped. "When you run from the suits, you need a more convincing story, and a better name. And right now, who I am is my business."

"Run from suits? How'd you know that? Have you seen them? Where are they?"

"Seen 'em come and go like a foul odor, Mr. Stand-In Muck-Duck," the fireman said authoritatively. "Don't worry. Your friends are afraid to shimmy down to our neck of the woods."

The Inspector struck a pose, standing with hands on hips, and a slit-eyed grin on his mug.

"They're not friends," I said. "They want to kill me."

"As far as we can tell," he came back, "they just want to beat you up for making them have to work. Chasing you made one of them puke, and one of them bubble things went the wrong way, so they're pissed off."

He stuck his index finger right up to my face, like he was taking everything down.

"Say," he spewed on. "Standing Duck is an Indian name, ain't it? You should mabble-cam with Seamus Singing Elk. Ever hear of him? He's a wise, powerful medicine man. For an unwise man, who needs powerful medicine. Sounds about right, don't it?"

"How do you know about all this?" I asked.

No response. He just showed amigo teeth and pointed his finger at me like an advo.

I tried to get up but my body seemed stuck. The Inspector looked on in amusement while I struggled to pull myself to my feet. My arms and legs didn't obey; they were numb, drained of power.

"Standing Duck means a duck who is too full of shit to fly," he said.

The sound of laughing voices started again, jamming into an overpowering blur. Then it faded into a ticklish buzz.

"What is that?" I asked, starting to fear-frizz. "What's that noise?"

Again no answer.

I saw a flash of light out of the corner of my eye, an opening in my visual periphery. And instantly, there they were. About a dozen children, of every age, ethno, and gender, buzzing around me, humming a nekro sounding tune. They surrounded me 360, in a circle. Then they stopped humming and began chanting, pointing their fingers at my chest.

"Get up, get up, get up!" they repeated.

The ground began glowing in soft white. The glow spread up my legs, into my body. Then, all together, the kids laughed.

Zoom, my body shot upwards, three meters in the air. I screamed and blew out bleeps. From my vantage point I could see a long, straight, manicured, perfectly carved path through the forest, stretching out below. My stomach was churning. I hovered there, and the brats started snapping their fingers. Then, still in the air, I slid down the path, yelling and flapping my arms. The snot faced flock rushed after me.

"No! Stop!" I pleaded. "Let me down!"

They laughed. They seemed to be carrying me with some energy they shared, and the laughter was the conductor. Their wild sweat smell blended with the pine scent of the woods. It made me nauseous. Maybe it was dizziness, from being in the air. I passed out.

FADE TO BLACK - SWIRL FADE TO REOPEN SCENE

Describing a place you've entered while unconscious is tricky. When you come to, all the shapes and colors of the furniture and settings blurt out their identity without intro. Everything just suddenly appears, too much for the puny skull source to animix. I was on my back on a couch, groggy and unfocused. My neck tingled. The air was cool, humid. There was a loud electrical buzz close by. I looked around, trying to comp like an advo.

The wide shot scanned alien-times turf. I was on a rumpled, red and gold divan, next to a noisy, 1970's refrigerator. Half of the room's walls were slag stone, and the other half concrete block, all sandy beige, with geometric designs painted on them. A dim, old-era light bulb dangled from the ceiling, over a roughly rigged-up table of dense, green, unmilled wood. The smooth stone floor was covered with bright, Native Am style rugs. A large whisk broom leaned against the stone wall across from me. Above it was an old-era clock, stopped at 12:13.

"Coo-coo," I said out loud.

I was in a cellar. A big, deep, dimly lit cellar; oblong in shape, looking hand dug six hundred seasons ago. Two stone steps descended into a small hollow in the oblong's curved corner.

"Hey! Anybody here?" I shouted.

Standing up, still panning the room, I noticed a blotch of light seeping in from a transparent block laid in the wall, way up high. I scanned around for a door, but no go.

"You lookin' for a way out?" asked a husky, nasal, male voice. The voice had an indigenous, Native Am flavor.

The voice came from the shadows near the wall, out of the glare of the light bulb. I narrowed my focus to source, then the whole full shot blasted up in front of me. An American Indian medicine man, sitting in a cross-legged shaman-like pose. Almost like a canned shot, all rustic and historical drop-in.

The shaman's longish black hair was pulled back by a white cloth headband with multi-colored, beaded symbols sewn into it. A white feather was tucked into the headband. His blue jeans and long buckskin moccasins bore more sewn-in symbols. A beaded, three-hands-big buckskin bag lay at his feet. His unbuttoned, blue and white-trimmed cowboy shirt had only one symbol; the whirlpool design Nogo and I saw on the wall in Industros Tragicos.

A necklace of dried plants, both leaves and roots, rested on his bare chest. The mug shot showed a clean-shaven, bronze complexion, classical features, a few wrinkles under large hazel brown eyes. Light from the transparent block above crept over his head, illuminating the mug shot.

"Who are you, Neighbor?" I asked, frizzing incred.

"You're seeing it right," he replied. "I'm a medicine man. Indidge, Original, whatever. Have a seat."

He gestured to a spot on the floor in front of himself. Taken by the mystery, I sat down quickly. A closer look revealed who he really was - Paul Greyleaf, the underground comic, long gone fly. Or, as the Inspector called him, Seamus Singing-Elk. Unlike the others, he didn't stink.

"Where's the Fire Inspector? Where's Francis?" I asked.

"Francis is out picking mushrooms and herbs for his birthday party," he answered. "And the Inspector is mowing my lawn. I hope."

"Where are we?" I asked, trying to comp. "There aren't any doors. How do we get out of here?"

"This is my kiva," he said with a proud smile. "Built it myself. Nice, eh? I built a sweat lodge, too."

Then, from out of nowhere, with one hand, the shaman produced a fistful of smoldering herbs. With his other hand, he took the feather from his headband, and waved smoke into my face with it. It smelled like some spice, maybe cinnamon.

"What the hell?" I asked, all frizzing and incred. "Did you chroma-key that? Is there a green screen here?"

He frowned. A sharp wind whistled through the exitless cavern, like the intro tag for a Yaqui Sunset spot. Cobwebs flipped by, dust swirled. The sound of a medicine rattle shished through the wind.

"I ain't gonna bullshit ya," the original said in his smoky drawl. "I got no clue. This place is spooked. Still got some kinks to work out. But don't worry, we'll be leaving soon. So just relax. We can get acquainted and talk about things."

The wind stopped. The smoldering plants disappeared.

"What things? What do you want to talk about?" I asked, staring at his empty hands.

"What brings you here?" Singing Elk asked, all amigo curious. "You looking for something?"

"I was running from goons, who wanted to make me a prisoner," I answered. "And now I'm your prisoner, right?"

"No, no. You're safe." he said, shaking his head. "But why did you run to us?" He mugged dopey like the Dave smear, then asked, "Were you looking for a good time?"

"Was that supposed to be funny?" I shot back. "Are you a comedian, a comic?"

There was recognition in his eyes, and a malignant smile, but no break from interrogation mode.

"Were you running from life?" he asked, still smiling, reaching into his shirt pocket and retrieving a crumpled piece of paper. "Some folks think life is hell." He looked at the paper, then put it back in his pocket.

"Hell is not knowing what's going on here," I said.

"You've incarnated, on the earth plane," he deadpan droned, folding his hands. "Your sorry-assed soul took the plunge for life on earth. Ergo, Standard Mozuck. If that is your real name. Of course your parents were involved, too. You do know about that part, don't you?"

Before I could pan his material, he produced the smoldering herbs again, and wafted more aromatic smoke in my face.

"But what are you doing here?" he persisted.

"Why are you doing this?" I skwacked, waving away the smoke. "I ran from a good gig to save you people, and you treat me like interrog. Can't you just let me know what's going on?"

"Aha!" he said, as the herbs disappeared. "You came here to save us people. Good answer. Now here's your answer. If I knew what was going on, I'd tell you. But right now in this neck, us people are nervous about conjecturing with strangers."

The parlor tricks, the confusing patter, were frizzing me. In the cool, humid room, I felt parched. I looked over at the refrigerator and imagined ice water.

"How long before we break the set? I'm a busy man. I'm a fan of native schtick, but this is going nowhere. Plus, I think I'm dehydrated. Can I get a drink of water?"

The indidge smiled, then reached behind his back. Instantly he produced a large, yellow, dried gourd bearing clear water. I seized it and drank like a marathon runner, spilling while gulping it down. Cool, delicious. I gave the gourd back, hoping for more. He put it behind his back, it quick-vipped into zero space. He said nothing. I said nothing.

The shaman glared at me with an impatient pout, then rummaged through his beaded buckskin bag. He pulled out a long wooden stemmed pipe, and held it forth in an offering gesture, with eyes closed, mumbling something. The pipe had a reddish brown bowl, with beautiful eggshell blue spots. I looked at it in awe, smiling. He stuck it right in my face.

"Smoke," he said. "It's one of my backyard blends. I call it Truth Thunder. A little salvia, cannabis, magic mushroom, red willow bark, other things. Smoke it."

I didn't know what all those herbs were. But to bring light to the smalls and the strange rituals of the Weirds into focus, I took a puff and held it in, like with Bob Sideways. Then, handed back the pipe and released the smoke, a dirty, tongue-coating taste.

Boom, there was a shattering clap of loud thunder, right in that little room. A green, sulfurous-smelling haze arose before my nose, pushing my head back from the stink. The room started spinning, everything looked kaleidoscoped. My head throbbed. I thought the shaman was trying to kill me.

The instant that thought came up, the haze ended, and the room smelled sweet, like fruit and spices. Seamus Singing Elk smiled, wide eyed. Suddenly there were four doors in that room, dear N's and A's, with big bronze knobs, one on each side and each end. They opened a bit, banged shut, and disappeared.

A small fired-clay doll-like figure, half a meter tall, popped up where each door had been. Each doll wore a red tunic, with a different yellow symbol. Their faces were wooden masks, hand carved into grotesque expressions, like the faces in my nightmares.

"We don't use wires," he said. "There's no set, no green screen, no tech."

"Ok, ok, I'm sorry," I said, groveling in fear-frizz.

"I've been focusing on the Four Winds Path lately," he said, in a forced modest tone.

The dolls turned blue and evaporated into zero space, like the water gourd and doors. Singing Elk paused to slow-drag me into close-up, then pointed at me with his pipe.

"You show promise," he said. "I see potential. You have big ears."

I instinctively grabbed my ears.

"What does that mean? I've got medium sized ears."

From somewhere, Native Am drum singing began pulsing through the cellar.

"Don't worry, you've got standard sized ears, just like your name," he said. "It means you're always listening, you hear things. But you're a boxhead. Promising, but still a boxhead."

"You can hear the drum singing?" he added.

I nodded. He smiled.

"Good," he said in helpful older brother mode. "Just something to help you relax and focus, like the smudge."

"Changing the sound track changes the meaning of visual information,"

I said. "Advo rule numero uno."

"So, you know how the mind uses the sense organs to create reality?" he asked like a teacher.

"Well, as an advo, I have some working opinions," I said. "But I don't …"

"Do names like Shushumna, Tao, Pillar Of Equilibrium, or Serpent Path mean anything to you?" he interrupted.

"What? I think one of them is from yoga."

"Can you feel your brain? Can you ignore verbal delusion and shut off thought?" he asked hopefully.

"I don't think so," I said. "I'm not sure. What does that have to do with anything?"

"Oh boy," he said, shaking his head in disappointment. "Just another boxhead."

He lowered his eyes, looking distracted.

"The other ones who made it to our chicken neck weren't just boxheads," he said. "They were morally defective."

"Who?" I asked. "Where are they?"

"They croaked," he said without emotion. "Maybe they'll have cleaner spirits when they reincarnate. If not, we're dealing with the evil ones."

The Elk shrugged, then scanned me seriously, searching into my eyes for a reaction of fear.

"Who are the evil ones?" I repeated.

The claustro-zamp was suffocating me. I wanted out.

"Soul suckers," he said, plucking an herb flower from his chest. He bit into it, chewed, swallowed. "When they die, they haven't learned anything, so they get reborn quickly. But they still don't get it. Kind of like spiritual repeat offenders. They knock the world out of balance. So we put it back in balance."

Singing Elk, Greyleaf, picked on a tooth with his pinkie finger.

"Just like ants fixin' an ant hill, eh, Standing Duck?"

Evil ones? Soul suckers? Was my career made, or what? My head felt hot. The room suddenly looked much bigger, and the atmo felt all goo-gooey. Then the kiva appeared smaller, and the claustro grew threatening. We looked at each other in silence. Singing Elk made thumb gestures, scribbled lines in the air, drew signets of confusion, sigils of fear. Truth Thunder.

"Were they advos?" I asked, afraid of the answer.

The drumming and singing stopped abruptly. The singers shouted "Hu!"

"No, they were the ones you called goons," he grunted. "They've been coming here for too long. We had to hold up the mirror."

"The mirror? What does that mean?"

"The mirror is a balancing tool," he said. "It prevents people from doing evil things."

His words came to life in my mind, with advo's directions. Fade in scary music, dissonant string quartet. Fade in feelie-realie gooseflesh.

"Wanna see the dead goons?" the Elk asked in a hoarse whisper. "See what the mirror can do?"

I remembered my grandpa's funeral. He was on one holo-screen, pre-recorded alive, feelie-realie, with the smell of K-factor funeral flowers. My mom and dad and sister cried and stared in anguish, feelie-realie, on other screens.

"Flesh and dirt? Real dead guys?" I asked with a lump in my throat. "I don't think so."

"What?" he asked, astonished. "An advo who doesn't want to v-u the hard and cold?"

Weirds were primitive culture stack. They loved visceral stuff, like all wild people did. But maybe it was a quick way out, through one of those doors.

"I don't want to," I said, unconsciously covering my eyes and rubbing them. "But as an advo, I have to."

I uncovered my eyes and looked down at the floor, then gazed around the exitless basement cell, at the walls, the lightbulb. My idea of time; then, now, and shaping up, was meaningless to the medicine man. He saw time as moments strung together on a mobius necklace. How long had I been here?

"First, what did those kids do to me?" I asked, trying to rebound into advo mode.

"They took you for a toboggan ride," he answered. "Fun, isn't it? More fun for people of great intellect, though. Our appreciation is finer."

.Singing Elk pointed to a spot on his breastbone under his necklace, smiled, coughed lightly, then spat. The saliva evaporated the instant it hit the ground.

"No, I mean, is my mind being controlled?" I asked, confused, but still trying to work.

"You can hear the subliminal squares, you know you're whispered-in," he answered flatly. "Not many people can nowadays, especially advos."

"Are you whispering-in?" I pressed. "Isn't a break-in mind control? Isn't all this mind control?"

"I'm not controlling your mind," Seamus said indignantly. "I control my own mind, and create reality for all to share."

His face grew angrier, until it finally resembled one of the doll masks.

"NeighborWorld controls minds," he blistered, pointing at me. "It makes people slaves."

He smiled abruptly, a puma cat smile.

"That's why I joined these Weird sons of bitches. To destroy

NeighborWorld."

He paused, freezing the wildcat grin, proud to be a dangerous malco.

"You'll see," he said. "Come on! Let's go look at the dead goons!"

The drum singing started pounding in my ears, the chanting, "We-ter, we-ter, eh, we-ha." There was a strong, sage-like herb smell everywhere. Either the original was controlling my mind, or I was growing courage. I rose to my feet. My mouth tasted bitter, the right side of my head felt fuzzy.

Singing Elk stood up, tilted his head, and thumb pointed at my backdrop. "Hey, look behind you," he said.

Splatto, all across my entire field of vision, the Fire Inspector's face screamed into my skull, a full frontal nose-haired attack. I reflexively jerked away from him. He smelled like very old, dirty laundry.

"Standard Muck Duck! Hiya, hiya, hiya!" he whooped.

Then he stood back a pace and source pointed in my face, a perfect bust shot. The drum singing faded under. The Inspector's huge poly fire boots squeaked as he stepped back towards me. He patted my shoulder with one hand, and held out his other to shake.

"Shake, Senor Pato Erecto. But not too hard, or you'll crack the floor."

I shook his hand.

"Ayyy!"

My palm tingled with a mild shock

"Sucker!" he snorted, wearing an ugly grin.

A clown with a joy buzzer. What a find, a personality package not seen for one hundred and twenty seasons. He probably had old-era scopes that gave you a black eye. A lethal one.

"Mabble, mabble, mabble," he gobbled like a turkey. "You and Seamus must be getting close to the secret of secrets, uncovering the mystery everyone's dying to find out about. Literally dying."

He winked at the Elk.

"I took care of them weeds in your yard," he added.

Seamus shook his head disapprovingly, waving his hand in front of his face in a squelch-frizz gesture.

"He said he ran from a good gig to save us," the Elk said quickly.

My knees got weak.

"Listen," I said. "I'm not worth killing. No one likes me back there, so it wouldn't help you. Besides, I don't know where I am, or what's going on, so I can't give anything away. Please."

The mabble-mouth and the beaded original looked at each other and smiled.

"Advo Standard is afraid of us," said Seamus.

"Don't fret, student monkey," the Inspector said, source-pointing at me. "We got bigger plans for you."

Then, on cue and mark, the shaman pulled the wrinkled paper from his shirt pocket, examined it again, and put it away. The fireman looked at an old wristwatch, then at me.

"Step lightly when the train's a-movin'," the Inspector said, rubbing his palms together gleefully. "Once she's gone, she's gone."

The fireman took a step, his fireman's boot squeaked; then he spazz-darted towards the end of the long oblong chamber, followed woozily by his pink and blue light streams.

"Here's the real door," he yelled, his voice and squishy footsteps panning, padding, fading out of range.

The range of illusions the wireless Weirds were capable of was incred. For all I knew, these guys were feelie-realie holozigs. Not sure if there was indeed an opening in this mineshaft of hallucinations, I shut off and followed him, with the shaman close behind.

As we got to the rounded depression at the end of the room, it suddenly appeared almost convex, as if something was pushing through the surface. The Inspector pointed at it, and released a tirade of head-wounded blither.

"Sheep flick gumbo double! Bone garden scroll bludgeon! Turgid gospel hog jelly!" he shouted. "Behold, I am vile in your sight, yet I seek honkmah! I'm the goose that laid the golden op. My gonads are swollen. Let me out!"

The shaman laughed, grasping his medicine bag with one hand, scratching his head with the other.

Suddenly, an enormous wooden door, like the ones banging on their hinges before, appeared in front of the Fire Inspector. It swung open. He hopped in on one foot, then looked back, mugging teeth.

"All aboard," he sang out.

Then the Elk yelled, "Let's go! Train's leaving." He rushed past me and jumped in after.

I took a tenuous step forward, crouching, to keep from hitting my head on a door that might be holozig or hallucination. A Weird sound track started, like the drum singing; a jeri-era big band imitating a steam locomotive. Presto, I found myself in a long natural hallway. The corridor's ceiling and floor were sandy pink rock, glazed with opalescent, pearly cream. Sharp, green stained, mineral formations jutted from the walls on either side. I had to run, struggling frantically to keep up with the shaman and the fireman. The sound of our loud footsteps echoed everywhere. Darkness at the corridor's end beckoned all gloomy, fast forward, subjective eye.

"Laugh, idiot," the Elk said, turning to face me while still running. "Laugh! We're in a hurry!"

The choo-choo train music swelled.

Why? Would laughing make the trip more pleasant? Then the Inspector yammered a few tenor chuckles, joined by the Elk in a bass key. They were both pointing at their breastbones. Then I laughed - at them. Boom, it happened, that unmistakable feeling of levitation. Laughter was the conductor. Down the hall we zoomed.

-11-
"THE MIRROR"

Dear N's and A's, if you've bought this far, please stay connected-in, because the truly incred, spooky feelie-realie begins now. We zoomed down the rocky hall into an entirely different world. We were spat out of the natural corridor into the air, over a wooded park, all green and spring focus. The music stopped. We fell.

The Inspector laughed and flailed, running, swimming, mid-air. The original held forth his hands in an offering gesture and chanted. I just screamed, and careened towards the ground.

We hit the grassy warm earth with force, to the sound of a loud thump, but we landed without a scratch. Mind control, break-in, drug hallucination, dream? Insanity? Seamus and the Inspector rose up, dusted off the dirt, and began babbling.

"Welcome to the house of horribles," gleamed the Inspector, indicating with the sweep of his hand. "Just walk along with a sorrowful look, and we'll give ya the gruesomes."

I stood up, and tried to attune to the remarkably smooth flop.

"Appear amazed and repentant for our camera crew," the medicine man said.

The Inspector source-pointed at me.

"Why is it so warm?" I asked. "Are we outside?"

Green-leaved trees and tall bushes enclosed the shot. Birds twittered. The sky was mid blue, but there was no real horizon, no trace of the sun.

"Is this place enviro, or feelie-realie, or...?"

"Shhh..." the medicine man interrupted, raising an index finger to his lips. "There's evil spirits in this place."

He looked at me tentatively, then at the Inspector. Some birds tweeted, a dog barked, there was the sound of a distant conversation. The shaman and fireman laughed.

The Inspector put one hand over his heart, and pointed in the direction we were walking with the other. "Welcome to Summerland," he said reverently. "Where incorrect intent and action get their payback. Day after day."

"It's for our children," Seamus said sweetly, making the sign of horns with his index and little fingers.

A pair of swallows dived between us, shocking me, causing no reaction from them. A euro-ish little girl with long auburn pigtails, one of the levitation kids, walked by, holding red, yellow, and blue balloons. A brown haired, afri-ish teenaged boy wearing a t-shirt with the whirlpool logo approached us. He stopped, looked right at me, and then ran away.

"It's like a museum," Seamus continued. "A place where they can learn about the mirror."

The mirror. I looked down at the wound on my hand I got while snooping at Bob's hideout, and remembered the broken glass. Goons must have been nosing around, and ran into the mirror. Which was probably an elaborate parametric protection system, which could have killed me, too.

"Yes, Mister Advo Duck," the Inspector said with satisfaction, "In the old days we wandered around in tin foil hats, with luggage and small furniture on our backs. But now, look around. We have a beautiful place, where people can enjoy nature, and learn."

A vivid shot came up in my mind, of the fireman under a flaming red sky, leading scores of bedraggled people, like Moses.

We continued walking, towards an old-era playground; with swings, jungle-gyms, merry-go-rounds, the whole jeri look. Before getting close enough to scan it, the fireman halted abruptly, then the shaman. With a grandiose gesture, the Inspector cued up a large rock lying on the ground with his pointy finger.

"Beneath that stone is the stone cold truth of what your murderin' info-goons have been up to," he said in a low rasp.

He paused and looked sourly at me, his first genuinely nekro mug. Then he removed his fireman's hat and placed it on his chest. With a somber look, he lifted his eyes upwards.

"Jesus H. Christ rolled away the stone, so that we all may live again," he said dramatically.

The Inspector and witch doctor stepped aside, and stared intently at the rock. The shimmer was dull on the psi fireworks, so I stepped aside too, and awaited the eruption of the stone from its seat. I ducked.

"Don't duck! Push!" the shaman scolded. "Push the damn rock away! We're waiting."

Real funny guys. I moved towards the rock, resigned to be a dummy box for an obscure old-era kids' TV personality and a former cult comic. For the sake of a gold op spot, or a nekro m-line, once again I obeyed.

"But may these bastards never live again, anywhere but hell!" the Inspector cried out in a sharp, pained howl. Then he made the sign of the cross, said "Amen," and put his hat back on.

"A-mental case," the shaman said, twirling his finger around his ear, making the sign of the crazy.

"Thank you, Paul," the Inspector said. "For helping teach this young man."

Like a dupe novice, I got down, slung my culo in a low arc, thrust my hands on the rock, braced my shoulders, and pushed. The rock popped from its seat, leaving me flat on my stomach, with my lungs empty, gasping. A perfectly circular opening to an underground cavern, about three meters wide, appeared where the rock had been. A dim, bluish light emanated from inside, forcing me to shield my eyes.

"Go on in," the Inspector urged, staring at me with a raised eyebrow.

"Go on, advo," the shaman commanded. "Go inside."

Nekro chilled and fear frizzing, I declined. Seamus looked at me with disappointment. The fireman shook his head disapprovingly and his boots squealed. Then they both jumped in and disappeared, to the sound of a muted pop. Suddenly alone, I didn't know what else to do. I popped into the blue light, and landed on a small platform inside.

A long playground slide extended from the platform, emptying into a cavernous, well- lit set with a vaulted ceiling. The light was full 360 source, and the walls vibrated in fallopian colors; red, fleshy pink, and slender veiny blues, like the inside of a womb. The Weirds were at the bottom of the slide, waving at me. I hopped on, and swooshed down.

"Careful," the Inspector said, greeting me, grinning slyly from a bust shot. "Viewer discretion. Adult content."

Then, dear Neighbors, what a grim visage to greet the naked eye. Up close, the place looked like some old-era wax museum chamber of horrors. The viewing area was only about ten meters wide, with a black poly-tile floor. On pedestals spaced a meter apart, were scenes, lit displays, enclosed in transparent walls. As I approached the first one, it played, like a feelie-realie holo-zig, in flow-through animix, in the now, Point A.

In the first diorama, a purple hat band-looking Surcord goon was about to zap some young Weird sister's brain with a frying pan. Suddenly he slipped, and the lit taser crossed his forehead, cooking his skull. He rolled down the hill. Unaware of the goon's undoing, she skipped happily away.

Immediately it replayed. Throughout the entire holo-zig, Seamus and the Inspector peered over my shoulder. I moved on to the next holo-zig diorama.

In it, a goon was shown climbing over rocks in a wooded park. About twenty meters below him six Weirds dined al fresco. The goon pointed his zapper at them, then tripped, falling, breaking his neck. Unaware, the picnickers kept eating, until one child looked away, sensing something. This registered. They walked over to look at the goon.

Then the entire holo-zig replayed. I moved on to another display.

In this one, three tough looking goons pursued a teenaged boy, running into medium close-up. The kid veered left, into a long shot. The shot tilted up as they ran towards a deep gully. The kid bounded over it easily. All three goons tried, knocking into each other. An overhead shot showed them slipping into the gully; yelling, striking the bottom. Alive, but with the wrong bones broken, they groaned, bleeped, begged for aid. The kid reached to help, but a goon tried to pull him down. The teen slithered from his grasp, and ran off source. The goons howled in agony, faded to black slowly.

Then the scene replayed. I heard the sound of the Inspector behind me, weeping.

"Terrible, ain't it?" the Inspector sobbed softly in my ear.

Phony tears spurted from the tops of crying-clown glasses, a great package from psi-fi hell. He was mocking Biff's rain dances. He had probed my stacks, and viewed my memories.

"Yeah," I said.

The old dicks would say, the truth burns like bad whiskey. It was nekro focus on all monitors. The goons were dead.

No, it was just an animixed holo-zig, and Weirds could make you believe whatever they wanted. The mirror was just another illusion.

Truth did more than burn. It incinerated, evaporated, obliterated. Were we not in material reality, which cannot be changed by mind?

"Hey, advo," Singing Elk said. "Stop thinking so hard. You're burning a hole in the wall."

"Pay attention!" the Inspector yipped. "Look at these here fake tear squirters. Took me two damn days to rig them up, and you don't even care!"

I was in one of my nightmares, forced to view the hideous.

"Let's look at more dead guys," Seamus ventured, all nekro teeth. "Sooner or later we'll find one that scares the shit out of you."

The place's womb-like walls looked garish, grotesque. There was a smell that reminded me of blood, and the same weakness and shortness of breath as after my run from the goons. I got the message.

"Why do you want to scare me?" I asked.

"To show you that Mother Earth protects her own," the shaman said with an angry bite.

"The mirror's a beautiful thing," the Inspector said. "A three-in-one tool that carves, dices, and slices, with no mess."

The shaman chuckled. They were clown witches, reshaping reality with mind, flying, joking, spooking, maybe even killing, in an old-era style nightmare.

"Hey, hey Seamus," the Inspector added. "Standard's thinking about his dreams. He don't know he's lucky to have his own dreams."

He paused, gazing at me warmly, toying with a frond of nasal hair. His boots squeaked as he shifted his weight from foot to foot.

"What about my dreams?" I asked. "Are you controlling people's dreams?"

"See? He thinks we've been controlling his dreams," the original said with contempt. "If it wasn't for us, he wouldn't have any of his own dreams. He don't even know he ain't the real MC."

"The real MC of what?" I asked. "How do you know about my

dreams?"

"The indigenous people were very big on dreams," the Elk mused, eyes fixed on some historical distance. "The Sonoi had 200 dream classifications. They got advice in dreams, learned secrets, received wisdom. Think of what a top-juice advo asshole like you could do with dream knowledge."

"Cut the happy horse shit, Paul," the pyrophile said bluntly. "Tell 'im what's up."

The shaman gave the fireman a faint smile and turned to me, scanning deep.

"You work for monsters," the Elk said slowly, savoring each word. "Monsters who totally control your consciousness."

He kept looking right into my eyes, and brought up his wildcat grin.

"So we had to rescue you," he said. "In your dreams."

"You rescued me in dreams?"

"We called and you came," said the shaman.

The walls began throbbing slowly, pacing into a steady heartbeat, the only sound track.

"What do you mean by MC? To me it's the host, the set-up guy for a spot," I said. "How could you rescue me in a dream?"

The Inspector's heavy fireman boots squeaked as he rocked back on his heels in time to the pulse.

"Hah!" he laughed. "You're a host, alright! You set them up, and they set you up! Hah!"

He stopped laughing and looked at me, waiting for me to get it.

"Mind control. MC means mind control, ya dolt!" he rattled, all full of feisty teeth.

"Audio signals are hot, video signals cold," said Seamus, stepping closer. "Audio attacks emotions. Video, critical belief systems. It's your sex-death formula, the subliminal squares, whispering-in, all of it."

Advos used these principles daily. I was immune. It didn't make sense.

"But if I was mind controlled, how could I escape and wind up here?" I came back.

"Hmmm," the Inspector offered, rubbing his unshaven chin.

"You said you wanted to save us," the Elk said enthusiastically. "So we let it happen. The goon gear don't work too good around here, as you can see. It glitches, and goes against 'em. But we didn't control you. We invited you. And you came of your own free will."

The Inspector nodded in agreement.

"The minute you ran from NeighborWorld, you were free," the pyro said, twirling his finger in the air. "Running away broke the link. It automatically triggered repressed abilities in you, and a repressive reaction from goon central."

On their own cue, they looked at each other with pained expressions, then at me.

"We broke into your Home prepro to show you censored old-era footage," the pyro said. "We been watching you for a while."

"We were looking for someone in your world we could parlay with," Seamus said sheepishly. "You advos are so MCed, we thought it might be impossible. But you could be the one."

"We're sorry we had to do that," the Inspector said with an embarrassed look.

So the Weirds had broken into my Home prepro. They called me. Maybe they were vipping squares into my skull, violating my sacred, not the G-O. Maybe they called those goons, too.

"The mirror is your defense system," I said, starting to fear-frizz again. "You use psi ability to discover evil intention or something. But I've always been in control of my own mind."

"Not in years," Seamus said, pulling a dried herb from his chest. "Maybe never."

The fireman nodded again. Seamus crunched the herb and waved it under my nose; a sweet but pungent aroma.

"I whisper-in what they tell me, and it works for the average Neighbor," I said blankly. "The signpost up ahead. Pinpoint means evolution. Everyone is information."

"You're all yakking artichokes," the fireman said.

"You live in a mind control prison," Seamus said. "That's why you can't do what we can. Our minds are free."

"We're a brotherhood," I continued. "We work for the global Neighborhood."

It sounded stupid. I felt shame. Tears welled in my eyes.

"There, there," the Inspector said in a sarcastic-sounding, comforting tone. "It must be tough, learning your info-scam brotherhood is just a mind and evolution control tool. And probably a front for some secret society, too."

The fireman raised an eyebrow. Seamus narrowed his focus, looking right into my eyes. The womb walls pulsed.

"But I'm an advo," I said, wiping tears. "Advos bring hush mode cults into focus, shine the light on them, ECU."

"Listen, boxhead," Seamus said, chuckling. "Just because you uncover a few secret societies doesn't mean others don't still exist."

"You're paranoid," I said.

"It's not paranoid to know the powerful secretly control minds and evolution," the Elk said.

"What about them splicers with the nice jewelry?" the Inspector asked, waving a ring finger. "What's their little secret?"

"Your techno-media superstate creates paranoia, so folks don't know what's real," the Elk concluded. "It's all lies, info-scam, to control them."

"But you can't lie to people forever," the Inspector added with a threatening tone.

He source-pointed, scrutinizing me with a distant look, then shook his head.

"I can see you still don't understand why we would never Spotlight, or join your Neighborhood, or be any part of your info-scam," he said.

"NeighborWorld doesn't help people evolve or live better," Seamus scolded, waving his hand. "It just jerks off their nervous systems when they should be seeking their true natures."

I was zoombie to their jango, totally accepting, and depressed. The Weirds had penetrated my stacks, and the nex was wide open. One thing seemed certain. This goose would never lay the gold op. These folks would never Spotlight gooey in the right. And I would never see the advo gig the same.

"The key to evolution isn't technology," Seamus continued. "It's the teachings. Tech changes. The teachings never change."

"The mirror is a beautiful thing," the Inspector said with a grin. "Beautiful."

In synchro-cue, the chamber got darker. Crushing stillness moved through the room, forcing us all into awkward freeze-frame. I had a feeling a bunch of those Weird kids were watching, invisible.

"My diaper's full," the Inspector said, looking sadly at the ground.

"Mission accomplished," the shaman said, nodding in agreement.

"There's only one way out," said the Inspector, shuffling slowly towards a plainly marked exit, near the last, omitted display. "And I'm the only one who knows it."

"Amen-tal case," Seamus said, holding his nose with one hand and making the sign of the crazy with the other.

The shaman placed his hand on the fireman's shoulder. The pyro-freak mumbled incoherently and made oblique gestures, his pink and blue streamers glimmered weakly.

"I lift my face to the invisible sun, for an invisible tan," the fireman muttered. "Beauty's only skin deep. By Fool's Day, everyone will glow."

They walked to the exit. I followed my witch clown masters, a crazy man in a volunteer fireman's outfit and a comic turned shaman, without understanding them. I lowered my eyes in humility, and relinquished my personality.

- 11-B-ROLL -
"SOULFUL RENDITION"

We marched through the exit, down another hall carved into stone. Then we turned right, directly into another dim, musty smelling room. The room was lit only by a relic from an old-era carnival midway; a Spanish Lady lamp, resting on a nightstand. The lamp had wide pink skirts as its base, with a light bulb stuck in black, lofty hair, which grew into an aqua blue lampshade. Next to the night table stood two ceramic flamingoes covered with blue and pink sequins. This was the fireman's basement. The Weird underground was connected cellars.

The light from the lamp quavered, creating wraith-like after-images. It was bright enough to make out more things; a card table, an old fashioned refrigerator with a heraldic insignia. The concrete block walls were dirty, painted urine yellow. A decrepit blue sofa, pocked with holes, rested against one wall. Against another wall sat an ancient TV set with a rabbit's ear antenna. The floor was gray cement, covered in places with throw rugs. Almost hidden, close to the farthest wall, was an old-era ping-pong table.

"Wait here, advo," Seamus said. "You need to learn more."

"Now watch!" the Inspector commanded, pointing at me, then at the TV.

"We don't use wires," Seamus repeated.

"Where are you going?" I asked, starting to fear-frizz again.

"Time for a change!" they both shouted, holding aloft clenched fists. They hustled off shot, and disappeared.

The TV turned itself on, flickering in black and white. Scenes began playing, with classical music and a Voice-Over, but the shots were incongruous, none of it made any sense. Still, I plopped down on the sofa, and watched. Fuzzy images marched across the screen, backlit with ultra-white. Occasionally an image broke up, but retained persistence of vision. So I went with the flickering scenes, unconcerned about whether they were cross fades into higher consciousness, or Weird mind control. It scanned like early videotape. The crawl on the screen bottom was from a jeri-era workplace video, possibly some kind of research lab log.

The words MC-ORDO flashed across top screen-right, then reappeared and settled into the bottom left corner of the screen. The words ULTRA and BLACK vipped in a few times. Then the screen gray wiped, and a new scene popped up.

It didn't look like a lab; it looked like an old-era apartment. Inside, a pale, dark haired man paced around a dining room table, picked up a calendar and looked at it, then walked to a phone. He picked up the receiver then put it down. He smiled, frowned, held his hands over his eyes.

He sat down, then sobbed and moaned.

Audio mastered to nova standard, it still had an old-era field mike flavor, with the ambient sound of tears striking paper, distant music, birds, old-era machinery in the background, cars, busses, trucks, water pipes groaning from the other apartments. I was witnessing case history footage from someone's nervous breakdown. The cold, clinical package made it more disturbing. The camera had the early covert surveillance look down. It was ugly. Frizzing from anxiety, I kept watching.

A fast pan of the guy showed him blowing his nose with an athletic sock and talking to himself.

"Please stop popping me," he wailed, like his soul was threatened. "Stop popping me."

The guy rubbed his hand against his forehead, his eyes gazed aimlessly, busy with internal sights.

"Pop goes the weasel, pop goese the weasel," he repeated.

He paused, and then grabbed a razor knife from a table near the phone. He unclicked the razor from its sheath, and with his face suddenly rearranged all berzerko, began slashing his arms and abdomen. Luckily the screen quickly faded to black. It also was like feelie-realie Point A, like I was right there with the guy, present tense.

Dear Neighbors, the next scenes came up even more feelie-realie. A metal insect appeared on screen, a combination floating camera and hypodermic, suspended on a mesh of grid white, on a cool green background. In the days before NeighborWorld, the meanie-monks and goonies boffed with biochems, drugs made in factories. More ugliness was on the way. A buzz-hop music track faded up and under.

"The MC Ordo Suspension Remote is a high resolution videotronic surveillance monitor," a flat female Voice-Over intoned. "Dynamistic Laboratories has taken the future one step further, with our new suspension remote. Complete with observation components, the remote now contains bio-flux regulators of every kind, for every variable."

The remote bug twisted and whirled slowly on the grid axis.

"This system is self enclosed," the voice continued. "Everything from covert surveillance to bio-elimination is right here, right now, in one package."

The screen faded to brilliant carmine red, as the flying, spying, hypodermic bug turned to show its massive mosquito driller. Then it zoomed right into my eyes, an old tech holozig that shocked me with its potency.

Next, the bug was shown in dozens of quick cut scenes; above jeri-era houses, streets lined with cars, and sidewalks full of people. It honed in on one among hundreds, then spurted chemical prescriptions, flashed destabilizing light, and pulsed e-mag waves. It made sense. Smart bombs back then, and smart little flying eyes. Not only monitor malcos, but terminate them too, in the same sweep. Squirt hurt, dose them with primitive nekrolim patterns. Early NeighborWorld components weren't brave artists with bold vision. They were on-camera, remote-control murderers, spy-guy goons. What did Bob Sideways say? Where did all those homeless people go? Were Weirds homeless, malco, psi-plus fugitives from the old era?

The touch of a heavy palm weighed on my shoulder, jerking me back into the F and D. I turned to see the Inspector standing behind the couch, smiling. His hat and huge coat were gone. His real hair was dark, with shards of gray, and a bald spot where the cherry fire hat was. Clad in a blue jacket and brown sweater, with wide cuffed brown pants, the look was jeri-era professor. He kept the boots, with the cuffs riding high.

"This is only the beginning, boy," he said, eyes wide. "When you leave here, you'll understand."

"Yup," the shaman agreed, emerging from a shadow. "You'll know what we know."

No more native medicine man regalia. In a green windbreaker, sport shoes, black jeans, he also fit into the jeri-era casual look; a high school athletics coach at the mall.

"Where're the looks?" I asked them.

"What looks?" the Inspector asked.

"It's time to learn from people, not characters," the shaman said.

He paused, with an expectant mug.

"Well, what do you think of the footage?" he asked.

"What does it all mean?" I asked, playing advo for the devil. "I watched some ancient surveillance work tapes. How does it connect with NeighborWorld? This is old-era tech."

Still trying to comp like an advo, I made an offended look, but I was gagging on the truth. The Inspector withdrew his hand. They looked at each other in bewilderment.

"You never heard of information warfare or e-bomb technology? Seamus asked in disbelief. "I thought you were so old-era savvy. You're ignorant."

"Don't ya get it?" implored the Inspector. "Early NeighborWorld components was dosing and popping everyone. Big fry, small fry, all French-fried. Anyone who didn't fit in the plan. You know, Stan, the plan? Weed the garden?"

He looked at me like Nogo did when he talked about smeared Neighbors.

"That's nekro scan, compadres, painful to v-u," I said. "Why show me this?"

"Because the guy on the video tape was me," the original said dramatically.

"Me too," the fireman said, choking back rage. "I lost everything. They engineered evolution to make a slave planet. They ruined lives, and didn't give a shit."

"They blinded us with subliminal light, dosed us with hypnotics, and popped our skulls with e-mag pulses," the indidge accused, narrowing his gaze on me. "Mind control worked best when you watched TV, or were on the Internet. It made you so depressed you wanted to die, or so paranoid you wanted to kill."

"The guy on tape was a journalist in Cleveland!" the Inspector hollered. "He was working on a big expose about info-tech royalties and the Hungarian trade delegation. He killed himself over a bad haircut!"

One hundred-twenty seasons old history. Cleveland was the name of Local 15, before NeighborWorld. Right next door, Neighbor.

"What does that have to do with NeighborWorld?" I asked, knowing the inspector was insane. "Did you know the guy?"

The Inspector's pink and blue aura lines moved in time with his agitation. His boots squeaked.

"No! He was just another guy who didn't fit with the plan!" he shouted. "He later jumped out of a window. The suicide note said he had a bad hair day, didn't like his haircut. They used to call being dosed with waves a haircut!"

"Suicide destroyed their credibility," Seamus said. "A lot of old-era journos who got close to the real truth about the plan for the Nova Century and NeighborWorld died that way."

"How's that for a story?" the pyro-tink spat. "You should appreciate that one, a guy like you, who don't fit in. A guy who wants to make Neighbors stars in his Spotlights, a guy who wants to save us Weirds. Hmm?"

"Everything they did was about control," Seamus said. "Genalts were invented to breed cold soldiers, to help the Grandees weed. The Bigs created psychic soldiers, and war warlocks, too. Secret weather control, information control, control control. All for profit."

"Lots of stories for an advo who don't mind doing his job," the Inspector said.

"Woah. You're going too fast," I said. "I don't know what you're talking about, or if there's any way of verifying this stuff."

They scanned deep into my eyes, they couldn't shut up. I couldn't focus.

"Light!" the Inspector yelled. "All they need is light. You think nekrolim is a pirate pattern? It's got to be NeighborWorld's, an inside job. All flesh and dirt fades to black, don't it? That's what all your wonderful light's used for. Now there's your climber Spotlight."

While they shouted from the soapbox, images of despair marched through my mind, an endless line of atrocities; murdered malcos, smear and zoombies, genocide, nekrolim, mirrored goons. The TV zizzed noisily in the close background, brilliant white static shifted aimlessly over the screen.

"What do you want from me, then?" I asked, feeling numb. "What?"

They stopped yakking abruptly and just stared. Still studying me, the shaman burped and rubbed his belly. Then he walked to the refrigerator, opened it, grabbed three antique-looking beer bottles, and walked back with them.

"Where's the pizza and homemade wine?" Seamus asked the fireman.

"You don't even ask anymore?" the fireman asked Seamus, looking at the beer.

"Let's have a beer and talk, like he did with Bob," said Singing Elk. "Let's approach this on a level he can understand."

"Bob? I didn't say anything about Bob Zeitweiss, did I?"

"Yesss!" the Inspector exulted. "Headband head is right as usual. Let's talk to the loser from our vantage point, as fellow losers. But sorry, boys, the wine and pizza are all gone."

"How did you know about me drinking with Bob?" I asked again.

The fireman quickly grabbed a beer, popped off the top, then guzzled; with light trailers waving around his head and shoulders, his eyes bugging all whacko over a satisfied smile.

"I can't drink again," I said. "The idea makes me sick. How do you know Bob Zeitweiss? How did you know he gave me booze?"

"Bob, Bob, Bob. Give it a rest," the fireman said. "Bob's a good student, he's interested in learning. You ain't. You're a bullshitter."

The Inspector scrutinized me seriously, and released a loud sigh.

"Ever hear of them psychic study institutes back in the old days?" he asked. "Probably not." He turned to the medicine man and nodded before I could answer. "Hit it, Paul," he said.

"The spy-guys stole gifted kids from their families," the shaman said with a disgusted moosh. "Used 'em as remote viewers, psychic spies, messed with their minds."

The medicine man took a long slow drink. Then he turned towards the TV and snapped his fingers. An image shimmied onto the box, broken and bubbly, another old surveillance or lab journal vid-cam adventure. It looked like a classroom or structured study place, with children sitting at desks. Each desk had a monitor screen. The children stared intently at the screens, with determined expressions.

A little girl jumped up with her hands over her head.

"I did it!" she screamed. "I made it go backwards. I did it!"

Every face in the classroom turned to look. Then, cut to a teacherish man with a beard.

"Show us what you did, Naomi," the teacher said. "Show us how you did it."

Eyes to source, the dimpled, honey haired seven year old explained, with comp much vaster than her age.

"We were told to watch the numbers, and then to imagine them going backwards," she said. "Whenever we felt like it, we were supposed to push the record button, and try to make the numbers go backwards."

"I imagined the numbers were coming out of me," she added. "I closed my eyes and imagined them going backwards. Then it just happened."

She was typical of kids with this power. Quickly a new series of shots appeared, showing the link they shared. There was Naomi, surrounded by an early NeighborWorld crew with feed lines, mikes, TV monitors, diva lights and mini-pots. Next to her stood a perfectly coiffed diva-Jane of indiscriminate age, true to the v-u of our brotherhood. The anchor dug for an emotional response. Little Naomi's mother died. Slice her, Mona, then back with more action coverage. A little boy had a similar experience - the scene showed a bloated little brother floating by. Children with horror stories clawed out from the screen. Grief was the key.

Eleven kids, mostly around eight years old, from different studies in different parts of the country, had the ability. All gifted with psi-kinesis, capable of sending things flying. All exploited through personal tragedy, gooey in the wrong. The kids looked aware of their powerful knowledge, like scientists discovering a secret weapon, in a jeri-era B. The tape bubbled again; yellow, ruby, and blue, the volupto color finale of most old tapes. Then it was over.

What horrible dream grotto had I crawled into? Hard School, Soft School, Ozzy and Harrier's Last Dream, all nada. The old corporate governments controlled evolution, through elimination and propagation. NeighborWorld was born from that. And I flung its manure in Neighbors' eyes, and helped weed the garden. Box beaters and Weirds weren't nekro malcos. Advos were. I was.

"I don't know what I've seen, or even what it really means," I said. "But please, stop. I don't feel well. I can't watch anymore."

"Moloch," the Inspector said, gritting his teeth. "Sacrificing kids."

"Here, Standard," Seamus said. "Here. Drink the beer. You're in over your head."

"I can't believe it was so sick back then," I whispered, taking the beer bottle. "You mean this kind of shit is still happening?"

"Still happening?" Seamus said with a smirk. "It's ten times worse."

"You ever seen what really happens to someone who's been erased and dubbed over?" the Inspector asked.

"Really happens?" I came back, popping the bottle cork. I took a long, tasteless swig.

"Yeah, let's show him what really happens to someone who's been overdubbed," the Elk said.

He snapped his fingers again.

A mug shot of Deluxe Broadmoor appeared on the screen. Broadmoor was young, only eighty seasons, but he had an old headache. A couple seasons ago, he frizzed and murdered his hab mate, on screen, while millions watched. Sure, you could commit feelie-realie murder. Just like feelie-realie sex, with anyone. But no murder in the flesh and dirt.

Broadmoor's crime was even shocking to the smear, so play it in your own minds, dear N's and A's, because only your own can convey the horror. The faceless, docile, almost genderless hab-mate struggled helplessly against Broadmoor's whirlwind of destruction. A capital gag-slam. Then cut to something worse. Broadmoor was shown being exposed to the flicker rates and subliminal light geometry that erased his personality. He blinked uncontrollably, and then stared wide-eyed, open mouthed.

Then cut to this frightening creature, Neighbor Deluxe Broadmoor, self sequestered in his hab, bio-electronically docketed, apprehensive, pawing at his shoulders, alone. His personality and memory were removed, even his childhood erased. He'd been remade into good Neighbor Delmore Blank.

Although not physically painful, overdubbing hurt. The memory of the crime was removed, but there was no overdubbing the guilt. Delmore Blank was clean of Deluxe Broadmoor, the man who betrayed him, the murderer of an innocent Neighbor. But overpowering remorse was a keeper, forever. No moment of joy ever sparked in him, no happy distraction came up teeth. The conflict lingered without reason.

"Why?" Neighbor Delmore Blank kept asking. "Why, why, why?"

It was worse than anything I'd seen at work in 838. In the releases we ran after his overdub, Blank Broadmoor was portrayed as rehabbed, sweet, and religious. But it was all animix. In truth, he was in a confused state of heightened grief and anxiety at all times. It was cruel, unnatural, just like everything else I'd been shown.

"I've seen enough," I said, putting the bottle down.

"Do you know the real story, advo?" the Inspector asked. "Broadmoor was a malco, and they got into his brain. They made him murder, in focus, and then finished the script by writing him out. All the way out. Now, that's your sex-death formula in action."

"NeighborWorld corrupts natural law," the Elk said, peeping my stacks again. "True evolution follows inspiration from nature. Not computers or greedy kooks."

"But why, why, why?" the Inspector asked in a pedantic tone.

He shook his head, then rolled his eyes up, as if searching for the answer.

"To keep bags on our heads!" he shouted, pointing to his forehead "To keep them on top, and us on the bottom!"

He made a face like he'd eaten something bad, then rambled on.

"The tech got too simple," he said. " It resembled a human nervous system. Along with knowledge of nature and the teachings, people could break free. So they had to mystify it, make it incomprehensible."

He grinned like mad smear.

"Understand?" he asked.

"No."

"Control minds and you control belief, desire, taste, emotion, personal wealth, even personal identity," Seamus said. "People pay you to tell them what to feel and think and do."

"The masters of the most powerful technology always control the masses," the fireman said. "In NeighborWorld, the masters are the most current techs."

The Inspector laughed, then began coughing, making his boots squeak. Seamus pounded on his back and the cough subsided.

"But why do the Bigs want such power?" I asked.

They looked at each other and smiled. The Inspector's eyes were red and watery.

"Pure power for its own sake," the shaman said. "That's history."

They looked at me like I should have known. The fireman source pointed at me, squinting. On their own cue, they chugged their beers, all the way down, adam's apples bobbing.

"Shadowy Bigs pulling the puppet strings of the info-scam, secret societies ruling over the unevolved," the fireman said.

"There's two control classes," Seamus went on, holding up his index and middle finger. "The wealthy aristo-class, and the scientist-sorcerer class. This has been going on for thousands of years."

"Yessir, yessir, yessir," the Inspector agreed. "Way past time for a change. Time to fight back."

Seamus gave me a somber mug. "We had to," he said. "It was survival. We had no guns. We were marginalized and despised. All we had was our minds."

"We didn't want to hurt anyone or anything at first," the Inspector said apologetically. "The first break-ins were accidents, screw ups. But goons kept coming around, trying to get us into NeighborWorld."

"Or kill us," Seamus said.

"If you'd been tortured for a long time - psychically, mentally, physically, any way - and you could strike back, wouldn't you?" the fireman asked.

All our speculation about the Weird break-ins, the live-in hype, was b-roll. The goons had located where the break-ins were coming from long ago, maybe when Nogo squeaked. The only reason why the Weirds weren't all faded to black or in the unhouse was that bleeping mirror.

"But where did you all come from?" I asked. "Why did you settle here?"

162

"People without homes or hope have been coming here since before your info-scam, advo," the Inspector said. "For generations."

"Our population's growing," Seamus said. "And the eye is on us. But remember, Mother Earth takes care of her own."

"But how did it happen?" I asked. "You mean you all just suddenly had this sorcerer power? You woke up one morning and wished gear would blow, and it did?"

They looked at each other as if they'd rehearsed what they would say when I asked them that.

"For me, it just happened, even though I'd been working on it," Seamus said. "It was a while ago, but they still had bugs that looked like the bubble that was chasing you."

He pointed upwards, as if pointing at the bubble drone.

"One of them kept following me around, especially after gigs or visiting friends or family," he went on. "I knew it was beaming some kind of MC at me. I'd been doing my people's shamanic power drills, trying to bring it down, for a long time. Once I ran naked in a snowstorm, suppressing all thought, for fifteen minutes."

The pyro-tech looked at the medicine man with admiration, smiling. The images in the shaman's mind began coming up in mine. The essence of something that took years to learn was going right into my stacks, on the internal monitor.

"One time," Seamus continued, "I just stopped trying, and imagined it tumbling from the sky into a vacant lot, without any thoughts in my head, just witnessing, and creating somehow. It wobbled and tried to right itself, but couldn't. Then boom, it crashed."

He grinned like a little kid getting candy for being good, so did I.

"Watching that freakin' thing go down made my heart leap," he said, beaming. "I ran home laughing. I kissed my wife and gave the dog and cat treats. It was great."

So that was before things got real bad for him, why he went underground Weird. I drank the last of my beer, and gently put the empty bottle on the card table.

"Some of us got addicted to it," the Inspector jumped in. "You could see how they'd think it was fun, especially since they couldn't be caught by NeighborWorld mind control tech."

"So it was drones first, then NeighborWorld system break-ins, then the mirror thing?"

"I guess so," he answered. "We actually had to threaten some gifted kids with a big slap-down if they didn't stop drawing attention. But now they support the mirror."

"I had to study all Native Am shamanistic traditions," Seamus continued. "Not just my people's. Study hard. I wasn't gifted like some. I also studied Kabbala, Sankhya Raja Yoga, Gnosticism, you name it."

"I think it has something to do with the pineal gland," said the Inspector, pointing to a spot between his eyebrows. "And stimulating gamma wave activity in the brain."

Some of the religious stimsublim spots I did for Cerevello had gamma-stim and delta- stim buried in. Could you become Weird from watching religious spots? Or fade to black?

"What about you?" I asked the Inspector. "How did you acquire these powers?"

"I had some gifts, but didn't pay them any mind," he said. "When cable TV went under, Toytown went off the air, and I lost my job. Then my wife died from some new virus nobody ever heard of before. So I started wandering, with my little daughter, Elsie. Now, she had powers. She could tweak computers with will power. But she died in a fire, in a house a bunch of us were squatting in. It was started by some goons working for developers, but they blamed it on us."

The fireman stopped, pushed up his glasses, and rubbed his eyes. He was crying for real.

"I guess she died. Maybe they got her. I got her out first but I ran back in to help an old woman. When I got back out Elsie was gone. I never found her."

Was little Elsie a little Naomi? The indidge put his hand on the pyro's shoulder and rubbed, quietly saying, "Pete... oh jeez, Pete."

"I had powers after that," the fireman went on. "Mostly I prevented or put out fires or saved other burned out squatters. But whenever I saw them bubble bugs, I dropped them. I might have killed one of them pricks who started that fire, with my mind, but I ain't sure."

"We all developed on our own," the shaman interrupted, saving the fireman. "All kinds of people, over time. But we sheltered each other, made a place for ourselves, and learned from each other."

"What about Francis?" I persisted. "What's his story?"

"Francis is what they used to call mentally challenged," the shaman said.

"Loco," the Inspector corrected. "Todo loco. He also fancies himself as a woman. His mother and sister dominate him."

"But he's harmless," Seamus said. "Except when he shows off his powers. He's like an idiot savant or something. He didn't mean to hurt anything."

"Why don't you ask him yourself?" the Inspector asked, pointing towards the room's corner.

I turned to look. Francis the Sissy waddled into the room, with an overflowing sack of light purple mushrooms draped over his shoulder. He held a large one above his head like a trophy.

"Look!" Francis shouted. "Look, nem nem nem, look!"

"They look great," Seamus said to him, giving the thumbs up.

"Come to my party nem nem nem," Francis said. "Come to my party nem nem nem."

Francis's mother followed him in. Her face was the same, but her body had puffed up. Instead of a wispy crone, she was now ten kilos fatter, a tubby tugboat hag. She strolled with an ethereal sashay, making gulping sounds. A black cloth fishnet web covered her fleshy body from head to toe, with the loose parts draped over her face and hand-stained hair.

Then in walked Laya, the dark princess MC of my dreams. She looked hot for eroto-slam. I realized she was one of the faces in my nightmares, and the same girl on the path and snooping around at Point A. And Francis was one of them, too. They'd been soozing me for a long time.

Suddenly, a large, wide halo encircled all three of them, the same light as at the table in their home. It softened the edges, foreshortened the figures, like an old-era oil gel shot. They looked self absorbed, sinister, a nekro holy family, with Francis as the mentally challenged, psychically gifted baby. On cue, together, they turned and began walking back out the way they entered.

"Let's go to the party," Seamus said. "Screw this talking shit."

"I shall eat an elephant," the Inspector said. "And drink a hundred beers."

They began walking towards the door as if I wasn't there, so I followed, wanting to be included, I guess. There were no thoughts of escape, or even of interviewing Francis. The halo went before us, through a short narrow hallway covered with stained, drooping red and white wallpaper, up a short, time-worn, wooden stairway, and out of an ornate old wood door.

We walked out onto the front stoop of an 1860's period house, with the haloed trio ahead of us, continuing down the street. It was unseasonably warm, and there was a pleasant, sugary scent in the air. Like with Bob's neighborhood, nothing was as it seemed at first. The ghost town, Industros Tragicos, was alive.

Kids with books and backpacks and elderly people with bags of groceries went about their business, walking around the halo, unconcerned. Cyclists pedaled by, and one green- fuel guzzler, which made no sound at all, passed through.

The old buildings were well-kept, even restored, yet inconspicuous, thanks to the mirror. Incred, and uncomp, the Weirds had hidden in plain sight, and made their neighborhood invisible. Or transdimensional. Large trees sprouted from every corner, tall bushes lined the avenue. There were houses and old-style shops and walk-up businesses, even a fruit stand at the end of the block.

We approached the fruit stand. It was covered by a green and red canopy, bearing the name 'Mars Bellhop' in white script. The shop was tended-to by three men in shredded old-era bellboy uniforms. Antennae sprouted from their bellboy caps. Wooden partitions contained huge clusters of pink, green, purple, and gray-blush grapes, and apples as big as grapefruit. There were vegetables, nuts, squash and pumpkins; abundance from somewhere. Even in early winter?

"Stop gawking and keep moving," the Inspector barked, and I dummy-box obeyed.

Just past the fruit stand was a large neo-classical looking building with stone lions guarding the entrance. The halo crew walked in.

"That's where the party is," Seamus said, nodding towards the building, as we grew closer.

"That kid's too young to drive," the Inspector snapped, glaring back at the silent electric guzzler, now gone off shot.

"We'll deal with it later," Seamus said.

We ascended a wide and long stone stairway past the lions. In blue mosaic tile below the metal and glass door were the words Public Library. Above the door was the figure of a woman, carved in stone.

"Athena," Seamus said, pointing to the figure. "Minerva, Wisdom."

We passed inside, and were greeted by someone wearing a gorilla costume, a cheap toy princess crown, and a too-small advo's tuni. The royal advo gorilla grunted, and indicated the way to the party. We passed a counter, some couches and chairs and full racks of old books and magazines, but nobody around. Then we turned down a hall and walked on a checkerboard floor towards a sign that read 'Auditorium.'

The sound of a crowd, and drums, accordion, and trumpet bounced around. Delicious aromas poured from the auditorium. Maybe the old ladies from the social halls were doing something gourmet with Francis's mushrooms.

The haloed trio had already entered the room, and the place was packed. There was a bar and buffet, overwhelmed by ham-jamming revelers. The halo evaporated suddenly as Laya and the scow mother and the sissy reached the middle of the floor. Francis's mother began cantering and bowing, making come hither pouts.

"La la la la la, I am the wind, I am the wind," the fleshy carnival mom sang. "The five of pentacles, the queen of hearts."

Then she turned and showed her massive behind, her gigantic buns, those abominable twins. One sex destroying oggle was enough. A roar of approving laughter shook the auditorium

"Those are cards you don't want," Seamus chuckled, wiping his brow.

Laya began clapping and egging her on.

"Sing, mamma, sing," she said, laughing.

Laya's dark hair was swept back into a red ribbon. Her clothes had changed. The brown frock she wore before was now a black, 20th century school uniform, with dark stockings and shoes, and red ribbons.

"Happy birthday to him, happy birthday to him," Francis's mamma sang.

"Sing, mamma!" she exulted, clapping harder. "Dance!"

Francis squealed a high-pitched laugh, then started dancing and mumble-singing. "Happy birthday to me, nem nem nem," he sang, with a mouthful of purple mushrooms. "Happy birthday to me."

Francis picked and rubbed his enormous, tuber-like snot packer as he whirled and twirled, accenting his mom's lewd comments with nem-nem-nems. Laya was coming up in staccato stills from some genetic wellspring as Egyptian, Minoan, Etruscan, ancient Greek or Roman. The Elk tapped his toe on the floor. The Inspector shook like a sleepy epileptic, with his colored wave lines jangling along.

"La la la la la, I am the wind," ma hippo sang.

"Nem nem nem," Francis intoned.

"Sing, mamma, sing!" Laya shouted.

I chanted along. The bio-flux regulators, the instruments of genocide, the whispers in the ear and squares in the skull, were being rejected, washed away. The Weirds were reshaping my brain. Laya was full of juicy, eye-peeling eroto-slam. The school uniform made her look earthy, but spiritual. Boners and buying go hand in hand, and I was buying. Then the whole place filled with light, as a giant old-era disco ball lowered from the ceiling. The ball began shooting out blue, citrine, and red colored streams.

"Do the tarantella, Francis," the Inspector coaxed.

"Dance, Frannie. Shake your ass!" the shaman said. "Shake it but don't break it!"

"I won't, nem, nem, nem," Francis answered.

Laya shrieked a gleeful giggle. The gnarled sissy saint's mother howled like a mutt in heat. The band jumped into a Neapolitan tarantella, with drunken sounding male and female voices shouting out approval. Laya came up on all internal monitors, pounding on caveman drums. In the auditorium, the drums sounded jeri-era disco. Here comes some gristle, dear Neighbors and Associates. If you've been swallowing so far, keep chewing. It may take a while to digest.

The ceiling disappeared, and a huge turquoise moon rose, over the disco ball. The auditorium was now huge, stylish. Some kind of skull-syrup poured down from the moon, with a color base running from turquoise to light purple. The room began filling with more Weirds, like some primitive Point A experience. Everyone was clapping to the byzantine tarantella rhythm. Accordions and mandolins and guitars wailed away.

As they emerged into F and D, one thing became clear; the denizens of Industros Tragicos were smelly. But there was cologne and freshly cleaned clothes in the olfactory mix, and that delicious food aroma. I could smell Laya's perfume and sweat.

There was every kind of jeri-look. Some appeared as Amish Hassidic Imams, some like hippies, beatniks, punk rockers, house rappers, stock brokers, soldiers, nurses, bikers, and other forgotten unshaven grupos. In the blurry mass, women with green hair and thumbless gloves danced along with men with mohawks or guru-hair, in blue overalls or well worn business suits. Every ethnic crew, every jeri-era gig seemed to be there, nexed-in, one and different. Even an advo gorilla.

I saw the chessboard black and white Generalissimo, who was morphing into different people. I saw the Dreaming Woman arguing with the devil. I saw the Martian Bellboys carrying fruit-laden luggage, in shredded bellboy uniforms and hats with antennae. All the Weirds were there. This was the gold op find. A true global Neighborhood, made holy. These yammer heads created miracles, played God in the basement. The crowd murmured, like the ride or show was about to begin. I strained to focus on what might happen next, through the anonymous bubbling lava of faces.

The sultry call of Laya's brain juice broke through, forcing me to seek her in the maelstrom of dancing body parts. She came up on all monitors, Point A, with a feelie-realie pre-caress, felt only between us. I touched her for the first time, but we weren't in the same space. Her hair brushed against my lips, her shoulder nudged mine. Her breasts rubbed against my arm. A warm current of air played under my nose, a driblet of sweat tapered from my septum to lower lip. The sensation was gooey in the right, and my brain began shutting down in favor of angular heat below my belly button.

Laya vipped-up in the F and D, wearing a pig nose mask, laughing all eroto-slam, with her school uniform blouse unbuttoned. In the early days of my combo with Sylvia, nothing could stop the urge for squish. Connector on or off, in the world of drooling voyos, or with as much sacred space as advos had. But this was different.

I pulled off the pig nose, and laid a throat gobbling beso on her. Then I pulled off her blouse, and kept kissing. Then she pulled me down onto the soft grass. Soft grass? In this library auditorium, where a hundred dancers were swirling?

"Bells are ringing, for me and my gal," the Inspector sang, all nasal.

The bobbing, bouncing heads laughed, while the dance streaked into a demon tempo. Then it all happened, in the animal flesh and dirt. It was more than a roll in the mud, but the feeling of Point A had faded, and descriptions desecrate. I was in way over my head.

Then, dear N's and A's, a total brain squeezer. It rained. It rained a gully washer, in mid-summer like torrents, with distant rumbling, fecund smells, and purifying water. The crowd let out another squeal, like the show was getting really good.

And just like that she was gone again. I could see her face in my mind, but she was nowhere. All I could think was that her eyes looked familiar.

Then all the faces in the room blended and recombined and re-emerged, and everyone looked familiar, like we were related somehow. As the recognition grew, the rain subsided into a mild mist. I could physically feel her absence; she took something out of me. I wondered what her name meant, it sounded like liar.

There were suddenly only a few puddles in the room. The washout was drying quickly, leaving places for everyone to sit down and rest and chat. Or sleep. Soon more and more Weirds sat down, or collapsed. As far as I could see, Laya and I were the only ones who actually made squish. The rest just seemed to have acted crazy a while, then fell asleep. All except Francis, who although half asleep, continued levitating a few centimeters off the ground, circling the auditorium, mumble singing, "Happy Birthday To Me, nem nem nem."

In the old-era dicks, the hero kept getting knocked out by mickeys before the scene changed. Either the Weird drugs were too strong, or this advo was too out of shape to keep up with the world out of focus. The sleepy brain shut off quickly, after suffering in the vastness, searching for meaning. Fade to black.

-12-
"THE TRIAL"

Whatever was happening brought me around again. It seemed like a dream, in and out, waking in different scenes. I was jolted into this one by the sound of angry voices. I was in the auditorium, but it looked different.

Closing the mesh, the wide shot emerged, animating the shouts. There were hundreds of people, all in very jeri-era costume, ancient garb from the American and French and Russian and other revolutions. At least that's what I comped, from history spots I'd taken on. A mish-mash stew of rags, dignified only by revo-malco meaning, was strewn on rabid-eyed children. They waved crude weapons, brandished sharpened sticks. A crowd of sore-headed jers stuck out in sharp contrast, shaking fists and threatening with knives, pieces of sharpened metal. Guns?

They were shouting at me. Menacing me.

I couldn't accept it. A blissful experience had come up a shrieking nightmare, in a moment. At the top of the shot was the puker, the revulsion of one glimpse of recognition. Laya was on a platform, or stage riser, yelling insults at me.

Francis was up there too. And Francis's mother, and the Inspector and Seamus, and all the other big face Weirds. And all sat behind an enormous long table, with hands folded, sullen-potched and scary to v-u.

The sound of a scratchy antique record filled the auditorium, followed prontito by a booming chorus singing a jeri-era revo-malco anthem.

The Inspector held a cupped hand to his ear and said "The Internationale."

"Weirds of the world unite," said Seamus, posing heroic.

"Whoever controls information controls reality," the Inspector said. "And vice versa."

They all snapped to attention, and held up clenched fists. They sang along to the anthem in out of tune voices, the Inspector in an old ladyish falsetto.

The song ended, and they sat down. Each, in turn tapped on the table with their left hands. Then they began pounding with their fists, then rose to their feet, spouting insults and accusations. And cute little Laya was the first to rail and rant, the first to scream like a knife, the first to cut.

"You are a priest of a false cult!" she bellowed. "You lie to the people. You're a sack of filth!"

"You're a big phony," the fire inspector chimed in. "A goddamn liar and a phony!"

"You're a soul-sucker disguised as a priest!" Seamus barked over them. "You work for murderers, in the getup of a holy man!"

The shaman shook his rattle at my heart, perhaps trying to kill me with the mirror. The sound of the rattle was loud, overpowering. This blob of heads wanted to rip me. I forgot the words, but deliver us our daily bread, and no trespassing allowed, hey Mary, Phil is great, Lorne is witty, amen. It was Point A in hell.

"You stand accused, phony priest," Laya roared. "Defend yourself or go to the wall"

"A priest of what?" I asked, all humble and small, sounding tinny and panned.

"Stand in the light," the Inspector demanded.

There was no goofy yuk in his voice now. His cabeezer showed the slant of an ancient inquisitor, confirmed in the outcome of my predic. I stepped into the light, which appeared to come from everywhere, 360. The light grew, panning everything else in the room to shadows. From below the floor, came the sound, the tremendous pulsing vibration of an old-era grand organ. Then in walked the choir, pounding a big bass drum, singing nekro, retching in some antique language or jango of their own. It felt like the gallows goodbye of the priest. Then a loud boom, as the room shuddered, knocking me to my knees. But everyone else seemed rooted, immovable.

"Let him see what he's done again," the stern fireman said, his eyes lifted to the almighty. "He'll pay for his crimes, but he must know why."

A huge monitor screen dropped down from a ceiling rig, to about three meters above the judges. The crowd mumbled in a hundred voices, drooling at the prey. A cross glowed on the screen, and I prayed again, to whatever. Then it changed to the Crescent and Star, the Star of David, a Yin-Yang symbol, all these different religious logos. They were the same designs I'd buried in religious stimsublims earlier in the week. All I could think of was that wall scrawl, All Flesh And Dirt Fades To Black. We buried that slogan in religious stims to remind Neighbors that life was fleeting, but the light went on forever, amen.

"But what am I accused of?" I said. "What have I done? I'm not a priest. I can't remember if I even believe in anything."

"Who authored and authorized religious spots with subliminal messages imbedded in them?" the Inspector asked.

"Not me. I just helped," I said. "They made me do it."

"Just watch if you want to enjoy a few more moments living," the shaman said.

There were dark circles under his eyes, but he looked younger, like the reddish brown pipestone, rubbed smooth. He was Buddha or Christ, with fangs. The screen above the judges swirl faded, and a scene popped up immediately.

From what I remembered of the old era, it was an aerial of Bayland 7, or San Francisco, in the jeri-jango. Land of concrete canyons, crooked streets and cliff perched houses. The shot zoomed into a quaint pink Spanish colonial mom and pop bodega. There was that flying bug again, drifting in the wind like a witch. It glimmered and beamed, then schpritzed down the bad gag. A man emerged from the shop, holding his hand over his eye. He sneezed blood, then dropped. Then another man, a woman, a little boy, and an elderly man careened from the shop, waving the stink from their noses. Too late for the jer. Intended for one malco, the misload, an overdose, graved all over, leaving translucent slime on the sidewalk.

"This is the work of monsters," Laya's mother croaked, lifting her head to speak. She pointed an accusing finger at me. "Your bosses."

"But this is old stuff, digi-cam, from then," I floundered. "Whoever did this has probably faded to black by now."

Maybe this grandma could connect me in.

"Please," I begged. "Stop this. You people have enough power to blow up the in focus world. You don't need to do this to me. I'm not responsible for any of this."

"You're a traitor!" Seamus howled back. "You got internal power, but you work for them. You don't want to Spotlight us, you want to lead the goons to us. You're the bad seed that needs to be weeded!"

"Alright, alright," the Inspector jumped in. "That's enough. His brain is so subliminally whacked he don't really know nothing for sure. We ain't gonna find out nothing this way, I can see."

"I say let the kids beat the piss out of him, and then see which way he points when he runs to his mommy," Laya spat.

Laya's mother cackled, Seamus laughed, and the Inspector shrugged his shoulders. Then, to a growing murmur from the crowd, Laya slammed her hand down on the table.

"I'll do it myself!" she yelled.

Then she jumped up, scrambled over the table, and leaped at me.

Before I could lift my hands - wham! She punched me right on my nose. I fell backwards onto the hard floor, and blood gushed out all over my moosh, neck, and chest. The pain almost made me pass out. It vibrated; a crackling sound was coming from the center of my forehead. Everything was like wavy lines on a blown screen. I instinctively fell into a fetal slouch, jerking my paws upwards in a boxing kangaroo move to keep her from hitting me again. Then she swarmed around me like angry bees, slapping me wherever she found an opening.

"Stop it! I don't know what I've done!"

A chorus of bleeps and crude laughter swelled. There was no escape; the room was filled with an angry mob. A woman I just made F and D squish with was beating me up.

She kept slapping, and she was hitting the mark. Something violently protruded from the side of my head, some brain-pain erection. She must've had a ring on a knuckle or something. Then she kicked me in the ribs, knocking the wind out.

"How could you associate with them? You're scum, like they are," she accused. "How could you?"

Gloomy prospects for that shiny gold op. After all, I was only here to correct some things, to straighten things out. I pulled myself to my feet.

"Kick his ass!" someone yelled.

"Yeah!" scores of Weirds agreed. "Kick his ass!"

"No! Show him more!" a voice screamed. "Show him everything first!"

Great. More old video, more rotten, nekro scenes.

"I never did anything to you!" I shouted, blood staining my teeth. "I never even knew about it!"

I never dropped tox on Neighbors, yet I was the object of this injured gang's hate. The surroundings grew further from me, dream-like, disconnected. As the menacing grumbles grew, vision returned, and focus.

"Take a number and wait," a voice yelled from the crowd, to crude laughter.

Laya laid in a deep, vile sneer, then walked back to the table, knowing she got in good shots, and that now I'd be subjected to another barrage of splattered meat and unhinged emotion. The room went black and the screen blew fuzzy. Then the pain scenes ambled on screen center, montages of people unscrewing themselves with guns and knives, jumping off bridges, driving jeri-era cars into bridge abutments. These hopeless peeks, this onslaught of suffering, took me to the brink of another convenient fade to black, but I waited for my number instead, and covered my eyes.

"Watch!" Laya screamed.

The old world was sick. I was a lightbringer, not a pawn of the state. I didn't want to manipulate evolution or perform human husbandry. I wanted to Spotlight folks. And now I was a victim of history, a fried little fish, while nature balanced itself.

A tiny lady with a huge bouffant hairdo came over and gave me a kick, too, for good measure. I remembered her. She was one of the little olds who cooked urban squab at the social hall. She had big feet for such a small woman, and the shock knocked the wind out again. My eyes almost popped out. I was fading to black again, under a swell of angry jeers. Tell the truth, a voice in my head said. The buzzing grew. Then they killed the sound.

EXT-DAY-SHOT FROM UNDER OF THREE PAIRS OF LEGS

That was the only way to decrible the shot, so that's how I put it up. Francis, the pyro-phile, and the witch doctor - their legs looked like tree stumps. I couldn't see above that, but I could hear everything. Somewhere in the garbled background, a Linda's Homestyle Cookies commercial played, with that horrible jingle in the bed, Latin style. Go. "When the gates open and the resplendent sun shines through the big monitor, don't you know it's time for mouth-watering, lump-smacking Linda's Homestyle Cookies?" Mmm, mmm. The flute hooted, the congas pounded.

"Jesus H. Christ in a business suit!" the Inspector whined loudly. "Now we done it. He's dead."

"Let's cook him, nem nem nem," Francis said. "Cook him and eat him, nem nem nem."

"Calm down, Pete," the Elk said. "Don't wet your pants. He ain't dead."

"Look at him! He's not moving," the Inspector whispered frantically. "What the hell are we going to do with him? They must have got a fix on him by now. Goons are going to be swarming all over us, any minute."

The Inspector tree stumps shuffled uneasily back and forth, and the chubby Francis stumps danced in mimicry, getting faster in time with the Inspector's agitated movements. The shaman tree trunks were immovable.

"I thought you knew what the hell you were doing, Paul," the Inspector babbled on. "Any minute now. Any minute."

"Hey, stop overreacting," Paul Seamus shot back forcefully. "Your nose hairs are smoking. We got plenty of time."

"But is he dead?" the Inspector persisted. "Or just passed out? Maybe he had a heart attack. Boxheads are delicate, ya know? And they'll blame us for it. Oh why do I let myself listen to you? Why, why, why?"

"Stop acting like a baby!" Seamus shouted. "We all agreed. It's no one's fault. We needed to know what he knew, so we had to scare him. How were we supposed to know he'd take it all wrong? We screwed up, that's all. We all did."

"Nem nem nem nem nem," Francis gurgled.

"But what now?" the Inspector lamented. "What can we do?"

"Let's get him out of here," Seamus said. "Grab his feet. We'll drag him."

I couldn't speak. My throat felt thick, like I'd swallowed something to numb my vocal chords or something. All nekro somnab, catatonic, like in the dreams with the Weirds and the religious stimsublim. I couldn't move my head, or even blink. And they thought I was dead.

"Jesus Christ on a crutch, Paul!" the fireman exclaimed. "You're not thinking of taking him to Summerland! He wasn't one of them. The poor stiff was clean, probably even tryin' to do what he said he was."

"We ain't taking him there," the Elk grunted. "Takin' him to my place. Get out the herbs. Maybe he ain't dead."

Then Francis's tubby potato face zoomed into extreme close-up, beaming like a thousand suns, each blackhead in his enormous pores a magic mountain, the blue veins on his red nose screaming.

"Nem nem, he's alive! Nem nem nem! He's alive!" the tuber-head slobbered, splattering juices on my chest. With a sad lilt, he added, "Now we can't eat him."

Then the inspector's knob noggin burst into ECU, across from Francis. He looked down on me, smiled, and then laughed.

"Why so he is!" the Inspector exulted giddily, breathing incendiary breath down on me. "I knew you were going to be fine, I knew it! What happened, boy? Havin' too much fun down here with all us strange folk? Let me help you up, Senor Duckie."

He grabbed my hand and pulled me up. My knees were weak, everything was spinning. We were on a street corner near the library, across from places with signs that read Pumper's Bicycles and Bubblehead's Bakery. Francis released another silly, high treble laugh.

"Now when you go back to your world, in peace, of course," the Inspector mused, "you must forget everything you've seen. Sure you're feelin' all right?"

"I guess," I ventured, feeling like my muscles were on the wrong skeleton.

"When you go back, tell them we're all crazy, smeared," the indidge interjected.

His smiling moosh appeared as another extreme close-up. He shook my hand.

"Like I said, advo, you got real promise," he went on. "But I don't think this is the life for you. You don't even know what happened. Do you?"

"Not really," I offered lamely. "She was trying to kill me, I guess."

"So you almost died," he answered quickly. "See? You aren't ready yet. She, or we, never laid a hand on you. You liked how it looked, so everyone played along. You know, upstairs. You did it right, and made reality for all to share. But you took it all wrong."

"Yup, yup, yup," the Inspector agreed. "Just go back and tell 'em a few crazy smear live here. Give us time to dissipate, blend back into the woods, see? The unhouse is slower track."

"I got a secret, a secret," Francis sang to himself. "You're mind-controlled, on a secret mission, nem nem nem. Nothing happening here, nem nem nem, nothing happening."

"It's too big a problem any other way." the Inspector explained.

"You don't want to Spotlight us, kid," the shaman said, smiling. Then he stepped into the close background. "We're all looney. Laya, Maya, Francis, the guy with the fire hat, me, all of us. Sorry you took it the wrong way."

"Bullshif," I said in a hoarse, painful slur, then correcting myself, "bullshit."

They all shut up and smiled.

"Nem nem nem," Francis gurgled.

"You got guts, advo," the shaman said. "In the old days my folks would have called you a warrior."

"Indeed," the fireman said. "We wanted to scare you, to see why you really came here. We called you in dreams, because we thought we could teach you, and you'd help us. But we still weren't sure what you really wanted."

"I want to Spotlight you, I already told you," I said.

"But why?" he begged. "Can't you see what a mess the world is in? You passed out again before we could show you the nekrolim stuff. That would have really made you fade to black."

"Mess, mess, mess!" Francis shouted. "Nem nem nem."

"I hope your heart's in the right place, advo," the fireman said. "If you go back there and tell them everything, we're done for. And they'll erase you, for knowing about it. You're knocking over the applecart."

"Those genalts aren't going to stop until no one's left but them," Seamus said. "That box you live in is going to be a lot colder when you get back. Like a morgue drawer."

Quaint jango. The truth works miracles, bringing dry bones and rejected meat to life again. I came here to do something, and didn't get the job done.

"Thinkin', duck-boy?" the Inspector asked. "Think long and hard, with your heart, not just your cabeezer. Folks down here don't like confinement. They'll die from all them sources in their faces. Just as sure as you'd die from not havin' it. Think."

"I have to go back to the world of zoom and lume," I said with finality. "Neighbors have to know. And you all have to be protected somehow."

"After we've Spotlighted and are in focus, we'll all be erased," Seamus said grimly. "You don't know what you're doing."

"Goons could be here any minute," the Inspector agreed. "Then what? Whose side you going to be on? You gonna shoot us with a source while they shoot us with zappers?"

"If the mirror doesn't work, nem nem nem?" Francis fretted, rubbing his nose. "I don't have a funeral dress, nem nem nem."

"We ain't immortal, advo!" the Inspector shouted.

"Go ahead," Seamus said. "Get us all killed."

"I'm just going to do my job, like I'm supposed to," I said.

"You can't say there's a bunch of folks living out of focus with powers," the Inspector said. "It's that simple. The mirror we use to keep you pricks away is weak, thanks to you."

I suddenly understood as well as they did that the mirror was just the Weirds' collective mind; not retro-tech. The only reason I wasn't dead was that they didn't sense evil in me.

"If you understand what we tried to teach you, use it now, advo" Seamus said seriously. "You know we can't hurt you."

He looked into my eyes.

"We can only plead with you," he said. "Don't do it."

That's when the screeches became dimly audible, cranking and peaking into a deafening whine. We could hear them coming from a kilometer away. Gas guzzlers, maybe even fifteen of them, were roaring towards Industries Tragiques. The first two cars to hit the muddy road near Bubblehead's Bakery skidded out of control, colliding into each other with the sound of crunching, jangling, broken glass and metal.

Weird faces materialized in the window of Bubblehead's Bakery, semi-solid, translucent. The forms became full torsos, and all the people who were in on my trial were peering from the windows of the bakery, gawking at an old era accident. Then the startled onlookers vaporized before the frustrated, jarred Sur-goons could see them. Then boom! Four, five, six, seven more guzzlers slammed into the first two in a colossal pile up. I could hear la-la-las and nem-nem-nems grow into laughter. I heard each individual voice, and all of them together. I heard them with my mind.

Everyone across from the bakery had vanished, too, except for me. Me and the accident. While I gawked, too close for comfort, not one goon noticed me. The goons cursed each other and ouched their ways out of the cars, holding their backs and heads and other body parts. They pointed at the steam rising from the old radiators, gave each other meaningless orders, then remembered the cold, and rubbed their shoulders and stamped up and down.

They looked around, covering bare ears with their hands, and slowly geared into contingency planning. Then they got into the cars that weren't locked into place by the crash, backed out of the mangled wreckage, and drove away. The guzzlers whipped right by me, and some goons looked right at me. But there was no hint of recognition; no one saw me at all. I was as invisible as a Weird.

I ran along after the caravan, bleeping at the goons, and screaming, "I'm over here, you morons! I'm right here! Hey, I need a ride!"

I picked up a rock and threw it at the car. It struck the rear window. A goon looked back, but not at the rock or thrower, only to notice something different in the enviro. I kept yelling, but there was a sense of omnipotence, different than before, when I cut from the lab. It was both physical and spiritual, magical. I ran after the car, still pissed off but laughing, feeling a warm spot on my breastbone. Then I started mag-lev zooming over the frozen, sloppy road and fields like a bird.

But where were the Weirds, the medicine man, the pyro-geek, the sissy, the eroto-slam goddess, the skinny-flabby mommy? Was I Weird now, or just their pawn? Or was it all hallucination? Was I just forever smear on a big bad one?

The questions didn't match the exhilaration of pure flight, low maglev zoom, riding the great dragon. I caught the goons distancing themselves from the traffic frizz, snapped away from Industros Tragicos by the mirror's left paw. All at once I knew what I had to do. I looked for a ridge or hill. Then something guided my feet to a soft, wet plop on frozen brown weeds, on the highest ground. It was feelie-realie way beyond Point A, just willing it to be. I was grounded, and it was time to test my will.

-12-B-ROLL-
"A NEW FEED SOURCE"

EXTERIOR-TWILIGHT-BUST SHOT OF ADVO-OUT TO WIDE OVERHEAD

I was going to break-in all over the Great Lakes, come out in Mrmz Av Neighbor's living room. I was an outlaw, a Weird. Why not tell my story? What did I have to lose? There was enough info to reconstruct me in 838, live at home, maybe in a bio-collective. The spotlight on me would dim, while they deleted my career and deconstructed me. Home would monitor tech and flow, and cue my credit. Then one fine day I'd be overdubbed, or erased, smear forever kind. Or I could jump ship, and help fight the meanie-monk splicers. And do it not for me, or the Weirds, or the poor smear being weeded by nekrolim, but for Average Neighbor. I would be weirdvo.

The scenery sucked. I was tucked into a vague gray background, weeds thrown amblesidedly from the earth in black and brown, with white ice knobs slimed around. In the then, remnants of a good idea. Shaping up, power and the promise of climbing and helping the Neighborhood, the gold op on the monitor everywhere. In the now, a big grunt to touch the global influencing box, to go right into the mad, MCed over-brain.

I opened my arms wide beneath the starry canopy, preparing for a dictation given by angels, or Weirds. There was a giant obelisk somewhere, beaming control into the hearts and minds of the mummy-like Neighbors, and I had to cut right through it.

"Friends and Neighbors of Northam," I yelled in a voice with flames. "I must seem loco, bewildered and abandoned, wandering through this archaeological site. But I'm less confused than I've ever been. Why? I've just spent an enchanting time with folks who don't need screens or their noise. I'm talking about those folks you call Weirds. And how weird are they? Well, for one thing, they walk around, outside, and look at the stars."

On cue, the faces of the Weirds appeared in my skull, smiling in approval. It felt like my brain was breathing somehow. But I was spent, weak-kneed.

I looked at the stars, certain I would be heard, sure of transmission and reception. I stood there for at least five minutes, waiting for something to happen. Then I saw it. A little speck of light, a tiny luminous dot, getting closer, quick-zooming in on me. It was a bubble, the descendant of the flying bug, the locator, the messenger, the judge, jury, and executioner. I had broken the link, left the flock. Now it was coming for its wayward sheep.

Then I felt real sick, like the climate control was way off, and I couldn't stop the dizziness, the vertigo. Whether the bubble was vipping squares, or it was just apprehension, I didn't know. Until I felt the disabling frying pan zap the back of my neck, and then vaguely felt my body hit the cold ground.

I awoke again, this time to the roar of gas-guzzler engine, the blast of a car heater withering my face, and the car slamming and bumping me around as it rolled over a long unused road. I was stretched across the back seat. There were no locks and the windows were black. I was in focus again.

"He's awake," a gruff voice said.

"He's going to have fun telling his Associates what happened to his mug when we get back," another, higher, voice said.

"Pounding this creep is going to be an extreme pleasure," the gruff voice said.

They both laughed. What happened to my Weird powers? Then it all jumped into my head. I could fly, but I couldn't fly away. It was all just hallucination. How could this happen? Why didn't it work?

It worked all right.

"Hey, asshole," the gruff one said. "Know what you did? You dorked up a bunch of screens all over the place, just like your friends."

"You're a menace," high voice said. "That was all the proof we needed. You're one of them."

"Yeah," low voice joined in. "And we'll be working with those Neighbors real soon, won't we?"

They laughed again, one of those hollow splicer goon laughs. I pulled myself all the way up, instinctively trying to make good focus. I could finally see them through the transluc-seal barrier. A creepy duo. One was flamboyant, with a pair of wrap-around shade sources on and an arrogant look. The other had a tired, middle-aged humper thing going, maybe that's what he wanted. He was the driver.

"Who knocked me out?" I asked. "Was it you or the bubble?"

"Sometimes know-it-alls like you try to leave the Neighborhood," Senor Flambo said. "They think they're better than the rest of us."

"Was it the bubble or you?"

"Your babble did it," the smugnose said.

He smiled.

"You're in deep mierda, compadre," flambo-goon continued. "Much deeper than your sick, mutant amigos back there."

The brown shoe pappa goon whistled an upbeat tune, then turned to smile at me. This irritated the flambo.

"Watch where you're going," he said nervously. "Watch."

Then fashion goon turned all the way around to give me a very nekro look. Like the old dicks would say, it was the shell game. Which shell had erasal under it, which one a hand slap and another chance?

"So what happens now?" I asked.

Flambo stared at me vacantly.

"You're screwed," he said bluntly.

Pappa goon chuckled maliciously.

The fearscape was gone, only raw disgust and anger remained, as hard to suppress as an exposed nerve.

"You think you can scare me that easy?" I asked. "Go ahead then, kill me. Kill me, you goon garbage."

I was so mad that both feet instinctively popped up and kicked out the transluseal barrier keeping me in the back seat. I kicked the thing like Weird-Fu, on one small point. I'm sure those substand bits of genetic waste never saw anything like it. The brown shoe squeaked and involuntarily punched the gas. Flambo-bo jerked back, reacting to the acceleration, then his head banged against the dash panel, as the car braked to a screeching halt. Then they both jumped right out of the car.

Flambo ran about five meters before lurching around, holding his cabeezer, and brandishing a frying pan menacingly. Brown shoe stood frozen, about a meter from the guzzler, clawing at his vest pocket. Then finally, he whipped out a skull zapper that was retroed to look like an old .38 pistol.

"Put those heaters away, you mugs, or someone's gonna get hurt, see?"

There was one second of doubt, of non-Weird lume. The mugs had the power of life and death over me, and my tantrums could get me killed. All the stored-up hate had vanished, leaving me wondering if they really came to kill me or rough me up, or just make it through another workday. One second of doubt. Before I could scramble out via the hole I made, the goons seized the moment, and quickly clambered back into the guzzler, shoving their skull zappers up my nose.

"I need rest," the flambobo monkey-in-wraps said with an exasperated tone, trying to keep from zapping me. "I need rest. It's late and I need rest."

"You shouldn't aggravate my partner when he's sleepy," the old bear said, almost out of breath. "It makes him mean. Look, Mozuck. You behave, you live. Misbehave, you fade to black. It's that simple."

I didn't say anything, and they were too tired to press the issue. My silence meant I agreed, so they instantly went back to work. The goon star turned away from me and ordered up a blink, a sleepy stimsublim.

I would go somnab on them for now, until there was a chance.

"Can I have a blink, too?" I asked. "I promise I'll calm down."

"Now you're talking," brown shoe said. "Make this a lot easier for all of us."

So we all got lumed. Good cop won, and I was cooperative.

The stimsublim ran twenty minutes. The K-factor was strong, but I couldn't remember the smell. Although I fumbled around in the back seat for what seemed like forever, getting comfortable, I got more lumed than I had ever been, and soon the car and goons, the whole enviro, slipped quietly away. Maybe I had cross-faded into higher Weird awareness. I was there for the ride, but everything once again slid into fast-forward.

Suddenly we had arrived in Car Town, and transferred to e-mags. And just as suddenly we were back in 838.

EXT/TIME?/SLOW CROSS FADE OF TEK CENTER AND MAG ARRIVING

I am no one's enemy. But sometimes justice is required. Ok, so the goons were an evolutionary throwback, they had a bad splice somewhere. Ok, so I wanted to break away, to save the Weirds, to be famous for longer than my fifteen, maybe be Weird, too. But I didn't deserve this shit. That was my b-roll as I scanned it. I was going up to Point A on the internal monitor. The background music was one of those tiny trumpet toy soldier marches, as we cut trim steps back into the lab, for another informal, fun, get-together with friends and Associates. My heart was beating too fast.

As I walked in, Nogo and Biff stood almost as they did before, only more rhythmically animixed. I looked back to scan the goons who'd been escorting me back to the party. Then I noticed the arrogant flambo had been concealing a skin condition, which was better focus for me.

"Where the hell have you been, Standard?" Biff asked all frizzed. "You should know how worried we've been. Looking all over for you, all over. Where you been?"

He winced, poked his specs, and made an expansive gesture, holding out his arms to Nogo. Not me.

"Nogo's been a wreck, a complete and total wreck, thinking you were dead or something."

"Yeah," Nogo said with a faint smile. "I thought you were dead."

"Well, there you have it, boy. He's concerned, I'm concerned, and you can see we're all concerned."

"So what?" I came back cool, almost nekro.

"So sit down and tell us where you've been! Tell us all about it. You know, some individs were just going to not include you in this whole thing any more. Just write you out of the script, let you walk off the set. Even m-line your work, erase everything. But Nogo and I stood up for you, son."

"So what?" I asked again.

"So talk to us!"

There was nothing I could tell them. They wouldn't believe the truth. I would tell them something resembling the truth, to gain time. It didn't make sense, but I wanted to tell my story to someone important, even that evil beak in the obelisk beaming squares into my skull.

"I want to go to Pinpoint," I said, dropping into a sincere profile.

"LA Pinpoint!?" Cerevello laughed, incredulous. "In the F and D?

That's impossible!"

He cleared his throat, a clatter of hesitant puffs and near coughs.

"You don't need to go to Pointpoint to make your point," he added quickly. "Talk to us, your crew, your brother advos. We can shake it at LA Pinpoint, feelie-realie, Point A, when we're stars. We don't need them now. This is our spot, isn't it?"

"I want to tell my story to some kind of Big at LA Pinpoint," I said, almost hush mode. "I need protection for the Weirds and myself."

"You've got it! Right here with us!" Cerevello said. "We can work this out. This is our property, and nobody's going to take you off the credit roll, as long as I'm gig supremo. You can bank your lucky strokes on it. On it."

The Weird power was low, my strut was all refound confidence. Why did they want my slant and POV, when they already had a world-stopping m-line that worked for them in the can?

"I still want to go to Pinpoint, F and D," I said. "But I will tell you this. Weirds are not villain of the age guys. They're people. A bit odd, but good, nice people. Not hallucinations. People."

"Well, hell, I knew that all along," Biff said eagerly, like a sales rep. "Just individs like you or me. But I mean, the break-ins are hallucinations, or else there'd be wrecked gear. So how do they do it? How can they control our minds?"

He paused, but not long enough for me to answer.

"It's like old-era nook science, isn't it?" Cerevello gushed, panting and grunting. "They went all the way back to the then, and figured it out!"

"No, no, no," Nogo jumped in. "These malcos want the pie, not just their slice, and that's the problem. They have new tech and they don't want to share. So cut the nice people crap. We're on one side of the chessboard and they're on the other. All we need to know is how can we get in there, clean them out, and get that tech."

"That's it," I said finally. "I'm not talking until we're in front of some Big heads at LA Pinpoint who can guarantee protection. I want everyone to know what I know. No m-line slants based on lies."

I pointed my finger at Nogo's heart.

"And I don't want anyone frizzing me or fucking with me!"

"No outbursts, knuckle dragger, or we'll do this all over," Nogo spat back. "We sit down and talk, or this time, you won't get sent home. You'll be in the unhouse."

"Ok, wow, man, now you're making sense," I said, totally unafraid, laughing. "All this pressure yakk was sending down my hidden survival reserves."

"First off, where the hell were you? Where have you been?" Nogo hissed.

"Nogo, we know where he went," Cerevello broke in. "We need to know how he..."

"Shut up!" Nogo commanded, to el jefe, el padron.

He shut up.

Nogo's elasticity was gone, his suave blown, the splicer star reduced to a blithering red mug like Cerevello.

"Ok, I was down there getting naked and rubbing bodies with the Weirds," I confessed.

"That's it. Screw this idiot," Nogo barked. "I want to go to LA Pinpoint too. The criteria's all in, two out of three agree, we have to go. And I'm going to tell my side."

"All right!" I yelled. "Yes! Si, si, si. We're going to Pinpoint in the F and D. Advo prio uno, sacred space, no sources up culos, and no goons."

"No way on the security," Nogo said, leaking frizz. "You're dangerous."

Biff was shaking like a leaf, looking down at his shoes.

"I guess there's no other way to resolve this," Cerevello said, punctuating with a long sigh. "That's it, end slate. What if we have to wait for weeks for our fifteen?"

"Put in for it now," I said.

"Yeah," Nogo agreed.

Cerevello looked ready to collapse. Trembling, he dragged himself to the big overhead monitor.

"Advo prio uno to the G-O," he said to the screen.

An animixed female secretary with a headset and an office cubicle backdrop appeared on the screen.

"And you must be Biff Cerevello," the attractive middle-aged secretary said.

"Yuh, uh, I'd like to ask the General Offices for some time for a project being realized in Local 838," he said. "Could we put in..."

"Come whenever you like," she said, cutting him off. "The General Offices will make time for you."

"What? Oh, well, then..."

"Can you come now?" she asked, cutting him off again.

"Of course," Biff said humbly. "We'd be honored."

The screen faded to black, without a goodbye.

The Bigs, the Grandees, saw and knew all. They were watching everything, instigating, probing, shaping and slanting the whole time. Maybe Hard and Soft were created to keep us insane, and there weren't any Weirds. Just Bigs pulling strings.

"I guess were really going," Cerevello said, looking down, as if the world was lost. "There's no other way."

Things were bad. I'd backed myself into a corner. But I had bought more time.

-13-
"PINPOINT"

The high-speed e-mag train came twice a week, but no one ever rode. Nova tech took us to this miraculous station, but no one showed up. The station was servo, with servo tended palms trees and shrubs, servos dispensing tickets. This week, it was tickets, for another illusion, of old-era discovery and adventure. The holozig billboards on the circular walls proclaimed the trip to Pinpoint as a trip to the end of the rainbow, with the thrills of a physical ride to the other side of Northam. In red, white, black, blue, and yellow; somehow the billboard still seemed stark and foreboding, warning unwary Neighbors to stay home.

Cerevello coughed and fidgeted all the way here in the mag, and in the station, and when we boarded the train.

"Too late now," he kept mumbling. "Too late."

Nogo was absorbed in countless feeds and sources he wore and carried, and ignoring us conspicuously. He was making focus for his ring-fingered splicer aco-lackies, playing to his crew.

Where were my Weird powers?

The train sealed hermetically to a clang, a snap, and a whooshing sound. Scented air filled the cabins, and directions and instructions appeared on each monitor in front of every seat. The push of a button turned seats into beds, for those who still could sleep. The monitor screens recognized each traveler, arranged the appropriate stop, and cued credit for payment.

It was an eight hour trip to Pinpoint, and most of that time you were somnab or internap. Time, and the scenery, were scoped. An old-era traveler might sit in a windowed roof lounge and take on the sights rushing by. But on the train it was all instant review and stimsublim.

My space, marked 36A, had a window. I could look outside and avoid the barrage on the monitor, even my own need for a blink.

Biff took a cubicle ahead of me, strapped in and took on. Nogo took another cube further ahead, and was connecting as soon as his butt hit the seat.

The train rose to a hover slowly, like a snake, making too much noise for a nova-cent machine, with grinding metalloid cyber-vertebrae. Then suave set in, and the snake spurted forward, all parts connected, rushing towards the other side of Northam.

I couldn't see the goons who followed us from the lab. They must have gone to another cabin. Or maybe we had sacred space. We were still monitored. The Weird power was depleted, something was missing.

I wanted to bring the Weirdness back, by looking out the window, and trying to make something simple happen, like changing the shape of a cloud. It felt like I was far apart from the shaman and the fireman now, and completely back in the world of blinking zoombies.

I dimmed the lights, faded the space to dark gray. The train clawed through the expanding west, under clouds and moonlight.

A cloud passed by the moon. I wanted to turn the cloud into the face of an old witch. I tried to pull the nose out longer and longer with my mind, make those eye sockets hollower and hollower and have the moon glow right through them. I was going to make a crooked smile, with three teeth.

The cloud witch was connecting with me, telling me it was working. Her chin grew longer, and I gave her a wart. For the final touch, a long, pointed black hat.

Then I heard the Weird kids laughing, and it gave me the chills. Yeah, they had me in focus, we were connected. Was the witch cloud them or me?

We rushed over the eastern watershed towards the continental divide, the great center, into almost empty plains, filled only by the slow moving moon's light. Everything looked perfectly still, animixed into slo-mo. I, we, made the witch cloud pass over the mag train, then quick-dissolve into zero-space.

In the other cubes and cabins, deep, empty, awake sleep. In the expanded Weird state I could hear squares being vipped into Cerevello and Nogo, and feel the stimsublim moving the light around in my own sacred. Traces of chocolate K wafted in from Biff's brain. Then, no one was peeking, not even Weirds. I was alone somehow, maybe for the first time in my life.

I suddenly understood I could blow the train up with my mind if things kept up at this pace. Luckily so far no one had seen the witch cloud, except maybe some servo-goons or an eye in Pinpoint. It was outside.

My arms tingled, they felt strong. Little flashes of static electricity danced around my body, and I could feel every muscle.

I wanted to try something on the monitor, but be untraceable. No scram yakking out to the zombie Neighbors. Just see if I could animix into the train's entertainment system and not get caught.

"Let's go to Holland in the old era, in the 19th century," I said to the monitor screen. "Make that Amsterdam in 1840. Make it a cartoon."

"Let's travel into the past, in the Netherlands," the travelogue's flat female V-O said. "It's the year 1840, in the old era."

A moored canal barge appeared on the screen, which I assumed anyone else watching might see just as I did. It was expressed mostly through early newspaper style satirical cartooning. And soon it became a feelie-realie experience; all lit like it was then, with the flavors and rank smells, the reconstructed essences of the time. There was the boatman, complete with wooden shoes, blousy shirt and baggy pants. His whiskered chin sported a clay pipe. The sound of a concertina sweetened the mix, and wove through the lume.

He began pulling a huge moor line. Draped over a rude moor post was one of those thick dwelf woolen jackets. There was the smell of autumn leaves and pitchblende. A slight chill registered in the brain.

How could I enliven this wonderful historical feelie-realie lume? Make that concertina sound squacky? I thought of making the boatman jump rope with that moor line. Real fast. Yeah, and making the concertina go faster, and wipe that steady boatman's expression into crazed fear of skipping rope. Boys and girls around the world, welcome to my own private cartoon time! There was a moment of instant precision, an eruption of total control, as thoughtless as a virtuoso's fingers. I made the poor Dutchman's face so ridiculous, and the rope skip so fast, that I started laughing. Stop, go back to the way it was.

Suddenly the Fire Inspector was whispering in my brain. "Listen, moonduck, listen. I need to talk to you. It's me, your ninth favorite person in the world."

"Yeah," I whispered. "The Fire Inspector guy, Pete Toytown, whatever your name is."

"And me," Seamus said, in my Weird-brain. "We didn't abandon you, advo. I knew you had promise."

"Well? What's Go?"

"Let's get right to it," the fireman answered. "Your power is growing, but it's still spotty. We don't know if you're prepared for Pinpoint. Got any ideas of what you're going to do when you get there?"

"No," I said, almost out loud, then continuing in mind jango. "No idea. I'm not sure why I wanted to go there, why I wanted to go over everyone's head. I didn't know what else to do."

"You don't plan, advo," Seamus said in my head. "You need to plan. Do some kind of warrior empowering thing, make a decision, then try something drastic."

"Like what?" I asked in skull jango. "Say it was all a hoax?"

"Just do what you're trained to do, advo," the fireman said. "There's a lot you don't seem to understand, even though it's right under your nose. Shiny-tiny, light to the smalls, right?"

"Work on invisibility, invincibility, escape and survival," Seamus said. "Stop or redirect the train. Throw a monkey wrench in, then hike."

"He can't," the Inspector disagreed. "He doesn't know what he's doing. Or what he's dealing with."

"I guess I'm going ahead, Pinpoint bound," I said in thought jango. "To tell my side, and get protection. Who knows what these splicers might do if they aren't stopped."

"We were hoping you could force their hand somehow, so they'll have to deal with us," Seamus said. "I can see it's not in you to blow up the tubetrain."

"No, I'm enjoying the scenery," I said. "Watching the clouds."

"We could tell your medicine was growing," Seamus said. "But you're still not ready."

"I knew you were thinking about me, duckboy, you needed help," the Inspector said.

"I need help," I said. "But not direction. It's still my spot."

"Shh," Seamus said. "Someone's coming."

"What do you mean, shhh? We're not talking."

"Shhh! Pay attention," the Inspector joined in. "Someone's coming."

Then Biff's head, with his glasses drooping, jerked around the corner of cube 36A.

"Standard," Biff burbled, full of fake amigo teeth. "You know, I was thinking. You and Nogo should try to get along. If you two would've got together, we wouldn't have to be jeopardizing our careers like this."

Biff was sweating right through the snappy twenty-years-younger clothes he'd chosen for the continental crossing; with the same beaten hat and rumpled shirt look.

"You're sweating, Biff."

"Oh, heh heh heh, you know how I get. Uh huh," he said. "Anyway, you and Nogo should bury the hatchet, join forces, get the team back together. Uh, by the way, Stand, I was a little let down by what you did."

"What? When?"

"Walking off the set, of course," he said. "Changing the rules, posing malco..."

"Oh, uh, I did what I had to," I said, bracing myself for a lecture. "It's not like nothing happened to me. I left that lab because I wanted to do my job, and you and Nogo and those goons and probably the G-O, didn't want me to do my job."

"That's not it," he shot back. "I was trying to keep you from going off half-cocked. I wanted a simple operation, to keep our production costs low."

His neck wiggled, like an unruly rage kept pushing up, and kept being repressed.

"I was trying to keep you from getting killed, or erased," he said, sounding sincere. "I was trying to make sure we still had jobs, and a future."

"It's more than our jobs," I said. "It's about how we live. The scum is rising now. We need to pay attention to what we're doing to the Neighborhood. That's real live flesh and blood, in the flesh and dirt, in Industros Tragicos. Not chews of feelie-realie. We have to do the right thing."

"Alright, Stand," he said. "I'll try to help your side of the story be told. I'm not saying you convinced me, because I don't know what you convinced me of. I just don't know anymore."

Then Cerevello looked nervously to his left, then right, as if an invisible panther was ready to pounce. He rearranged his shoulders. His eyes appeared bigger behind the source specs.

"Just don't let me down with any more bad gags," he said in a rasp. "This is the very, very big time. Stay professional. Hang in toe to toe until your side's told. Then we'll know if it's the gold op and Andy, or the unhouse named Joe. You got me?"

He looked behind, as if someone was coming, then back. He clenched his tie and pulled on it, waving a finger with his free hand.

"Just don't let me down," he added, unable to fade it.

"I'll do my best," I said. "If you stand behind me, I won't kick or cry."

"Oh," he said, almost sounding surprised. He looked at me quizzically, and wiped his nose with his fingers. "Well, I just wanted to talk to you about that, and I guess we did. I'm going back to my cube then. I'm doing a little prep on our presentation. So, that's it, on it."

My cube felt cold, like a gene bank, or as Seamus said, a morgue drawer. As soon as C-man left, the flambo goon stuck his head around the corner. He smiled and waved, then disappeared. Then Nogo walked by my cube, with a sandwich in his hand.

"There's food on this thing, Stand," he said. "Want a sandwich?"

"No, man, I'm not hungry. I might need to take a leak though, if I can figure it out."

"Hmpf," Nogo said, mouth full, like I wasn't even there. "He probably doesn't need food anymore."

He split, hanging the mug scowl. It felt like nothing, like the absence of any emotion, emptiness. This world was crap, and individs like Nogo made it that way.

"Nem nem nem," I heard in my mind. "Nem nem nem. It's me, Francis. And my sister says you should come back and stay longer. She likes you now. You satisfies her. Just like Satiscope satisfies unhouse Joe. Hee hee hee, nem nem nem."

"Yeah," I said in skull jango, "I'll come back, if there's an 'I' to come back with."

"Don't worry, Standard, you can do anything you want," he said. "Nem nem nem nem nem."

Then abruptly, he said "Bye."

Unhouse Joe loved Satiscope. Good Neighbor Deluxe Broadmoor, I, we, Nogo, Cerevello, even Delmore Blank, everyone loved Satiscope.

All at once it hit me. Satiscope. The almost comic name, sad-a-scope, we advos called it sometimes. Satiscope was blessed oblivion, peace, the lume that nova-cent types used to weave dreams that didn't come undone. It brought huge ratings and credit for the producers, and plenty kickers for the carriers. And it was the foundation for all our religious stim patterns, the giga-goo lume we used to quiet the minds of troubled Neighbors.

All Flesh And Dirt Fades To Black. That was the last message buried in our religious spots, in the last spire of a Satiscope pattern. Only a few tweaks to that foundation, a few more delta brain waves in the pattern, could turn it to nekrolim.

Satiscope enfranchised the entire system. Just a blink ended domestic squabbles, existential pain, and disillusionment. And anyone, any box beater, could make it nekrolim, and disguise the shift. Any splicer whiz kid would find it easy. As more Neighbors smeared, more nekrolim seeped into the unhouses. Nogo and his splice-brats were turning Satiscope into nekrolim, somehow. That was it. I knew it. I jumped to my feet without thinking. I was halfway down the hall, on my way to strangle Nogo, when I realized I had to nail him with some real evidence. I didn't have any.

But I knew it was true, the two waves of evolution colliding, the psi-fi war and genocide with no culpable mass murderers, weeding the garden. The stakes were big.

So there I was, staring into his cube, seething, with no way to unravel it yet. He turned away from his screen and looked at me. The e-mag train hummed briefly.

"Change your mind?" he asked, chewing, holding out his half eaten roast beef on rye.

"Satiscope," I said, looking into his eyes.

Nogo stopped chewing. A huge lump of unchewed sandwich formed a pouch on the left side of his mouth. He swallowed.

"You want a blink on my monitor?" he asked with a puzzled look.

"Satiscope," I repeated.

"What about it?" he asked, putting down his sandwich, looking directly back into my eyes.

"What about it, indeed," was all I could say.

"Well, I can see your brain swelling hasn't subsided," he said with a disgusted smile.

He picked up his sandwich, turned back towards his screen, and resumed eating. That was my cue. I turned and walked away without saying another word. I didn't know what to do, but planting a seed of doubt seemed right. Now, he would wonder.

At this artificial moment in history, this wicked twist on the path, Neighbors would rather have sex with photon beams and electromagnetic fields, be fed by prepros, washed by inhuman hands, and drugged by a good blink of Satiscope. Some genalts were running the most nekro m-line on the planet since Day One, and no one was doing anything about it. Except the Weirds.

I turned into my cube and sat down and looked out the window, into the empty night. A bunch of Neighbors had psycho-kinetic powers, and Nogo and Biff hushed it and shaped it to avoid scandal. That's one thing I had on them. But there was no hard and cold on genalts tweaking nekrolim from Satiscope.

"What was the crack about Satiscope supposed to mean?" Nogo said, pushing his scowling mug around the corner of the cube.

"What crack?" I came back.

He was wondering.

"Listen, I don't have time for your head whistling," Nogo said. "If you want to convey something to me, go ahead."

"I just thought it would be easy to make nekrolim by tweaking a few spires on the top of that Satiscope pattern," I said. "Just think of it. All these Neighbors blinking on religion and God and spiritual fortification. But they're getting nekrolim instead, luming on their own suicide. You've got to admit, it's good thriller flimmer, no?"

Nogo was as white as milk. He looked scared, and pissed off. I could feel him thinking I had to die.

"Well? What do you think?" I asked through a low dense panic. The words seemed meaningless.

"About what?" he said, full of hate. "What the hell are you talking about?"

"It's a great scenario for a thriller," I repeated. "I can't believe someone hasn't thought of it already. Like an old-era dick. Man, just a few tweaks would do it."

"Satiscope? No way," he said with one eyebrow raised. "That stuff's written-in soft. But those last few spires are written-in hard. They can't be broken."

"Yeah, I know," I said. "All those religious spots are soft. Covered in hard, nice and tight. But it's conceivable, no es?"

"What's up, boys?" Cerevello asked, leaning around the corner. He was bubbling over with interest, and almost looked horny. "What are you barking about? I sincerely hope the team's ready to make a comeback."

He smiled like an idiot and rubbed his finger across his upper lip.

"This has nothing to do with the spot, Biff," I came back. "Nogo and I were just talking plot slants for a nekro thriller spot, fiction. About smuggling nekrolim through religious patterns."

"Fiction, indeed," Nogo said, chuckling. "He's talking Satis-cope as the carrier signal. Knocking down spires in the light pattern that were written-in to be soft, nice and harmless. It's like making heavy water out of regular drinking water."

"What in hell does that have to do with Weirds and our thing we got going here?" Biff asked. "You mean Standard thinks Weirds put nekrolim in the Satiscope?"

"No, Biff, just relax. We're talking thriller slants, that's all. There's nothing else."

"Then why the big pow-wow? Are you working on the spot?"

"Hey, Nogo, why don't you offer Biff a sandwich?"

"This whole discussion is stupid," Nogo said, then turned, and walked back to his cube.

"Does this mean we're still bickering like kids?" Biff asked. "Everything for nothing. Spoiled kids. Everything for nothing." Then Biff turned and walked away, too.

Biff didn't know. That meant it was a genalt deal, not the credit scam. Biff had no idea of why nekrolim was seeping into the unhouses, or why so many Neighbors were smearing.

The buzzing, frog-chirping beeps of squares vipped into my skull. Pinpoint was peeping, we were being observed very closely now. Would they be waiting with synchronized watches, would we stroll together for all the local climbers to gawk at? Or would it be a subdued affair, with only the pointiest pinhead brass - with the noose in hand? I had to make good focus. The Weirdness was low again.

Time had been scoped somehow, maybe by the squares. Thinking of Pinpoint seemed to make it appear sooner. Just an awareness at first, crossing desert, then climbing the archangel in the distance, the San Gabriel Mountains, then the bowl on the Pacific, the basin carved into gray green and olive hillsides that dropped into canyons of dark green. The shackles of the world were forged here. Then, now, and shaping up.

The scope grew more intense as the tubetrain rushed into the Los Angeles Basin, and focused on Pinpoint. The lights went out, and we descended into the tunnel below the station. We were there.

It wasn't anticlimactic as much as it was fearscaped. Everything was still full of promise here, in the land of climbers, where I used to want to be. But it seemed poison laced, with the doom clock on fast forward.

We stepped out of the tubetrain and I was still uncertain of what to do. Nogo was doing arrival poses, and Cerevello kept muttering "Too late."

The lift raised us lightly, soundlessly, into the main concourse. This week's theme was "Encantando Por La Noche," "Enchanted By Evening." Charmed by twilight? Being at Pinpoint was indeed charming. Mariachi music was everywhere, no changes with the scenery.

The lobby's weak decor, the zoombies tromping past the dwarf palms, all gave the place an unhouse feel. The number of people walking around in the F and D was amazing, and unsettling. Most were pointy-pinheads, the young, web-footed children of the dinosaur. The Pinpoint dinosaur's bureau class was all around us, moving fast but looking worried and defeated, weighted under the most current lie.

A retarded paradise, where the high fashion coiffure fit the pointy-pinheads, like the underwear hats fit the unhouse smear. The looks, the hairstyles, were extreme personal statements, and each had a competitive edge. It wasn't as bad as hickrug, skin-min 838, maybe. It just seemed like my dreamland, Pinpoint, was just another shallow-bed catfish farm, a spawning pool for boxhead vidiots.

An old-era radio voice announced an event in the concourse.

"Militant Malcos Dance In The Fake Holozig Recroom At 2 a.m.," the 'enemy media' sounding V-O said.

Nogo smirked, an inside joke.

Pinpoint was a place where Cerevello could fondle his hat and specs and mumble, it had climb. It was where Nogo and the goons could broker deals. These gabby hallways would have felt much friendlier with the howling of a demented cowboy.

Then a milk commercial blew over the mariachi as we walked further on. Then the holo-zig ads became incessant, one after another.

"Attractive," a deep, middle aged, male voice said.

"Important to good grooming," a young diva-Jane chirped.

"Por los ninos," a reassuring, motherly voice soozed.

There were so many spots, so much soup, it was impossible to comp what they were talking about, and head was going balky. Nogo's brows were furrowed, giving him a weasel mug. Cerevello was looking up at the ceiling's well lights, counting them like summer stars, hatching excuses.

The goons gaggled along at a distance, supposedly honoring our mandated sacred space. The palms were beginning to scan like funeral K-factor, and the nausea was always near. The old-era turnstiles were a nice touch. I felt like yelling out to Sylvia across the continent. Sylvia, are you still alive? I hadn't seen her in six shifts, over two days now. A knock-knock would zoom her soon, if it hadn't already. She might not even be there when I got back.

Cerevello began yammering, barely audibly, to his lenses, as he hankie washed them. I needed a blink of Satiscope. I tried to make good focus. I smiled.

"Do you mind picking up the pace a little?" said a pinky ring and shades goon, who had moved right up behind. Sacred space was gone.

"Taste the refreshing taste of...."

"Feel the fresh spring air with..."

"I have to go to the bathroom," I said.

"Just keep moving," the goon snorted.

"No time for that now. There's the belt to the mags," another goon grumbled.

"Standard, can't you wait til we get there?" Cerevello winced in pain jango.

You going to take off again, Mozuck?" Nogo said, sneering.

Obviously, they had Seamus's monkey wrench and hike strategy figured out.

"Am I under confinement or what?" I asked.

"Let's just say we want to keep going in a straight line," the pinky ring goon said. "No time-wobbling and no Weird sidetracks."

"Good lord, yes, Standard," Cerevello whimpered. "We're going to straighten this out with no tricks, remember?"

Nogo was strangely quiet; he looked sad-a-scoped. Everyone was scanning the station concourse nude, no sources. Except the ring-goon. He was watching a monitor that measured or detected psychic activity, I could tell, I knew it.

"I hope my bladder doesn't pop before we get to the belt, let alone the mags," I said.

"You'll do just fine," he said, full of false reassurance, staring at his psi monitor.

"What are you watching?" I asked.

"Just keep moving," he said, after looking up with a suspicious moosh.

-13B-ROLL-
"WELCOME 838 ASSOCIATES"

The mag was a silver and blue takeoff on a 1940's DeSoto guzzler. The thirteen- minute ride scanned great, but I was bound in knots from el agua, and not knowing what might happen. A lot of quick, well-produced holozigs flashed by before we got to MacArthur Enviro Park, but it was all a blur.

Suddenly Pinpoint Village emerged, looking like something from an old film noir, a cluster of buildings scorched by Santa Anna winds, with pink terra cotta roofs and white stucco, near a brightly multi-colored 1880's-style Victorian courthouse.

Maybe somewhere out in the hollyweeds, Weirds in adobe and scratch-thatch huts were scaring the bleep out of Pointy pinheads.

Then the forty-level citadel appeared, the combo art deco-and-bauhaus masterpiece that celebrated our brotherhood and our society. Pinpoint, the last step on the ladder of lights. We slowed to a halt in front of the building. I got out of the mag, ready to burst, but still paused to marvel. And to try to make good focus.

The entryway and main lobby hall at Pinpoint was decked out with gold chandeliers, intricately carved marble fountains, plaster sculpted mythological gods and heroes, and all that Palace Theatre splendor of the old-era movie houses. The gold plated elevator doors were something right out of an ancient cartoon. It all made the goons look even sillier.

"I have to go right now," I said to the ring-goon.

"Go ahead," he said, looking at his source.

I ducked into an opulent bathroom with twenty sinks, and an animixed servo valet whose hair was parted in the middle. I was monitored at a decent distance by the goon without a source. The other one monitored for Weirdness outside. The crying-hat and the splice-wank mumbled nearby. I could hear them.

When I walked out the first thing I saw straight ahead of us was the sign that read Welcome Local 838 Associates. We took the gold-plated elevator mag-lev to the 40th floor, in seconds. The sign that greeted us as we exited said 838 Conference, Salon 8. As we entered, a music bed swelled, "Twilight Time," accompanied by some audience laughter in the conference salon. Then, boom. The lights went down, and the song changed to "There's No Business Like Show Business." The lime green overhead light poured down, but not on us.

A little man, maybe under a meter and a half tall, emerged from behind stage curtains at the end of the salon, and into the limelight. He had silver-blue hair, pulled and twisted - pointed - into different directions. I guess his personal statement hairdo meant he was a pointy-pinhead who could pick up signals coming from all over. His face had a light green cast, maybe old-era greasepaint. Wearing a red tuni with no step light and blue costume elf pants, and pointy shoes, he looked like one of Santa's little helpers, or Mr. Jingle-jangle, the keeper of the keys to Toytown. He made the Weirds look like very average Neighbors.

"Signori e signorine, damas y caballeras, dammen und herren!" the little man riffed like an old-era boxing card announcer. "Ladies and Gentlemen! Loiterers and germs! Welcome to Pinpoint - Welcome Local 838 Associates! Let there be light!"

There was a titter of effete smarm from the salon audience as the little man crossed his eyes and tilted his head.

"I'm your host, Pico Grandee," he said.

The laughter faded into coughs and crosstalk.

"Well, well, well," he said. "What do we have here? It looks like a burned-out old man and two dangerously ambitious young men. A combo created for trouble."

There were a few deep voiced laughs from the audience. His eyes narrowed when he said 'ambitious' and his left eyebrow arched high enough to touch his pointy elf hair. He called it the way it was, in the form of disrespect reserved for those about to be corrected and penalized. As the jeri dicks would say, the jig was up, all way around.

"Now what do I mean by ambition?" the little man asked as he turned on his heels, then brought his hands to his lips. "Now what could I mean by that?"

Then an old rhumba played, sounding like it was coming from an antique stereo - a horrible cacophony of toots and honks and untuned conga and bongo drums.

"Ambition..." he sang to the music, while wiggling his large eyebrows. "Ambition, ambition, ambition."

The edges of the limelight expanded, ever so slightly. It lit the room just enough to show a supper club atmo, a full house of formal tux schmoozin' schmoes. The old fleshy dirt Grandees laughed. The G-O was calling us onto the carpet. And they were going to do it like one of those old-era style TV celebrity roasts.

Of course, it could all be Point A, Pinpoint feelie-realie. How would we know? Live in-person F and D would mean they were upset enough to show up. But feelie-realie would mean we were unimportant. Or they were afraid Weirdness could hurt them. It was hard to tell why they did anything. Maybe it was Alan Dingleman's idea. Where was he?

"Standard... Standard had ambition," the little green man sang. He pulled out two small maracas from his pocket and began shaking them.

I scanned around to see how the supper club audience, Nogo and Biff, and the goons were reacting. I couldn't really make out the Grandee Bigs' mugs, just hear the titters of laughter. Nogo's eyes were closed; his mouth was frozen into a smile. Biff's mouth was wide open, his eyes were popping out of his eyeglasses sources. He couldn't believe it.

Then the music stopped and the little green host stopped shaking the maracas. A cabaret pot shone gold, right on his head. He looked back over his shoulder, and the conference room's overhead monitor showed his mug in extreme close-up. A fake tear welled in one eye.

"My boy, we trusted you all the way," he said, pointing his finger at me. "Believed in you. All the research said you were our guy. And you were going to do it the old-era way. But you lost your objectivity, son."

He pouted.

"You identified with the individs you tried to bring into focus, confused yourself with your Spotlighters," he went on. "And you tried to steal the Spotlight. You wanted to go where no one individ should ever try to go."

He looked angrily at me, with frosty eyebrows wiggling.

"You knew you were in over your head, and didn't confab with your team. You knew Weirds were a threat, and didn't let anyone know!"

The rhumba swelled again. Nogo looked almost overjoyed; Biff shook his head and talked to himself.

"Ambition, you had ambition..." the little MC sang.

Now throughout this entire spot, Biff was Soft and Nogo was Hard, and both the marshmallow and the steel-hearted splicer tried to sabo it, to further their own blue and gold. I had been mauled, held captive, slapped around, and threatened with fade to black. But I still tried to zoom the credo, tell the truth. Now my culo was on the line again. At least I knew enough to defend myself.

"Wait a minute," I said, as loud as I could muster. "I didn't keep anything from anyone."

Nogo laughed, Biff grimaced and held his hand to his forehead in dismay.

The MC looked pleasantly surprised by my speaking out, then riffed into a schtick.

"Wait a minute, yourthelf, big boy," he lisped, camping it up, waving a limp wrist dramatically in the pale light. "You'll get your turn."

The audience howled. Nogo laughed again and Biff sighed loudly. There was the sound of a snare drum, a high-hat cymbal, then bass drum.

Then, changing character, the MC laughed, gestured towards me with his thumb, and spoke to the audience, saying "I love this guy, really, he slays me."

Then he held up his hand and shouted "We'll be right back, with Welcome To Pinpoint, Local 838 Associates, right after this!"

An old-era late night talk show studio band went into the bumper, the interlude music. The lights went back to supper club cabaret lighting, and the room returned to pre-feelie-realie flux. There was the buzz of rich Bigs annoying F and D waiters, the noise of gear and bar equipment, and background gab.

Pico MC walked straight over to us, with his hand extended.

"Great stuff, you guys, great stuff," he said, shaking my hand, then Nogo's.

"You look great, Biff," Pico said, shaking Cerevello's hand. "Great. Who's your embalmer?"

He laughed and pointed at Cerevello, da-da boom. Then the bumper music swelled.

"Oops, here we go again," the MC said looking back towards the spotlight, all teeth.

Green MC trotted back, then turned to source one, and came up on the overhead.

"We're back," he yammered, to prompted applause. "We're back with Welcome Local 838 Associates, on Welcome To Pinpoint. Now, Standard, didn't you once say in your personal log that the Fire Inspector was dangerous? Hmm?"

The thermo control was off again, hot, cold, more nausea. Did I call him dangerous? When did I...?

"I never told anyone in 838 he was dangerous," I said. "It was a common feeling in 838 and nearby Locals, that's all."

"Standard, the last time you told the truth was the last time you bathed," Pico quipped. "Let's see how accurate that is. Roll it, play it back."

Everything went up to Point A, the whole place was a monitor again. The room filled with the sound of my voice, but I wasn't speaking. My old title graphics for the spot appeared for all to experience in the feelie-realie: Transdimensional Paradise Or Psi-Fi Hell? Where Do The Weirds Really Want To Take Us? Deleted Excerpts From the Making Of The Spot.

Then Bob's "Ghost Riders In The Sky" swelled. I couldn't make out what my voice was saying over the music. It was unfamiliar.

"Full up on the guy in the near foreground," my voice said. "Make him look menacing. Wait. Freeze his face. We'll take it back to the unhouse and super him over some real smear. He's not creepy enough."

The conversation was fake. I never whispered-in this stuff. I wanted to scream out the words nekrolim and Satiscope, but couldn't speak. The claustro-zamp was crushing.

"Don't screw around so much, ok?" another voice said. "It makes it harder to get right."

The voice sounded like Nogo's.

"Standard," pico-poco MC said, over the sound, "I'm sorry if it seems like I'm teasing. You look ready to burst. Need to go to the bathroom again? Give them my name, they'll give you a good seat."

There was the sound of dada-boom from the drummer again, and more audience laughter.

"Ok. Let's get right to it. Roll the Fire Inspector!"

Appearing instantly on every screen, a small lap monitor whirled in black space. It whirled closer, until finally a face was visible. As it zoomed-in, a close up of the Fire Inspector's mug filled the screen.

Then a trailer-like V-O ripped through the roast hall.

"Is this an emanation from the subconscious minds of millions of Neighbors?" the voice shouted.

There was the sound of wind and tinkling bells. The Fire Inspector's head twirled like a gyroscope, flattening a freeze here and there. His tongue flipped in and out like a snake.

"Or the work of a group bent on destroying the world?"

There was the sound of a child singing, and a dog barking. From full front, little firemen's hats popped out of his face, and marched into the viewer's eyes.

"A deliberate attempt is being made to maximize public hysteria, without waiting for a suitable saturation length. Arousal is blown, and malco jokers are on the internal lawnmower."

The crowd laughed, but I couldn't understand it. It didn't seem like it meant anything to Biff, either. Nogo looked nervous. Maybe a weed-the-garden joke.

On screen, a red haired blanko-Joe appeared, watching something on his screen, unaware that fire hats were rushing into his head. The individ began twitching violently, jerking from side to side, then looked away from the monitor.

"I can't take this frizzing noise!" he yelled. "This frigging, frizzing noise!"

His tall, afri, Diva-Jane hab mate looked alarmed, and kept fussing with him, imploring "Honey, what's the matter? What's wrong?"

A nasty sounding voice squacked from the screen.

"What's that silly hat you're wearing, craptain cortex?" the voice asked. "The boat show's over." Then the voice cut out abruptly.

"Some things the Weirds do cannot be explained," the trailer's V-O boomed. The scene faded to cut.

Another extreme close-up appeared on the screen, another Neighbor twitching. The shot tracked back to show him in a fat chair, in a dimly lit, cell-like room. He tilted his head upward, as if speaking to an interviewer.

"Fireman wasn't a real person," the guy burbled. "In my mind, he wasn't the real MC. But one time I visualized an old-era grocery store, with cans of fruit on shelves. And the labels on the cans told me to k-k-kill everyone."

The guy's face froze up, and a title rolled over it - Deleted Excerpts

From The Making Of Transdimensional Hell by Standard Mozuck.

I didn't know where they came up with the shots. They took a pastiche of my Home stuff, and animixed the rest. I wanted to say nekrolim and Satiscope again, but no-go.

"Kill everyone? Kill everyone?" the poquito green man bellowed. "If that isn't dangerous talk, I don't know what is. Oh my."

The crowd chuckled.

"Psychically dangerous," Pico went on. "And since you've converted, you are too. Maybe you can turn your unhouse-Jane Sylvia away from the flame with your power. That would be something."

Pico's material was weak, but the audience laughed dutifully. It made me pugnacious.

"This stuff is all feelie-realie fake, b-roll rigged, animixed," I said.

Some Grandees booed; Nogo too, in hush mode. I tried to set up a zinger.

"Seriously, folks," I said. "Pico's wit dwarfs me. A man of Pico's stature is hard to find. Literally, hard to find. Many people find 'I Was A High-Personality Urinal' his best short feature... "

Dada-boom, no laughs.

"People?" he huffed, like the word had rotting genitalia. "People? Don't you mean individs? People commit murder, larceny, cheat, and abuse themselves, then invent gods to forgive them in another world. Individs make good focus, butter our bread on both sides. Can't you see that this Neighbor was hurt by this? Weirds are dangerous."

"They didn't mean any harm," I yelled. "The damage was accidental. If there really was any."

"Now, Standard," little green man came back slyly. "This Fire Inspector has managed to stay out of focus for how long now? I mean, he definitely is information, isn't he? He isn't interested. And he's flagrant. He causes trouble, wrecks gear, scares Neighbors. Oh, well, blah blah blah. Show the next spot."

"But Weirds are on to something," I almost whined. "They've gone beyond the idea of life as school. To them earth is a playground and it's always recess."

The crowd laughed loud and hard. Greenie pushed his hands up to his mouth to stifle his laughter. Nogo was growing fur, too.

"If what you said is true," Nogo said, "the whole structure would evaporate. So they're dangerous to NeighborWorld. But it's all bullshit, anyway. How big a bullshitter is Stan? The last time we ... when he...uh..."

Waves of laughter rolled through the conference room. What the hell was so funny? Nogo was losing his acid; he was on the edge of frizz and couldn't roast.

"Standard," Cerevello spurted in a high voice. "What in hell are you saying? I told you to keep your damn head on your shoulders here. You gave me your word."

Cerevello jiggled his glasses sources with both hands, and the place went crazy. Some of it sounded like jeri-era canned laughter. Maybe for illusion, to sweeten the track.

"If break-ins are so harmless, let's see how you like them, Standard," the MC said, still chuckling. "Welcome to Transdimensional Hell."

"That title sucks!" Nogo shouted, right before the awful sound effects scorched across the room.

The deafening howling of fire engines, the wee-ow, wee-ow sound of old emergency vehicles, all kinds of sirens, pounded the room. A red light popped right through the monitor, and panned across the room. Then K-factor jumped in with nostrils flaring, the eye-watering smells of a raging fire; ozone, burning poly-plast, smoke.

Then the Fire Inspector rode in on a little kid's tricycle, peddling furiously, panting like a dog, accompanied by toy bells. The studio band went into a guest intro, the song "Fiery."

At least it looked like him. It was a holozig or a double, a simulated Weird break-in, to make me toss my empty stomach and pass out again. But I didn't see any nines, or recognize any of his goofy schtick. So I didn't frizz, I just withstood the blast and laughed. Cerevello had curled into defensive body jango; Nogo was taking on everything like he was waiting for something.

The fake inspector's intro music and horrible sound effects padded and faded out, as he pedaled closer to the pointy-headed green MC. But the fearless fireman didn't extinguish the little Grandee with some head-exploding trance; he extended a free hand instead. Then the MC started singing, to a very jeri-era romantic comedy, radio orchestra-style.

"Wouldn't it be lovely?" he crooned in a deep voice. "Wouldn't it be grand? If after all this fighting, you would only take my hand..."

The fireman got to the MC and dismounted, then turned and waved to the applauding supper club audience, before shaking hands warmly with him. Instantly they feelie-realie appeared at a talk show panel.

Pico MC made a pensive mug, then stormed on with his schtick.

"We're here on Welcome 838 Associates, with the Fire Inspector," he said. "Now you were a dangerous psychic terrorist, before being rehabilitated by a talented young 838 NeighborWorld advo and director, Standard Mozuck. What was it like working with him?"

The fake inspector nodded, then turned to glance towards me. That's when I could tell whoever put him together never saw him in person.

"Standard is the kind of advo who would give you his right arm," the fake inspector said. "Great guy, great working with him."

Before he could elaborate, Nogo frizzed, and popped.

"This is ridiculous!" he shouted. "This doesn't have anything to do with anything. It's bullshit!"

The audience laughed a culty insider's laugh, and the drummer went dada-boom.

"This whole thing is a hoax," he screeched hoarsely. "What is this crap?"

Nogo was way ahead of me, and he wasn't taking it well. He looked close to smearing or something. Biff's mouth was wide open in disbelief. The audience was howling. Forget the roast and toast, boil them in oil.

Poco-loco greenie looked shocked, and shielded his eyes from the lights with his hand, to see who was making the commotion. The laughter dwindled, as greenie's expression grew angrier, but there were a few short grenades of yuks from those who thought it was all part of the schtick. The fake inspector dissolved into a fade, an animix, indeed.

"Is that Ngo Blgo making all that noise?" Pico bellowed. "Who is blowing my flow?"

Nogo looked at us as if we had betrayed him, then to the supper club for sympathy. But before he could look back, the little green MC was marching towards us. He strode to Nogo, reached up to his lapels, and began trying to rip his step light off.

"Give me that step light, you spicer slut," he shouted. "Give me that light!"

Green man lifted his leg to gain yanking leverage. Nogo cringed and whimpered, almost crying. The audience was sure this time, and a torrent of guffaws erupted.

"No, please, no no no, please, I'm sorry," Nogo begged. "I didn't know what you were trying to do. I'm sorry. Please, I'm sorry, I'm sorry."

"You're sorry, alright," MC Pico said. "You sure are."

He let go of Nogo's lapels. I thought greenie was going to start slapping him, like an old-era gangster, but Nogo's face was too high to reach. The "Ambition" song started playing in the background again. Pico-poco verde MC stepped back from Nogo, with one eyebrow raised.

"Ambition... Nogo had ambition..." he sang, into an imaginary jeri-era microphone.

He pointed at Nogo. The music stopped dead.

"You are indeed a splice-baby," poco verdito dicted in a haughty tone. "I personally can't stand these spoiled individs. They think they've got it all, but they're missing one very gooey, chewey chunk. This world was made for MrMz Av Neighbor, blinko blanko Joe and Jane, not them."

He turned away from Nogo, after a disdainful snort.

"All Flesh And Dirt Fades To Black, doesn't it?" verdito MC said slowly. "A fad, folks turn blue? A fade and death for the boobs, a fake actual design for the beginning, bla bla bla?"

The room went dark again. Cerevello shouted out "No! Don't do this! Sacred Space!"

Pronto, the Grandee screen showed an elderly woman in a Sniffles bio-collective, wearing tissue repair gloves, holding a box of Sniffles tissues, doing her unhouse obsesso griff. Then she stealthily pattered into a screen lounge filled with monitors, looking around to see if anyone caught her entry.

"Man in the box," she whispered to a screen. "Let me in."

Then she began monitoring the screen, and the eyes-and-ears logo of a Satiscope stimsublim appeared. A religious spot, a prayer with punch, like the ones we'd buried. She blinked, she nodded, and the flesh faded to black. Man in the box had taken her to a prayer meeting on the other side, via nekrolim.

"All Flesh And Dirt was Biff's idea!" Nogo screamed. "Mozuck was burying it in spots, too!"

The crowd released a bored chuckle, verdito Grandee shook his head.

"That poor vieja, an abuela, a loving grandmother, so smeared, so addicted to her little man in the box," green MC pined. "Taken by a forbidden pattern."

Greenie grasped his crotch, and the crowd erupted, the drummer went dada-boom.

"Who cares, right?" he laughed.

"I was doing what the G-O proscribed," Cerevello broke in. "We didn't know those signals could be altered to do harm."

"Shut up poppy, you jeri-jerkoff, just shut up," Pico snipped. "We are the G-O, the Grandees, the Bigs. We know and see all."

He paused.

"Whose idea was it to put nekrolim in the religious spots, right when that message of divine powerlessness reminds us that life is fragile but light goes on forever?" he asked.

I knew for sure. How the smear were getting nekrolim, why Neighbors pulled the credit scandal and split, or died. It was Nogo and his ring crew. But I didn't finger Nogo with a readymade m-line. I just laughed along with the crowd, and applauded.

Greenie did a broad sweep with his finger source, pointing first at me, then Cerevello, then locking in on Nogo.

"You," MC said bluntly.

"It was an idea for the times," Nogo blurted out. "A way to assure the Nova Century's survival. Why are all these individs allowed to keep taking up space, anyway? They have to make room for those who can produce."

There were only a few chuckles, but the drums went dada-boom.

"We allow them to take up space because it's lucrative," green MC said in a loud voice, twirling one of his hair points. "But we don't allow anyone to kill the goose that laid the gold op, and we don't allow anyone making room for just themselves. Not in our Neighborhood."

"Why can't you see the big monitor," Nogo pleaded. "They don't contribute. They take and don't give back. We did nothing wrong."

The crowd let out a big laugh, punctuated by two dada-booms.

"That's the spirit, boy, keep it up," verdito poco-loco gummed. "You have ambition. But it's too late."

The drums broke into a brushes and snare walk. A saxophone or something honked off key.

"For Nogo's ambition, his reward is an international spot of his own," greenie said. "But it's an m-line, amigo, a spot on what you and your ring wearing compadres have been up to. And you'll be confined to your hab, until you get your day."

"No!" Nogo cried out, then covered his eyes with his hands.

The crowd laughed, with some whistles and cheers thrown in.

"For Biff's lack of ambition, his reward is an international spot on how he missed three important stories, why he asked the wrong questions, why he couldn't see the big monitor, all that," Pico added. "An m-line, but not as bad as you probably deserve."

There was scattered laughter and applause, and one boo, while Cerevello held out his hands for forgiveness, looking devastated.

"For Standard's ambition, his reward is an international spot on the Weirds, exactly as he wanted," greenie said. "But that doesn't mean you'll be able to pull it off."

The crowd booed. There was some scattered laughter, but it was a long chorus of jeers before greenie stopped it.

"That's it, we have spoken!" he yelled. "Now get out of here, get those sorry buns back to 838!" He looked at the audience and shrugged his shoulders. "Don't blame me; I'm probably just a holozig. Thanks for being with us, on Welcome to Pinpoint, Local 838 Associates!"

The band played the outro, and greenie trotted towards us again, a wrap.

"You three slayed!" greenie gushed. "Hilarious stuff. I can tell this Welcome to Pinpoint will go gold."

Nogo was a quivering blob. Cerevello mumbled in agony, his blue and gold faded to black.

"Nobody's going to put you in the unhouse, Nogo, take it easy, boy," MC consoled. "You'll be climbing in weeks. All for the show, everyone good guy bad guy good guy. We won't let anything untowards happen to one of our own."

Ngo Blgo wasn't cheered up, he was frizzing catatonic.

"You can't do this to me," Nogo said, struggling to speak. "You don't know who you're messing with. You're not one of us, you can't..."

"I told you, I'm just a character, you're taking this all wrong," greenie responded.

Nogo froze. The fat and skinny non-genalt goons appeared and moved around Nogo, like they did to me. He let them lead him out like common smear, escorted by his elbows, without a word. Cerevello followed dejectedly, and greenie MC called out to him.

"Lighten up, Biff, you're made for life!" MC yelled.

"We don't use wires," I said.

"At least one of this comedy trio understands," greenie came back.

"Just a holozig messenger for the Bigs?" I asked.

"I'm real, just working a feelie-realie room from another source," Pico said.

"We weren't important enough for them to make the scene?" I asked.

"No, no, this was important. They made special time for the Welcome, didn't they?" he retorted, all amigo teeth. "We were in an adjacent conference room, in the F and D. I swear."

"Are the Grandees afraid of me?" I asked.

MC smiled on, scrutinizing me with wide, whiskery eyes.

"Maybe they don't think you can pull it off," he said. "Maybe you're smearing. That would solve a lot of problems. Maybe you just can't grip the key anymore. But you liked doing Spotlights on Local 838 Neighbors. It won't be hard to go back to."

"I'll take my shot, shorty," I said.

"Then get your sorry buns back to 838," he said. "Show's over here."

A new goon with a psi monitor sidled up to me, to take me back to safety, freedom, and lies in 838.

-14-
"FIVE STARS"

The mag train ride to 838 was uneventful, dear N's and A's, but the end was sad. I wasn't strong enough to explode the planet or break-in everywhere, just enough to take my shot. And when I got back, Sylvia was gone.

She left me a message. I watched her medium close-up on my monitor in Stansville, where she used to go somnab. Her eyes looked duller than usual, her face twisted into a vague, questioning expression. The shot's barren white background betrayed its meaning. It was a farewell message from an unhouse, one of the format goodbyes sent out to reassure friends, Associates, and hab-mates. Ironically, I had written it, without the current mug shot. I had written all this season's farewell messages.

I cried a little. But when it sounded like someone else crying, I felt better. I didn't need a blink, either. There were other messages.

One was from Francis, with scenes showing him dying in an explosion, in a guzzler in CarTown. He had broken-in and faked his own death, and made the image stick. He knew what was up, and didn't want to Spotlight. Francis declined.

Other Weirds had left break-in messages. One was from the Martian Bellboys; a proto-Spotlight of them giving advice and demonstrations on how to grow huge vegetables with mind power. La Suenadora, the Sleeping Woman, left a proto-spot showing her giving advice on exorcisms and removing evil influences.

There was nothing from the Inspector or Seamus the shaman, but it seemed we were in business. There would be no more break-ins, just positive new focus.

Later in the shift, things got even harder to comp. Laya broke-into Home's message box, rather than breaking into my head. She looked more beautiful than I remembered, and a little unfamiliar on the screen. Laya wanted to stay with me, because her mother had disappeared along with Francis, and it was chaotic in Industros Tragicos.

My own Weird power seemed to be just some kind of potential. But I still didn't need to blink or zoom the lume every hour, and the skull squares I was bombarded with constantly never seemed to stick.

That was Day One of Day One. Within a week, everyone wanted my slant on the Weirds, and Weirds were coming into focus in droves. But this Cutting On The Action spot still wasn't ready for nex-al-mundo until Cerevello nexed-in with me. The international spot on his incompetence was making him rich. He was the cult comic of the week.

When Biff appeared on the screen, he looked younger. He was wearing a Hawaiian shirt, and instead of his usual sweat drenched full shot, he sported a dry, medium shot. His bazook mannerisms; the eye-source slapping, the collar grabbing, the nervous glances, had a free, whimsical flavor.

"It's almost too much for me to believe, Stan," he said. "Who would've believed it? But you knew all along. And you deserve that Andy. It's amazing. To think they were living among us all these years. Really makes you wonder, doesn't it?"

Biff grinned broadly, showing teeth and climb. Then he lifted a tall glass with a cocktail umbrella to his lips. He stopped before drinking and tilted the glass in a toast.

"Real stuff, Stan. Just like Bob Sideways drinks. Cheers."

He drank a long slow swig, then puckered, reacting to its tartness.

"Ahh. That's it, Stan. Old-era all the way. I knew it had a ring, I knew it was go. And I really want to thank you, uh, I mean about Bob Zeitweiss. That was really fine of you to let me share in picking up his contract this season. Your little bundle made me a bundle, too."

He smiled again, then lifted his glass in another toast.

"And we're going to make a whole bundle more!"

He took another drink. The smile lingered a while, then Cerevello erupted into a cackle.

"I just can't believe it," he shouted on, waving his drink. "Andy, Andy, Andy!"

He turned to a three quarter profile shot, and stared.

"Wait a minute," he said before I could track a word, talking to someone else. "I'm connecting with Stan, my man, my main burner."

He turned to face me in a private close-up and smiled.

"I'll nex back," he said to whoever was trying to connect with him. "I got biz to take care of."

Biff acknowledged the nexer's fade with a nod.

"Well," he said flatly. "I know you're busy, so I won't creep you. But it is strange about our amigo and Associate Nogo. Shows you never can tell. Of course, on the other hand, I had my doubts all along. Guys like him keep everything inside, then pop like an oyster."

Nogo and his ring crew's nekrolim conspiracy spot was going gold, too. But Nogo wasn't around to cash in on the badguy spin.

"Well thanks for taking time to connect-in," I said quickly, before he could yammer. "I still don't understand what happened to Nogo. It doesn't make sense."

"It doesn't make sense to me either," he answered. "One of our own involved in a hush-mode genalt cult, thrill-killing Neighbors for the sake of a bad gag POV. Then smearing, to top it all. I thought he'd be climbing back by now. And how could he smear anyway? It's as wild a scenario as the Weirds."

"I can't believe they thought they could get away with it," I offered.

"Well, thanks to us, partner, they didn't," Cerevello said, making climber focus.

"Have you seen him? I can't do it yet," I said.

"Artichoke salad," Biff said solemnly.

"First Sylvia, then Nogo," I said. "It's too much."

"You think the Weirds smeared Nogo?" he asked, looking for a bigger bundle. "What about that angle and slant?"

"I don't know," I said. "We'll talk about it another time."

"I'll be nexing again," he said.

"I know you will," I said, and the screen went black.

Weirds were hot focus everywhere. Industros Tragicos was coming into the Spotlight, and the CarTown refugees were returning with gear. I was a shoo-in for an Andy. And of all things, Nogo had somehow smeared, from the stress of seeing himself made a villain. Maybe the Bigs did it. No one, especially the Bigs, wanted m-line focus on hush-mode cults weeding the Neighborhood.

And nobody wanted Weirds to compete with NeighborWorld. Most Weirds came into the Spotlight and quit breaking-in. But some kept it up. There were hush-mode rumors they had killed some Grandees with mirror-mind. There were fewer break-ins, but they were more violent. The G-O Bigs pronounced it victory, saying only a few desperate Weird malcos were left.

My own Weird power was confined to briefly changing the colors on my screen once, and knowing Cerevello was going to nex-in with me. It was nothing like on the way to Pinpoint. Seamus and the fireman still hadn't nexed with me; psychically, or in the F and D.

Home's personalities, like Gert and Bill and Mina and Stansville, seemed to miss Sylvia, I don't know why. It seemed Mina was trying to make me feel guilty. I was apprehensive about Laya moving in, and avoided dealing with it. Instead, I got busy with the last shots of Transdimensional Hell.

This Cutting On The Action would mean more than an Andy, it would mean the Neighborhood was saved, the Weirds were saved, and I was going to climb the ladder.

But it didn't seem like the Neighborhood, or the Weirds, or I, could handle it. As more Weirds popped up around the world, more genalt cults would pop up to fade them. Soon, younger advos would sprout up with a totally different take, and I'd be Goodguy Badguy, sliding down the ladder into smear, clutching that Andy.

In a world where homes had personalities and supplied all their occupants' needs, where holo-screens handled every aspect of life, where everyone was info in the Spotlight, where some were genetically altered and bequeathed with talent before conception, where unhouses were filling with smear who no longer had personalities, where everyone was peeped and probed and mind controlled; life sucked.

It was finally time for the last shots of this spot. "Ghost Riders" cued up again. I stepped into a full shot before the source, wearing my old-era journo's trenchie and bogie hat.

"Gracias tan mucho, Dear Neighbors and Associates," I said. "Thank you so much for nexing into 'Cutting On The Action,' my personal diary of today's events on the connector. And now, you've seen it, just as I did. This is Standard Mozuck, wishing you all a good night, and good focus."

The full shot cross faded into a long shot of me walking towards the door. It was cold outside, but I had on warm gear, so I wasn't worried. I walked out of my hab and into the touchlot, and a wide overhead shot. I didn't know where I was going, but I knew I couldn't stay in focus. Like Bob Sideways said, I was done.

The last scene heading crawled over - END SLATE: EXTERIOR-TOUCHLOT - EVENING-WIDE OVERHEAD OF TOUCHLOT.

I walked off screen. FADE TO BLACK.

ABOUT THE AUTHOR

Dave DeLuca is an artist, writer, musician and reporter in Ashtabula, Ohio. With Wes Jenkins he authored a previous novel, *Dorkus and the Affairs of Lord Willing*. He has sung and played guitar in bands including The Chronics, The Clocks (aka Radio Alarm Clocks), Cooky, Einstein's Secret Orchestra, and The Mondo Retardo Band. He is best known to radio and podcast listeners as Lonesome Cowboy Dave of *The SubGenius Radio Ministry Hour of Slack* as well as *ESO Swamp Radio* and *Brain Rot Radio Theater*, all originating at WCSB-Cleveland. He has been a major contributor to Church of the SubGenius projects since 1992. He has written for numerous magazines, newspapers, and TV specials (including *John Lennon Remembered*). He is the only person on the planet who can do what he does with words and sentences.